THE LONESOME HEART IS ANGRY

The Lonesome
Heart Is Angry

Paul Charles

NEW ISLAND

THE LONESOME HEART IS ANGRY
First published 2014
by New Island
2 Brookside
Dundrum Road
Dublin 14
www.newisland.ie

PRINT ISBN: 978-1-84840-339-0
EPUB ISBN: 978-1-84840-340-6
MOBI ISBN: 978-1-84840-341-3

Typeset by JVR Creative India
Cover design by Nina Lyons
Printed by OPOLGRAF SA, Poland

New Island received financial assistance from
The Arts Council (An Comhairle Ealaíon), Dublin, Ireland

10 9 8 7 6 5 4 3 2 1

Dedication

This book is for Catherine.

Acknowledgments

Thanks are due and offered to: Andrew my father, Oisin, Darragh, Eoin, Edwin, Justin, Emma, Mariel, Lucy, John Mc, Ja, Christopher, Duncan, Larisa, Brad, Christina, Ann, Kathleen, John C, Peter, Lindsey, Richard, Maddee and Craig.

Also by Paul Charles (www.paulcharlesbooks.com)

The Detective Inspector Christy Kennedy Mysteries:
I Love The Sound of Breaking Glass
Last Boat To Camden Town
Fountain of Sorrow
The Ballad of Sean & Wilko
I've Heard The Banshee Sing
The Hissing of the Silent Lonely Room
The Justice Factory
Sweetwater
The Beautiful Sound of Silence
A Pleasure To Do Death With You

The Inspector Starrett Mysteries:
The Dust of Death
Family Life

Other Fiction:
First of The True Believers.
The Last Dance
The Prince Of Heaven's Eyes (A Novella)

Factual:
Playing Live

BOOK ONE
The Matchmaker

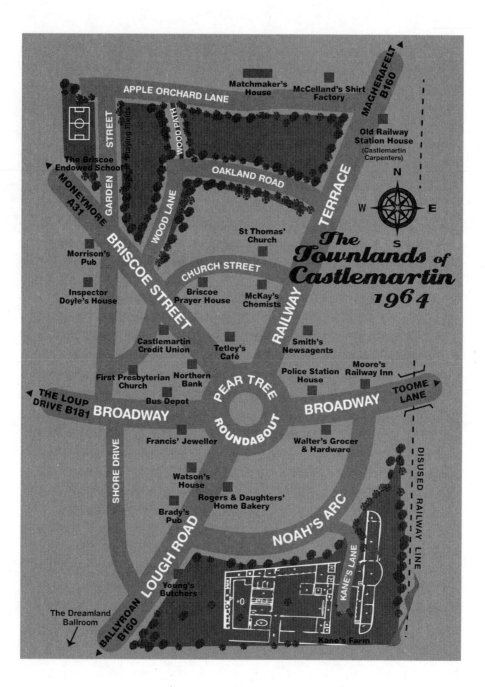

Chapter One

Life went on in Castlemartin, like it had been doing for nearly one hundred and thirty years. That was how long it had been since the first church had been built on the rich lush land, not so far from the shore of Lough Neagh. This small Ulster village was nestled between two orchards, one with apples and one with pears. In Castlemartin another day began the same; (mostly) the things the six hundred and seventeen residents did they'll do again.

This particular day hadn't been a day to remember in a way that say, for instance, 22 November 1963 had been a day the world was incapable of forgetting. No, nothing like that day at all. Michael Gilmour, matchmaker to the parish of Castlemartin, County Derry in Northern Ireland, could recall in great detail the events of 22 November 1963. He could remember every single thing he'd said and done and, equally, he could recollect every personal thought he'd had.

But save for a meeting with the Kane twins, Michael Gilmour could remember precious little about the other day we are discussing. It had been a Sunday, of that he was sure. Sure because farmers could not, and would not, take time – excepting the Sabbath – from their fields or their chores for the recreational purpose of finding a wife.

The matchmaker's wife had shown the Kane twins, Joe and Pat, into the 'good' room, just like she would have done with any other prospective clients. This particular room – sometimes referred to as the Sunday room, the parlour or even the sitting room, but mostly the 'good' room – was so named because it was saved only for special occasions. As such, it had an unused smell and feel to it. The furnishings were nearly all good as new, not because they *were* new but because they, like the room, were hardly ever used and whenever marks accidentally appeared on the table, chair, sideboard or anywhere else, the matchmaker's wife could be seen, apron and spittle at the ready, frantically removing the offending stains. This precious furniture always smelt freshly polished, unlike the battered pieces in the living room, which the furniture from the 'good' room would eventually replace but only when the matchmaker and his wife could afford to upgrade.

The sooner this could happen the better because the furniture in the living room suffered a continued threshing from the matchmaker's three children: Paul, ten years old, and Nick, five years old, separated by Marianne at seven years old. As well as the general wear and tear, there was also the negative impact caused by the continued smell of food, dogs and children.

The good room was at the front of the white-washed, pebble-dashed, two-storied house, although all callers to one of the oldest houses in the area entered by the back door. Neither Michael nor his wife Dorothy could remember the last time anyone had entered or left the house through the front door. In fact, in trying to recall such an historic event, they guessed it would have to have been some twelve years prior – before they were married and while Michael was still living under the same roof as his parents. Michael's father had used the front door – or, at least, it had been used on his behalf – while making his final journey out of the house following a wake the entire village of Castlemartin was to talk about for years.

It was not intentional, nor however a disadvantage, that people in search of husbands or wives would have a chance to view the happiness of the matchmaker's family as they looked through the living-room window while crossing a busy and toy-packed yard to the back door.

No, Michael could remember little about that fateful day. He knew that his wife would, as ever, have encouraged him to fasten the top button of his shirt and tighten up the knot of his tie. She would also most certainly have gone to their bedroom and fetched Michael's 'good' jacket – a Harris Tweed – and helped him to put it on before answering the door.

There is also an odds-on chance that Dorothy, on showing the twins through to the front room where Michael would have been waiting to greet them, large leather-bound notebook always nearby, would have offered the twins tea and home-baked shortbread. And she would have delivered the tea and shortbread shortly thereafter, serving it on their best china.

Before the arrival of the liquid refreshments the matchmaker would have indulged in small chat with the twins. Then he would have used Dorothy's timely interruption as a key point to shift the direction of the conversation. After his wife had left the front room, social chores accomplished, Michael would have gotten down to the business at hand: the matchmaking.

Michael Gilmour knew of the twins, having gone to the same school as as they had. They were still what could loosely be described as fresh-faced. They were definitely good looking, in a Paul Newman kind of way. They were identical, slim, green-eyed and about five foot ten-and-a-bit inches tall. Michael the matchmaker could tell them apart only when they smiled. Joe had a stern, begrudging and somewhat unforgiving smile, whereas Pat had a warm inviting grin that lit up his entire face. It seemed to Michael that Patrick Daniel Kane, to give him his full name, liked to laugh. On the other hand, Joseph David Kane laughed only when he felt it would be inappropriate not to do so.

Their arrival at the matchmaker's house, on that Sunday in the long distant past, went pretty much unnoticed and unheeded by all apart from the matchmaker himself. Even Dorothy soon forgot they were in the house; Michael was in a session so she helped herself to a cup of the freshly brewed tea, turned on the radio and resumed her knitting – a large barrel affair of a jumper, supposedly for her husband but which threatened to grow out of control and become a multi-coloured bedspread unless she took command of the constantly swishing needles.

No, the Sunday we are discussing, that Sunday in the long distant past, had not been a day to remember – it was just another non-descript lazy Sunday afternoon. A Sunday afternoon when you are happy to have nothing to do so you can relax and lounge off your large meal, maybe go for a bit of a walk over the fields or steal a nap on the sofa, with your peace being disturbed by nothing other than the distant chimes of the ice-cream van.

But this particular Sunday was a day that drove the twins, the matchmaker, Dorothy and a few others onto an path of unavoidable conflict. A path which would become etched in the brains of all those involved and a path that, in its own way, proved to be as significant, volatile and life-changing as the event which had forever rattled the foundations of the entire world a little over a year earlier on Friday 22 November 1963.

Chapter Two

It should also be pointed out at this stage that Michael Gilmour was not in the least surprised when Pat and Joe Kane turned up on his doorstep, seeking out his specialist skills. He was nonetheless shocked, as in very shocked, by their unique request.

If truth be known, the matchmaker had been expecting a visit from one, if not both, of the twins. They were both of that awkward age of either finding a wife or being forever doomed to bachelorhood. They were in their late twenties – so late in their twenties, in fact, that their next birthday would see them leave their twenties forever, if Michael was not mistaken. And Michael made it his business never to be mistaken in such personal details.

Two summers past, the twins had been made parentless when their mother, 'who'd a good innings', passed away peacefully in her sleep, outliving her husband by ten years.

The matchmaker had guessed that right around the time they came calling on him, the two would have just begun to miss a woman's touch about the house. He had guessed correctly. Neither Pat nor Joe had much time in the day, or inclination for that matter, for domestic chores. No, they were forced to work all the hours God sent them, and some more besides, to make their small farm just pay for itself.

'Well, gentlemen, what can I do for you?' the matchmaker asked, as he reached for his leather-bound book, which he had rested on the sideboard to his right. He spoke with a distinct Ulster accent, which was part hurried, part jovial.

The twins had chosen to sit together on the sofa. They looked so out of place both in the somewhat formal setting and from the discomfort they were experiencing wearing their Sunday best.

Joseph Kane, the twin seated furthermost from Michael, used the opportunity of the matchmaker's opening question to raise his teacup to his lips, thereby encouraging his brother to answer.

Michael considered Patrick and Joseph Kane as he awaited an answer to break a silence as bleak as a dawn walk by the nearby shores of Lough Neagh.

The twins' suits were matching in cut and style but differed slightly in colour. They were perched on the edge of the sofa, like two hyper magpies on a fence, juggling teacup, saucer and shortbread. The matchmaker knew full well that should the brothers be in the comfort – and disarray – of their own farmhouse, the tea would be in rinsed-out mugs grasped firmly in fists while the other hands shovelled biscuits, or usually something more substantial and nutritious, like a sandwich or a chicken leg, down their throats.

But here they were, jet black hair permanently dishevelled due to receiving the threat of a comb only once a week, usually on Sunday mornings following their weekly shave. They were trying so hard to fit in with the matchmaker's surroundings, to show him that they *could* fit in so that he *would* 'take them on'. But they weren't (fitting in) and the harder they tried, the more awkward the opera became.

Patrick smiled, half to himself, noting that Joe was keeping the teacup to his lips, frozen in a mock sucking pose, for an incredible amount of time, and half to the matchmaker indicating that he, the twin with the natural smile and sparkling eyes, was to be the spokesperson on this issue.

'Well, it's like this. We've been told – Joseph and me, that is – that you can … that you could find a wife for a man. Is that true?' Patrick enquired, thinking that it seemed such an easy solution to their problem – well, at least the first part of their problem. He now raised the white china cup to his lips as a signal to the matchmaker that he had completed his question.

'Yes.'

Michael Gilmour smiled as he opened his well-worn book and removed a fountain pen from his inside pocket. He unscrewed the greenish marble-patterned top and fixed it on the other end, exposing a nib that betrayed signs of blue ink. There was nothing unusual in this except that he executed the manoeuvre with one hand, a trick neither Joseph nor Patrick had ever seen before. They both openly marvelled at this display, impressed as though they were children discovering for the first time that there are not, in fact, little men sitting inside your wireless.

'Yes, that is what I do, Pat: I make matches. You see, in the first half of this book of mine,' Michael paused as he used his thumb to flick through the pages, 'I take down all your details, along with all the other men I deal with. And in the second half of the book,' again, for effect, he flicked through the pages, 'I have the details of all the women looking for husbands – and I see if I can match them up. Mind you, my father, when he passed all this over to me, he told me never to forget the words of Oscar Wilde: "Men marry because they are tired; women, because they are curious." So the perfect match may not always be the perfect match to start off with.'

The matchmaker felt, as ever in these circumstances, it was inappropriate, not to mention untimely, to reveal the end of Wilde's quote, it being, 'Both are disappointed'.

Pat looked at the book on the matchmaker's lap. Joe's eyes were still glued to the fountain pen as he tried to work out if he could pull off the same trick.

'Let's get the business bit out of the way first, shall we?'

The twins nodded in agreement.

'Fair play to you both. I charge you ten pounds to register with me, in this special book of mine, and then if and when I match you up satisfactorily and you get married or move in together' – the matchmaker showed a sign of disapproval regarding this last option but he was, first and foremost, a businessman, and if a couple chose to commit the 'big sin', they weren't going to be allowed to commit another even bigger one by not paying him – 'I charge a final 100 pounds – that's calculated as fifty from the lady and fifty from the gent. In my experience, the man always tends to pay the hundred; whether it's the lady's cash or not is none of my business.'

The twins, without consulting each other, nodded agreement to the matchmaker's terms.

'So, who do we get then?' Joe chipped in at last, speaking with his mouth full of biscuit.

'Ah, well, it's not as easy as that, I say, it's not as easy as that. As I've already mentioned, I need to take down your details, all your particulars as it were: your age, build, height, weight, hair, teeth – you know, all those personal kind of things, plus all my own notes and observations. And I'll need to know about your financial position, details about the farm, the stock, the debts, all your assets. All this stuff might seem a bit nosey, lads, but it's all stuff I need to know in order to allow me to make a good match. And then I need to know, well, if you would want to have children and how many, or, equally, if you are not prepared to have children,' Michael advised them. He'd already started to make his notes and after a bit of nib scratching across the clean page he continued: 'Then I'll need to know what each of you is looking for in a wife. Looks, age, whether you want your prospective wife to have a dowry. You have to think what you're really looking for – a wife? A housekeeper? A mother for your children? Financial support for you and for your farm or –'

'Isn't that all the same person?' Joe enquired.

'No. Well, no, not really; some people don't really want anything other than someone to look after them and after the marriage has been consummated, well, they don't really want to be called upon for, well, to … look, shall we just say they won't want to be responsible for those kinds of chores any more, if you know what I mean.'

The twins nodded, signalling that they knew exactly what the matchmaker meant.

The matchmaker refilled the twins' cups with tea and invited them to help themselves to milk and sugar (three for Joe and one for Pat).

'So, Pat, shall we start with yourself? Shall I take your details first?'

Pat did not reply, rather he merely allowed his face to transmit a dumb grin, just like a drunk who has fallen on his behind and finally realised he doesn't have the wherewithal to resume the vertical.

'Look, ah, would you feel more comfortable if we did this part separately?' the matchmaker offered, thinking he'd found the reason for the resistance.

'No!' Joe replied, very nearly shouting the word. He eyeballed his brother with a 'you tell him' kind of stare.

'Look, this is a bit awkward,' his brother began, putting his tea down on a small pinewood coffee table in front of him and slipping back into the full wealth of the sofa's comfort. Joe followed suit but kept his cup and saucer with him, one hand supporting the saucer from underneath and the other thumb and forefinger poised on the handle of the cup, ever ready to raise the cup to his mouth when either silence or thirst decreed the necessity.

'Well, I'm sure you'll understand, Michael, we've only a small farm.' Joe rolled his eyes.

'And you know it's barely able to support the two of us,' Pat continued, ignoring his brother. 'You know, I'm amazed at how our parents managed to get by – I mean, when we were growing up I don't remember being poor.'

'We certainly weren't rich,' Joe interrupted.

'No, perhaps not,' Pat continued unperturbed, appearing almost to smile at the memory. 'But I don't remember us ever going hungry, or going without clean clothes on our backs, or suffering the embarrassment of hand-me-down school uniforms. I never really thought about it at the time. I suppose I really was guilty of taking for granted what my parents did for us. But now that I am aware of their limited resources, I appreciate it all the more.'

The matchmaker couldn't be sure, but he thought that Joe faked a yawn behind his brother's back. In the end Michael gave the apparently reluctant twin the benefit of the doubt, graciously figuring the yawn came not from disrespect but from the hours on the fields.

'We've had a few bad years since our father died,' Pat offered. 'It's been touch and go sometimes, I can tell you. Any time we get a few bob in, the bank manager is there, knocking on our door, threatening to call in the papers on our loan and take the farm away from us. But now we're getting the hang of it and I think we are beginning to make it work, but only just. However, since our mother died, well, her part of the housework – her chores – well, that's all been a bit of a disaster, if you know what I mean.'

'Fair play, to you,' was the matchmaker's only reply.

'Some days we don't even get a chance to eat at all we're so busy and then by the time it gets to the end of the day we're too tired to worry about cooking or cleaning or washing or anything other than sleeping,' Pat Kane said, as he continued to circle the point.

'Yes, I understand. That's perfectly understandable. Now you want wives and you don't have a chance to go to dances or socials or parties to meet the women, so you've come to me. That's all perfectly normal, nothing to be ashamed about,' Michael coaxed, as he proceeded to write Patrick Daniel Kane in the left-hand column of his opened page.

'Yes, we know and we're fine with all of that – aren't we, Joseph?' Pat said, not venturing from the safety of his circle.

'Yeah,' came the indignant reply from his brother.

'But, as I was saying, well, it's a small farm and the money from the crops is spoken for and, well, you know, I don't think that it could support two more people, well, at least not at this stage … but ….'

'Oh, I *see*! One of you wants to get married immediately and the other one wants to wait?' the matchmaker prompted hopefully.

The twins looked like they were Native Americans trying to converse with Palefaces for the first time.

'Well, lads, which of you drew the short straw?' the matchmaker gamely asked, not realising he was risking his own scalp. His long ginger mane would have made a fine trophy on anyone's belt.

Joe stared at Pat with another of his 'you tell him' stares.

'No, no – it's not like that. You don't understand … I … well, we … you see ….'

Joe placed his cup and saucer firmly on the coffee table, his impatience getting the better of him.

'Look, Mr Gilmour, what my brother … what Pat is trying to tell you is that we – the both of us – want to take the same wife!'

Chapter Three

'Absolutely out of the question! Totally impossible,' the matchmaker hissed, spluttering his most recent mouthful of tea in a spray over the carpet and his shoes. He regained his composure, but only slightly, to continue, 'Not to mention illegal in every county on the island of Ireland. What do you want to do to me – put me out of business?'

Joe started one of his 'I told you he wouldn't understand' stares at Pat who, now he was able to come in from his circling, was happier to get into the conversation with the matchmaker.

'No, no, not at all!' he said, sounding enthusiastic for the first time. 'Tell me what part of what we're suggesting is illegal?'

'I'm sorry, lads, but there's a little thing called "bigamy". God, if anyone even knew I was having this conversation with you I'd, I'd, I'd …' When the matchmaker obviously couldn't imagine anything worse that could, or would, happen to him, he took a different tack. 'I don't know whether to laugh or throw you both out on the street.'

'Look, Michael, we don't want to get you in trouble, nor do we wish to get into trouble ourselves and we certainly wouldn't like to start a relationship off with a poor girl by having her commit bigamy,' Pat started.

'Well, that's good to hear,' the matchmaker stated, feeling compelled to interrupt. 'I say that's great to hear.'

'But don't you see, Michael, she wouldn't be? She wouldn't be committing bigamy; she'd only be marrying the one of us!'

'What? But I thought you said—'

'No, no! Look, let me explain. We've thought about this, thought about it a lot, and believe me there is absolutely nothing illegal about what we are suggesting. We just need to find a partner who will agree to it,' Pat said, as he smiled at the matchmaker.

The matchmaker had the feeling the twin had reasoned this through a lot in his mind. Even Joe forced a smile of hope as his brother, circling over, continued to plough the field.

'Firstly, you find us a potential wife and on the wedding day only one of us will be at the wedding. As you know, we both have "D" as a middle initial so this, this lucky woman will be marrying a "D. Kane" and even on the day she won't know which one of us turns up, which one of us she will actually be marrying.'

The matchmaker couldn't believe he was hearing what he was hearing. In all the years he and his father and his father's father before that had been matchmakers there had been some weird and wonderful twists, but never, ever one quite as far around the corner as this.

'There'll be no fuss,' Pat persisted, as Joe twisted nervously on the sofa. 'We'll go down to Belfast and do the business in a registry office – no-one from here will be aware of anything and then *our* wife will move into the farm with us and look after us *both*.'

'I can't believe you lads. I really can't,' Michael said, staring only at Joseph, since he felt Joseph D. Kane was the real culprit behind this folly. Joe refused to meet his stare so Michael continued. 'How on earth do you think you'll ever find a woman to agree to this? Eh? And I suppose you mean by "looking after you both" she'll also be expected to have sexual relations with the two of you? God, if the wife knew I was even in a room where this conversation was taking place I'd be for the high jump!'

'Come on, Mr Gilmour, it's no big thing,' Joe began. 'It's not a big thing with us – you know we'll be too busy most of the time to even *talk* to our wife, let alone bother her, and we'll give you a guarantee that our joint demands on her time, you know, in the bedroom, well, it will be no more than if she were married to just the one husband.'

'Would you ever listen to yourselves, would you? You mean, of course, "if she were married as normal", don't you?' Michael began to laugh. 'I really can't believe this – I'm sorry, but I really can't.'

The matchmaker started to pour himself another cup of tea only to realise that his cup was still nearly full. He sat down and scratched his head with his thin fingers and sighed a few times before saying: 'Look, part of the thing here is that when I am, in normal circumstances, asked to do this I take down all your details. I make a few notes of my own. I consider all the information I have. I then go to the back of the book and I check through the details of the ladies I have on file to see if there are any of them who I feel might make a good match. You have to know that I think about all this for a long, long time. I like my matches to *work*. Don't you see? Good, solid, successful matches are like my best advertisements: successful matches are my reputation. I'm not like you. I don't deal in things I can sell, things like potatoes, like milk, like hay or like cattle. I'm not a carpenter; I can't make a great table or chair and take it into the market next Thursday in Magherafelt and sell it and feed the family for a week on the proceeds and have enough left over to buy some more wood to make another table and so on.'

The twins looked on and listened in amazement. They were like two kittens being chastised for playing with a ball of wool and now they watched, hardly daring to move a muscle, as their master rolled the wool back into its ball, all neat and tidy. However, given an opportunity, they would be right back in there, in the thick of it, messing with the wool again. The twins realised this was the time to remain quiet, so quiet they remained and let the matchmaker continue uninterrupted.

'No, I'm a matchmaker, I'm proud of that. It's a grand thing to be and it has served the last two generations of Gilmours well, *very* well. But, as I say, it's all down to reputation. That's all I have to sell – my reputation and to a lesser degree the reputations of my father and grandfather. So you can see I'm very careful and before I even suggest my matches I'm pretty sure something will work out. You know, even if it's not love at first sight that's OK. I'll tell you what I believe to be true: where there is no love, put love and you will find love. My granddad always used to tell me that and I couldn't get to grips with it when I was younger. But the older I grow and the more I see people together and working with each other, the more I believe that to be true. Of course the couple in question has to at least *like* each other in the first place. There has to be a basic bond and trust there. There has to be a willingness to try and make it work.'

The kittens were growing restless again but the matchmaker continued unperturbed.

'So I make my match. I don't work out a wish list in advance – I make my match and suggest it. I don't have a second and third choice ready in the wings just in case the first doesn't work out. A lot of people think that I do. But, Pat and Joe, let me tell you: it's much more of an exact science than that, this matchmaking business. Obviously if it doesn't work we go back to the drawing board and I consider *why* the match didn't work before I'm willing to try another recommendation. But anyway, when I make the match I insist on a few casual meetings between the potential partners. You must remember we have to try to make this as natural a process as possible,' the matchmaker added.

Four arched eyebrows confirmed that his audience was confused.

'OK, for argument's sake, let's say that you are not as busy as you are and you both have some time to spend in, em … shall we say, "recreational pursuits". So you go to a dance, you go to a pub, you go to a party or you go to a friend's house for a bit of craic. And you see a girl, a girl who catches your eye. Now, nine times out of ten you won't do anything about it the first time you see her. You'll wait until you see someone *you* know who knows *her* – could even be her brother or sister who happens to be a friend of yours. And you ask about this girl: what's she like? Has she got a boy? Does she go to dances? Where does she hang out? You'd have lots and lots of questions. Then you'll maybe go to a dance or a party or your friend's house with an excuse to see her again without actually doing anything about it.' Michael smiled – the twins didn't realise he was recalling the exact way he'd chased his then wife-to-be, Dorothy.

'Maybe you'll be introduced, find an excuse to say something, just make that vital connection. So next time you see her, no matter where it might be, you'll have the confidence to talk to her a bit more. And then you might check back in with your first friend to ascertain if she likes you. You might ask one of those hypothetical questions, you know, "Em, you know, so and so, well, em, I was thinking: do you know what would happen if I … There's this friend of mine and he really likes her and he was thinking, and I said I would check for him, so do you think if he asked her out, you know, would she go, you know, out with him?" And the friend will probably answer, "Oh yes – where were *you* thinking of taking her to?"'

Pat and Joe smiled, forgetting the underlying concern the three men in the room were feeling.

'Then you ask her out. You go for a walk, you talk a lot, you leave her home, but before she's returned to the safety of her parents' house you ask her when you can see her again, and bit by bit you get to know one another and start to like each other and it develops from there and maybe, just maybe, after a couple of years you will discuss marriage. Whereas when *my* potential matches go out for *their* first date, yes, even on their first date, marriage is on the agenda. It might be in the very back of the minds of both parties, but it is still there. So I'll go along on the first two or three meetings and stay with the matched couple for the entire time. Then I'll talk to both of them separately and try to gauge how sincere they are about each other. Then and only then will I suggest the couple go on a date with a chaperone. After they've had a few such dates I'll chat to them again – separately and together – to see how it's going. I'll encourage the two of them to openly discuss with each other what they're feeling and then, if it's going to fly, I let them get on with it. But it's important, vitally important, that the early stages are as natural as humanly possible. Do youse understand that?'

The twins nodded.

'So at what point in this procedure were youse two perverts going to tell the sorry lass that she'd be sleeping with both of you?'

The matchmaker stood up, undid the top button of his white shirt and loosened his tie. Dorothy would be cross at this but he would do it back up again before she saw him. He always felt very uncomfortable with all his shirt buttons and tie done up, to the extent that his wife had started buying him shirts a size bigger to help him out, but all her efforts proved to be in vain. He was fine now though, at ease in his brown cords, light tan shoes, Harris Tweed jacket, starched white shirt and brown tie. He had a light frame at five foot eight inches tall and clothes hung well on him, the way they tended to on school teachers. The heat in the front room, either from the conversation or from the continuously burning peat and wood fire, had brought a flush to his cheeks to match his hair. He opened the window, allowing the sounds of the countryside to spill in.

'Nah, nah! You're making it all sound sordid,' Pat complained.

'Well, look at the facts, gentlemen; from where I'm standing it all sounds pretty sordid to me,' the matchmaker replied. He had remained by the open window to bask in the cool breeze. 'If I went and told the wife, if I said, "Oh, by the way, Dorothy, you know the meeting I've just had with the twins? Well, they're looking for a wife," and she'd say, "Oh that's nice, Michael, they're good people," and I'd say, "That's what I always thought, but get this: they just want the one wife between the two of them." And do you know what she'd do if I told her that?'

If the twins did know, and they could only guess, neither of them was saying.

'Well, I'll tell you – she'd have us all out of this house and over in the mucky ditch across the other side of Apple Orchard Lane, Sunday clothes or not!'

'No, look, Michael – it's much simpler than that,' Pat began.

'It is?' Michael replied, stretching the 'is'.

'Yes, look, here's the thing: we – Joe and me – each go separately to these meetings and dates and whatever and when you feel the time is appropriate we can make our suggestion. It'll have nothing whatsoever to do with you. No-one will be aware that you know anything about it. In fact, no-one, full stop – except for her, Joe and I and yourself – will be aware of the details. But when we make the suggestion, well, if it goes down as badly as you think it might, then we can make out that it was a joke all along and that we were only kidding.'

'A joke? Only kidding? I'll tell you, youse two with all your jokes and kidding about, you're funny enough to get on *Sunday Night at the London Palladium*. Fair play to you, aye, I say, fair play to you, but it's certainly on the stage youse two should be.'

The twins could see that this particular ball of wool was about to be put away on a high shelf and out of their reach forever.

'OK, why don't we do this, Michael – why don't we just give you all our details now and we pay you a tenner each today? We'll go away and then you can think about it for a while and if you decide that you can't or don't want to do anything about it, well then that will be absolutely fine. There it will stay forever. Just think about it will you?' Pat pleaded.

Forty minutes later the twins were walking down Railway Terrace, homeward bound to their small farm on the opposite side of Castlemartin on the way to the townland of Toome.

While the matchmaker was redoing his tie, Pat was hurriedly undoing his and the top button of his factory blue shirt. He walked in silence, deep in thought, for about fifty yards before he addressed his brother.

'I told you he wouldn't go for it, didn't I?'

'Oh, I wouldn't be so sure if I were you. Don't you remember Gilmour at school? He was a tight bastard then and if he can make two hundred and thirty quid for the one match, and providing he can prove to himself that it's not illegal – which it's not – then, just as sure as the Pope's a Catholic, Gilmour'll go for it. Just you wait and see.'

Chapter Four

Michael Gilmour had heard many strange requests during his dozen years of matchmaking. Even before that he'd heard, on numerous occasions, his father's forty years of matchmaking stories. But he'd never heard, never even heard of, a request as bizarre as the one the Kane twins had made to him.

Discussing the situation with Dorothy was purely and simply out of the question as far as he was concerned. However, should he have had the courage to entertain her opinion on this he would have found, to his surprise, that she would have had a much more liberal slant on the situation than he would have given her credit for.

Instead, he chose to discuss the unique circumstances with his wife's sister, Margaret Watson. The matchmaker and his sister-in-law had always been very comfortable with each other and had often sought each other's counsel on a variety of private and personal subjects.

This dated back to Michael and Dorothy's courting days. How, in fact, does a matchmaker make a match for himself? In Michael's case it was easy: he'd been good friends with Margaret at school and, as such, he'd discussed each and (well, very nearly) every move in his budding relationship with her sister. So in point of fact, you could say that Margaret had acted as matchmaker in that particularly smooth romance.

Margaret Watson had inherited her father's spirit and her mother's sculpted looks. Dorothy was much the opposite, but that was fine for Michael, since he found her qualities more reassuring in a wife. Margaret had shunned the attention of many a bachelor, some eligible with looks and money, some eligible with looks and no money, some eligible with money and no looks and some with none of the above but tempting nonetheless. Although tempted she seldom was. Not yet for her the married life; no, instead she helped to marry off her sister and, in the process, retained her own freedom to search for adventure. Dorothy, on the other hand, had been at that stage in her life where she needed a husband, needed to start a family. She'd been unlucky in love, but only, Maggie felt, because she'd been more preoccupied with the hurt she'd suffered, rather than considering that she'd had a lucky escape from a life spent with the wrong man.

Maggie adopted her sister's new family as her own and by doing so she was filling a very evident gap in her own life – well … evident, that was, to all excepting herself. She liked Michael more than she ever felt she should like a brother-in-law, but because they both shared a genuine love for Dorothy there was never a moment of awkwardness between them. And on top of all of that, Paul, Nick and Marianne got to enjoy the unselfish love of their dear aunt.

'Eh, you know the Kane twins, Joe and Pat, don't you?' Michael began tentatively as they walked away from his house and up and over the field that the neighbouring farmer rented from Michael to graze his small herd of cows and two horses.

'Yes, yes, of course. Sure, weren't we all at school around the same time? Oh God, Pat had such beautiful eyes – that was the only way I could tell them apart,' Margaret replied, as she side-stepped a still-steaming fly magnet.

'Well, it's funny. I mean, it's not really funny, but they came to see me a few Sundays ago and …'

Michael hesitated to such an extent his silence encouraged Margaret to offer: 'What were they looking for – wives?'

'No,' he uttered hesitantly, shaking his head slowly, his ginger hair blowing this way and that with the wind, 'not really.'

'Not really? Sorry, so this *wasn't* to do with your wedding factory?'

'Em, well, kind of, but they weren't exactly looking for *wives*.'

'Oh Jesus, come on, would you ever tell me? What's the big mystery?' Margaret smiled. He loved it when she smiled. She had natural blonde hair but she didn't look blonde until she smiled.

'Well, it's kind of … kinda like *unusual*.'

'And?' Margaret was beginning to get annoyed with Michael. Here it was, a beautiful spring afternoon; the sky was blue, a deep blue whose perfection was spoiled only by a few small fluffy clouds. It was quite sharp, as in refreshingly cold. That was in contrast to an Ulster cold that you could feel through your coat. She enjoyed their walks together – they had become less and less frequent with the passing years, so now they had managed to steal one, she felt it was too precious to waste on the twins. No, she wanted to discuss her favourite topic – a topic she wouldn't dare discuss with anyone other than her brother-in-law: namely how and when *she* would find her true and great love. Margaret was confident that she would, and her confidence was encouraged by the matchmaker – not as a matchmaker, mind you, but as a friend. Margaret often joked with Michael that if a matchmaker didn't know when, and from where, a true love was going to appear, then no-one ever would.

'And?' she repeated.

'Well, they're both looking for a wife!' Michael blurted out as he looked away from her over the fields to their left.

'But you just told me that they weren't ….'

'Weren't what?'

'Oh, Michael, for heaven's sake! Weren't looking for wives!'

'But they're not,' Michael explained, now starting to enjoy the confusion he was creating.

'Sorry, Michael, stop!' Margaret took her hand out from the warmth of her pocket and caught the matchmaker by the arm of his sheepskin jacket, turning him towards her. 'What on earth are you going on about?'

'They want *a* wife!' Michael whispered like the seagulls whisper mid-ocean. 'They want to take *a* wife – one wife between the two of them!'

'What?' Margaret shouted.

'Yes, I thought the penny would eventually drop and I'd get your undivided attention.'

'Oh Jesus!'

'Yes, and it's probably a new one for Him and all.'

'What did you say to them, Michael? Which of them did the talking? What type of woman are they after? Would she have to sleep with the both of them? Can you charge them double? God, what would they do when they went to church?'

'I couldn't possibly tell you. Patrick. Anyone who'd be available. I think so. Not exactly and God only knows. I think that answers all your questions, and in order!' Michael replied, smiling – not at the fun of it, for he was sure the situation wasn't in the least bit funny, but a) at the look of disbelief on Margaret's face and b) at the relief of finally being able to share this unique, disturbing request with someone else.

'Amazing!' was all that the matchmaker's sister-in-law could utter as she let go of his arm and returned her hand deep into the pocket of her warm, well-worn brown leather jacket with its snug snow-white wool collar. They both headed out further into the pleasant northern wind.

The matchmaker had expected a much bigger reaction from Maggie; in fact, he was surprised at just how quiet she was as they strolled back to the house.

Chapter Five

Gentleman Jim Reeves was on the wireless singing 'Welcome to My World' and Margaret Watson found herself unconsciously adding a top harmony to Jim's dark-brown dulcet tones. She also found herself thinking about the Kane twins' strange request.

Maggie had begun to dwell on the previous week's revelations from her brother-in-law. Dwell on them quite a lot in fact. Well, if Maggie was being truthful, and we need her to be so, she would have to admit that she now rarely thought of little else. She couldn't help imagining what it would be like to be one of the three principals in this rural drama. For instance, would they all sleep in the one bed? That would be just too weird – or would it? After all, why not? The reasons for it to be too weird were social ones, weren't they? Wasn't that how she was supposed to think?

But would the reality be the total opposite? A woman with two men continually vying for her affection and attention: shouldn't that be an ideal scenario? Each one aware, because of their twin, that they could never, ever take her for granted. Mind you, when Maggie thought of 'her' she didn't mean herself, of course – no, she meant the hussy to take the both of them on. That was, of course, if they should ever be lucky enough to find a hussy brazen enough.

The single factor that intrigued her most about this scenario was that two other people – the twins themselves – were already considering the possibilities. Now maybe even her brother-in-law could be added to the short but exclusive list.

And what about the twins? There had always been something about Pat which had intrigued her, but Joe had always left her cold. So what would the prospective wife be taking on? What were they like now? She knew what they were like in public: quiet, handsome, clean and well-mannered, but not the best-dressed boys in the parish. When she'd known them – that is to say, when their mother was still alive – if their clothes lacked something on the fashion side, perhaps even growing a little threadbare, no-one could ever fault them in the hygiene stakes, as their garments were always spotlessly clean and smelling fresh. But now, with their mother gone, what would they reveal about themselves behind closed doors? Would they be exactly the same or completely the opposite? Would they find their ideal woman in all of this?

Her sister, Dorothy, claimed that she knew immediately after her first date with the matchmaker that she'd found her ideal man in Michael. Maggie had advised her to be cautious due to her sister's notorious previous train-wrecks. She'd long given up trying to work out whether Dorothy's frequent dark moods descended upon her because a boy had broken up with her or if the boys broke up with her because of her dark moods.

The matchmaker was different though: he was sensible and he and Dorothy seemed to hit it off pretty early in their relationship. They had become engaged at Christmas, four months after their first date, and were wed the following June.

But Maggie herself hadn't had much luck with her choice in men over the years. Her main flame to date had been a musician, Davy, who played bass with the local showband, The Playboys. But the flame had blown out very quickly for Maggie when she discovered Davy was two-timing her with a hairdresser from up in Cookstown. Apparently, as well as comforting Davy on his away nights, the hairdresser was also throwing a bit of black hair-dye in for good measure. Now how could Maggie possibly compete with that?

Poor Maggie had been devastated and she'd spent days crying in her room. Going out with a local celeb had done wonders for Maggie's profile, but equally the very public falling-out was impossible to hide from. Even the sanctuary of one's own room barely kept the storm at bay as wave after wave after wave arrived at her front door to enquire, discreetly of course, 'Is Maggie over her man yet? Is she ready to come out?'

Maggie's mother and father had advised the very worried Dorothy not to be overly concerned about her sister: she'd be sure to get over it. 'Time is the great healer in affairs of the heart,' her father had offered in comfort.

Maggie would get over it – in fact, she duly did nine days later when she happened upon Freddie Miller, a shop assistant in Dawson Bates', a large grocery store in neighbouring Magherafelt.

Freddie had his own car, a Black Ford Vauxhall, and Maggie was made up to be driven the length and breadth of County Derry. The novelty of this constant road work soon wore off when Freddie tried his seldom practised Ulster Octopus technique in the back of the car. The octopus in question did live to tell the tale, albeit slightly wounded and speaking half an octave higher.

At this point Maggie had decided that she was off boys for good and she was as good as her word, remaining unattached for a full two-and-one-half weeks until she met a friend of Michael's at her sister's new house. Michael's friend was nice. That was the problem – he was nice and all the girls grew to learn that nice boys are boring.

So began her discreet journey into the unknown in search of a man.

She wanted a man she could feel good with, a man who would excite her, could surprise her, but also a man who would always treat her well. Following many a failure, Maggie envied Dorothy's luck in finding her man – her brick – relatively easily. In fact, she began to worry that this was the secret: you find your man, your one true love, your partner for life, first time. Or you don't – not at all, ever. Dorothy had a few partners before this who were chased off by her dark moods.

Despite her failed relationships, Maggie felt her virginity was not something to savour but a gift to give away – so she did. At first she had simply wanted to gain experience in that area so she could meet her man on an even plane, but she was shocked, surprised and extremely pleased at how much she enjoyed sex. She was overwhelmed by it even on her first occasion, out in Hutchinson's hay shed on the Magherafelt Road.

This particular ballroom of romance, an old run-down shed used to keep the hay dry in case of frost or snow, was so popular with those locals eager for a play in the hay that Maggie and her partner had to return on three separate occasions before finding room at the inn to consummate their joint virginal passion.

For that special night (well, more like half an hour) of passion Maggie had selected a former friend from technical college, Stuart Gibney, because he was good looking and honest, he didn't have bum fluff on his upper lip, he knew how to laugh, she knew he'd bring protection and, chiefly, she knew he didn't have a blabber mouth – and even if he did, he was no longer around much to do any blabbering, having recently left Castlemartin to study at Queen's University in Belfast. Besides all of the above, they'd nearly gone all the way during their previous four-month courtship prior to his leaving town, when they'd become all hot and bothered on several (more than seven) occasions. Perhaps the most important reason in picking Stewart was that Maggie knew he was also a virgin and she wanted to venture on this journey of sexual exploration as an equal.

Maggie was surprised, after all the horror stories from her friends about how unpleasant and painful the first time was, by how absolutely pleasurable the experience turned out to be. To make sure they weren't doing anything wrong, they repeated the race of the fiddler's elbow to get full value from the infamous 'packet of glee'.

Similar experiences had been repeated on rare occasions over the following eight years – twice more with Stewart, one over an exquisite weekend down at his digs in Belfast, and with three other partners. Maggie had hoped that one of these partners, Scott Grade, might be the one, but the sex had been so boring (he hadn't cared in the least for her pleasure) that shortly thereafter they stopped stepping out together.

Now, here she was pottering around her room in her parents' house, a detached bungalow on the Magherafelt side of Castledawson, listening to RTÉ radio and ruminating on the Kane twins and their search for a solitary wife.

On the spot, right there in her bedroom, as Larry Gogan came on the air to announce the next single, Liverpool's new singing sensation the Beatles with 'Can't Buy Me Love', Margaret Watson made a decision and the decision was to have as much impact in her world as the Beatles were to have in theirs.

She decided to pay a visit to her brother-in-law the following day.

Chapter Six

On the way to Michael and Dorothy's house – up the Lough Road, filled with terraced houses, to the Pear Tree Roundabout, second exit to the left and down the steep Briscoe Street, right into the uninhabited Wood Lane, straight into the narrow Wood Path, right along the tree-lined, sparsely housed Apple Orchard Lane and it was the fourth soldier's cottage (of four) on the left – Maggie raced over all of her ideas, which were whizzing around in her head like leaves caught in a wind trap. You don't know where they are going to land and for how long – you only know that they are sure to stay contained in the trap. She was trying to find a way – the easiest way – of announcing her intentions to the matchmaker. She certainly knew that she could never put a brave enough face on to tell her sister. No, Michael was going to have to look after that one, not to mention selling the entire project to Dorothy.

Michael greeted her at the door. It was the back door and normally she would just have strolled in, but tonight she wanted the comfort of greeting Michael first. Protected by the cloak of darkness, she knew the man of the house would answer her gentle tapping.

'Guess what?' Michael announced to the family indoors, reading the apprehension on Maggie's face and grabbing his jacket from behind the door. 'Margaret and I are off for a bit of a dander.'

Dorothy seemed to be pleased to have the both of them out of her hair, while Maggie was equally pleased at how quickly Michael had read the situation, although she neglected to impart all this information to the matchmaker. Instead they fell into step together and wandered off up the lane in the general direction of the hay fields.

How many times had they paced this journey? She felt she knew every bump and dip in the lane. They both knew instinctively when to veer to one side to avoid the long, dangling, thorny blackberry branches that hung out threateningly, like tentacles, from the hedge on either side of the lane.

The sister-in-law wondered when two people, such as she and her brother-in-law, wander in silence, was it because they were both lost in their thoughts, or was it because one of them was lost in their thoughts and the other was trying to find the right thing to say? Or could it possibly be because both of them were trying to find the right thing to say? Maggie found herself trying several opening lines under her breath as if she were a sailor holding a recently licked feather up towards the heavens to see what way the wind blew. However, in Maggie's case she could only guess which way the wind might blow because, of course, the matchmaker was not able to hear any of her proposed opening lines.

'How's it going?' the male voice eventually offered as he interrupted their silence. Maggie thought she could hear a little shake in Michael's usually confident hoarse tones.

His voice was amazing really – he always sounded, to Maggie at least, as though he had a cold or sore throat. In a way his voice was not too dissimilar to Dylan's raggedy vocals – you always felt they were doing permanent damage to their throats with their ever-present raspiness. Maggie had often tried to imagine how Dylan would sound if he sang in an Ulster accent, but her mind could never quite make the connection. However, once when Michael, Dorothy and she were drunk she'd had Michael sing 'The Times They Are a Changin'. That *did* work – that could have been Dylan if he'd had the luck of being born not in Minnesota but in Bellaghy, or Toomebridge, or Ahoghill, or Cullybackey or even Ballyronan. Now that would have been one, wouldn't it? What if Bob Dylan, the voice with the message of warning from the 'excuse me, it's our turn' generation, had been born and bred in Ballyronan? What on earth would the likes of the *Mid Ulster Mail* have made of that?

'Yeah,' was her only reply, barely whispered, making it obvious it was his turn to serve.

Michael looked like he'd been expecting a longer reply, perhaps a reply behind which he could better prepare himself to make his revelation.

'I think I've sorted out the Kane twins' situation.' Michael smiled, trying to pull off the air of someone casually oblivious to their ace serve.

Maggie stopped dead in her tracks, but obviously thought better of it and moved on, the break in her stride barely noticeable.

'You … you took it on then?' was all she could utter, hoping she was hiding her disappointment as she picked up the imaginary ball from the rear of the court.

'Well, not exactly.'

They were, by this point, passing the cowshed. Maggie remembered a few summers ago, Michael – much to the amusement of his family – had ridden up this lane on the back of one of the cows doing his best Clint Eastwood (as Rowdy Yates in *Rawhide*) impression. This was a time when making Clint's day meant no more than tending to a peaceful herd of grazing cattle while satisfied with a full belly of beans.

'And?'

'Let me explain,' Michael continued as he opened the door to the cowshed, which was empty since the cattle were over at the main farm, close to fresher grazing pastures. However, it most certainly was not free of the pungent aromas of their hide, droppings and hay – a healthy smell as quick to fill the nostrils as the smell of another brute made famous by Henry 'splash it all over' Cooper.

'As you know, I was more than a little uncomfortable …with the… am… situation. So. So I went to Pat and told him that I thought there might be a better way to go about doing this.'

'Yeah?' Maggie pushed, her eyebrows raised to the hay-packed rafters of the cowshed in disbelief. This was like … no, on second thoughts pulling teeth was easier, probably much easier. But she wondered if her impatience had anything to do with the feeling of emptiness growing in the pit of her stomach.

'And. Well, I … well, if you really want to know the truth,' Michael began, only to be interrupted by Maggie on his case.

'Look, Michael – you keep saying that, and Dorothy and I keep telling you off about it. It's so infuriating! "Well, if you really want to know the truth" – no, actually, could I have a lie, please? They're much more fun. Of course I, *we*, want to know the truth!'

'Sorry, I know it's a bad habit and you're right, Dorothy is always on about it, but I just kind of do it subconsciously. My dad used to do it all the time and, well, women didn't question their husband's use of the English language in his day. Now all that's changed so I had better, em … pull my socks up, hadn't I?'

The apology hadn't been one hundred per cent necessary as Maggie's words had kind of been in jest … if you really want to know the truth.

'Well, I explained to Pat that I was sure he didn't exactly want the whole town talking about their particular situation. So, I asked, why didn't he go about it in a more natural or usual way? I suggested he register on my books as a bachelor, part owner of the farm, a young, hardworking man, interested in starting a family – a dowry would be nice, but not vital, and a few other things I would add but not tell him about –'

'Like?' she cut in, this time playfully.

'Oh, good looking, good head of hair, slim, strong, fine mouth of white teeth. You'd be surprised how many women look for men to have their own teeth, and white. I suppose it's just that they don't want to wake up in the middle of the night and see their husband's smile on the sideboard in a jam-jar half-filled with water. Where was I?'

'White teeth,' she prompted.

'Oh yes, teeth, and strong, hardworking,' the matchmaker tried to complete his list, unsuccessfully.

'We've already had hardworking. What about lips – do you talk about lips in your list? Like are they thin, hard, chapped and uninviting or full, soft, rich and enticing?'

'I'm quite sure I can leave the couple to suss out those and other such details for themselves, thank you very much.'

'True, I mean, I was just trying to save your clients some time. Some women could very well like kissing something that feels like two pencils covered with sandpaper.' Maggie smiled impishly. She liked being like this, flirting with an invisible man, with Michael as a witness. It was fun, but fun she would share with no-one but the matchmaker.

'Anyway, then I thought I could go about my task of matchmaking and then, when he met someone he felt good about he could … well, he … well, you know?'

'What, Michael, for heaven's sake, what?'

'Well, at that stage Pat could subtly introduce his – *their* – special requirements, couldn't he? Keep it all very private; in-house, or in-farm, as it were. You know, what people choose to do in the privacy of their own home is really only their business, isn't it?' Michael pleaded.

'I don't know, I'm sure. Are you saying that it's OK for them to break the law just as long as they do it behind closed doors and you and I don't know about it?' Maggie hopped on the bench at the work space created at the other end of the shed.

'Well, let's think about it. Just what laws are they going to break exactly?'

He sat down opposite her on a barrel and let her consider his question and then, without allowing her an opportunity to reply, he announced, lawyer fashion: 'She's not going to be a bigamist, because she's only actually going to marry one of them. She's not going to be unfaithful, and even if she was she wouldn't be breaking the law and if it was a law – being unfaithful that is – then a good percentage of the adults of Castlemartin would be following her to her punishment. So she's not going to be unfaithful because she's going, well, they're all going to, ah, well, you know, be in it together.'

'What you mean is they're all going to end up in bed together!' Maggie roared in disbelief.

'Shush, *please*, Maggie. Dorothy will hear you.'

'You hypocrite! You are prepared to instigate all of this, put them all together, nice and cosy in their bed, all neat and tidy with an eiderdown – no doubt the patchwork quilt made by the twins' grandmother's fair hand and stuffed with a few Kane Christmases' worth of goose and turkey feathers. But at the same time you are scared that your wife, my sister, will hear me talking about it and be offended?' Maggie said, forcing a laugh as sincere as one of Hughie Green's lopsided smiles.

'Well, you know, if I make a match for Pat Kane, I'll have done my job. What they do after that is between the three of them,' Michael claimed and added, as an afterthought, 'and God.'

'Oh, Michael, come on. You can't just wash your hands of it as easily as that! If you make the introduction and take the money for it, then I'm afraid you have to accept some of the responsibility for what you are letting the three of them in for,' Maggie stated harshly, but then smiled at her brother-in-law, softening her stance. She appeared a little down – well, a cross between disappointed and distracted would be the best description the matchmaker could come up with. She tried to be honest with herself as to the genesis of her disappointment. She looked down at her feet, dirty from the lane, as she swung her legs beneath the bench. After a time of this coming and going motion she ventured into the unknown, an unknown she wasn't altogether sure she wanted to discover, but some little voice inside her head egged her on to ask the question. Eventually she voiced it.

'So, come on then. Tell me who you've matched them – oops, sorry – who you've matched *Pat* with?'

Chapter Seven

Three evenings later the matchmaker was sitting in Bryson's with two of his clients. Bryson's public house was situated on the corner of Hospital Road and Garden Street in Magherafelt. The publican, Mr Paddy Bryson, kept his pub clean, friendly and, surprisingly, free of drunks. His logic was a sound one: he wanted to offer his regulars, mostly survivors of the Second World War, an escape, particularly on Friday and Saturday nights, from the problems caused by their work, wives, teenage children and nineteen-year-old horrific war memories. He offered them a sanctuary with a comfortable space to drink, chat, play darts and dominoes, and to exchange the odd bit of local gossip.

A public house, mind you, was not the most obvious place for the matchmaker to introduce prospective partners, or even spouses. However, it had been one of his clients who had suggested – no, sorry, make that *insisted*, yes, insisted on that very location. The client? Joan Cook, a thirty-four-year-old who had, three years previous, caused a local scandal when she'd become the first woman in living memory in Magherafelt to divorce her husband.

Up to the 'Cook Affair', divorces were subject matter only for the Belfast or English newspapers, or sometimes even the wireless. Occasionally people divorced in London, rarely in Belfast but never, ever in County Derry. Eddie Cook, the poor man, had been disgraced for life and he left Magherafelt in shame to work the roads near Watford, north of London. The only thing Joan kept was his name; he on the other hand would have been pleased if she'd lost even that as she had always, post-split, particularly when she'd be in earshot of her husband, referred to herself as Mrs Cook.

Surprisingly the marriage had started off on happy enough grounds; it was when Joan found out that Eddie was never going to be able to father a child that she decided to go off 'in search of better stock, someone with a bit more lead in the pencil', as she put it, and she would offer this to each and every one of the locals, digging them in the ribs at the last part and bursting into a high-pitched whine, which served as her laugh. It also served to let other people know she was coming and most used it as a signal to take evasive action. The truth be told, Joan probably would have forgiven Eddie his round of blanks had he had sufficient funds to keep her up with the Joneses. He was not in such a position and probably never likely to be so. And so for the previous thirty months Mrs Cook was in the market for a husband.

Joan had searched the market herself for the first ten months but, frustrated at her lack of success and the imminent falling of another set of autumn leaves, she was prompted to enlist the services of the parish matchmaker.

Michael Gilmour, for his own part, thought Joan much too fussy by half. In fact, he found it amusing how his less-than-perfect clients always sought perfection from their prospective mates. But his latest suggested match was far from perfect; in fact, this match was based on the fact that if there was any woman listed in his book who was perhaps capable of taking on two men, it was Mrs Joan Cook. When he pushed himself, as he did when he first thought of her for this bizarre match, he couldn't think of one other possible link of compatibility. But now here they all were: the matchmaker with Pat, the newest client on his books, and Joan, the client longest on his books, meeting for the first time.

Bryson's large valve wireless, on a shelf above the door which led to Paddy Bryson's private quarters, was playing Roy Orbison's 'It's Over', which the matchmaker hoped was not an omen.

Introductions concluded, Michael left the two romance-seekers at the table in the snug as he visited the bar to buy a round of drinks – a pint of Guinness for himself, a half pint of Guinness for Pat Kane and a double Old Bushmills for 'yer woman'. One thirsty person who had completed the first stage of his matchmaking and wanted to satisfy his thirst; one who was restrained in his ordering so as not to create a bad first impression (not to mention he had to be up at 5:30 the following morning to start work on the farm) and one who cared not a hoot about the impression she created, keen only to take advantage of the matchmaker's offer of a free drink.

At the bar, Michael met local policeman and Sherlock Holmes fanatic Colin Doyle.

'Another successful match?' the detective asked, nodding at the table recently vacated by Michael.

The matchmaker turned his head and stared back at Patrick Kane and Joan Cook and quickly noted how one was trying to create a good impression for the other, who in turn neither tried nor cared.

'Well,' Michael sighed, through near-closed lips, 'I wouldn't be so sure there was a match there, Colin. Mind you, it's their first meeting, but I'm still not convinced there'll be another one.' He looked back at Joan as he said this. She was wearing some contraption which had probably looked great on the young slim model in the catalogue Joan had purchased it from, but that night in Bryson's it looked more like the three ugly sisters had pooled together their three worst items – one polka-dotted, one hooped and one tartan – from their pantomime wardrobe and not only forced their younger sister to wear the clashing garments but also tied her into them. Mrs Joan Cook's bottle-blonde hair was done up in a bird's nest bun, making her resemble one of the Beverley Sisters caught out on a windy night in Blackpool. Her make-up was thrown on and not really effective. The point of make-up, Michael thought, was to take what was there and enhance it; he felt no amount of cosmetics was ever going to transform plastic into marble. Joan appeared to think it sensible to fight even the direction of her eyebrows. 'Nope, I wouldn't bet on there being a round two, Colin.'

As was his way, the matchmaker always accompanied his clients on their first date: one, to smooth the way; two, to fill any potentially embarrassing silences; and three, to avoid the randy male taking advantage of their date. You know, some of these farm lads, after a few months away from civilisation with only their sheep or cattle for company, think that anything in a skirt is pretty darn attractive. Some of them would go to any lengths, including paying the matchmaker the ten-pound registration fee, to get their leg over.

Also Michael, like the majority of matchmakers, insisted on having the final say on the match. Should, as was rarely the case, he feel the match not workable or durable, he would advise the clients of this and help them find other potential partners. Should they then choose to ignore him, he would have nothing further to do with the relationship, including, surprisingly enough, the final billing.

It has to be mentioned, though, that this was very rarely the case because Michael had a brilliant reputation for setting up successful matches and in order to protect his hard-won reputation he was not prepared to risk a doomed marriage. On the one occasion in his career when the couple had gone against his advice they had, sadly, lived to regret it. And now, seeing his two clients together at that table in Bryson's, he accepted that perhaps his reputation was at risk a few feet away from where he currently stood.

Colin Doyle reached into his inside pocket and took out a spectacle case. He removed the pair of silver wire-framed glasses, easing the pressure that had caused two red marks to form on the bridge of his long thin nose before placing the glasses into their case, which he had opened and rested on the bar in anticipation of such movements. He used his stubby forefinger and thumb to pinch his nose, just by the two red marks. As he did this he closed his eyes gently in order to soak up the relief. He turned to the matchmaker's table.

'Now,' he began in his ever confident tones, 'oh, let me see now ….'

After a few minutes' consideration the small detective offered: 'He's a farmer, not much land, not a lot of money; he's honest, hardworking; I'd say he has a brother – could even be a twin brother – but he's definitely parentless. On the other hand, our desert beauty queen, she's a different kettle of fish altogether. Divorced, I'd say. Getting on a bit, last chance romance and all that, and I'd bet she's probably had more men than you've had fadge, and she doesn't mind charging for it.'

To say that Michael was impressed was an understatement.

'What?' he uttered in sheer disbelief. 'You can tell all of that just by looking at them?'

Colin Doyle smiled his impish smile. 'Now don't be foolish, Michael, will you. Sure it's Patrick Kane and Joan Cook – don't I know them as well as I know yourself?'

With that the detective replaced the spectacles on his person, flicking the jet-black hair back up from his forehead as he did so. He'd let his hair grow quite long on top so that on occasion it hung over his forehead and needed to be pinned back behind his ears. However, the back and sides were so short you could easily see his very white skin. He snapped the glasses case shut, took his freshly poured Guinness from the bar and disappeared in search of a quiet corner to steal yet another read of a Holmes mystery.

Chapter Eight

Meanwhile, back at the table, Pat was trying hard to strike up a conversation with Joan. He was being as unsuccessful in his endeavours as all the pop artists were in trying to keep the Beatles from the number one spot upon the release of each of their new singles. They'd done it again late last year with 'I Want to Hold Your Hand', the first ever single in the UK to have a million pre-sales. Joan was as quick at getting to her point as the Beatles were at reaching the coveted top of the charts.

'So, how many acres do you have?'

'Forty-seven, we, my brother and—'

'How many head of cattle do you have?'

'Sixty-four, all good milk—'

'You would be expecting me to take care of youse, would you? You and your brother?'

'Well, actually—'

''Cause I won't be a skivvy for anyone, you know. I've done that, you know. Oh boy, have I done that! And no thank you very much, sir, enough is enough,' Joan announced as Michael interrupted them with the round.

'So, how have you been getting on?' The matchmaker smiled as he placed the drinks in front of their owners, thanks offered from Pat but not from Joan.

'Well ...' Pat smiled his wonderful smile. Michael noticed for the first time the warmth in his eyes that his sister-in-law had been talking about, 'we were just –'

'I was just telling him, actually, that I wouldn't be his skivvy,' Joan interrupted again.

'Yes, well, I'm sure that's a long way down the list of things to discuss,' Michael cut in, trying hard to lighten things up. And things obviously needed lightening up: Pat looked like he was about to bolt for the door and seemed well relieved by Michael's return.

'Well, I believe in telling the truth, calling the kettle black – no point in hiding behind politeness.'

'No fear of that,' Michael thought but said nothing, using the gap instead as an excuse to take the first sip of his delightful Guinness. He came away from the glass with a thin white moustache.

'I won't be a skivvy for anyone, Michael Gilmour, and you know that. And I'll need an allowance, a good allowance at that, mind you. And I'll want—'

'Ah, that's good,' the matchmaker interrupted firmly and loudly, smacking his lips and removing his newly formed moustache quicker than any Gillette would. 'No, no, listen, Joan, let's not get ahead of ourselves.'

His plea was received with relief from Pat Kane, who, Michael feared, was beginning to feel he may be going home with a deal done for a wife without having had one word of say in the process. Michael was impressed by the way Pat had taken the trouble to turn himself out. Clean shaven – shaven so close, in fact, he looked like one of those people who never, ever had to shave (Michael, on the other hand, had had complaints from Dorothy a mere two hours after shaving one Saturday evening). Pat wore his black boots, well-polished but a little out of place in springtime – they were probably his best footwear, Michael figured. He wore the fawn trousers from a suit, a white shirt – open-necked – and a snappy black blazer. His hands, neck (for Michael checked such things) and face were clean – spotlessly clean, in fact. All skin exposed to the elements was taking on a weather-beaten colour, midway between red and tan. He looked sharp, slim and healthy. To top it off, at least from Michael's point of view – and he was sure that Joan hadn't even noticed this – there wasn't a speck of dirt underneath his fingernails. Not bad for someone who had been out working the land since the crack of dawn.

'Now, what I like to do at these awkward first meetings is just talk a bit, generally, you know, nothing too deep – just a getting-to-know-each-other type of situation. Then, as discussed, I'll talk to both of you – separately of course.' The matchmaker smiled at both of them in turn, lady first. 'Yes, I'll talk to both of you over the course of the next few days, see what you both thought of each other and then if you both feel good about the situation,' he paused for a drink and thought 'and if pigs fly' before continuing, 'we'll all meet again, maybe not in the pub next time, I say, maybe not in the pub next time,' the matchmaker repeated, as he stared at Joan who was totally beyond any subtle hints and matched his stare with her own unsubtle one into her empty glass as she twiddled it around between her fingers. 'Yes, maybe we could meet for tea and a bite to eat in Teyley's Café back in Castlemartin. Yes, that would be nice, wouldn't it? And then I'll talk to you separately some more and if things are still fine then perhaps you could go out on a few dates with each other. You know, just the two of you. Then we all can have another chat together and see how it's going. Talk as a group – it's good to be able to voice one's opinions in front of one's potential partner – and maybe we'll also have a separate chat, you know, just in case, and then we'll take it from there.'

'Is there any chance that all of these cosy little chats could take place before I'm in my grave? You know, they all sound *so* enticing I'd hate to miss them 'cause I'd passed away in the meantime. It would be great to be there, wouldn't it? Don't you think?' Joan laughed in her high-pitched whine that had all the drinkers in the pub turning and staring at the matchmaker's table. Pat's red-to-tan complexion returned very much to red again. Joan took another extravagant drink from her empty glass.

From there it all went steadily downhill. Pear-shaped, as they say. Joan was bored and obviously more interested in a guzzle than a match with a potential suitor. So, at a time Michael considered that both he and Pat had fulfilled the labours of politeness, he offered as a closer: 'Well, I think that's good for the first evening. Pat and myself have to cycle back to Castlemartin so we best be on our way. Can we walk you anywhere?' he offered, taking civility to an extreme never experienced before in Bryson's.

'No, no thanks. I think I'll stay here for a while,' Joan returned, eyeing up the remaining talent in the bar.

Chapter Nine

'The poor feller,' Maggie offered. 'Of course, it can't have been easy for yourself either, Michael. But I suppose the main difference was that he had to pay to be subjected to that abuse – at least you were getting paid by both of them to be there.' There were several questions Maggie wanted to ask the matchmaker. But she felt she had to pick them carefully. Her next question obviously wasn't going to be about the weather but at the same time neither could she ask the questions she'd really like answers to. So she struggled to find the question anyone, anyone having received the information she just had, of course, would. She kept it simple and nonchalant. 'What did he say, what did Patrick say, when you'd left Bryson's?'

'Well now, that's a funny one. I say, that's a funny one. Sure didn't the poor chap only go and ask me if he would *have* to marry her?'

'No?'

'Yes! He seemed to think that if I decided to make the match he'd have to take it whether he liked it or not,' the matchmaker reported, gracious enough not to laugh or even smile for that matter. 'We walked the hills on the way back. It's not that we were too tired to pedal them or anything, I just think he was happy to have the extra time to chat.'

'Aye, that's the matchmaker for you. You're the easiest person around to talk to. I'm not so sure that you don't do the clergy out of some of their business!' Maggie remarked, only half in jest. They had returned to his house and resumed a spot in the kitchen, the hub of the matchmaker's home.

Michael decided to leave the sisters and a friend together to update notes of recent meetings and what-have-you. Maggie looked enviously at him as he made his excuses to leave; what she wouldn't have given to read tonight's entry in his famous matchmaking book.

Maggie, Dorothy and Audrey Clayton, an old school friend of the Gilmour sisters, tended to meet up every Wednesday night (alternate weeks at Dorothy and Audrey's homes) for some TSG: tea, sandwiches and gossip. This week's gossip had centred around Thelma Bliccey, a seventeen-year-old girl who was fast gaining a reputation as the village bike. Supposedly her father had caught Mr Gallen, the headmaster at Castlemartin Primary School, in a highly compromising position with her. Sadly he couldn't get the local police to do anything about it – allegedly several members of the local constabulary had some intimate knowledge about the subject of the case themselves.

Maggie, as the only unmarried member of the Wednesday night trio, usually found the other two trying to exclude her from the really juicy bits of scandal on the grounds that since she was still single, despite the fact that she was in her late twenties, she wasn't really supposed to know what they were talking about.

Anyway, after Thelma's father found no joy with the police he went to a local firm of solicitors and it was through a source in this office that the information burned the wires of the local bush telegraph to melting.

Apparently the seventeen-year-old Thelma had been with, as in the biblical sense, a shopkeeper, a member of a local showband, the milkman, the aforementioned headmaster, her next-door neighbour – who in fact had a daughter the same age as Thelma – a few local corner boys and, as was discovered, at least one member of the local police force. All were now under investigation for having sex with a minor.

Following a couple of hours of this Maggie was happy to take Michael a cup of tea, to 'give him a break from his books', as Dorothy had requested.

Maggie was happy to get back to discussing the Kane twins' unique situation, which was fascinating her more than she felt healthy.

'And did you know,' Michael offered as though the two-hour break in their conversation had never existed, 'that in the early days the clergy themselves were involved in a bit of matchmaking? They obviously had a vested interest in expanding their congregation!'

'So, do you have any other potential wives lined up for the twins?'

'For Patrick – surely you mean do I have any other potential wives lined up for Patrick?' the matchmaker corrected Maggie sternly.

Chapter Ten

'What do you mean, she won't do? Since when did we get to be so choosy? Ma always said you were too fussy for your own good. That's all very fine when it comes to yourself, but you're not going to be too bleedin' fussy for my good. I'll tell you that for nothing.'

Joseph had been waiting up for Patrick in their very small kitchen. He'd kept the peat fire alive with logs and their conversation was punctuated with the crackles and snaps of the fire.

'Listen to me now, Joe, will ye? Her first question to me was "How many acres do you have?" and then "How many cattle?" followed by "I'm not going to be skivvying for youse" and finally "I'm going to need an allowance!" and—'

Joe went to interrupt his brother, but Pat's eyes interrupted the interruption so that he continued: 'And she was drinking whiskey – and doubles at that! You should also know that she has a reputation for being liberal with her favours and, on top of which … Oh, it's useless. You know what? If you're so desperate, I'm sure Michael will fix up another meeting. But just for you this time; I don't want to have anything else to do with her. I'd prefer to go without for the rest of my life. But you're welcome to her. My advice would be to stock up well on the whiskey for the wedding though – you're going to need it. But as for me, I don't want anything to do with her.'

Patrick was mad. Mad as hell. Well, as mad as it was possible for him to get. He'd made the effort to go and see this … this excuse for a woman and had been totally humiliated by her right there in a public house. Sure, wouldn't all the chins be wagging about it tomorrow morning? And another thing, Pat thought: what was a good woman doing in a pub in the first place? Yes, humiliated in front of the matchmaker. He'd felt greatly out of his depth and had been caught wanting. How could he ever go back to Bryson's again? Not that he went there a lot in the first place, but he liked the friendly, warm atmosphere of the bar and if he had a local it was there and not Morrison's, Moore's or Brady's, Castlemartin's unholy trinity. But now all of Bryson's regulars knew for sure what had been going on. He – Patrick Kane, proud Patrick Kane – was trying a match with Joan Cook. And she a bleeding divorcée at that.

But what had made him really mad was the fact that Joe had hit him hard, very hard, on a very raw nerve.

Their mother *had* always said that he was too fussy. But she'd also complained, just as frequently, that Joe wasn't fussy *enough*. Mind you, that hadn't been much comfort to him then or now. The really annoying thing was that Patrick Daniel Kane realised and accepted that he was too fussy, too fussy for his own good, and he certainly didn't appreciate his brother pointing it out to him once again. When he'd been at school, and to some degree at the tech, and mixing daily with girls, he'd always mentally dismiss them as being too fat, too thin, too tall, too short, too quiet, too loud, too whatever … he had an endless list.

He found himself compelled towards a vision of perfection. Joe had always been unmerciful in sending his brother up over this.

But they were both good-looking lads and they'd had their fair share of female attention.

Barbara Hutchinson was generally accepted as the most beautiful girl in their class, if not in the entire school. She'd made it known via her friend Margaret Gilmour via Joe that she'd like to 'step out' with Patrick.

Patrick shared the universal opinion of Barbara Hutchinson but, because she had been *too* forward in asking him out, he had refused to have anything to do with her. Joe then tried, unsuccessfully, to step into his brother's shoes. There had also been other instances when Pat had dumbfounded his brother with his interest in nothing less than the perfect woman. Joe was convinced that such a creature, if one existed, could only be found in London.

Now here was Pat, ten years later, still without his woman and the passing of each year making such an eventuality a highly unlikely one.

And equally Joe certainly wasn't as fussy as his brother, but try though he did he could never find a way to make a lasting connection either.

'Look, Pat, we've agreed we need a woman around here. Personally I don't give a flippin' fig what she looks like. I'm not interested in any of her faults as long as she takes care of us, takes care of us in every way. OK?'

'Yes, I know, Joe. But honestly … honestly I didn't even have a chance to be fussy. We'd be the laughing stock of the town if we—'

'There you go again, Pat. You see, I don't give a rat's waste disposal point what they think in the town. It seems that this is to be our lot – this is all that's been marked down for us in the great book in the sky, so we're going to have to learn to live with it and get on with it. And get on with it I will. But I do need a woman to get through this miserable existence. We need a woman to help us get through this ….' Joe trailed off.

'I know, I know. The matchmaker said he'd have another look for us and I'm to go and see him again on Sunday afternoon,' Pat – thankful for Joe's slackened pace – took up the conversation again. He was tired, tired from all of this, not to mention his hard day's work. He was equally tired in anticipation of another hard day's work promised for the morrow.

'Well, OK, but see that you keep your fussiness in your back pocket this time. Don't dismiss the next one after the first meeting. I'm serious, Pat! I'm sure you'll prefer the woman you choose to the one I would choose, but any more faffing about and *I'll* find a woman for us. You better believe me.'

Chapter Eleven

The next woman the matchmaker introduced to Patrick Kane was indeed perfect – perfect in every sense of the word, even from Pat's grand viewpoint. The only problem, the one ever-so-slight twist in the potato drill, was the fact that this woman was Margaret Watson, the sister-in-law of the matchmaker.

Well, this really shouldn't have been a problem; it was just that when Pat met Maggie by accident the house, he was embarrassed that she, being so close to Michael, would probably know that he was looking for a wife through the matchmaker's services. In fact, he thought, he was only lucky that she didn't know the half of it.

The reality, however, was that Maggie Gilmour knew the *whole* of it and in her privileged position of knowledge she didn't think any less of him.

In regards to his growing attraction towards Maggie, the thing that niggled Pat most was that she had been there, in his circle, all along. She'd been in his life the whole time: he'd gone to school with her and he'd seen her around during the intervening years. There had always been something about her that made him stare, something that meant she remained in his thoughts (some he wouldn't have shared with anyone and certainly wouldn't have wanted Maggie to know about) for a long time following their infrequent meetings, which were often just mere sightings. But she'd been there, or thereabouts, all the time and he'd been just too blind or busy to have done anything about it. Then he kicked himself, told himself in no uncertain terms to wise up, that Margaret Watson would never in a month of Sundays be interested in someone like him.

That particular Sunday afternoon Pat had, as planned, paid Michael Gilmour a visit. He'd found the matchmaker clothed exactly the same way he'd been on their first meeting, but this time he was in the kitchen sharing a cup of tea with his sister-in-law. They invited him to join them rather than visit the front room. Pat seemed happy in the more casual environment and soon forgot the real reason for his visit. Maggie seemed in no hurry to leave them to their business and soon a natural conversation flowed as freely as the supply of Dorothy's moreish Paris buns.

'How's your brother doing? What's his name – Joe, isn't it?' Maggie enquired as Michael poured the three of them a second cup of tea. Of course, Maggie knew the other Kane twin's name but she thought this little question might serve to persuade Pat that she and Michael had never spoken about his 'situation'.

Michael surprised all of them by suggesting, at this point with teacup replenished, that they move into the front room, where they would be more comfortable.

'Oh, he's fine, he's fine you know. There's just the two of us up on the farm since our parents left,' Pat answered, as though his parents had just moved to another house, village, city, country, even planet, instead of the other non-physical state they were now both enjoying. 'So neither of us has a chance to get into the village too often, but he's fine.'

'I always thought he'd be the one to leave. You know, go to Belfast or something – I'm surprised both of you stayed around,' Maggie volunteered, removing her black woollen cardigan to acknowledge the new level of heat, revealing a beautiful and simple high-collared white blouse, hung loosely over a pair of tight-fitting black slacks.

'That's funny. Seems as though you're able to tell us apart – not many people are able to do that.' Pat smiled, happy that he was being recognised as an individual and not one half of a duo for once.

'Oh, you know,' Maggie replied, blushing ever so slightly, 'it's easy when you smile. You always had – still do, in fact – lovely smiling eyes. I was always able to tell you apart by your eyes.'

Maggie and Pat shared an unembarrassed and intimate moment of direct eye contact. At one point in the silent exchange Pat felt Maggie was aware of some of his secret thoughts about her.

'And besides,' Maggie continued when the moment had gone, 'at this point Joe would have been pretending to be you.'

Pat started to smile and then gently laughed, not commenting upon her observation. He was relieved that he still had the ability to relax and enjoy himself in other people's company and be happily involved in a natural conversation. He and his brother only discussed topics of necessity; they never just talked for the sake of it, which meant that Pat would sometimes go weeks without a chat. 'I wondered where you had gotten to – I thought you were going to move to Belfast with Stuart Gibney,' he finally responded.

'No. No, not at all. We're still good friends, of course; I see him now and again, but, am … as they say, we're just good friends – not that good friends should be qualified by the word "just". But as you know it's shorthand for we're friends, we're no longer lov—no longer dating,' Maggie replied, nearly letting the word 'lovers' slip. She and Stuart had certainly been lovers; it's just that she'd never used that term in a conversation such as this before.

But then what exactly was this conversation? Although she'd railroaded the matchmaker into stage-managing this meeting, she couldn't work out why she'd forced him to do it, despite his obvious reluctance; she only knew she had to.

The matchmaker sugared his tea and stirred it so much he probably ground each and every little grain of sweetness into his wife's best white china. He was watching the two visitors closely. He noted the way Maggie was drawing the twin out of his normal reserved shell. He also noticed the way Pat spoke confidently with Maggie; the way he was relaxed and enjoyed talking to her. And why wouldn't he, thought the matchmaker, sure wasn't she the finest single woman in these parts? And so fine she surely wouldn't want to be having anything to do with the sorry situation Pat and his brother had dreamed up. But Maggie, as her sister had a habit of saying, was always playing the fiddle to her own tune.

'And what about yourself, Pat – any girls in your life at the moment?'

'Well,' Pat looked nervously at the matchmaker, the man he felt might have discussed his rather bizarre situation with at least his family, even if it hadn't gone any further. But obviously he'd misjudged him. 'Ah, I came to see Michael about, ah, about … well … that is, you see …' He sighed, took a deep breath and went for his oft-used line when discussing this particular topic. 'You see, it's like this: we work all the hours God sends and I haven't much time for ....'

Maggie was looking at him, her face betraying no thoughts or judgements, just encouraged him to continue and will him to be brave enough to just be honest with her.

'And I've never been very good at it, you know? Chatting people up. I find the entire process so awkward and false,' the painfully honest twin continued.

'Yes, I agree,' Maggie cut in, 'both sides – man and woman, boy and girl – are guilty of putting on this "front". We're convinced we'll attract a partner by doing so, but after all the searching through the woods of words, you eventually find out what, if anything, is *really* there. Unfortunately, I'd bet that sometimes this process continues way into a marriage when it's sadly, clearly, too late. Of course, that's not always the case.'

She smiled as she looked at Michael the matchmaker, the man with his perfect match.

'I know,' Pat replied, as he relaxed even more by undoing his top button and loosening his tie, an action that bought the matchmaker out in sympathy. 'But at the same time I feel I missed out in a way 'cause I didn't even try and, you know,' he glanced across at Michael, 'I have a feeling it might just be too late.'

'Ah rubbish,' she laughed, 'you're barely thirty, right?'

Pat nodded in agreement with her assessment.

'Barely thirty, with a whole life ahead of you, and believe me it's better spent with the right person. Not everyone is like our Dot and Michael here – they both knew from the first time they met that they were meant for each other. Although it probably took them a little time to admit this to one another. I remember Dot getting home from her first date and coming into my room and gushing, pure gushing – just like the Moyola after the rains – and saying that she'd met *her* man.'

Michael was becoming a little hot under the collar but held his counsel.

'Mind you, I tried to convince her to shop around a bit, but no, she had met her man and wanted to get on with it, with him,' Maggie said, as she noticed the matchmaker's usually red cheeks were glowing from the rush of extra blood to them. 'And now he tries to work the same magic for others!'

'Well, I'm obviously not going to further my career tonight so I'd better do what I'm really good at,' Michael replied as he lifted the wooden tray filled with china and added his punch line, 'washing the dishes.'

After Michael was gone Maggie and Pat remained in their seats.

Pat was the first to speak. 'Do you think it's weird, you know, using Michael to find a wife?'

'Well, I know from the tone of your voice that *you* certainly do,' Maggie replied.

'Yeah, you're not wrong there. But what else is there for me to do? I've got to get someone for the farm: we need someone to look after us and help us on the farm don't we?'

'Yes, but why does it have to be a wife? Why not a housekeeper?'

'Well,' Pat blushed slightly as he moved one hand on top of the other and then turned the palms and rubbed them together, the way one does in front of the fire in order to circulate the heat from the flames, willing it into your body, 'it's more than housekeeping, isn't it?'

'Is it? Does it have to be? Do you not think that it's wrong to turn romance into a chore for someone?' Maggie suggested, hoping she wasn't pushing him too far.

'Yes, yes. Yes, I agree with you one hundred per cent. I couldn't agree with you more. But, it's Joe. He wants ….'

'Let Joe find what he wants for himself. Pat, you're not going to put some poor woman through misery just to keep Joe happy,' Maggie offered a touch impatiently. She was nervous about letting on just how much she was aware of the special requirements but continued anyway. 'I'm sure if one of you finds a wife, she'll still look after the other – you know, feeding and cleaning and clothing and such like.'

'Of course, but it's not just that, is it? You know, the farm is small and we're barely breaking even as it is – we're just getting by.'

'But look,' Maggie started, 'the important thing is at least the farm does work in these times when we are all struggling just to get by. Problems always seem much bigger than they are. Today it might be tough, but it's not always going to be this way, is it? And when your parents were leaving you the farm I'm sure they didn't mean for it to be a millstone around your neck.'

Pat nodded with a 'that's true' kind of smile and Maggie encouraged him further.

'Use it as a start. Build on it, take it somewhere. Make it into something. Make it into something which is going to serve you and Joe and both your families and not the other way around, you know, with you all serving the farm. That's not the way it's meant to be.'

'Yeah!' Pat sighed. 'I hear you, but what about yourself? What's going on in your life? What building are you doing?'

'Oh,' she replied with a twinkle in her eyes, 'I've got a wee project I'm working on that I'm quite excited about.'

Chapter Twelve

Three days later, before he'd even had time to think about it properly, Patrick Kane found himself on Margaret Watson's doorstep. Actually, on the doorstep of her mother's house, located down on Lough Road amid terraced shops, houses and Brady's noisy pub. Should the Kane twin with the warm smile have thought it all through carefully he would never have picked up the courage to make the house-call.

Indeed, if the truth be known, and it must for this is to be a true account of this sad, if painful, tale, he had also ventured there late the previous evening. Pat had not developed a yellow streak; no, he had merely gone round to familiarise himself with her house, perhaps even to imagine which of the windows allowed the light and the days into Maggie's room, perhaps to wonder if she was in the room he imagined to be her room and, if so, to ponder on what she might be doing.

On the second night of making the Watson house's acquaintance, the yellow light escaping from the window directly above the door to the house was mixing with the inadequate street light in the twilight of a darkening spring evening.

He wondered what the Watsons' lounge looked like: did they use it as a family room or, like the majority of Ulster folk in similar terraced streets, was that job left to the kitchen at the rear of the house?

Maggie's mother answered the door. She recognised Pat immediately and invited him in.

'Am, I was wondering is Margaret in?' was all Patrick could find to say as he was shown down the narrow hallway and into the warm kitchen at the rear.

'Margare*t*!' Mrs Watson called up the stairs at the top of her voice. 'It's for you – there's someone down here to see you,' she continued, shouting in the general darkened direction of heaven.

'Who is it, Ma?' Patrick could hear a familiar voice call out from above.

'Sure it's Patrick Ka–'

'Tell him I'll be right down,' the voice ten feet closer to heaven interrupted.

'Let's have some tea, shall we?' Mrs Watson smiled at Pat. She was dressed in a combination of aprons, frocks, blouses, cardigans and bibs, which all moved together in a system so complex Patrick couldn't rightly work out where one finished and the other started. He imagined the process of dressing and undressing must take forever. Pat liked Mrs Watson – she was permanently bent over, ever so slightly, and her head was tilted to the right, again ever so slightly, and one of her eyelids (the left) half-hooded her eye, so when she smiled at you it looked conspiratorial, almost with a hint of devilment.

Maggie's dad was out, over in Magherafelt at his favourite pub, Bryson's, Maggie's mother reported. Pat crossed his fingers in his pocket hoping Mr Watson hadn't been in the pub the night of the Joan Cook disaster.

Maggie's mother was entertaining a neighbour, a lady Pat recognised as Mrs Gilreath, the local taxi driver's wife. Mrs Gilreath was a wholesome fun-loving mum and she bade Pat sit beside her.

'And now what would bring a handsome farmer such as yourself to these parts?' she began, as she winked knowingly at Mrs Watson.

'Oh, I met Margaret out at her sister's and, well, we kinda agreed I would drop in next time I was passing. And I, ah … but you know if it's inconvenient in any way,' he paused and looked from Mrs Gilreath to Mrs Watson, 'in any way whatsoever, I'll … well, you know?'

'Oh no, not at all! She's up in that room of hers much too much as it is already. I wonder what she does up there all the time by herself – I'm always telling her to get out of the house a bit more, you know. Milk and sugar, love?' Mrs Watson enquired.

'Am, yes, actually – a little milk would be nice.'

No sooner had he raised the cup to his lips than Maggie burst into the room, causing a disturbance similar to a pouncing cat interrupting a flock of feeding pigeons. Her recently washed blonde hair swirled around her shoulders. She smiled at Pat, a smile that made him very glad he'd called, very glad indeed.

'Don't get too comfy,' Maggie began as she took a black duffel coat from a hook on the back of the door, 'I fancy a bit of a walk, I do.'

'Oh, let the young man finish his cup of tea, will you?' Mrs Gilreath mumbled through the nibbling of her biscuit. She was keen to see them talk together. She was keen to see if this was a man with gumption enough to take Maggie off her mother's hands. Sure, even Mrs Gilreath knew how tired and how keen that same pair of hands was to pass Maggie on to the next player in her life.

'Nah, it's cold out. If he gets too comfy and warm he won't want to go out again – you know what these farmers are like: if they bend down in a seat for more than a few minutes their bones set. Besides, we can always stop in Teyley's Café for a coffee.'

Patrick didn't have a choice. Before he'd a chance to mumble an apology, much less take a sip of the tea, Maggie had placed her hand under his right arm and was quite literally prising him from his mucho comfortable chair.

She'd initiated their first physical contact.

It was purely functional to her, but nonetheless totally electrifying to Pat.

When Maggie was dealing with her mother and Mrs Gilreath, Pat was able to steal a look at her. He hoped he wasn't being too obvious but he couldn't stop staring. She just vacuumed his breath away. She was so stunningly beautiful – in a Barbara Parkins kind of way – that all he wanted to do was look at her. If he was allowed to enjoy her the way he was currently doing that just might, *just might*, be enough for him. He could hardly believe that she had just physically prised him out of a chair and clearly wanted to spend some time with him. Pat knew he couldn't afford to become preoccupied with this thought for fear of scundering her.

Maggie had been right, though – it was a lot colder outside of the house and they took the icy air straight on the chin as they headed back up the Lough Road towards the hub of the town, Pear Tree Roundabout, and down the steep Briscoe Street to Teyley's Café on the right-hand side as you headed towards the Briscoe School, which was just a wee bit out the Moneymore Road with all its fancy houses where all the teachers, shopkeepers, solicitors and general well-to-do professionals lived.

They were both happy to get out of the cold and settle down in Teyley's. After she'd ordered, Pat Kane looked nervous, like there was something he wanted to say, needed to say.

'I hope it was OK to call and see you – we had talked abou—'

'Yes, Pat, perfectly OK. I'm quite glad you came actually. Apart from which, I'm very happy to have an excuse not to spend another night in my room alone.'

'It's just that I enjoyed chatting with you,' Pat began, seemingly intent on imparting important information to Maggie regardless of her part in the conversation. 'I enjoyed our chat the other day. I mean, it's such a change talking to a beau—er, to a woman such as yourself.'

Maggie liked his innocence in these delicate matters – the fact that he didn't have a list of lines ready to spin her was a big plus. She was quite happy to let him stumble on, using the break in her part of the conversation to hold the coffee cup between her hands and then in turn using her warmed hands to generate some heat in her cold cheeks.

'I don't mean Joe's not nice or anything like that, but,' Pat shrugged his shoulders, 'we're twins, you know – we know everything there is to know about each other and even when one finds something new to say, the other one knows what it's going to be about – not because of any kind of special powers or anything like that; I'm not sure how much I believe in all that. No, it's a lot simpler than that: we've spent every waking moment together for nearly thirty flippin' years.'

'Yes, I know,' Maggie said as she nodded. 'Well, I don't know really, but I feel I know what you mean, about it being nice to have a change.'

For a moment the two were silent and the room in Teyley's was filled with the sounds of three girls laughing over their Coke bottles in the corner, the clashing of cups and saucers and orders being shouted into the open hatch behind the front counter.

'Why do you stay, I mean in your room, you … I mean you surely could …?' Pat offered, trying to break the silence which was building into a storm between them.

'What's my alternative? Go to the Dreamland, the "ballroom of romance", and pick up, oops, sorry, I mean *be* picked up by a spotty youth wanting to practise the Ulster Octopus? Sorry, no way. I say good luck to the girls who enjoy that sort of thing, but it's positively not for me.'

'But then how else are we meant to meet people, Maggie?' They were leaving Teyley's now, Maggie having paid for the coffee, and they headed off down Briscoe Street towards the Moneymore Road and the regal Briscoe Endowed School.

'Perhaps at the fairs.' She smiled as they passed the very large, extremely flat tree-lined playing fields on the right, which the annual fairs and amusements camped out on each year. Duffy & Sons' Travelling Circus, which arrived to the field every summer, added a multitude of colours to the usual varieties of green.

'I used to love the fairs,' Pat began, as he broke into one of his smiles.

Maggie loved it when Pat smiled; it was such a pleasing, unconscious smile, and it lit up his entire face, maybe even the whole of his body.

'The swing boats: I remember the first time I went up in those it quite literally took my breath away. It was such an unusual experience. I'd never felt that feeling in the pit of my stomach before. It was a magic sensation,' Pat offered, realising it was a similar experience to one he'd just enjoyed as he'd studied Maggie while she was talking to her mother.

They walked on up the Moneymore Road, both content with their thoughts, neither trying to engage the other in conversation. However, Pat was experiencing another unique sensation. He didn't feel awkward during the silences with Maggie. He didn't feel compelled to try to fill the space, to try to find something – anything – to say. And when he did talk to her, it wasn't laboured: the words just came out of his mouth. Flowing would be too strong a word for it, for Pat was not a man of many words. But on the two occasions they had recently met, once at the matchmaker's house and now again tonight, Pat had spoken more to her than he had to anyone since leaving the technical college.

This was a very sad but true fact.

'It was great in those days, wasn't it? When all your feelings were new and you didn't really know how to deal with them, you just sailed on through them ....' Pat heard himself say.

'And the music. I just loved the music blaring out over the fairground speakers and spilling up the streets of the town. Do you remember 'From a Jack to a Queen'? Oh, I just loved that ... and anything by Elvis, I mean 'Wooden Heart' – how could that possibly do anything other than send you to bed in tears? And those boys, the ones who worked the dodgems, in their tight jeans, pausing to comb their hair back into their DAs, following every body movement,' Maggie recalled.

They both laughed and continued laughing at their shared memories of those times as they took a right along Garden Street, a smaller street with views of the school but without houses, save a very small two-roomed cottage, the only one in the town still with an external toilet. No-one knew much about the owner, Francis Mellway, except that he liked, and kept, a lot of animals and he never, ever, even on the coldest winter day, wore socks. Francis kept to himself, preferring instead the company of his pets. For those facts alone he was considered strange and the locals were happy to give him a wide berth.

Garden Street runs out abruptly when it happens upon Apple Orchard Lane, which in turn goes off to the right and coincidentally past the matchmaker's house. Michael and Dorothy Gilmour's house, like the other four houses on Apple Orchard Lane, was a soldier's house, built for the brave men who risked life and limb in the First World War. Over the years the inhabitants had carried out their own individual work on the houses – both internally and externally – to the point where they now shared little in common, excepting, that is, the address.

The only other building on Apple Orchard Lane was McCelland's Shirt Factory, which, like the soldiers' houses, overlooked a small meadow surrounded by mature trees, none of which were actually of the apple species.

The two new friends automatically took this right turn, for in truth it was either that or turn back. In fact they walked on past the matchmaker's, neither commenting upon his fine abode, up to the Magherafelt Road, which went off to the left. Then they took the sparsely populated Railway Terrace to the right and back into town around Pear Tree Roundabout, anti-clockwise across the Broadway, so-called because it was the broadest street in Castlemartin (it had to be to take all the Ulsterbuses). They ended up continuing around the roundabout for about 400 degrees and retraced their steps down Briscoe Street and straight back into Teyley's Café.

'Two coffees please!' Maggie ordered as they walked past the counter and into the side room, the main room of the café, which had been full last time. The jukebox in the corner was now surrounded by three giggly girls and two boys trying to impress each other with their knowledge of the records on the box. The Dave Clark Five's pumping hit, the first number one of the year, 'Glad All Over' rang out from the turntable. You could tell how popular the song was by the heavy amount of crackle – caused by the wear and tear of dodgy needles – that accompanied the tune, which mixed, somewhat sympathetically, with the new Tottenham Sound.

They took a table by the window. Maggie liked to sit by the window. Occasionally when she was bored from the loneliness of her room, she would come to the café to sit and have a coffee. Her mother didn't keep coffee in the house, so it was always a bit of a treat, and she would either read or watch the town go by the window. She enjoyed both distractions equally.

Pat felt less comfortable. Before tonight he hadn't been in Teyley's Café in ages, not since he'd left the tech, in fact, and he preferred tea to coffee, but he was drinking the horrible American liquid twice in the one night. He did like being with Maggie, though, so the coffee was a small price to pay: a very small price.

'So what do you do all day? You don't sit in your room do you?'

'Goodness, no, of course not. I work. I need to work to keep my independence. If I didn't have a job and my own pay packet I'm sure my ma would have had me married off long before now. I wouldn't have had a choice in the matter – I'd have lasted as long as snowflakes in the fire.'

'What do you do?' Pat asked, just as the coffee arrived with Maggie's usual (and favourite) Kit-Kat. The owner had taken the liberty of bringing one for Pat as well. Pat would have preferred one, possibly even two, Jacob's Orange biscuits, but if the Kit-Kat was good enough for Maggie Watson, then it was certainly good enough for him.

'I work in the administration office at the technical college. The pay is good but I used to work in a shop: I was shop manager for Dawson Bates', up in Magherafelt. I'd been working there on and off since I left the tech. He was a good boss: I knew what needed to be done and he let me get on with doing it, and the pay was OK – very good for these parts but not as good as I get up at the tech.'

'Do you like working there?'

'Yeah, it's fine. But I'm by myself most of the time. That's why I preferred working at Dawson Bates'. The shop was great for the town gossip, I can tell you!' Maggie laughed and leaned in over the red-topped Formica table, signalling to Pat to do the same. Their faces were now only about six inches apart. 'In those days I knew who was sleeping with whom and, equally importantly, which husbands were not sleeping with their wives. I also knew which housewife had a taste for schoolboys.'

Pat leaned back and stared at her as if to draw from her the name to fulfil every schoolboy's dream. None appeared to be forthcoming so he leaned back in over the table. When he was close again Maggie continued, a wicked smile creeping across her face, as sly as a fox bordering the edge of town in search of his evening meal.

'I couldn't believe how candid some of them would be in a crowded shop! They all laugh about it, but in a way, I suppose, it serves as some kind of therapy,' Maggie said, as she leaned over the table even nearer to Pat.

He was now so close he could hear her breathing and smell her distinctive scents: clean and fresh with no evident aroma of perfume. He liked that she was natural – 'nothing manufactured', as she would have put it. 'Hmm, all the stories I could tell you, Patrick Kane – it's enough to put you off marriage for life, or even longer!'

Pat smiled, for he silently hoped this was not the case.

Chapter Thirteen

'So, what did you find to talk about for three and one half hours?' the matchmaker asked his sister-in-law.

'Nothing I was conscious of. The time just seemed to pass. I'd forgotten how much I really like him. And that smile, Michael, his wonderful smile.'

'Hey, listen here, Maggie, this can surely come to no good. You know exactly what he's after,' Michael warned.

'So?'

It was the following evening and Maggie and her brother-in-law were in the garden behind the matchmaker's house. It was dusk and they were being lit by the light from the kitchen window as it spilled out in a yellow glow. From inside it looked dark, but from the outside, because they'd both been out for a while and their eyes had grown accustomed to the twilight, they could see pretty clearly – maybe not clearly enough to read a book, but enough to see each other.

'Maggie! Sure you're not going to be a wife to two men! If your sister even knew what you were thinking, she'd have my guts for garters!'

'Ah, away with you, will you ever. We've only just been talking – I'd say it's as far away from having two husbands after one chat as it is from getting pregnant from a kiss on the cheek. Unless of course,' she left it hanging in the air for a while to wind him up even further, before adding, 'your name happens to be Mary.'

They both roared with laughter, so much so in fact that Dorothy came to the window to see what was going on. She didn't seem amused.

'Hush, woman, wash out your mouth,' was all Michael could utter as he tried to compose himself.

But there was no hiding the fact that he was scared by the look in Maggie's eyes. He could not believe that she was actually considering the Kanes' proposition, but it seemed likely that she was. He was sure that his own father (also called Michael, but always referred to as Mickey) had never come across anything as strange as this.

Mickey Gilmour had been a matchmaker when it was a big thing to be. He'd told his son about old men, as in ancient old, looking for teenage girls; young girls in search of old men: the shakier the walking stick, the closer the bank balance – well, rarely a bank balance, actually, more like a stuffed mattress around these parts. (The talk about town was always about how well some of the older people slept at night, meaning how soft their mattresses were. A mattress can be as soft as a feather floating in air when it is packed to overflowing with red ones (ten bob notes), green ones (pound notes) and sometimes even the much rarer blue ones (five pound notes).) He'd told his son of widows looking for teenage men, someone's shoulder to read the newspaper over. He'd even heard of three sisters looking (unsuccessfully) for three brothers. Until the present, the funniest one Michael had heard of was a forty-three-year-old, twice-married brunette searching for an eligible bachelor. She wanted a man with good teeth, his own hair (on his head not his chest), who was a non-smoker and non-drinker, independently wealthy, able to cook and a hard worker in his own business. A tall order? Yes, but not impossible. However Michael felt it important to point out the one small additional problem he foresaw. The woman was already married and her husband, although not about to challenge Roger Bannister in a re-run of the four-minute mile, was still very much alive. 'Ah, sure don't I know it,' the brunette had said as she laughed, 'but I reckon I'll either wear him out or he'll drop off in the next six months and I don't want to be wasting time looking for his successor!'

Needless to say, Michael declined her retainer.

But now Maggie, his dear wife's sister, might be considering – although not admitting as much, and probably not even to herself – becoming a wife to a set of twins. A set of twins who had very calmly and casually made their unique request to the matchmaker and had gone to great pains to point out to him that it was all perfectly legal.

He also knew that the more he tried to persuade his sister-in-law against the unholy alliance, the more likely the union was going to be. It wasn't that she was obstinate or anything like that, it was just that … well, she had often explained to Michael, on their long walks, that 'all of us have to take our happiness where we can find it'. The only rule never to break, she claimed, was not to hurt anyone in pursuit of your happiness.

'Look, Maggie, listen to me – I say, listen to me!' Michael began, his voice raspier than usual as he tried to summon up all his powers of reason, yet trying to remain dispassionate about the matter, or at least attempting to give off that air. 'Consider this: consider exactly what you are thinking about doing. Yeah?'

'Consider what, Michael? I've seen him twice, briefly. Well, one brief visit, one kinda long. So what's this, this concern of yours all about?' she replied, giving him the wide-eyed and innocent look, hands raised, palms outstretched in a classic 'what on earth are you going on about?' pose.

'Yes, yes, I know, don't give me all that,' Michael stated firmly. 'Look here now, I don't for one moment believe a word you're saying. There's a lot more scheming going on behind those eyes than you're admitting to. But listen to me, Maggie, do me this one favour, will you? Imagine that the situation was different and Dorothy was considering this proposition. How would you feel then? What would you be saying to her now?'

Maggie patted Michael gently on the arm. 'You listen, Michael, dear sweet man that you are – I'm not considering anything … I *like* this man, I like Patrick. I like him a lot. I find myself being drawn towards him. What can I tell you?'

They stood there in the garden, by the light of the kitchen. Michael looked up at the sky. Maggie looked at Michael and started talking again, this time very quietly.

'I see something in him: an innocence, a kindred spirit. I don't know what it is exactly and, you know what, I don't care. I trust him. I've never ever felt this way with a man before and he hasn't even touched me, hasn't even tried to touch me.'

Michael kept looking up at the sky and the stars while he continued listening to Maggie speak, never daring to glance at her in case she stopped. He felt they were about to reach a point, a point they had never reached before in their friendship, where she was about to let him into the biggest secret in her world.

'I don't know if it's love – I don't even know what this love thing is apart from maybe a packaging used to pair men and women off with each other so that they will do what comes naturally to them, breed like rabbits, and so help to keep mankind going.'

'Maggie?'

'No, please, I was only joking … but then I wasn't really. I mean, love could be as simple as that. That makes a lot more sense to me than a lot of the rubbish I've been hearing. But you know, Michael, the thing which scares me about Patrick Kane is that what I am feeling for him may be greater, bigger, or whatever, than love. In fact, I'm scared to compare it with love because in a certain way that belittles it. It even belittles it to talk about it, to talk about it in human terms when in reality what I feel for him is more animal, more primal. I feel that there is something between us that would have drawn us together even if we had been in separate towns. I know that probably sounds too dramatic, maybe even a little stupid, but it's what I'm feeling, Michael. I feel now that this gut- and heart-wrench would have pulled us together no matter what had separated us. You've seen me, Michael: I've been hanging around waiting, waiting for something, waiting for someone, waiting for the bus to come and take me somewhere. And he's been the same, although trapped in another set of circumstances – you know, this farm thing that he and his brother have been struggling with – but it's as if now we've found each other, it's like we've both found the other part of ourselves and now we can *really* start our lives.'

She squeezed his arm again.

Michael thought she was close to tears, but at the same time, as he now looked at her just as the clouds cleared and let the moonlight through, she looked radiant, beautiful, spiritual and more. The matchmaker couldn't really pin it down but he'd never ever seen her look so magical.

'And you know what else, Michael?'

'There's more?' he joked.

'Here, just now talking to you about it was the first time it all made sense, even to me, the first time it all fell into place. I haven't even talked to Pat about any of this and I might see him tomorrow and think to myself "what was I on about?" But I don't think so, Michael. I know it's a cliché, but I think I've really found my soulmate and I'll do *whatever* I need to do to make sure we can be together.'

'That's all very well, Maggie, and fair play to you, I say fair play to you,' the matchmaker began, after a few seconds and the enormity of what she had just said sinking in, 'but tell me this – do you think you might like him?'

They both cracked up and laughed, again so loud the matchmaker's wife came out to the farmyard to see what all the commotion was about. 'Come on in, will youse, or you'll be catching your death!' Dorothy called out from the door.

'Oh, I think she's caught something much greater than that,' Michael said, as he crossed the yard with Maggie in his arm, giving her an extra strong hug and taking her into the warmth of the kitchen. Not that Maggie needed the heat of a fire at this point.

Michael had noticed that she seemed to have her own internal glow tonight.

*

Meanwhile one of the twins was trying to find a way to tell his brother that perhaps it may not be a good idea after all for them to take the same wife.

There were lots of ways to try and achieve this. The easiest way, the twin with the smiling eyes thought, was just to concentrate on the point and his brother would pick it up telepathically.

'There's something troubling you, isn't there?' Joe said, following fifty minutes of silence.

'Oh God,' thought Pat, 'this shit really works!'

'And I know what it is,' Joe continued.

'Yeah?'

'You don't want to wash the dishes, do you? There, I knew it. Well it's your bleedin' turn and if you weren't so flippin' useless at finding us a wife it would be none of our turns to do the washing up, would it?'

Pat nodded to the positive.

'No, it would be *her* turn all the time, so the sooner—'

'Eh, Joe,' Pat interrupted.

'Don't "eh Joe" me, Pat. We're discussing this!'

*

Joe had been pushing Pat, advising – no, not advising, more like instructing, yes, instructing – him not to be wasting time on this Watson woman unless she was going to be 'the one', unless she was going to be the one for *both* of them.

'It's not as easy as that, Joe,' Pat had said desperately during one of their late-night conversations across the sturdy, ancient stripped-pine table. They'd grown up around that table; they'd played beneath it when they were small enough not to bump their heads on the under-side when they stood up. It was sturdy and had been chipped, marked and cut by three generations of the Kane family in this same farmhouse. Most family members had their own signature somewhere on the table, be it an indent made with a knife, an initial carved awkwardly with a nail or just a secret mark made somewhere in memory. For some strange reason Pat had even taken to sleeping on the table when he was six years old. It was a table they had eaten at, had rowed around, had shared conversations, of both good and bad news, and it had been the platform for some of their father's wonderful farming stories. It had also been the table they had prepared tea and sandwiches at for the funerals of first their father and then their mother. The table had been the focal point of each and every family crisis and celebration in their lives and now it was the table around which they negotiated the details of their proposed wife.

Pat had made his statement through sheer frustration at his inability to remove himself from the awkward predicament.

When they had first discussed the issue and made a joint decision to do something about their domestic arrangements, this proposed 'wife' had neither face, name, heart, character nor soul, so it had been easy to talk of her as an object when she lacked a voice and an opinion.

Now Maggie had every single fibre of Pat's body screaming for her twenty-four hours a day and he was no longer quite so comfortable to discuss the 'sharing' aspect of their relationship.

'What do you mean it's not going to be as easy as that? As easy as what?' Joe had snapped before banging the table, causing the half loaf of bread to jump a few inches into the air as the crumbs all around it provided a target upon which to aim its return. It fell outside the target, landing instead upon the knife used to cut it. 'It's simple, very simple. There is no room, nor money, for two extra people here. We've discussed it to death and we've reached our agreement. If your fancy woman is not going to be the woman for both of us, she's not going to be coming in here at all and … listen to this, I'll go out and find the first bag willing to live with us and look after us and get her hitched and back here before you've been able to work up the courage to give your fancy woman her first kiss on the cheek!' Joe banged the table again, to make his point – this time the half loaf fell back amongst its crumbs – before continuing, 'Now I'm warning you: get it done or get rid of her!'

Get rid of her? Pat thought. No, no, siree, not even possible. I nearly passed through my life without really getting to know her and now that I have, I'm certainly not going to lose her.

Chapter Fourteen

Pat's mind, but not mouth, was entangled with such thoughts as he walked out onto the Ballyronan Road with Maggie on their next date. Joe had been way off the mark with his 'peck on the cheek' line. They'd already passed that. In fact, they were long since regular 'guests' at Old Man Hutchinson's hay shed and what Joe didn't know and would never ever be allowed to find out was that the more they tasted each other's bodies, the less Pat wanted to share the treasure with anybody, least of all his brother.

'You know, Pat, you're going to have to make an honest woman out of me!' Maggie announced as she skipped on ahead of him so that she could turn around to face him and grab his two hands. They continued walking: he forwards, she, confident in his care, backwards.

'Ah shit.' He sighed.

'Ah shit what?'

'This should be the happiest day of my life, but it's ….'

'Hold the happiest thought, I like that one.'

'Well, Maggie, look … am, you see … it's like this … I … *Oh shit!*' Pat shouted. He was getting more frustrated the more he couldn't tell her or, perhaps, the closer he came to telling her what was on his mind. It didn't matter which was the case, the end result was exactly the same. The cat who'd escaped had spilt the milk and was enjoying it, but now it was about to get a right good clip on the ear for spilling it in the first place.

'Look, Pat, I know about the situation up on the farm,' Maggie began, dropping her voice to a near whisper.

'The "situation"?' Pat cut in, as steady as a new foal trying out its legs for the first time.

'Well that you need to share—' she started.

'God, does everyone in Castlemartin know our business?'

'Come on, Pat, surely I'm not everyone?'

He suddenly dropped her hands and froze right in the middle of the road. 'I can't believe you – I can't believe this.'

'What? What's the matter?' Maggie implored.

'After all … all we've been through, all we've done, you stand there casually and say, you mean that you would accept this situation …? You would … you could?' Pat was now stammering badly, and worse than that, he was about to start crying.

'Look, Patrick Kane, let's be real about this. OK? You know what I feel about you and I know what you feel about me and we haven't even actually discussed it. Don't you think that that point just there in itself is amazing? Hey, and we're not even twins!' This didn't manage to draw even a smile out of Pat so she continued, 'It's not just love and all that crap, it's … oh, you know *exactly* what it is we have. I see it in your eyes every time we make love.'

Maggie stopped talking at this point to consider what she had just said. She could tell he was doing exactly the same thing and she noticed the lines of strain flow from his forehead.

'So,' Maggie started again, 'to have that, to keep that, to protect that, to stay close to this soul I've been lucky enough to find, I'll … I'll do … I'll be whatever you need me to be. I'll be your woman, your wife, the mother of your children, your housekeeper and, yes, I'll even … even look after your brother. Hell, I'm going to be working with you on the farm and I'm sure there will be lots of things I'll have to do which will be a lot more unpleasant.'

'But I thought it was special between us – I thought it was, you know, just *us* and, you know, I wouldn't want to share you, I couldn't share you!' Pat stated defiantly.

'Well, of course you won't be sharing me, you idiot,' Maggie lectured, as they resumed their walk, arm in arm this time.

'I'm afraid I don't understand. I would be sharing you, but …?'

'Listen,' Maggie began. It was when she was like this, all fired up and full of passion and conviction for a subject, that Pat loved her the most. It was just … just, well, that he was feeling sorry for himself that the subject in question had to be about her sleeping with his brother.

'I'm not. I'm just damned if I'm going to lose you over this! I want – I need – for us to be together,' she continued. 'I want to be with you and I *will* be with you.'

They kissed lightly as they walked on off out the Ballyronan Road.

'I will sleep in your bed, and only in your bed. I will do whatever other chores I have to do to help your farm run smoothly so that we can start to make it successful. And the quicker we can make it successful, the quicker we can either buy out Joe's share of the farm or, if he's not disposed to that, move to another one ourselves. OK?'

Pat nodded his agreement; so far so good.

'Now, the chores will be whatever they have to be: milking the cows, cleaning their shit out of the cowshed, feeding the chickens, cleaning their shit, making a home out of that pigsty you call a house, cooking, cleaning, washing and doing whatever else I have to do. If it also means … that on occasion I have to give Joe some relief, then so be it – it will be no more or less pleasant to me than cleaning the shit out of the cowshed. Both will be mandatory chores and my mind will be as much on one as on the other. I will wash myself thoroughly after both.'

A longer pause for thought and the only sounds were those of Pat's hob-nailed boots upon the tarmac, the rustle of leaves in the trees and a few blackbirds croaking to their mates that the day was over and it was time to go back to the branches before the night fell too far in on them.

'You have to realise, Pat, that what we have is not special because of what we do to each other's bodies, pleasant though it may be, but, hell, we can do that by ourselves, and I imagine we've both had a lot of practice,' Maggie continued impishly.

Pat smiled for the first time since the conversation had taken this turn.

'But what is important is what's in our hearts, what's in our souls, what's in our eyes, as we do it which … which,' she searched hard for her words, 'which exalts what we do to each other from the animal act it so often is.'

'But what if you were to become ….'

'Pregnant?' she helped.

'Yes.'

'Not a possibility. Either he wears protection, or that's one chore I'll certainly refuse to do. And you, you're going to have to wear protection as well, 'cause I don't want us starting a family until we've been by ourselves for a good nine months. No more of this "it's OK, I can feel it in time" malarkey.'

'But I'm careful!' Pat protested.

'Oh, maybe you should patent that method – I'm sure we could make a fortune selling it at McKay's Chemists down in Magherafelt and then we wouldn't have to work the farm! Anyway, let this be an end to the conversation,' Maggie suggested as she pulled her interlinked arm (and Pat) closer to herself. 'Let's put an inch to our step and check into Hutchinson's Exclusive Hotel for a wee while. You know the one I mean? The one where men are men and the sheep run scared.'

Chapter Fifteen

And so it came to pass, six weeks, two days, twelve hours, thirty-four minutes and ten seconds later, that a Miss M. Watson and a Mr D. Kane were married. Yes, married! The twins (well, at least one of them) and Maggie married in a small registry office just off University Road in Belfast.

Maggie was not so sure that her idea was as great as when she had first suggested it to Pat, so, in order to take control of the situation, she decided to have a meeting with the twins, insisting they both be present. She advised them both that as far as she was concerned she was Pat's wife and that is exactly what she would continue to be. Moreover, she agreed in advance precisely what her 'chores' would be.

Joe had originally hoped that he would be sleeping with Maggie on alternate nights, but all such dreams died a quick and nasty death during that first joint meeting. Maggie proposed once a month, Joe fought for once a week, and eventually they settled upon once a fortnight.

Joe Kane didn't really stand much chance of winning his argument: through the magic of mathematics, two always out-votes one. Nevertheless, to avoid an atmosphere around and between them, Maggie had previously told Pat of her offer of once a fortnight so that they could join forces in the meeting.

Maggie was also keen to get the first of her chores out of the way as soon as possible, having realised that for all of them – particularly Pat – this would prevent their nerves being withered down raw to their stumps. Her plan was to get Joe so worked up in advance that the chore would be as short (but never as sweet) as possible.

Maggie found her opportunity on the third morning they shared the house. Pat, as ever, rose at six, made his own breakfast and was off out to the fields before Joe was even awake. On her trip to the bathroom, Maggie noticed that Joe had awoken and was lying in his bed, looking at the ceiling. She kept the bathroom door open and caught sight in the mirror of Joe ogling her. She knew that he could see the outline of her body thought her nightdress. In fact, the twins' wife delayed her bathroom procedure intentionally to put on a bit of a show for Joe.

As she left the bathroom she pretended to be shocked that he had seen her so. They both remained silent as she went into his bedroom and closed the door behind her.

She went over to the bed and lay down beside him. He reached out to fondle her – somewhere, anywhere: he just wanted to touch any part of her beautiful body. She politely caught his hand and gently moved it away from her. He awkwardly placed it behind the back of his neck interlocking the fingers of both hands now behind his head. She felt beneath the cover for his manhood and mouthed, but did not say, the word 'protection'. He reached to his bedside table and soon they were ready.

Maggie lay on top of him, refusing to either undress herself or kiss him. In a matter of forty seconds, with a certain amount of fumbling, grunts, groans and sighs, it was all over. She was very pleased with herself: she had managed to fulfil her fortnightly chore without having to be involved in full intercourse, a fact she proudly relayed to Pat who agreed that he was extremely glad that Joe's attempts at a union had been thwarted. He just could not deal with thinking of them – his twin brother Joe and wife Maggie – together.

The awkwardness of the first month over, the three of them coexisted effortlessly. Joe was happy for Maggie to play wife to Pat. For his part, he was now getting his clothes cleaned; regular, well-cooked meals; a clean house to come home to following a hard day's work in the fields; a clean sheet on his bed and, occasionally – twice a month to be exact – a bit of the other.

Perhaps, but only perhaps, Joe thought he may be missing out on something to Pat. But from where he sat, his brother had all the potential grief and earache that comes from having a woman around all the time. Meanwhile, at last, everything was rosy in his garden.

Hey, and you know what? Even the matchmaker was happy with the way things turned out. Pat had insisted on paying the balance of his fee, his logic being that if he hadn't gone to the matchmaker he'd never have met Maggie.

Michael never asked his sister-in-law about her domestic arrangements, neither did Maggie volunteer the information. However, the matchmaker was very happy to see her in love and happy at last. In another way it saddened him that he had lost his confidante and sounding board.

Dorothy, prompted by her mother, dropped the usual unsubtle hints about the patter of tiny feet, but all such suggestions fell upon stony ground. Maggie had committed to 'working all the hours that God sends' (to use the Kane twins' most frequently spoken quote) to help make the farm work. She wanted – needed – to change their domestic arrangements as quickly as possible because she was convinced that in the end the whole situation could only lead to disaster.

That said, the honeymoon had to end. And it wasn't a case of 'if' – rather it was more a case of 'when'.

Chapter Sixteen

And eventually they all lived happily ever after.

But what *really* happened to Snow White and Prince Charming the morning after the credits making this proclamation had rolled up the silver screen? Did they live happily ever after and become the first couple in the world to be bored to death? Or did they deal with the reality of toilet seat up or down, toothpaste cap on or off, toast buttered before applying jam, pot bellies, fag ash, dirty dishes or dirty boots on clean floors? Did the seven dwarves singing 'Hi-ho, hi-ho, it's off to work we go!' eventually get on her wick? Would she have called after them, 'Can you keep that racket down, please? I'm trying to catch up on my beauty sleep – it's not easy keeping this skin so soft and pure!' Thankfully Maggie didn't have seven dwarves and one Prince Charming, but she did have a set of twins with the combined height of eleven feet and eleven inches to attend to.

For the first couple of months they all pretty much kept on their best behaviour and, in fact, they found living together easier than they'd expected. Pat noticed that Joe now made an effort with his appearance and he was even seen to be tidying his bedroom on one occasion.

All three of them worked hard, very hard, so when Maggie thought it was time to invite her sister and the matchmaker out to their place for Sunday tea, the farm was no longer running fast just to fall behind, financially speaking. They were in fact standing still, and that in itself was progress.

Dorothy was still unaware of the 'arrangements' up on the twins' farm. In fact, Michael had chosen not to discuss it even with Maggie since their early conversations. He knew that if Dorothy were to scent even a hint of what he imagined the slumber arrangements to be, then his remaining life would be most certainly not be worth living. But he wouldn't even be allowed off that easy: she would let him live and his resultant life would be his biggest punishment.

Anyway, it all appeared to be very civil and, following lunch around the crowded table, Joe took the Gilmour kids off over the fields for a walk, leaving the sisters Watson, the matchmaker and Pat to chat amongst themselves.

'So … youse seem to be doing well here?' Michael offered.

'Yeah, we're getting on OK. Maggie's been great: she's organised, so organised. She puts together systems for everything and,' Pat paused to tap the table with his fingers, 'touch wood, we can see the light at the end of the tunnel.'

'We shouldn't be getting too excited though, Pat – there's never going to be enough here to support the three of us,' Maggie offered, not as a rebuff to her husband but as a way to get a discussion going amongst the three of them about formulating a plan for the future.

'Not to mention a family,' Dorothy chipped in.

Surprisingly, Pat Kane smiled fondly at this remark, a fact not unnoticed by the other three.

'Is there anything we can do to help?' the matchmaker offered.

'What, with starting a family?' Maggie smiled and put her arm around Pat. 'No, we're managing OK in that department, thanks.'

'No, silly. I meant with the farm, I say, I meant the farm.' The matchmaker blushed.

'Well, we'd certainly welcome all hands next weekend with the baling of the hay?' Pat laughed; he was looking forward to seeing how Maggie was going to cope during their first harvest. Traditionally all able bodies from neighbouring farms chipped in together. There was a lot of work to do in a short period of time. The host farm was responsible for non-stop cups of piping hot tea and an endless supply of sandwiches.

'Count us in,' Dorothy volunteered.

'Great.' Pat smiled. 'Many hands make light work.'

Actually, I *meant*, is there anything we can do to help you get the farm on a sound footing,' the matchmaker persisted.

'Well, at this stage it's just a matter of paying off the loan to the bank, and Maggie's made great inroads in that direction with getting old Walters to pay us properly for the potatoes and vegetables we sell him. She also negotiated a discount with the old fox for the we have from them. In those dealings alone we're so much better off and Joe and I haven't had to lift a finger.' Pat smiled proudly at Maggie.

'Yeah, I couldn't believe the pittance old Walters was paying them. I told him we'd move all our business to Dawson Bates up in Magherafelt. He's a fair man, I told Walters, he'll look after us. So then he gave me all this rubbish about how his parents had looked after Joe and Pat's parents, and their two families had been doing business together for years. So I said, "Well, it's not hard to see who's been doing best out of the arrangement." I thought I'd maybe pushed him a bit too far and he'd throw me out, but he broke into this great big grin and said I was exactly what the twins needed and he was happy because he thought the farm now had a chance with someone like me looking after the business. I wasn't sure whether to take it as a compliment or an insult.'

'Oh, a compliment, Maggie, definitely a compliment, coming from the mouth of Ernest Walters, and, don't you see, a particularly big compliment seeing that it was addressed to a woman,' Dorothy offered.

'Yes, well, whatever,' Maggie stuttered, for she too wasn't a great one for the praise. 'But he said his office was open to me, and if I need any advice or information all I have to do is come and see him.'

'Maggie reckons with the extra money we're making on our sales to Walters and the discount we're getting from all the provisions we'll be able to pay off the bank loan in fifteen months,' Pat announced as Dorothy poured them all a fresh cup of tea.

'Then when we've that paid off we'll be able to use the next income to invest in things for the farm – a lot of the equipment has been run down over the years with Pat and Joe struggling to get by. But if we can get some of it repaired and some new bits and pieces then the two of them can be a lot more efficient in their work and at the same time generate more money,' Maggie continued.

'That's great, Maggie!' Dorothy said, as she poured her sister's tea. 'I never thought I'd see you so thrilled and excited to be working on a farm.'

'So what if we loaned you some money to speed up the whole process?' the matchmaker offered. He had a bit of a reputation for having short arms and deep pockets, but he was fearless about investing his money in Maggie.

'No, really, thanks – ah thanks, Michael and our Dot,' Maggie gushed, 'but it wouldn't really help – we'd still owe the money if it was to you or the bank or whoever. But thanks, I … sorry, I mean *we* … of course, we really appreciate it.'

'Well any time, you know all you have to do is ask.'

'We know, Michael, and thank you both very much. Even though we can't take it, it brings considerable comfort to know that it's there.'

'What about Daddy, Maggie? What about going to him?'

Maggie looked first at Pat and then at the matchmaker. She looked as if she was trying to decide whether she was going to tell them something or hold her own counsel. 'Well, he said he would like to help us. We had a chat before our wedding. But Pat and I agreed we would leave that until we were ready to get our own farm.'

'Is Joe aware of all of this, about the plans for your own farm?' the matchmaker enquired, his permanently hoarse voice adding some drama to an otherwise simple question.

'Well, no.' Pat's short answer cut off Maggie who was about to reply. 'I mean, he knows, or should know, that we're not going to all stay here together forever. I mean, that would just be impossible.'

'Impossible and unhealthy,' Maggie managed to contribute this time.

'Yes, but you can't just dump him,' Michael suggested.

The problem with the fluency of this conversation was that one of the participants was not aware of the subtext. Furthermore, neither Maggie, Pat nor Dorothy's husband had any intention of enlightening her.

'No, we weren't planning on dumping him, Michael. But who knows what might happen in the future, with the farm becoming more secure and all that? He might meet someone and want to be on his own anyway,' Maggie said with a certain hint of finality.

'Maybe Michael could help Joe out with a match?' the matchmaker's wife replied, finding herself in the lucky position of being able to find work for her husband and make her sister's life easier in one gesture. She wasn't to know just how much easier such a match would make things for Maggie.

When no-one appeared to be showing any enthusiasm for her suggestion she had another go.

'He'd be a great catch for someone,' she offered, clearly trying to head the conversation in this direction.

'Nah, I don't think our Joe would take too neighbourly to that suggestion; he's much too shy for Michael's book. No, don't worry about Joe – he'll find his own way through the woods. He's not great at finding the most used pathway but he is very good at barging his way through whatever's in front of him and eventually he always comes out at the other end,' Pat replied, hoping Dorothy wasn't following his tracks too closely.

'How would you work out what to do? Would you buy him out or would you want him to buy you out?' the matchmaker asked, seeing the potential for problems to crop up and wanting to cut them off at the pass.

'Oh, that's too far away to even be considering, but I'm sure if Maggie and myself were the ones to introduce the subject then Joe should have the first right to either buy us out or sell his share. If the situation were reversed that's what I would think fair.'

'There's logic in that ... or maybe you could buy more land, the adjoining farmland, and build another hou—'

'No, no, we wouldn't want that,' Maggie cut in, just a split second too quickly for the matchmaker to assume that the subject hadn't already been discussed.

'But listen, as I say, we're getting ahead of ourselves and the only thing we really need to be discussing here are the plans for the harvesting next weekend,' Pat added, taking another, much safer path. 'Dorothy, do you think you and Maggie here will be up to helping feed the five thousand?'

'God, how many people come to these things, Michael?' Dorothy asked, the usual playfulness disappearing gradually from her voice.

'Oh, pay no attention to him, Dorothy: there'll be a dozen people max,' Maggie, a veteran of the princely total of zero harvests, offered, with the confidence of a farmer who knew why he should tie string around the bottom of each trouser leg while out in the fields.

'Good guess, Maggie – we'll make a farmer's wife of you yet,' Pat replied proudly as he winked at Mrs M. Kane.

'Ah, not so much a guess: I overhead you and Joe discussing who'd be turning up and I just added our Dorothy and Michael to the total – see, as I keep telling you, not just a pretty face,' Maggie teased, as she affectionately tickled Pat's sides from behind.

'Ah now, Maggie, don't you see Pat's not green himself? He's not the one who'd think that,' the matchmaker said in a quieter rasp.

Just then the noise of the three Gilmour children being chased by their uncle-in-law could be heard at the back door. His firm hand turned the stiff handle and all four sprang into the warm kitchen.

'Now you've all the plans made for the harvesting, Pat, I hope you've told whoever is making the grub that I don't like flippin' tomatoes in my egg sandwiches – make me throw up on the spot,' Joe announced to the catering committee sitting around the table.

'No, he hadn't,' Dorothy offered, 'but you just have and in a manner I'm sure none of us will forget.'

Chapter Seventeen

And the sun shone on harvest day – what more could one ask of their God?

But the sun wasn't up first – that honour, if indeed it was an honour, went to Maggie and Pat, followed twenty minutes later by Joe. Five days earlier it was Joe who had been awake first because that particular day, the previous Tuesday, was one of Joe's special twenty-four days of the year. Once again, Maggie had fulfilled her obligations without being fully physically unfaithful to Pat. Long may it continue, she wished. Well, not actually for a long time, if you see what she meant. But, as long as it had to continue she wished for it to do so with Joe fumbling about, not really knowing what he was doing as he searched for his twice monthly relief.

By the time Joe joined Maggie and Pat in the kitchen on harvest morning the pan was well fired up and stocked to overflowing with a fair stock of George Best's (alleged) favourite sizzling Cookstown sausages – if they were good enough for Ulster's favourite son, they were certainly good enough for Castlemartin's only set of twenty-nine-year-old twins.

On hearing Joe's movements on the creaky floor Maggie had added three rashers of bacon to the pan plus a couple of pieces of fadge. This, with the couple of eggs she would crack open carefully into the pan the minute Joe walked into the kitchen, would create the legendary Ulster Fry, the bedrock of each and every farmer in the country. This, supplemented with porridge in the winter months, kept the vital workers of the land well-nourished and in energy until they became a bit peckish around lunchtime. In fact, all their helpers from the neighbouring farms would be sitting demolishing a similar meal at that exact moment.

The matchmaker's ten-year-old son, Paul, who created projects for himself by collecting such statistics, noted, following detailed interviews with all the men and women on the field, that for breakfast the workers had eaten a combined twenty-four eggs, thirty rashers of bacon, fifteen sausages (sadly, though, further research indicated that not all of the workers had taken Georgie Best's recommendations literally) and a staggering forty pieces of fadge, once again placing the potato at the top of yet another chart (Paul was working on a theory that if someone could persuade the Beatles to release their records on some kind of potato bake they would double their already astronomical Ulster sales). Believe it or not, there was more: to be exact, eight pieces of fried wheaten bread and eleven pieces of toasted loaf, all washed down with twenty mugs, and three cups, of tea. His mum and Maggie were the only ones to have cups of tea and Paul wasn't surprised that it was the sister who lived on the farm who had two cups to his mother's one.

The team, milling around in groups of twos and threes that fine late summer morning, was Bobby Patterson and his son Tommy; widower Harry McKinney; Wesley McIvor and his wife-to-be Valerie Scott; the Lone Ranger (aka Daniel Stevenson) and Tonto (aka Ray O'Sullivan); Dorothy and Michael Gilmour with their aforementioned eldest son, Paul, and their hosts, Joe, Pat and Maggie Kane.

The matchmaker was intrigued by the whole harvesting ritual and spent his time distracting himself from the ever-growing pain in his lower back by amassing as much information as possible. Bobby Patterson, at sixty-three, was the oldest man on the field and an expert, not shy at sharing his knowledge with the matchmaker.

'The corn is sown in the springtime. Well, actually the proper name for the produce is "oats" – corn comes from the American fields, what we would call sweetcorn, or corn on the cob – but it goes by "corn" most commonly.' Bobby advised Michael that the oats would be recognisable by the way the grains, on balancing stems, flow gracefully in clusters, which are called panicles. 'The crop first came to the British Isles in the thirteenth century and our cool moist climate suits it well,' the old farmer said, imparting his history lesson to his wide-eyed student. 'Tractors plough up the fields, over-turning the earth, the seed is sown and six weeks later the stems break through the ground. When summer arrives, well, just look around you,' Bobby said, as he and Michael surveyed the scene directly in front of them, of the Kanes' fields, awash with the ripened four-foot-high golden rays of corn blowing in the gentle summer breeze.

And just as the lesson was coming to a close, the proceedings commenced with a tractor – driven and owned by the Lone Ranger – pulling a David Brown binder, or reaper, owned and attended to by Tonto, through the fully mature corn crop. The reaper was so noisy that Michael could no longer hear the elder Patterson, whose voice was low and dull at the best of times. The pathway being cut by the reaper's turning wheel, slapping the corn down and against a cutter bar, was a good five-foot wide. This particular binder could cut about two acres an hour, meaning this particular task was no longer the backbreaking laborious chore it once was, 'in the olden days', when the corn had to be cut by scythe. As the binder made its way through the towering corn it produced sheaths of the grain – a slim armful of corn tied together with a few stems of hay – which dropped to the side in its wake.

Bobby Patterson demonstrated how you take three of these sheaths, pull a few strands of hay from the centre and bind them together to make self-standing stooks. These stooks would remain standing for about two weeks to allow them to completely dry out.

Within a couple of hours, the team had completed the work in the smaller four-acre field, so they moved on to a larger field, perhaps twice the size of the first, in which the hay had already been cut and stooked. Now the job was to break down the dried stooks into sheaths again, and build those sheaths into huts.

Michael soon learned that you took the driest of your sheaths to make the base of your hut. He used about a dozen for the base, stacking them in an upright position in a circle. Then he built up from this base, tapering it in so that the higher he built, the less sheaths he needed. Pat joined Michael and the eldest Patterson in their hut-making efforts. It took about one hundred sheaths of corn to make a hut, which meant, Paul Gilmour advised his father, that they were getting about ten huts per acre. They crowned each hut, happily for it afforded them a few minutes' rest, with a hud, which was used as a water-diverting device, not too dissimilar to an umbrella. The hud, Michael worked out, was pretty much a stook but with the three sheaths tied closer to the top – although, apparently, some farmers were known to use long grass to get the same effect.

They completed work on each hut by using baling twine to encircle it about half a dozen times, to ensure it would not be blown apart by the vicious lough winds. The corn would remain in these huts for a further two to three weeks, whereupon it was either taken for threshing or built into stacks, where it would remain until it needed to be threshed.

'And the threshing is where the corn is separated,' Bobby Patterson continued, 'by the threshed into grains for flour; chaff, which we mostly burn now, but in the good old days we used it to stuff our mattresses, a great way of hiding your fivers, don't you see; and hay, which we use for animal feed.'

The twins had planned for the threshing to take place the weekend after next when they would, again with most of today's crew, thresh about two-thirds of their crop. The remainder they would thresh as far away as the following March, where some of the freshly threshed corn would be taken and planted as seed to start the cycle all over again. This cycle had outlasted Joe's and Pat's father, and their grandfather and would, they knew, outlast their own time on this earth.

'You know,' Pat began as he and Michael sat by one of their recently built huts, tearing away into the egg sandwiches and tea just delivered by Dorothy, Maggie and Paul, who was still taking notes on everything said, done and eaten, 'a few summers ago I – well actually Joe and I – would have viewed this as hard work: you know, *all* of this.'

'Well, don't you see, you won't have me contradicting you there,' the matchmaker replied, rubbing the lower part of his back.

Pat smiled; he was grateful for all the help given but particularly by the matchmaker. All the others on the field, excluding Michael and his family, were there because they were local farmers and it was impossible for them to do their own harvesting, so they would all eventually chip in their labour on each other's fields. All, that is, except for the Lone Ranger and Tonto: they owned the machinery needed for the harvesting so they made their income by hiring out their equipment and their labour; but they also enjoyed a fine reputation for working hard and putting in the hours required as opposed to the hours hired. Their double act, which they kept up all the time, served to keep good humour in the fields they worked.

But Pat knew the matchmaker was not there to return a favour from the past or in the future: he was working up a sweat because he was family. Pat allowed himself to savour and enjoy having family with that spirit and commitment again. He knew for certain that the following morning, when Michael would try and rise from his bed, he'd be rewarded by discovering his body would refuse his commands and he would ache for the first few hours until his limbs loosened up again. That was when he might rue his day in the fields. But today he was certainly enjoying himself.

'But now,' Pat continued, picking up the thread again, 'when we're not just slaving away to pay back the bank, you know, never getting our head above water, it's different. It's like, now, for the first time, we're doing all of this for ourselves, for our future. And the great thing is, it actually looks like we might even have a future.'

The matchmaker knew exactly what his brother-in-law meant but remained silent, happy to munch away on his thick sandwiches and swig the mouthfuls down with piping hot tea, forcing the sweat through his brow quicker. Pat stole a look at Maggie, who was joking and kidding with her sister and Paul as they delivered the rations to the owners of the silver bullets. Tonto was kneeling down on the ground with his head turned and his ear close to the earth. Drawn by the Watson sisters' laughter, most of the workers, including Pat and Michael, were making their way across to witness the Lone Ranger and Tonto show.

'What is it? What do you hear from the ground, Tonto? What does the earth *tell* you, blood brother?' the Lone Ranger began as he blew the imaginary smoke from the top of his outstretched index fingers now that he had his audience.

'Well, Kemosabe, a stagecoach just passed,' the other half of the double act, ear still to the ground, replied.

'Incredible,' the Lone Ranger announced to the audience.

'Ha, Kemosabe, the stagecoach was a late 1870s Wells Fargo wooden-suspension model drawn by six magnificent horses – the front two were pure white, the second two were piebald and the two closest to the stagecoach were black.'

'Incredible!' the Lone Ranger continued, now coaxing his audience.

'Yes, Kemosabe; the paleface riding shotgun wore a pair of red trousers, green shirt, pink waistcoat and a scarlet necktie.'

'Sounds more like someone from Barry's Arcade down at Portrush,' Bobby Patterson interrupted. Unperturbed, Tonto continued.

'He had one of those Winchester repeater rifles. The horse man was dressed from head to toe in black, even fine black leather gloves to protect his hands from the reins. On the shotgun-side, rear window, a young beautiful lady dressed in a white bonnet and pale blue dress sat weeping quietly. She was clutching a letter, obviously the source of her tears,' Tonto concluded.

'Incredible, Tonto, just pretty darned amazing!' the Lone Ranger grandstanded. 'And you can tell all that just from listening to the message Mother Earth passes on to you?'

'No, Kemosabe,' Tonto moaned, 'they only went and drove over me, didn't they?'

Young Paul led the laughter as they broke up, throwing their tea dregs to the earth, walking back in twos and threes to their work positions. The craic on the field, as they say, was 'ninety' and all the jaws – for voices couldn't be heard unless you were close up – were moving like fiddlers' elbows.

Michael led Pat back to, and beyond, their earlier conversation.

'So, is Joe as happy with the new set-up?'

'He seems to be,' was all Pat would reply.

'Look, I've been thinking, Pat. What if I was to try and do a bit of a match for Joe?'

'He'd never go for it,' Pat replied as he kept on working the sheaths. The sun had long since passed its peak and was now an artist's delight as it covered the workers and hay in a golden hue, set off brilliantly against an ice-blue sky.

'What if he didn't know about it?' the matchmaker pushed.

'Like how?'

'Well, don't you see, he's basically a fine young man; he's just very shy and that tends to make him appear a little arrogant. So he's probably found himself, well … unpopular with the girls and consequently that's why he's not interested. So if we, well, if *I* could find a suitable girl, one we all thought suitable, then maybe we could stage a few dinners at our house? We invite you, Maggie and Joe and have this other young lady come by, and then we light the match and see how the fire grows.'

'I don't know, Michael – if he got a whiff of something funny going on he'd be off on one and he'd never forgive Maggie or me, and you know what, it's going OK at the minute, Michael, I'd hate to –'

'It's not going OK at the minute, Pat,' the matchmaker cut in firmly, very firmly, but delivered in more of a hiss than a shout. 'I said, it's not going fine at the moment! Please don't forget that, as well as being my sister-in-law, Maggie is also my good friend. She'll do whatever she has to do to be close to you but that certainly does not make it OK, Pat, at the minute or any time. We have to do something about this!'

At that point Paul wandered over to advise his father that, at their current rate, they would finish work within the hour. Paul was working up the courage to ask Pat if he could come back out to help on the farm next weekend as well when they all heard a violent retching about two huts down the field.

Pat instinctively ran across and found his brother doubled over in agony, throwing up his guts behind the hut. Maggie ran and grabbed Pat by the arm in fear.

'Look, Maggie, just keep people away from us, will you?' Pat began. He then whispered in her ear, 'Joe gets very embarrassed at this – I'll look after him.'

Joe mouthed the word 'tomato' to Pat, who nodded and held Joe's forehead tenderly with the palm of his hand while using his other arm to prevent his brother from falling into his own sick. When the entire contents of Joe's stomach were spent, Pat pulled his brother's left arm around his shoulder and grabbed it with his left hand, using his right to support him from behind across his back, gripping his waist firmly. Arm in arm, they walked alone down the field towards the farmhouse.

Maggie couldn't help but swell up with emotion as she watched the sorry sight of the two bothers as they hobbled off in the direction of the farmhouse. With all the subterranean conflict between the three of them she'd forgotten that first and foremost they were brothers and it had taken what she had just witnessed to realise the genuine love Pat had for his brother.

Joe's work on their farmland was now concluded, at least for that fine summer's evening.

Chapter Eighteen

The next time the matchmaker met up with Pat was the following Tuesday, when the sisters Watson organised one of their family dinners at Michael's house. Pat liked going to the matchmaker's house – he felt comfortable there and was always made to feel very welcome.

Pat, prompted by his wife, was in his Sunday best. For his own part, he felt this a bit extravagant, but Maggie insisted he always looked great when he paid a bit of attention to his appearance – you know, for instance, simple things like pulling a comb through his hair. But it worked: for once Pat felt like he was stepping into the shoes of someone a bit more sophisticated than himself and he had to admit, it made him feel good. However, he did draw the line at spending some of their hard-earned farm money on a new outfit for himself.

'God, Joe would laugh me out of the house,' had been his immediate reply.

Maggie contented herself with the thought that Magherafelt, the biggest of the local villages, hadn't been built in a day and in all honesty she couldn't complain about the size of the steps they were already taking.

At the same time there was still one thing and one thing alone she needed to change and would change, given half the chance.

'Listen,' Michael began in a hushed voice to Pat. They were alone in the kitchen – the sisters had gone out to the yard on the pretence of enjoying a bit of fresh air before sitting down to dinner, but Michael knew some major chin-wagging would be going on, which was fine, for he needed to have a private conversation with this twin. 'I think I might have found a suitable candidate, look, don't you see, for Joe, I mean.'

'Oh?' Pat replied, rising from the hard chair he was in and wandering over to the kitchen window to see where his wife and her sister were located: they were, in fact, up the other end of the picture-postcard garden. The garden was one of Michael's passions, not to mention his pride and joy. He had grown a hedge the entire way around the garden. At the end, furthest from the house, he had erected an arch over the gate which took you through to the top fields where Michael and Maggie had often walked to discuss the woes of life over the years. The matchmaker had various rose bushes around the garden, culminating in an elaborate display up and around the arch of this gate.

As Pat looked out from the kitchen window, it was just after 7:30 on what had been yet another beautiful late summer's day. The sun was accelerating in its descent and, in fact, dropping behind the rose arch, with the sisters leaning against the main arch posts, which would greatly annoy its creator were he to join Pat at the window and see them doing so. The sisters were involved in an animated conversation and they were creating a magical silhouette against the backdrop of the sinking sun. Pat merely gawked in astonishment at the beauty created. He wanted to call his brother-in-law over to share the proud vision but found himself speechless. He was drawn from his trance by the rasp of the matchmaker.

'Oh? Is that to be all, Pat?'

'I'm sorry, Michael, I was miles away,' Pat replied before rejoining the matchmaker at the table. They were enjoying a half pint of Guinness each and Pat replenished his white moustache before continuing. 'I'm nervous, Michael. It could upset everything. I mean, it's easy to throw Joe at the best of times, but he's still a bit weak after the weekend.'

'God, I never realised that tomatoes could be so lethal,' Michael offered as he too had another sip.

'He's always been the same, as long as I can remember,' Pat said, checking once again over his shoulder to ensure the sisters were not within earshot. 'They're pure poison to his system. They don't affect me in the same way, thank goodness.'

'How long will it take him to get over it?'

'Ah, not too long, it just leaves him weak for a few days. But going back to your other matter, I'm really not sure, Michael. I mean, apart from anything else there'd be no room for four up at the farm.

Don't you remember, this is how all of this started? The farm can barely support the three of us, and wouldn't at all were it not for the resourcefulness and energy of Maggie.'

'But don't you see that's part of my point in a way? I certainly know how special Maggie is and how fond youse two are of each other, but believe you me, this will all blow up in your faces if you're not careful. You are both putting up with things now just for the peace it brings, but what happens down the line – say you have a fight or an argument, don't you see? Naturally enough in a relationship it can, and will, happen. Will that drive her into Joe's arms? Have you thought of that? Have you thought of how she may think in a quiet moment, you know, "This man says he loves me, yet he lets, no … he encourages me to sleep with his brother."'

'Shush, Michael, for heaven's sake, or the girls will hear you!' Pat whispered.

'Exactly, Pat. Shush! Exactly! Keep it quiet 'cause it's not right. I say, it's just not right. Don't you see that I'm dreading the day Dorothy finds out? I bet you, Pat, I'll be out on my ear. She'd never forgive me. Pat, I'm telling you, she'd never, ever forgive me.'

Pat thought for a moment as he brought the glass of Guinness to his lips, paused and returned the glass to the table without tasting any of the dark heaven.

'So, this woman, the one you have in mind for Joe – tell me about her.'

Michael breathed a major sigh of relief. 'Well, it's Doris Durin.'

'Doris? Doris Durin, from the tech days?'

'The very same – she said she knew you,' the matchmaker replied.

'And what on earth does Doris Durin need the services of the matchmaker for – sure, isn't she gorgeous?' Pat asked in disbelief.

'Well, you're not exactly the back end of a double-decker bus yourself, Pat, and you came to me.'

'Ah, but that was different.'

'Sure, isn't it always different, Pat? I say, isn't it always different? She's got to the point in her life, and, listen to me now, Pat, never breathe a word of this to anybody,' the matchmaker pleaded.

Pat nodded consent and so Michael continued.

'She's reached the point in her life, don't you see, where she's been led on a merry dance one too many times and now she's serious about finding the right person, marrying, settling down and starting a family. She figured that if she came to me, having tried the "ballroom of romance" circuit on too many a Friday and Saturday night, that maybe a potential partner she may find through matchmaking just might be serious about marrying.'

'How much does she know, you know, about everything?'

'Nothing, Pat, sure there's nothing to know. However, what I've said is that I think the perfect man for her would be Joe but because of my family relationship with him I can't be seen to be the matchmaker. So what I've offered to do is introduce her, introduce *them*, don't you see, as friends and not charge for matchmaking. I've also advised her that Joe has not come to me seeking similar services so she should keep quiet about all that and just let it happen naturally.'

'Naturally ... but with a little nudge from yourself, Michael,' Pat interrupted.

'Hmph. Be that as it may, Pat, but I'll tell you, I'm desperate to resolve this situation. There's more than your life at stake here – there's mine and my marriage as well. Shush now, won't you? Here come the girls.'

'What were youse two conspiring about?' Dorothy enquired as she breezed through the door, followed closely by Maggie.

'I was just telling Pat,' Michael began tentatively, 'that I'd like, well, you know, I'd like to, don't you see, I'd ....'

'Oh for heaven's sake, Michael, spit it out!' his wife chastised him. 'Don't be a wimp! What he's trying to say is that he'd like to fix up Joe with Doris Durin.'

Pat and Maggie stared at each other, each trying to judge the other's reaction. After a time – fourteen clicks from the old grandfather clock standing five feet six inches tall in the corner, to be exact – Pat broke the silence.

'And I think it's a great idea.'

Maggie noticeably relaxed at her husband's proclamation.

Dorothy seemed to be the only one not so sure about all the scheming.

Chapter Nineteen

Maggie and Pat found Joe surprisingly responsive to, as in overly keen on, the idea of going to the matchmaker's for dinner with Doris Durin in attendance.

Doris had not failed to mature into the beautiful woman she had shown the promise of in their technical-college days. Her striking curly ginger hair had lost none of its fire – however, the overall total appearance was now more subtle, excepting of course when she smiled, which was often. She wore a loose-fitting black dress, with small white polka dots covering it, and white high-heel shoes.

She broke the ice immediately when she grabbed Joe by the elbow and steered him off to one side. 'So, we're to be each other's date for tonight.'

Joe forced a shy smile.

'Well, let's make the best of it and have a bit of a hoot and keep the adults,' Doris glanced at the two married couples to help make her point, 'happy, shall we?' at which point Joe, with a more relaxed smile, nodded agreement, which in turn encouraged Doris to break into one of her wild infectious laughs. Her laugh was so sensual it appeared to send a shudder up the entire length of Joe's body.

'Right!' the matchmaker called out, inwardly breathing a colossal sigh of relief. 'Let's see what's on the radio.'

'Ah, great it's the Beatles!' Maggie cried out, recognising the number-one summer hit 'A Hard Day's Night', which was also the title of their first album and their first film. 'They're just fabulous aren't they?'

Everyone but the matchmaker agreed and they discussed going to see the movie when it visited the nearest cinema, which was on the Moneymore Road in Magherafelt. Excepting ballrooms it was the only local palace of entertainment complete with its rear soft expensive seats for the families and for couples stepping out, hard cheaper seats at the front.

He added, 'I wouldn't hold my breath – it'll probably take about a year and a half to reach Magherafelt. Anyway, let's move through into the front room for dinner – Maggie and Dorothy have done us proud.'

'It must be a special occasion – they'll be using the white china again,' Joe half-whispered to Pat in conspiratorial tones, remembering the last occasion he'd been afforded the same luxury in the front room.

The dinner went well, although the men weren't perhaps as relaxed as the ladies. But the ladies were having such a good time it didn't seem to matter. It was as though decisions had already been made and the men were merely playing bit parts in this rural drama. Joe, cautioned earlier in the day by Pat, was restricting his intake of beer but he seemed to be enjoying himself on his first social engagement in perhaps as long as six years. He seemed happy, but yet not smug, to be Doris' date for the evening.

'We'll clear the dishes away,' Dorothy volunteered on behalf of those present sharing a marital status, 'and youse two can chat while we brew up some tea.' The sisters winked in turn at Doris and led their husbands off, but not before loading them with the dishes.

'Juliet', a sad, slow, melodic ballad with tight harmonies by the Four Pennies, was on the radio and surprisingly, Joe was the one to start the conversation off.

'So, what have you being doing since the tech? I thought you'd have been married with a few wains by now,' he ventured, regretting the last part in case he was being too forward.

'Well, to be honest, Joe,' she said with as much sadness in her voice as the lead vocalist in the Four Pennies, 'I'd love to have been … married by now, that is. God, look at Dorothy and Maggie – they're so happy with their men, aren't they?'

'Aye, it certainly looks that way,' Joe replied, concealing his thought that, yeah, Maggie in particular was happy with her *men*.

'But the right one just hasn't come along; I seem to attract fools, or perhaps I'm just too fussy.'

'I know what you mean – our ma, she always used to say that our Pat was much too fussy for his own good. And it does get in the way though, being too fussy that is,' Joe replied, now so locked into the conversation that he was no longer stopping to consider what he was about to say before he said it.

'But if you're going to marry someone, Joe, and have children with them, they can't really be baboons, can they?' Doris said.

'Not unless you want very peculiar, not to mention hairy, children,' Joe replied spontaneously, sending Doris into one of her raunchy laughs, ginger hair flying everywhere.

She did that thing she had done with Joe at the beginning of the evening again – squeezing his arm as she said, 'This has been fun, you know. It could have been a disaster, all this blind date stuff – I was worried, I can tell you.'

'Well, it wasn't really a blind date, was it?' Joe asked.

'What?' Doris replied, a little panic creeping into her voice as 'Don't Throw Your Love Away' by the Searchers came on the radio.

'You know, us – it wasn't really a blind date. I mean, we knew each other, didn't we, at the tech?'

'Yes, Joe,' she said, smiling in relief. 'That's true, we did know each other, so I suppose you're right, it wasn't really a blind date. But it was fun.'

At that, Maggie and Pat returned to the room with a tray – pine with a woven basketwork rim – proudly bearing the Gilmour family's best white china and lots of biscuits.

Maggie resisted, but they were all aware she was resisting, the 'you two seem to be getting on well' comment, if only to acknowledge her, Pat and the matchmaker's nervous tension. Instead, she politely offered them tea.

Thirty minutes later, Maggie, Doris, Joe and Pat were saying their goodbyes to the matchmaker and his wife on the doorstep, yellow light spilling from the doorway, drawing the bugs. And ten minutes later, the twins with Maggie and Doris had reached Pear Tree Roundabout by way of a left out of the matchmakers, along Apple Orchard Lane and a right down Railway Terrace. They stopped at the roundabout.

Joe kicked his heels nervously, not really knowing what to do or say. Doris lived on the Ballyronan Road, which she would get to by going down the Lough Road, whereas the farm was up the Broadway, right onto Noah's Arc and left on Kane's lane to the farm. Now as Noah's Arc curved around back onto the Lough Road, they all could have gone down the Lough Road together and then Pat and Maggie could have swung a left up Noah's Arc and then a right onto Kane's Lane. However, Maggie was trying to will Joe to offer to walk Doris home and by splitting up at the Pear Tree Roundabout she felt she was giving them more time together.

Maggie was just about to say as much when Joe showed his bottle by getting in there first: 'Right, I'm going to walk Doris out to her house – I'll see youse later.'

'Great!' Maggie and Pat whispered in unison.

'I hope that walking you home is OK?' Joe asked when Maggie and Pat were out of earshot.

Once again she squeezed his elbow but didn't, surprisingly, interlock arms. 'Joe, that's fine, just perfectly fine.'

Five minutes and a little more conversation later, they had arrived at Doris' house. Actually, it was her parent's house – a purpose-built, two storey, four-bedroom and three-bathroom house – built two years earlier in 1962. Joe was trying under his breath the various ways to ask a question, a question he had been considering and attempting to form since halfway through the meal.

The night air was chilly and Doris' bare arms were goose bumping. Joe felt that if he didn't get something out quick, she'd leave him standing stammering on the doorstep. And although Doris' mother had been very conscientious when it came to polishing the red doorsteps, there were probably at least a thousand other places Doris would prefer to be standing. Maybe not even standing, but just going straight to bed. The thought of Doris removing her loose black and small-white-polka-dot dress and what there may be there-under drove Joe mad. He couldn't figure out why – he'd only just re-met the girl. She was beautiful, she was stunning and she appeared to be paying attention to him, so he figured it must be a combination of all the above facts. However, if he were not careful she'd be gone. All of which didn't mean it would be impossible to come around at some time in the future, but that would be like starting from scratch, wouldn't it?

'Ah, Doris, could we maybe go out some time again? Together, I mean, just the two of us, you know. I mean, don't get me wrong, tonight was great and I really like Dorothy and Maggie and Michael and Pat, my brother, as you know – I like all of them, but it would be nice, well, I was thinking it might be nice if, you know, kinda just you and I went out together?'

There, he'd said it – he'd gotten it out. Only just, mind you, and yes it had, perhaps, been a bit clumsy, but he'd done it, and as he was saying it, he was thinking, 'Oh shit: what am I going to do if she says no?'

He was persisting with these thoughts when she leaned down from her mother's proudly polished doorstep, squeezed his elbow once again and said, 'You dear sweet man. That would be very nice, Joe, I'd enjoy that. Pick me up here at 8:30 on Friday – we'll go dancing: Robin & the Breakaways are playing in Magherafelt at St John's Hall.'

With that she kissed him lightly on the cheek, removed the key from her purse, turned it, let herself in, turned again to wave him goodnight and closed the door, all in one well-orchestrated movement.

Chapter Twenty

'We are the Breakaways,' their leader, Eamon Regan, announced at the end of the night. 'If you enjoyed us, please tell all your friends; if you didn't, do us a favour and please keep quiet.' Pause for laughter. 'This dance is your last chance of the night. See you next time.' And with that Dixie Kerr led the band into a blistering version of 'Glad All Over', getting the audience to clap along in time to Davy Quinn's *bap-bap-bap* drum fills.

Joe hadn't been to a dance in years and he couldn't remember the last time he'd had as much fun, if in fact he ever had. It was different, though, going to a dance with a beautiful woman. Normally you go single in the hope of meeting someone you can walk home.

You see, here's what happens in the ballrooms:

Apart from the couples, all the boys sit and stand along one side of the ballroom and all the girls on the other. The band leader announces the dances. Each dance consists of three songs; the three songs in each set will be a similar pace – three slow songs for the smoochy set and three belters for the fast bopping sets.

When the band leader announces the set, the boys will make their way across the dance floor to invite the girl of their choice to dance. However, should the boy not be the choice of the girl and she refuses, then the way back across the dance floor by oneself is a long and sad journey with a few hundred sets of eyes beaming down on the back of your neck. Some girls, usually the older ones, are too polite to cause such offence by refusing, so they will accept the invitation to the dance only to break it up after the first song, claiming a visit to the toilet is necessary. What they won't have declared, however, is that the trip to the bathroom will have been necessitated more to save the lad's pride than to touch up one's make-up.

Now, the secret is that the boy will dance with a few girls in the course of the early part of the evening, not seeking repeat dances for at least the first hour. At this point you then revisit some of your earlier partners to see how badly bruised their toes are and for other important things like, you know, 'Do you come here often?'; 'Do you like the Beatles?'; 'Do you ever go to Teyley's Café?'; 'Do your parents let you stay out late?' and so on, and then, if you receive a few nods and comments of approval and generally seem to be getting somewhere, i.e. she tells you her name, then – and only then – will you be allowed to ask her the big big question, which is 'Will you save the last dance for me?'

The significance of the question is extremely important in that if your would-be partner's answer is in the positive, then it means you get to walk her home and … well, who knows. However, if she finds it impossible to respond to your charms and answers in the negative, then you've still got time to get out there and work your way through to the next choice on your wish list.

Some of the older boys, experienced in these matters and the art of drinking like fish, had developed a short version of this time-honoured mating ritual. They would walk around the dance hall, slouching up to their unsuspecting prey and hitting them with such finishing-school classics as 'Do you ride?'

Now, nine times out of ten they'd receive a slap in the face for their troubles. But on that one out of ten, that magical occasion where the willing lady smiled or winked discreetly and nodded or blinked in the direction of the door, well, then they'd be all made up, wouldn't they? Because even the chaps who were accepted for the last dance, well, they were on a promise of no more than a walk to the lady's house, perhaps a peck on the cheek or a bit of snog, perhaps even some awkward groping, but rarely anything more other than a very uncomfortable long walk home.

But none of this for Joe and Doris – they went to the dance that Friday night in St John's Hall together, stopping off for a couple of beers in Paddy Bryson's beforehand. Doris had already decided that she would let Joe kiss her that night – she had done more before on past first dates, but this was different: at least, she very much hoped this was different. This time she would have to let the man think he was making all the running, but with someone as obviously shy as Joe she was going to have to do a little prompting of her own to get him started.

Wrong.

How much more wrong could she have been?

Not much.

I mean, she accepted some of the responsibility because once they'd started kissing, back in the good (front) room of her red-bricked house, well, things just kinda flew out of hand. To cut a short story even shorter, they got carried away and had sex on the floor.

Doris gagged Joe's mouth with her hand at the vital moment; the last thing she needed was for either of her parents to walk in on them. They weren't undressed or anything – in fact, their clothes were in a discreet state of disarray, and they probably could have escaped the ultimate embarrassment with some highly tuned twitching and turning, but Doris would have preferred to have at least introduced Joe to her parents and been seen around with him a bit before … well, it was a bit late to be using the word 'before'.

Joe was not a great lover, or even a good lover – there was too much fumbling and he seemed perfectly unaware that his partner also needed to feel good but, Doris felt, he had potential. He was slim, tight, muscular, certainly in his own way tender and loving; it was just, well, that he really didn't know what he was doing. For Doris, the fact that he wasn't experienced was a good sign in another more important way.

After the sex, the evening kind of tailed off quickly. Joe felt there wasn't much else to do after that. There was quite a bit of whispering, of replacing one's body parts and getting one's clothes in order and then it was, for Joe, out into the cold night air. But as he turned off the Lough Road, left up Noah's Arc, there was definitely an inch to his step and a new form of grin was making an appearance across his cheek.

Doris had a long languishing bath full of mixed emotions. How had she let it go so far? What on earth had happened? Still, it had all been totally natural, so there was no real reason to feel bad, no apparent reason at all to feel as bad as she was starting to feel.

Chapter Twenty-One

'I can't believe it, Pat – you'll never guess what just happened!' Maggie gushed.

Pat did not utter the expected 'what?' No, he just stared at her. She was soaking wet with her big – much too big – white dressing gown on, and her hair was dangling like rat's tails over her shoulders. Pat reckoned it was one of Joe's twenty-four mornings of the year and he wasn't sure he was ready to share some of his brother and wife's intimate secrets. Sure, she kept telling him that they never had full sex, and he believed her – it was just that he didn't like his mind to ever wander to the space where he would picture them together in that way. Whether they were having full sex or not, it didn't really make the whole situation any easier for him.

'Joe came to the door of our room this morning, before I'd a chance to visit him.'

Pat stood up in anger.

'No, no, no, it's OK, Jesus, Pat – it's more than OK. It's great really. He said he had something important to tell me.'

'Yes?' Pat grunted, not knowing whether to feel happy or upset.

'Well, he hung around the door for a while, he didn't come in – he knows he's never, ever allowed in our room.'

Pat nodded his satisfaction that their golden rule hadn't been broken.

'Then he shocked me so much I found myself having to sit on the bed to steady myself. He said that he no longer wished to continue with our arrangement. *He no longer wished to continue with our arrangement.* Can you believe that?' There were tears in her eyes. 'He said that he no longer wished to continue with our arrangement,' she repeated, her disbelief evident in her emotionally charged voice.

Pat didn't know what to feel – he was still trying to assess if he was about to hear good or bad news.

'It's all over, Pat,' Maggie continued, tears streaming down her cheeks like rain flowing down the kitchen window. 'He told me he's started dating Doris Durin and that "it's getting serious".'

Pat moved across the kitchen towards Maggie and took her in his arms. They just stood there, gently rocking back and forth, neither saying anything. For the first time in their marriage it was their marriage alone; now it was sacred. It was hard to tell if the sacrifice had been worthwhile. Yes, it had all worked out like they'd wanted, like they'd planned, and, if truth be told, it had all worked out way ahead of schedule, but Maggie prayed that there would be no long-term repercussions.

So, the matchmaker had turned up trumps again with his subtle ways. Pat knew that Michael was worried that the longer the original arrangement continued, the more chance there was of permanent damage being done. Pat felt, at that second, as he held his wife, *his* wife, tight to him that they'd be fine – they were safe, they were good. But he couldn't hide the little niggle creeping into his mind that now neither of them had to worry about Joe, would they start to be too self-conscious of what had gone on before the past couple of months? Even Joe – now that he was out of the relationship, where were his thoughts going to lie?

These were all problems for the 'morrow, but now Pat did what he had never had done before: he took his wife back to bed during the day and they made sweet passionate love. They made love with an intensity that had been missing from their love-making up to that point.

Both were aware of the change; it was a spiritual thing. Neither spoke about it, though; they did all their communicating through their actions. In fact, hours passed before either of them spoke. Maggie was snug, curled up lying on her side with her head tight against the nook of his neck; Pat, lying on his back, had his arm around Maggie and was caressing her upper arm.

'I'd better get back to work,' he felt compelled to say, breaking the spell.

'I know Pat, but this is delicious – just five more minutes, five more, please?'

'Fine with me,' he replied. It was rare – that is, unknown – for the brothers not to be out in the fields working together, but Joe must have been tuned in to what was going on, for he appeared to be leaving them be. Pat resolved to make it up to his brother by working extra time himself over the next few days.

'We should get away for a few quiet days together, Pat,' Maggie suggested.

'Yeah, but it will be a while before we can afford it,' Pat replied.

'What if we just go up to the Port for a couple of days? The summer's ending so the peak season is almost over and we'll be able to get a good weekend rate in a guest house. And hey,' she laughed, 'the beaches will be empty when we go for a stroll.'

'And here's me thinking we were going for a weekend in bed together!' Pat said, laughing.

'Hey you, don't be greedy,' Maggie responded, laying a playful dig into his unprotected guts.

With that, a young woman once more participated in the oldest recreational pastime known to man-, and woman-, kind.

Thirty-two minutes later, Pat, with a hot flush on his face, made his way up to the top four-acre field where he spied Joe, not busy at work, but sitting atop the permanently open battered wooden gate, a pinch of straw in his mouth. He was looking out over the fields, deep in his thoughts. Pat wandered up to the same gate to join his twin.

'Hey, sorry I'm late,' Pat began. There were a million things he wanted to say but he couldn't find a way of introducing a single one of them.

'Did Maggie tell you what I said?'

'Yes,' was Pat's only reply, fearing the ice may be thin.

'I think it's better this way. I'm seeing Doris now.'

'That's great, Joe.'

'Yeah, it is, isn't it? I like her, I like her a lot. I think she likes me. Well, at least she hasn't sent me packing yet. I don't know what will happen ….'

'Hey, it's OK, it's too early to talk about it. Don't worry, we'll work it all out,' Pat interrupted, only to be interrupted in turn by Joe.

'No, man, I *do* want to talk about it. I *need* to talk about it. I need to know what to *do*. I don't know anything about any of this, Pat; I've never done any of it before. I'd like to be able to talk to you and Maggie about it – it would be great for me if we could.'

'Fine, absolutely fine, but I think Maggie is going to be more use to you than myself; remember, I'm not exactly a singer in a showband,' Pat replied. They were both still hanging around the gate, work the furthermost thing from their minds. The last time they'd had such a chat was when they were both at the tech and would rabbit on ten to the dozen about this and that, leaving their father to the weariness and worries of the farm.

'I mean, you and Maggie – how long did it take before you knew?' Joe asked, looking away from Pat and out over the fields again.

'Well, that was slightly different, Joe. There were, as you know, a few other factors going on in that scenario—'

'But—' Joe cut in.

'But,' Pat in turn interrupted his twin, 'for myself, I knew pretty quickly. Then I went through fearing I was going to hear the five words all men live in dread of hearing.'

'And which five words would those be, Pat?' Joe said, turning back on the gate so quickly that he nearly flew off it.

Pat reached out to steady his brother as he replied. 'Let's just be good friends,' he said and smiled at Joe, who smiled back, despite the fact that he didn't really get it.

'Oh, we're more than friends already,' Joe boasted proudly.

'Hmm!' Pat barely uttered as he nearly choked on his spittle.

Chapter Twenty-Two

Maggie persisted, as she often did, in search of things she wanted badly, and three weekends later she and her husband ended up in a charming little guest house just off the strand in Portrush. To anyone who knew Maggie, particularly Michael and Dorothy, this wasn't surprising. No, the surprising thing was that they were joined by Joe and Doris.

Anxious to quell the wagging tongues of Castlemartin, and there were many, the twins and their respective companions for the weekend kicked up a bit of a dust cloud to cover their tracks. Maggie and Pat were 'going up to the Port for a weekend'. Joe, on the other hand, 'didn't want to hang around the farm that weekend like a spare rooster at a hen's party so I'm going to Belfast to hang out with some old friends from the tech'.

However, Doris wasn't yet officially a member of the party. Sure, she and Joe had been seen out together a few times having fun, but then she was known as a fun girl and she'd been seen out with lots of other chaps as well. She didn't make any excuses – she merely told her mother, and by association her father (for she and he hadn't shared more than a dozen words in the last few years), that she was going to Donegal to visit 'a friend' for the weekend – more than that, though, she was not prepared to impart.

Pat was annoyed that Joe had invited himself along to his special weekend away with Maggie, but what concerned him even more was that he and his wife had not seen or heard from Doris since their first meeting at the matchmaker's house, and things between her and Joe seemed to be moving incredibly quickly. At least that was Pat's interpretation of the glaringly obvious fact that Doris was prepared to spend an entire weekend *together* with Joe in Portrush. Weekend, by virtue of the fact it implied a couple of days, at least, also clearly meant that a night (and a night *together*) was involved. Still, he couldn't have really refused his brother's request and, besides, the fact that Joe and Doris were getting along so well could only be good – not just good, but great – for him and Maggie.

As it turns out, the couples saw little of each other over their weekend away, with both parties clearly having privacy, not to mention intimacy, at the forefront of their minds. They met up on the Saturday night, though, and had a fish supper in Diveto's seafront café, wherein Maggie and Doris selected Cilla Black's superior version of 'Anyone Who Had a Heart' and the Animals' classic 'House of the Rising Sun' on the jukebox, before visiting Barry's for a bit of a hoot.

Barry's was an amusement arcade, built in the mid-1920s when the Northern Counties Railway company constructed a new terminal in Portrush, which is at the extreme north-west corner of Country Antrim, about five miles, as the seagull glides, from the world-famous Giant's Causeway. In order to protect the large investment of their easily earned cash, the railway company decided that they and Portrush Council needed to have something at the end of the rainbow (in this case the railway line) to attract, detain and entertain their predicted thronging crowds. They approached the people behind Barry's, a branch of the famous Chipperfield Circus family, with an invitation to move permanently to a site just off the West Strand, no more than a stone's throw from the station. Up to this point Barry's and several other travelling carnivals had used Portrush as a summer (or Easter to September) stop-off. It was to this lodestone – known throughout Ulster as 'the Port' – that Pat and Joe Kane and their sweethearts were drawn some forty years later.

Pat and his brother had been to the Port and Barry's a few times before, at various points in their lives, both as children and adults. Each and every time they found it so exhilarating that they could actually taste and smell the excitement.

The very second they walked through the double doors of the large glass bay-fronted building, located just to the left of the famous Barry's helter skelter – which, with its Meccano-type construction, was an obvious relic from their pack-up-and-go days – the smell, the buzz and the absolute thrill of anticipation hit them smack between the eyes with a wallop as mighty as any on the legendary Lambeg drums. They immediately felt their heart rates quicken as the adrenalin kicked in, and that was before their brains had a chance to get in gear.

Adding to this stimulation, the spontaneous cacophony of sounds included, but wasn't limited to, girls screaming at the tops of their lungs (screams of joy as opposed to terror); kids crying, heads swivelling in continuous 360-degree turns as they pitifully pleaded for a go on every ride; the intermittent sizzle of the Dodgem super cars' life force – electricity dispensed via a chicken-wire ceiling through the electrode, a piece of bent sprung metal attached to a flagpole on the back of the car; said dodgems loudly bouncing into each other (despite the numerous 'No Bumping!' signs); coins jangling through fingers eager to spend; the repeat from the rifles in the shooting gallery; skittles being hit and dropped; ping-pongs of the ride commencement bells; the old-fashioned music rolls of the magnificent carousel; the penny-induced chuckles of the laughing sailor; chanting barrow boys trying to drum up trade for their particular wares; the non-stop clatter of hard-earned pennies being fed into greedy machines and the rare – very rare – sound of a lucky punter's winnings flooding forth into their waiting hands (such pay-outs always resulted in a feverish revitalised feeding of all nearby machines); a multitude of ride-manager announcements from their individual PA systems – 'Keep your hands inside the car!', 'Don't lean out!', 'Hold on tight, especially to your girlfriend!'; the sounds of the recent and popular hit records blasting out to all and sundry on the huge PA system, which was piped into every nook and cranny of the arcade; all topped off with clamorous laughter and the continuous rain dancing loudly on the roof, the same rain which would drive even more customers into Barry's.

If that didn't get Joe, Pat, Maggie and Doris going, then there were always the visual hits of the vivid blues, yellows, greens and reds of the painted stalls and rides, or the shocking pink of the candy floss, or the beautifully painted horses on the carousel, or the dazzling neon of balloons discarded by pre-teen owners who'd become preoccupied with their thrill-seeking.

On the other hand, if it was smells that floated your boat (and boats to float in were also available for a mere sixpenny bit), then you were in for nostrilic (and if such a word didn't exist before the Kane gang visited Barry's, they certainly knew what it meant afterwards) delight, with the aromas, pongs and fragrances of a heady mix of motor oil and automobile engines; burnt electricity; fried fish and chips; the vanilla of ice-cream; slicked on Brylcreem; sinewy, sickly sweet candy floss; mint chewing gum; talcum powder; floor polish; fresh paint; hundreds of varieties of perfume and an even greater assortment of sweat; not to mention the faint whiff of salt from the nearby Atlantic Ocean.

The irresistible cocktail of sights, smells and sounds was, in total, more than enough to indelibly eat its way into your memory cells and remain with you for at least the rest of your life.

The Castlemartin foursome let their collective hair down from under their 'Kiss Me Quick!' hats and the feeling of goodwill was so strong that Joe and Pat were thinking, at precisely the same moment, it would be good if things could go on like this forever. It looked like, following the few years of darkness, things were certainly lightening up for the twins.

Maggie and Doris had retreated to the ladies' after a particularly exhausting couple of rides in the Cyclone to freshen their make-up. It was a funny duty really, as neither of them wore much of the stuff in the first place. But a little cold water on the forehead helped to reduce their collective temperature.

'How's it going then?' Maggie asked, hoping her question wouldn't be shot down in flames as being too nosey.

'Great! Well, it seems great to me – we don't actually talk about it much really, if you know what I mean. Joe doesn't seem to, well … Do you mind if I ask you if Pat has any trouble expressing his feelings?' Doris asked, the front of her ginger mane damp from sticking her head too far into the sink, to get near to the tap with its refreshingly cold water. She appeared eager and willing to strike up such a conversation.

'Not really, I mean, he was shy when we met and he might go around the houses a bit, but he eventually gets there,' Maggie replied, confident that she wasn't giving much away.

She looked in the bathroom mirror at Doris' reflection and as she spoke, a strange thing hit her: how incredibly similar they were in appearance. Apart from their hair colour, that was. But height, build, hair length were all pretty much as close as you could get. 'Is that what this is all about?' Maggie thought. 'Is Doris meant to be another me?' Then she reasoned that those thoughts were all a bit far-fetched and perhaps she was just being a bit vain; after all, hadn't it been the matchmaker who had introduced Joe and Doris? Joe had really only been a willing bystander.

'Yeah, I thought as much,' Doris interjected. 'Joe seems to think a lot about things, but when I press him as to what's on his mind he always makes light of it and changes the subject. In one way, sometimes it seems like we've known each other for ages and in another I'm not sure how far we've progressed beyond the first night,' she volunteered.

'Yes, well, please don't tell him I told you this, Doris, but Joe, and for that matter Pat, well, neither of them have really had much to do with girls, if you know what I mean,' Maggie replied, a bit more adventurous in her attempts to encourage Doris to stick with Joe (for obvious reasons).

'Do you mind if I smoke?' Doris asked, taking a packet of Players out of her black leatherette handbag. The handbag matched her shoes, which contrasted perfectly with her white, knee-length sleeveless dress.

'No, fine, go ahead,' Maggie replied, as she refused an invitation to join Doris in lighting up.

'Joe doesn't like me to smoke so I've been cutting down – well, as much as I can. But now I'm sneaking off for a quick drag more and more. I used to have to do that all the time around me da but not any more. I'll be glad to get out of there. God, they'll be glad to get rid of me.'

Maggie didn't dare ask the obvious question for fear of hearing a reply she didn't want or need. In a way, all this other stuff with Joe and Doris was happening too fast, she thought, but then she reminded herself that in another way it couldn't be happening fast enough. The sheer relief of stopping her fortnightly visits to Joe was bliss. She could remember clearly how she would always be a little apprehensive afterwards when she was with Pat, as though she was going back to her man after being unfaithful to him (although never completely, she reasoned). The more time that passed since her last time with Joe, the more unreal that whole episode had become.

Had it really happened? Could it possibly have all been part of her imagination? She and Pat had never, ever discussed it in detail. Was that his way of blanking it out? The morning she'd told him of Joe's big announcement, it seemed to take a while to sink in; could it have been that, before he could accept it was over, he actually had to admit it had happened at all?

'So how do you feel about Joe then?' Maggie asked, still communicating with Doris via the mirror. They could hear the noise of the amusements the other side of the thick brown-painted door. The Bachelors' masterful rendering of 'Diane' was playing on the arcade's PA system. There was no bass so it sounded a bit trebly, but the high-pitched whine of the Bachelor brothers, Dec and Con Cluskey, and (friend) John Stokes carried everywhere, even into the ladies' toilets.

'I like him; I'm trying to get to know him to see how much I really like him. But that part – the getting-to-know-him part – seems to be quite difficult. It's strange in a way, but he just seems to be content to hang out, just to be around me. I rabbit away to him all the time but he rarely asks me a single question. I have to prod him severely to dig out any information about him. But he seems to be loosening up a bit. I like a laugh, I like to have a bit of fun and he doesn't seem to resist that. You know, just a bit of encouragement and he's fine,' Doris replied. She turned away from the mirror and they addressed each other face to face for the first time since they'd gone into the toilet.

'You want to know the strangest thing?' Doris started and continued without any support from Maggie. 'That's the first time I've expressed my feelings about Joe – I mean, even to myself. I hope it's not because his quietness or darkness is rubbing off on me. I like to talk about things, you know, get them out in the open. If I like somebody I like to tell them – you know, let them know and get on with it.'

'Have you told Joseph how you feel about him?'

'Well that's it – I haven't, have I, really? 'Cause in a way I don't know myself, and, as I say, he doesn't encourage conversations to go in that way.' Doris was down to near the end of her Player.

'Well, don't forget he hasn't done this dating game much – if at all – and he seems very keen on you when he's talking to Pat and me,' Maggie lied.

The truth was, Joe never told them much about Doris, or anybody else for that matter. She'd been expecting him to open up a bit more after his conversation with Pat, but instead it appeared that he still continued to wander around disappointed with the world, as if accepting that all his childhood dreams were never going to come true and now he was just waiting out the rest of his life. It was sad, very sad indeed.

'Listen, we'd better get out there,' Doris began, stubbing out her ciggie in a cleaned-out base of a Fray Bentos steak-and-kidney-pie tin. 'Or they'll think we've run off with two of those slimy dodgems chaps with the tight trousers and the greasy DAs.'

'Ah, sure they're nothing but a pile of wee skitters,' Maggie laughed, as they exited the bathroom.

*

In fact, the Kane boys had not been thinking any such thing. Rather they had been engrossed in their own conversation, pulling away on two half-drunk Coca-Cola bottles as they did so. Even though they were country lads, dressed in their denim jeans and shirts – Joe's white and Pat's blue – and their off-white gutties, which they'd dug out for a first appearance in years, they fitted in effortlessly with the Barry's vibey scene. The main reason for this was that they didn't even know there was a cool Barry's scene, and so in actual fact they hadn't attempted to fit in with that or anything else.

Pat dragged Joe away from his music-induced trance, just as Dec of the Bachelors was requesting 'Diane' to smile for him before she wafted away.

'So, how's it going?'

'Fine, yeah, good weekend so far,' Joe replied, a wee bit non-committal.

'I *meant* you and Doris: how's that going?'

'OK, I suppose – I don't really know, do I? Pat, what am I meant to feel like if this is it? She's great, good fun, loves a laugh and she has a flippin' amazing body. But she doesn't make my heart miss a beat every time I look at her. Is that meant to happen? Or is that just in the movies?'

'Well,' the voice of little experience began, 'there's certainly meant to be more than just "feeling good" – it's meant to be stronger than that. Do you really not feel more?'

'Sometimes I feel a power but it's always when we're ... am ... kind of messing about.' Joe hesitated, since he and his brother had never discussed such an intimate topic before.

'But do you care about her?' Pat persisted.

'Have I known her long enough to care about her?' Joe asked.

'Probably, I would have thought so, yes,' Pat innocently replied.

'Well, I don't care about her in the same way I cared about Mum and Dad – is that OK?'

'Yes, Joe, it's a different kind of caring. Don't you feel protective towards her?'

'It's never been questioned; I've never had to protect her so I wouldn't know, but I'm sure if anybody was going to harm her I'd make sure she was OK, but I'd do the same for Dorothy or Maggie, for that matter.'

'But don't you, you know, when you're with her sometimes, don't you just want to put your arm around her and let her feel you close and know you'd never ever let her down or willingly hurt her ...?'

'I wouldn't raise my hand to a woman, any woman, Pat – you know that.'

'No, no, Joe, I don't mean hurt her in that way. I mean *hurt* her by not being there for her when she needed you, or by not being as good as your word. Or hurt her by ... by ... chasing other women.'

'Me? Chase other women? Chase women at all? Don't be daft, Pat.'

'Well, maybe not chasing other women exactly, but say one made eyes at you and she was giving you the come-on, would you first think of Doris or would you consider it?'

'Gosh, that's a hard one, Pat. I suppose it would all depend on who the woman was. Don't you think?'

'Nah, Joe, I don't think. You see with Maggie it's not that I would be faithful to her; don't you see that to be faithful means I would consider being unfaithful and then decide not to? Then I would be unfaithful in *truth*. But with Maggie, it doesn't even come into it. I'm not interested. I'm glad that I'm not interested; I've been living my life hoping that I would find someone like Maggie where it wouldn't matter, all this stuff – I'd just want to be with her above all else.'

'You mean to tell me that if you went up to Magherafelt tomorrow, or the night after,' Joe added, realising that they were all still going to be in Portrush tomorrow, 'and sitting in the corner of Agnew's was Dorothy, no, not Dorothy but Brigitte Bardot? You know, sitting there at the corner table by the jukebox, all blonde hair and those bleedin' amazing boobs resting on the table – she's all by herself and you've wandered in and played, say, the Stones' 'It's All Over Now' and she comes up to you, with her amazing French accent and pouting lips and cute tongue, with which to tickle your tonsils – you mean to tell me you'd think, "Nah, Maggie's the one for me" and be off out of there as quick as you could drink your glass of milk? I don't think so, Pat.'

Pat smiled at the image, then laughed and laughed out loud. Then they both started to laugh out loud, catching a fit of laughter like they used to in their younger days when they'd be left to amuse themselves. And the more they thought about it, the more they laughed until tears streamed down their cheeks.

Joe tried to stop to get something else out. 'Well, I know you wouldn't – because the only reason that she'd be in Agnew's in the first place is …' the howling took over again and it was a few seconds before he could quieten down enough in order to get his punchline out, 'the only reason that she'd be there at all, our Pat, is because she'd be there waiting for me!'

And they both roared again, even louder than before, so much so that Pat got a pain in his chest.

Just at this moment the girls exited the toilet to see the laughing twins were becoming the centre of attention.

Joe spied them first. He nudged his brother as he pulled on his Coke bottle for a swig and uttered as the giggling subsided, 'Here come the girls. Doris does look good, though, doesn't she? Ah, well, I suppose she'll have to do. Maybe I'll just have to learn to feel all those things for her that you feel for our Maggie.'

Chapter Twenty-Three

On Sunday, the Portrush heavens opened and it rained and rained and rained. And then it rained some more.

Pat and Maggie were disappointed that they were not going to be able to enjoy either the Wall of Death or Kit Carson, two of Barry's biggest attractions that summer. Both took place outside the main arcade and, as such, were at the mercy of the heavy clouds.

So instead, Pat and Maggie went to bed, and the young couple took to enjoying all the comforts of the small guest house up in Portrush. The smiling Kane twin was not at all unhappy that he'd been confined to close quarters. The downpour, which constantly beat away on the window, set up its own little rhythms, which encouraged Maggie and Pat to set up some of their own. They rose for breakfast – full Ulster fry as ever – and returned to bed grinning from ear to ear. Pat was dispatched mid-morning for some elevenses: Tayto Crisps, Kit-Kats and a large bottle of Cantrell & Cochrane's pineappleade.

They both sat up, partially robed, on the small double bed in their room. It certainly wasn't a palace, but it was clean. The window which overlooked the strand was tall, nearly the full twelve-foot height of the room. They had pulled the red-rose-on-and-off-white-background curtains back to their extreme to enjoy the full view, to see the charge of waves breaking against the rocks to the left, which in turn created large plumes of water, not dissimilar to the teddy boys' quiffs. To the right, and centre, the waves lost their energy and violence and merely washed peacefully, even playfully, up the sandy beach. They had repositioned their bed so they could recline on the pillows and fully enjoy this mesmeric scene. The moving of the bed was easy, as there was scant other furniture to block their movements. There were a few chairs, now draped with their clothes, and one basket-work easy chair. Against the wall, by the entry door, was a dressing table with a mirror at its centre, some notepaper, envelopes and hotel literature at one end, and a large bowl with a water jug set in the middle at the other, with a snow-white towel draped over the ensemble. The main toilet and bathroom was down the hall, three doors to the left.

Replenished, they tried to work the squeaks of the bed into the rhythm of the rain falling on the window pane and then happily dozed off, contentedly entwined in each other's limbs, as their sweat flowed freely together, mixing in a way which would have made them blood brothers in a game from Pat's childhood. But they couldn't possibly have been any tighter – physically, mentally or spiritually – than they were at that moment.

They awoke, Pat first, disturbed by the rain, now obviously annoyed that the couple were no longer creating back-up patterns to the incessant *rat-a-tat*, *rat-a-tat* on the twelve large window panes. As Maggie woke, the two of them thought they could hear voices, loud and argumentative, somewhere else in the guest house. It was about 3:40 in the afternoon. The voices grew quieter, the rain louder and they were eventually distracted from both by each other.

At 4:30 they decided that they would brave the rains to find somewhere to eat, as close by as possible so that they could dine in relative comfort, and then they planned to throw caution to the wind and venture onto the beach for a walk, the logic being that they would get drenched, but at least they could return to the warmth of the guest house and fall back into bed again, since their clothes, Maggie reasoned, would dry out before they had to leave at 6 a.m. the following morning.

Meanwhile, over in room number seven, the novelty of being stuck in their room due to the bad weather quickly wore off for Joe and Doris. They soon ran out of things to say to each other and the point of least attraction coincided with the point, or just past the point, of greatest attraction. Doris tried to find a way into his head, if not his heart. She was looking for … something – she knew not what, but she just felt that there had to be something more. At least, she wanted there to be something more between them.

She felt it odd that they had started the relationship on such a high and then she was seeing it all slip away, through no fault of her own. She found it incredible that although they both showed quite a degree of willingness to make the relationship work, it was floundering and about to hit the rocks in a crash as violent as any of the waves upon the boulders not too far from their window.

They had both reached a point in their lives where it was time to find and settle down with a partner. But, apparently, that wasn't enough.

Doris was forced to this conclusion through Joe's coldness towards her on that rainy Sunday. She felt grateful that they had stolen this weekend, in sin, together. Without their time at Portrush she might have fooled herself that, given time, it could work. But the trip had accelerated their relationship and given her an insight into what it may have been a couple of months down the line, when the novelty of their sex sessions wore off.

The annoying thing, or the most annoying thing for Doris, was Joe's inability to see this. He seemed quite happy, content even, to let things continue as they were without even wanting to try to get more out of it. Over the weekend, Doris had looked on with envy at the obviously blossoming relationship between Maggie and Pat. How could twins be so different? Weren't they meant to be like two peas from the one pod? This wasn't even like they were from a different pod; no, it was more like one was a pea and the other was a banana, or even a tomato. The tomato comparison amused her because Joe had told her of his aversion to that particular fruit.

The argument started innocently enough.

'Why don't you just go out by yourself?' Joe had responded to Doris' request for a walk along the rain-drenched strand.

'No! Why don't *you* go out by yourself in the rain?' Doris replied, maddened that he appeared to want to spend time away from her. 'Why invite me here for a weekend and then throw me out by myself in the rain?'

'But you said that you wanted to go out for a walk in the rain,' Joe responded, noticeably confused.

'Yes, but not by myself, Joe – it was meant to be romantic. I'm not sure you have an ounce of romance in your body,' she said, making an effort to laugh at this juncture, since she was fearful of things getting too heavy. She certainly didn't want to come across as a nag.

'You want romantic? You want flowers? You want 'Anyone Who Had a Heart' on the jukebox? You want me to go out in the flippin' rain and catch my death of cold and not be able to work the farm? What's so bleedin' romantic about that?' Joe replied sternly.

'Ah, come on, Joe – look at Maggie and Pat.'

That was enough to send him ballistic.

'Don't talk to me about Maggie and Pat or Dorothy and Michael, all lovey-dovey and all that! You don't know the half of it … The things I could tell you ….' Joe barked. He then appeared to think better of it and retreated into his darkness once again, point blank refusing to talk to his girlfriend. In fact, he refused to acknowledge that she even existed.

Even at that point – him drawing down the blinds, pulling up the drawbridge and anything else available that would help to shut him off – Doris was still exercising some damage limitation. She was concerned about their future together. Still, in the short-run she had to spend one more night with him.

But after a night with an incredibly frosty shoulder, she had accepted that any future she may have wished for – and even felt assured of on that first night at the matchmaker's – had completely evaporated.

'Look, Joe, this is not going to work out,' Doris began the following morning as they prepared to travel home separately (as planned) – he to catch an early bus and arrive back in Castlemartin with Pat and Maggie, and she to have a more leisurely time wandering around the now sun-lit beach killing three hours until the next bus home. 'I like to make clean breaks. We know it's not going to work out and there's not much point in wasting any time flogging a dead horse. I think, in all honesty, we want different things from a relationship. We can't just be together because we're both available to be together. There has to be more. There must be more. There isn't more with us.'

'Whatever you like,' Joe replied curtly.

They were standing on the pavement outside the guest house and he turned on his heels towards the bus station, leaving Doris standing alone.

As she watched him disappear into the distance, not once did he turn to steal a look at her. She couldn't help thinking that he was a lonely, sad and somewhat pathetic figure. In fact, she felt she'd probably just experienced the luckiest escape of her life.

Chapter Twenty-Four

Joe huffed the entire two-hour-and-ten-minute journey back to Castlemartin. The journey took that long because the Ulsterbus stopped to drop off and pick up passengers at Portstewart, Coleraine, Garvagh, Kilrea, Maghera, Tobermore and Magherafelt before depositing the weary threesome on the Broadway in Castlemartin. Maggie and Pat knew something was amiss but didn't venture into the area of uncertainty for fear, Pat cautioned, of what might be discovered.

The remainder of the working week passed with as little activity as there was between the Manchester United goalposts. Charlton, Law and local hero Georgie Best were always too busy causing grief at the opposite end of the field for Harry Greg, the United goalie, to ever work up a sweat.

The following Saturday was the last one in August and, if not officially the end of the summer, it was definitely the end for school children who were due to return to their hard seats and desk-tops, which contained a few generations of carved initials, some of which would belong to their older brothers, or even in some cases their fathers. *That* particular Saturday was the one that Pat and Joe had chosen to do the remainder of the threshing.

The Lone Ranger and Tonto had to cry off from the previously scheduled Saturday as the main drive belt from the tractor to their 1942 Garvey broke and then was completely destroyed when it became mangled in the thresher. But now, with replacement belt at the ready, the Garvey was fired up and ready to be fed mounds of hay, delivered as if by a posh restaurant waiter in the shape of a proud Massey Ferguson tractor, complete with fork lift. The trusted Massey

Ferguson, fork lowered, merely reversed into a hut, raised the fork and tore over the field, load bumping precariously as it did so, and deposited the hut as close to the thresher as possible.

The hut was then dismantled back into sheaths, which were passed, in relay, up onto the top of the thresher where one chap, in this case the matchmaker, would cut away the bind with a sheaf knife. Then the hay would be carefully fed – very carefully, mind you, as people were known to lose fingers, hands and even arms in the hungry, gnashing rotating spikes – into the insatiable, eager mouth of the thresher.

Bobby Patterson was waiting at the other end of the temperamental machine with a never-ending supply of hundred-weight white flour bags to capture the continuous flow of oats. Valerie Scott tied the necks of the bags with twine, while Tommy Patterson (Bobby's son), helped by Wesley McIvor, loaded the bags onto a tractor trailer. This way sweethearts Valerie and Wesley always remained within talking distance of each other.

Harry McKinney fed the hay into a 1942 Jones Baler, which transformed its food conveniently into manageable bales. The bales would then be loaded onto another tractor trailer and taken to be stored in the hay shed. The refuse in this feeding system – and no toilets rolls were required – the chaff, was taken away to be burnt.

During all of this the Lone Ranger operated and maintained the thresher and Tonto carried out similar duties with the baler. Pat took away the tractor-trailer loads of hay bales and Joe did the same with the bags of oats. Once again Maggie and Dorothy prepared, and delivered, the piles of sandwiches and Paul Gilmour came up with some more interesting facts. Facts like, for instance, one hay stack produces two tons of oats and one ton of hay. He didn't bother to come up with a figure for the chaff, since he reasoned it didn't matter how much waste was wasted.

Dorothy noticed that there was an air about her sister and the twins, but Maggie was not forthcoming with any information that could shed light on that particular situation. Well, she couldn't really, could she? She couldn't really tell her sister that early that morning while Pat was downstairs preparing breakfast Joe had knocked on her bedroom door and, without waiting for an invitation, had broken the farm's golden rule by entering his brother's bedroom. Joe had then quietly announced that it was all over between him and Doris Durin and that consequently he wanted a return to the original 'agreement'.

'Have you discussed this with Pat?' she had asked, trying hard not to lose her cool when all she really wanted to do was scream at the top of her lungs.

'No – it's nothing to do with Pat, is it? It's part of the deal, isn't it? It's part of the reason why you're here,' Joe had replied in a quiet, indignant voice, before hissing, 'but this time I want it proper, no more fumbling around.'

'Well, speaking for myself and Pat, all that nonsense ended when you took up with Doris. It's not our fault it didn't work out.' Maggie paused and then back-pedalled a bit to take a less aggressive approach. 'Look, Joe, surely Doris proved to you that you are attractive to women. Now, that doesn't necessarily mean that the first one you meet is going to be *the one*, but you should get out and about a bit more. You were having fun with Doris, weren't you? There'll be others you'll have fun with and one of them will be the right one – you know, the one for you.'

'I'm not interested in all that crap. I've had enough; I've wasted enough of my time; I couldn't be bothered with any of it any more. I want it to go back to the way it was and that's the end of it. I'm sure you'd be happier with that than Dorothy and your family finding out what's been going on?' With that he left Maggie, open-mouthed and staring at his back, lost for words and fighting to hold back the tears.

No, Maggie couldn't really have recounted that to her sister, but she did feel a desperate need to tell Pat. She chose a tea-break to do so. She had just reached the part where Joe was threatening to tell her family about the farm's sleeping arrangements when Pat threw his sandwich and half-drunk mug of tea to the earth and tore across the field as fast as his legs could carry him, jumping straight onto an unsuspecting Joe.

In the movies, or in comic strips, fights are always well choreographed and orchestrated. But on the field that day, this particular fight was little more than a brawl, with badly aimed thumps, a few hard, loud slaps to the face (they are the ones that really get your rile up, where the noise aggravates you more than the pain) and the fighters collapsing in a wriggling heap on the ground, fingers in eyes and up noses and the occasional grunt of 'bastard' (which, when you think about it, is a funny insult for a twin to utter to his twin) or other such crudities.

It had all happened so fast and was so vicious, blood now flowing freely from Pat's nose, that the battle took the entire field, excepting maybe Maggie, although she was still pretty shocked at how brutal the brothers were to one another, by surprise. The few who could stop their work did. The matchmaker, Tommy Patterson and Wesley McIvor tried hard to pull the twins apart and received a few ill-aimed punches for their troubles. There wasn't the usual 'hold me back, hold me back' gesticulating, where posturing replaced willingness to get hurt. No, these two brothers seemed to genuinely want to do damage, to cause great destruction to one another.

'Don't you see this is stupid? Stop this stupidity now!' the matchmaker demanded.

The Kane twins ignored him, fists flying furiously again now they were disentangled from each other's person. They continued grunting and groaning at each other. Maggie, her tears no longer flowing, was trying to protect her man and was taking a few swings at Joe herself. Dorothy was embarrassed and highly distressed at the very public family squabble and was trying to pull her sister away to the safety of the farm.

Joe broke free from Wesley McIvor and ran, legs kicking, towards Pat, who was defenceless, his limbs restrained by the matchmaker and Tommy Patterson.

'Come to order, lads – now! Stop this!' the matchmaker shouted. 'I say, come to order, lads, stop this now!' his anger rising all the time as he silently accepted part of the responsibility for the squabble.

Joe caught Pat with an almighty splat to the cheek, kicked him three times in the legs and landed a high right hook to the side of Pat's face. It was a lucky punch: had it been two and one half inches to the right, it would have smashed Pat's nose to pieces. But it was enough of a direct hit for Pat's legs to buckle immediately and he collapsed to the bare soil. The ball of energy that the matchmaker and Tommy had been trying to contain surprised them both when it transformed into a dead weight as Pat slithered through their hands.

Maggie broke free from her sister and ran to Pat's side to comfort him.

Dorothy went over to Joe to check if he was OK, but he pushed her away aggressively, looking on in horror at the damage he had done to his brother, who was out cold and not responding to Maggie's incessant pleading. Joe stared around the men and woman on the field. When he saw no look of sympathy on any of the faces, he barked: 'Well *he* started it – he started the fight!'

With that he started to run. First he looked like he was heading towards the farmhouse but he continued on past it, down Kane's Lane and away towards a place that was anyone's guess.

Paul Gilmour sidled up to the comfort and security of his father and said, at a level barely a gnat above a whisper: 'Why does Uncle Joseph not like Uncle Patrick?'

The answer from the matchmaker was at a level no-one on the field save himself could hear. Should anyone have been able to mind-read, they would not have believed the words the matchmaker nearly spoke.

BOOK TWO
The Detective

Chapter Twenty-Five

Nothing much ever happened in Castlemartin.

So thought District Detective Inspector Doyle, also known around town affectionately as 'Wee Doyle'. Doyle was day-dreaming once again about being stationed in Belfast where the real crime was. Even Cookstown had more ambitious criminals than the bicycle thieves of Castlemartin.

Hey, even Magherafelt had the great headline-grabbing under-age sex case the previous year. Mind you, Wee Doyle wasn't sure he would've liked the responsibility of arresting the headmaster, the police officer, the musician, the shopkeeper and all the other alleged offenders. The police officer's involvement seemed to have been hushed up. In fact, now Doyle thought about it, the case never seemed to get as far as the courts. The girl had been sent away to a home and the whole episode written off as a rumour.

Could all the inhabitants of Castlemartin, all six hundred and seventeen of them, be saints? Surely at least one of them must have had some sinister undertaking in his or her mind? Doyle prayed for some crime in his small village. The criminals were all out there stealing their chances, if nothing else, behind his back.

He had both his feet, comfortable in their brown and white brogues, resting on the corner of his cluttered desk. Wee Doyle wasn't worried about the fact it was cluttered – he could find anything he wanted to on it within a second. Besides which, unwelcome eyes would have trouble following his logic because there was none, and his filing system was much better than locked drawers or cabinets. He was dressed, as he dressed three hundred and sixty-five days of the year, and had done so ten years since, in grey flannel trousers with a crease as sharp as Lennon's tongue, a checked shirt, green tie and a Donegal tweed jacket, set off with his prize possessions – his brogues. He had four pairs and he took better care of them than some people did their children. Anyway, this was him winter and summer, and as a concession to the winter months, he supplemented the above with a dark navy duffel coat.

In the year of our tale of the Kane twins, District Detective Inspector Doyle had been on thirty-four of the earth's trips around the sun. He enjoyed a full(ish) figure but he wasn't fat, or even overweight. He kept himself fit by walking – lots of walking (he positively loved to walk). While he was out walking, the detective claimed, he did his best thinking.

Being a confirmed bachelor, he had enough time to satisfy his two passions: the aforementioned walking and the Sherlock Holmes mysteries. But the Station House was his kingdom; he was totally in his element there. He was perfectly comfortable and at ease there, and because he didn't have much of a social life to speak of, he spent more time in the Station House, which was east of Pear Tree Roundabout on the left-hand side of the Broadway, than he did at his home, a small, but tidy, recently built bungalow in Garden Street, about a three-minute walk from work. In fact, he was well known for his casual off-duty drop-ins to the station with his password greeting: 'Hello! I was in the neighbourhood and at a loose end – anything interesting happening?' It should be pointed out that everywhere in Castlemartin was, in fact, 'in the neighbourhood'.

And here he was, now officially on duty, feet on desk, drinking coffee, flicking his longish jet black hair from his forehead and in his mind's eye picking out each member of the village known to him. He was imagining the crimes they were all getting up to. The more important the villager, the bigger the crime; the bigger the crime the greater the punishment; the greater the punishment, the quicker the chances of promotion and a trip down the B160 to Magherafelt and on to Belfast, and maybe even the mainland.

His thoughts were interrupted by a knock on the door.

'Yes?' he shouted.

Mild-mannered Constable Edward Hill stuck his head around the door.

'Excuse me, sir.'

'Yes, what is it, Hill?' Doyle snapped, with all the charm a school teacher offered their pupils.

'Well, it may be nothing,' Hill apologised.

Didn't the most interesting of scenarios always start with that, Doyle thought, as his clean-shaven, fair face broke into a smile.

'On the other hand, it may be something.' Doyle smiled. He could smell a case whiffing its way around his poorly decorated, overfilled shoebox that some called his office.

'Yes, yes, that is true as well, sir. But it's just a missing person, sir,' Hill replied, well aware of his superior's zeal for a bit of detective work.

'Just a missing person?' Doyle's Scottish-tinted Ulster voice rose an octave as he repeated, 'Just a missing person? Oh, let me see now, Constable, but surely you're not *just* a missing person if you're *the* missing person. Are you, Constable?'

PC Hill thought for some moments, closing his lips tight as he did so. He closed them so tight, in fact, that he could feel the ends of his moustache on his bottom lip. He thought that if you were a missing person you wouldn't be a missing person to yourself because you'd know where you were, wouldn't you? Unless, of course, you were dead. In which case you wouldn't really care, would you? Well, you couldn't – care that is – could you?

'Come on, Hill, stop 'tache tasting and fill me in!'

'Well, Joan Cook, sir ....'

'Oh yeah.' Doyle sighed.

PC Hill continued without acknowledging Wee Doyle's dampener.

'Joan Cook came into the station about ten minutes ago and claimed that Joe Kane has gone missing.'

'One of the twins you mean?'

'The very same – Paddy's brother. She further claims that there have been strange goings on up at the Kane farm and apparently Joseph has not been seen for nearly two weeks.'

PC Hill now had DI Doyle's undivided attention, particularly with the 'strange goings on up at the farm' bit. Now *that* seemed like a mystery if ever he'd read one.

'We'd better bring her on in then, hadn't we? Why don't you show her through to the interview room, my good man?'

'The interview room, sir? Oh, I see, of course, you mean the store room, sir, don't you?' Hill offered.

'No, Hill, I mean the *interview* room; the fact that the Regional Office has chosen to deposit Mid Ulster's entire stock of paperwork there doesn't change the fact that it's still the interview room.'

'Well, it's just that we're in the centre, geographically speaking, so it's convenient to all—'

'Yes, yes, Hill – I know all the arguments; just bring the witness through, please, to the *interview* room. Let's just call it the interview room for now, if only because the witness is about to be interviewed in it.'

'The witness? Oh, you mean Joan, Joan Cook, yes, of course, sir,' Hill agreed.

Doyle rolled his eyes skyways. Give me strength, he thought. How am I ever meant to get on when I have to deal with all of this? As an afterthought he called after the constable, 'Oh, and let me see now … after you've brought her through, why don't you bring us a couple of cups of coffee and some of those nice chocolate biscuits.'

'Aye and what did your last servant die of?' Hill thought but didn't dare say.

'Disobedience,' Doyle called out after him, causing the constable to blush right down to the roots of his ginger hair.

As Hill's ginger top disappeared back around the door, DI Colin Doyle stood up and tightened his already tight tie, which was done up in a classic Windsor knot. He removed the fountain pen from his desk and placed it extravagantly into the breast pocket of his jacket and made his way proudly to the interview room where, hopefully, an interviewee would be waiting for him.

He felt so excited and charged that it might have seemed to anyone watching him on his journey that the only things missing were the deerstalker hat and large pipe.

Chapter Twenty-Six

Doyle clicked his third finger and thumb, creating a loud snap. He pointed to the basket-work chair, which he had carefully positioned on the opposite side of the table from where he intended to sit.

He was astonished at his supposed control of the situation; it was as though an astral lookalike had appeared out of thin air and descended into their midst and was now running the show.

'So ... what's all this stuff about Joe Kane then?' he began, positively unperturbed by the fact that cardboard cases, all with various official forms waiting to be filled out (in triplicate) by the Mid Ulster Constabulary, surrounded him on all four sides, space made only for the door. He removed his fountain pen from his breast pocket and placed it neatly on the desk by his papers. He took off his jacket and very flamboyantly swirled it around and onto the back of his chair in one movement. He ran his fingers through his hair and afforded Joan Cook a brief smile so that she would know he was ready, willing and able to receive her answer.

'Well,' Joan began, in a very gossipy tone. She removed her light-blue headscarf to reveal her recently permed blonde-dyed hairstyle, 'It's certainly the talk of the town. Joseph has disappeared and he hasn't been seen around these parts for two weeks now.'

Sometimes Wee Doyle could see things quite clearly. You know, where things start, how you can work your way through the muddle and arrive at a satisfactory conclusion at the end. It could be as clear as water or as transparent as a child's smile. But somehow he couldn't quite get the hang of this missing thing, this missing Joseph thing. If he was really missing then how come his brother, Pat, or his sister-in-law hadn't missed him? Why weren't they there in the Station House this very moment, reporting this missing Joseph thing to PC Hill?

So, if he had no beginning, no start to his case, then how on earth was he meant to proceed?

He removed the top of his fountain pen, a Parker with deep-blue covering and light-blue ink, a Christmas present from his only surviving family member, his younger brother. Doyle wrote the name 'Joseph Kane' in extremely neat, and very readable, handwriting at the top of a clean page. He put a colon after the name and underneath it he wrote the number one and then 'Missing two weeks?' The question mark was to remind himself at a later time that he wasn't exactly sure that Mr Kane was missing.

Underneath the number one he wrote the number two and then 'Reported by Joan Cook', this time no question mark. He figured the question mark to point number one would by association also cover point number two.

'So, Mrs Cook, where do you suspect Joe's gone to?' Wee Doyle enquired.

'Well, I'm not to know, I'm sure,' came the tetchy reply. 'But maybe you should have words with Pat's wife, Margaret.'

'Why? What on earth would she know?' Doyle asked. Now he was sure the local tongues were wagging, and if they were wagging a lot he was surprised neither he nor any of his colleagues had heard the rumours up to now.

'Oh more, I'm sure, than she'll ever admit to you.'

Doyle re-screwed the top onto his fountain pen. The twists were slow and deliberate, as was his smile. 'Mrs Cook – it is *Mrs* Cook, isn't it?'

'Yes, although I'm no longer involved with Mr Cook.' She stole a brief glance at Doyle's bare wedding-ring finger as she used her right hand to puff up her perm by the nape of her neck.

'Sorry, Mrs Cook. Yes, I have to admit that I'm surprised. Why have you come here to report Joseph Kane missing? Surely that is a duty for a member of his family? And how do you even know that he's missing in the first place? Perhaps he's,' Doyle paused to think, 'perhaps he's gone on holiday? Perhaps he's gone to stay with relatives? Perhaps he's even gone to work on someone else's farm? There could be any one of a dozen legit things he's doing, and besides: what on earth has Margaret to do with all of this?'

'Oh, I'm sure you've got me pegged for a nosey parker,' Joan Cook snapped, to the imaginary metre of a typewriter. She lifted her left hand and wagged her index finger at Doyle as she made this pronouncement. He could see the band of fairer skin on her second finger where once her wedding band had sat. 'But let me tell you, there is definitely something going on up there on that farm. Believe you me, everyone, but everyone, is talking about it. Miss High-and-Mighty wanted both men to herself, if you know what I mean?' Her finger was wagging ten to the dozen now. 'Oh no, one man wasn't good enough for her, was it? She had to try two and now that she's tried them both, well, there's one too many around, isn't there? Or there *was*, more's the like. Yes, one surplus to her requirements as it were.' Cook's lecture and finger wagging ceased at the same moment.

Wee Doyle could not help but laugh. And laugh out loud at that. He had a nervous laugh and a loud laugh. And this apparent mockery ruffled the newly coloured feathers of Mrs Joan Cook.

'Now you listen here!' she spat, rat-a-tat, barely containing her anger, her finger and tongue recommencing their feverish wagging.

'No, *you* listen here: stop spreading this rubbish and get off with you before I arrest you for wasting police time … She drove off her brother-in-law, indeed!' Doyle snapped, just like a school teacher chastising a consistently naughty pupil.

'Don't you be so quick to dismiss me. You'll live to regret it, just mark my words. And before you go getting all high and mighty with me, just answer me one question, will you? Which of the two brothers is she married to?'

Wee Doyle rose from his chair with the words 'Come on', and escorted Mrs Cook to the station door and verbally flung her down the three well-worn steps with, 'I'll be seeing you. *Goodbye!*'

*

Wee Doyle was visibly upset. He knew the Kane twins. He had known their parents; his parents had known their parents. They were hardworking, God-fearing farmers who wished and did no harm to anyone and here was the village gossip beating the bush telegraph with how Pat had done away with Joe or a variation on that theme.

For heaven's sake, this was Castlemartin. People just did not murder each other in Castlemartin. Sure, they occasionally slept with each other's wives and husbands – hell, sometimes they even slept with their own. And, yes, they did indeed sometimes cheat the tax man with their cash transactions and spitting on hands and all that palaver. And sure they drank too much – they even (and while intoxicated) tried to carry out stupid crimes which they were all embarrassed to read about a couple of months later in the *Mid Ulster Mail*.

But murder?

Not just murder, mind you, but fratricide.

And, to add insult to injury, the thing that made him the maddest about all of this was the fact that he was going to have to investigate it. He hoped that he was clever enough to be able to handle the matter with the delicacy it required. On one hand, he had to treat it as a potential murder investigation, but if he wasn't careful then people's lives, not to mention his own career, could be ruined … even in just trying to prove that no loss of life had, in fact, occurred.

Doyle decided to waste no time and jumped straight into the investigation. He didn't want some smart fellow in Belfast asking in the future, should this indeed turn out to be a murder, why he'd delayed. 'How come,' some superior, keen on apportioning blame to another desk, would say – such landmine questions always started out with that. 'How come,' he'd say down a long nose, 'when you had been reliably informed of the demise of Mr Kane, you took so much time to do something about it?'

So, Doyle agreed with his inner voice that there were, literally, no minutes to spare.

For the second time in five minutes, Doyle, all five-foot-four-inches of him, rose from his chair, except this time he paused to remove his jacket from the back of it and was hand-brushing the lapels in search of dandruff as he exited the station and made his way, through the various browns of the impending winter, towards Michael Gilmour's house.

The Castlemartin detective felt the matchmaker's house was the obvious starting point on the case. Michael Gilmour knew everything that was going on in the village and he was also related by marriage, via his sister-in-law, to the Kane twins. Doyle hoped that he could put all this nonsense to bed once and for all, nip in the bud any and all suggestions of wrongdoing before they blossomed out, and not as a rose but as a thorny branch, capable of surrounding, strangling and drawing the final breath from a few people's lives.

Chapter Twenty-Seven

Doyle was still experiencing conflicting emotions when he knocked on the door of the matchmaker's house some seven minutes later. He could tell from the look in Michael's eye that he thought there might be some matchmaking afoot. But Wee Doyle was happy with his most-eligible-bachelor status. He wondered, however, if the matchmaker would be so happy about the business the member of the local police force, acting in an official capacity, had come to discuss.

'Colin! Colin, come on in, why don't you?' was the warm greeting afforded the inspector.

'Thanks, Michael, I will at that,' replied the policeman, allowing himself to be shown firstly into the kitchen and then ushered, with Michael, by Dorothy into the front room with a promise of tea. The detective was one of the few men in the village who wore his Sunday best all the time, so it was hard to tell when he was dressed up for something special. She'd also given him the benefit of the doubt, Doyle figured. He had just reached the stage in his life where he was happy, extremely happy, with his uniform of grey flannel trousers, Donegal tweed jacket, checked shirt, green tie and brown and white brogues. It worked for him, he was happy and comfortable dressed this way and, more importantly, he was not self-conscious attired in this manner. He felt this gave him an advantage in his work – he only need apply himself to his thinking process. He worried not about how he looked. Although that was not entirely true, of course – in his own subtle way he was making as large a statement as those who were the first to try out all the new fashions. He certainly spent as much money as anyone else on his clothes – it was just that he repeatedly bought the *same* set … although he did allow himself a little variety with his socks and underwear.

'Listen, it's something and it's nothing, I suppose,' Doyle began as he sank back into the comfortable sofa, 'but the tongues are wagging about your Joseph Kane.'

'Oh yeah?' was the matchmaker's guarded reply.

'Well, you know what the imaginations are like around here once they're encouraged on a flight.'

'Yes, I do that. Sure wasn't Mattie Stewart meant to be the richest man in the town with all those years of cash? That rumour was soon put to an end when those two idiots broke into his house to find only a goldmine of beer bottles and consequently the solution to the biggest mystery of modern times. No, he didn't eat a lot, no, he didn't buy any clothes, no, he didn't have a wife or children but, don't you see, he certainly didn't mind a wee drink,' Michael fondly recounted.

'So, Michael, what exactly can you tell me about Joe and his whereabouts?'

'I'm sure I don't know. His twin brother doesn't even know where he is, so how on earth am I meant to know? I say, how am I meant to know?' Michael smiled, slightly nervously. He was rubbing his hands to generate warmth in them, a gesture he'd inherited from his father which was mostly, as in now, incorrectly assessed as being a sign of glee or happiness.

'Did they row?' Doyle enquired.

'They're brothers and what's more they're twins, so of course they rowed. Don't you see that family rows are rarely more than a storm in a teacup? Talking about teacups, I hear the clink of two making their way towards us,' Michael replied, giving a signal to stop the discussion until his wife had left. Well, at least that's the way the detective saw it. And why wouldn't the matchmaker want his wife to know what they were talking about – sure, wasn't it all innocent enough?

'Have you asked Pat about Joe's whereabouts?' Doyle pressed.

'Sure I have,' came the short reply.

'And?'

'And he hasn't a clue.'

'What, he really hasn't a clue? Joe just up and left without saying a word to his brother?' Doyle continued as Michael served tea. The inspector was a coffee man himself, since he found he received more of a hit from it, but now that the tea was here he didn't want any further interruptions.

'That's what Pat says and why should he lie?' the matchmaker posed.

'Let me see now …' Doyle began. 'When was the last time you saw Joseph Kane?'

'That sounds very official, Colin!'

'Be that as it may, Michael. The tongues are wagging. And they're wagging about the three of them: Joseph, Patrick *and* Margaret. It's all pretty unusual, the whole thing. And it is my experience that the wagging tongues of Castlemartin are not going to rest until we show them where Joe is,' the detective continued.

Michael nodded his acceptance of that truth.

'So, Michael, when did you last see Joseph?'

'Three Saturdays ago. We were all up on the farm, doing a bit of harvesting, don't you see. And I think that's the last time I saw him,' the matchmaker answered, appearing to be considering whether or not that was in fact the last time he saw the missing twin.

'Who else was present at the harvesting?'

'Oh, let's see now: there was Maggie and Pat, Dorothy and our eldest, Paul, Dan Stevenson and Raymond O'Sullivan, Bobby and Tom Paterson, Wesley McIvor and Valerie Scott and the widower Harry McKinney,' Michael replied, alarmed to find halfway through his list that Doyle was committing the names, by ink – Parker fountain-pen ink – to paper in his standard-issue police notebook.

'Would they all have seen Joe at around the same time you saw him for the last time, or would it have been staggered?' Doyle pushed, persisting with his line of questioning.

'Jesus, Colin, this is getting a bit like *No Hiding Place*, isn't it? Do you want to search my cupboard for skeletons?' Michael laughed, but the minute he said the words, he would have paid a fiver to be able to stuff them back into his big gob.

Doyle just stared at the matchmaker, content that by merely glaring at him he was not helping him feel any more comfortable.

'Well, it's hard to tell, isn't it? I mean everyone sees the same scene differently through their own eyes,' Michael started. He paused, thrown by Doyle's refusal to offer any words of support or encouragement. 'I mean, I suppose roughly all about the same time.'

'And you positively didn't see him again after that day on the field?'

'No, Colin, no-one has,' the matchmaker said, yet as he spoke the words and had a chance to listen to his own voice saying them, there again seemed to be a certain amount of unretractable drama now attached to them.

'Can I assume that neither your wife nor children have seen Joe since that Saturday?'

'No, no – we discussed it and, as I have already mentioned, none of us has.' Michael stopped to think for a few moments. 'Don't you think that it's something simple? Surely you don't think anything untoward has happened?'

'Well, that's exactly what I'm trying to find out,' Doyle replied, finishing off the cup of tea. 'I'd better be off now – thank the wife for the tea.'

As he rose to leave, both men felt a strangeness towards each other, a slightly unreal feeling, like at any moment one of them could crack a joke, just like they would often do in Paddy Bryson's pub in Magherafelt, and the whole episode would lighten up and everything would be back to normal.

But it was not to be. Doyle left the house amidst an air of discomfort. As he walked back up Apple Orchard Lane and turned right into Railway Terrace to head back down towards Pear Tree Roundabout, and then up the Broadway twenty yards to the Station House, he felt very uneasy. On his way into the matchmaker's house he had considered the business he was on to be no more than the result of a busy-body. But now, with the matchmaker's apparent and considerable discomfort, perhaps something *was* afoot; whether or not it was sinister remained to be seen.

He was convinced he had a mystery to solve. The mystery may only entail seeking out the current whereabouts of one Joseph David Kane and the discovery would be the solution. Should the twin prove to be in a permanent state of missing – from this earth, as it were – well, then that would prove to be a whole different can of worms.

Chapter Twenty-Eight

Doyle's next port of call on that beautiful late-summer's evening was the residence of Bobby Patterson, who'd been the oldest man on the field helping out with the Kane twins' harvest. Actually, to describe it as the residence of Mr Patterson was slightly misleading; it would have been more accurate to state that it was the residence of Bobby Patterson, his dog Samson, three old cats (Bobby had never given them individual names – they were simply known as the Beverley Sisters or, when venturing forth solo, one of the Beverley Sisters), fourteen chickens, two roosters and three ducks. One of the ducks was called Blind Pinky because she was exactly that: blind and pink.

The reason that Doyle decided to visit Mr Patterson first was because he was the closest to the station house. Patterson's two-room residence was situated behind Moore's Railway Inn, which was at the top of the Broadway on the left-hand side. When his cottage (which had been erected around 1820, as near as the locals could tell, mainly by the thickness of the walls) was originally built in that spot, there wouldn't have been many other dwellings in the area. Bobby had lived there all his life, as had his father, Thomas, and when his own son Tommy had built a new farmhouse out on Toome Lane (which is what the Broadway became the other side of the disused railway tracks) and had offered his father accommodation, either in the main farmhouse or a little bungalow of his own, Bobby had refused on the grounds that he had spent all his years thus far in the thatched cottage and he wasn't going to change his living arrangements at this late stage in his life.

Local legend had it that Bobby owned most of the land Castlemartin was built on. If this were a truth, then he certainly hid his wealth well.

As Doyle's shadow darkened Patterson's doorstep, the words 'Ah, come in, won't you' were heard from within, uttered in the old fella's deep baritone. This would have been a regular greeting because callers were many: Patterson sold the best eggs for miles and his regular customers remained regulars all their lives, as did their children. Aye, Patterson's eggs were the hits of the pan parade. The detective wandered in and closed the door behind him, hoping for a few minutes' peace within.

'Well now, if it isn't the most prominent member of our constabulary,' was how the smiling farmer greeted Doyle. 'You'll not be after my eggs and you're not here for a chat, so am I to guess you're here on official police business?'

'Aye, and that's a fact, Bobby,' Doyle replied cautiously. 'How are you keeping?'

'So far so good,' Patterson replied, nodding Doyle further into the crammed room. 'Sit yourself down by the table there then,' Patterson continued, taking a swipe at a couple of his prize chickens, sending them – and their feathers – squawking, gawking and flying in a million directions. As the dust settled, Doyle went to brush down the seat but then thought better of it.

'You'll be having a drink won't you?'

The reason for the twinkle in Patterson's eye now became obvious as he went over to his sink and swished a lick of water around a handle-less mug and returned to the table, just a mite unsteady, with a lemonade bottle, three-quarters filled with a clear liquid.

'A swig of poteen, won't you?' he offered, pointing the top of the bottle in Doyle's direction.

'Nah, never touch the stuff – never touch that type of auld alcohol, that is. But I do have a thirst on me nonetheless: have you anything that won't make my toes smoke?' Doyle enquired hopefully.

Patterson hobbled back in the direction of the sink and from a makeshift cupboard directly above it he produced a bottle – unopened – of orangeade. He returned to the table and plonked it in front of the policeman with such force that Doyle was convinced froth would explode from the bottle the minute he released the cap. In fact, he released it tentatively and let the gasses escape the confines, now they'd been shaken into life, ever so slowly. Patterson returned to his mountain dew and let out a loud sigh after a slow swig.

'Ah, just like drinking razor blades. Great stuff, sure, you don't know what you're missing. I'd bet you this fine liquid would put hairs on the chest of a nun!'

Doyle had seen enough men, mostly farmers, eyes turned inside out and lying face down in ditches to know exactly what he was missing and would continue missing for at least the remainder of this lifetime.

The room was filled with rich smells: the burning peat, the livestock, the closeness of the farmer's bed and the straw. Everything was black or dark brown – his pots and pans, kettles, furniture, bedclothes. His clothes even matched the scene: brown cords tied at the waste with a length of baling twine; white vest (clean, very clean), peeping out from behind a tartan shirt under a black waistcoat complete with pocket watch and gold chain (the farmer's one open concession to wealth); black, well-worn boots, close to the fire, warming for tomorrow. Even in the heat of this room he kept his dark-brown cloth cap on. Some say he wore it in bed. Some say he wore it all the time because he was as bald as a newborn baby. However this was disproved by those lucky enough to see his party piece – bending his head back until his cap fell off; he'd then catch it behind his back and in the same movement swing it high in the air and have his head positioned in the exact location to receive it as the cap returned earthwards. Such rare manoeuvres proved he'd a full head of hair, all snowy white and very curly.

'I've come to talk to you about Joseph Kane,' Doyle began.

'Aye, ye have, have you?' Patterson replied as he tried, successfully, to rest his feet on Samson. Doyle figured, for he was a detective and allegedly good at these things, that this was the reason for the dog's strange name.

'Yes, Bobby – I believe you were up on at the harvesting with them when he was last seen?'

'Certainly the last time the posse saw him,' the old farmer confirmed.

Doyle never entertained any ambitions about being a dentist – he had no interest in prolonging the agony – so he sought a way to speed up the conversation. This was going to be difficult – not least due to the fact that the farmer was comfortable in the room where he'd spent most of his life. He was not going to be 'interviewed' – he was in his home and if he was going to do anything, he was going to chat. If Doyle managed to get anything worthwhile out of the chat, well and good, but if he didn't then it would just be his hard luck.

Patterson, Doyle knew, was a God-fearing man and he wasn't going to lie. But equally he wasn't going to offer a neighbour up on a plate just because a member of the police force was drinking orangeade with him.

'Any ideas where he might be?' Doyle enquired.

'Some say he's down in Belfast. Some say he was seen boarding the Heysham Ferry and he's made his way to London. Some say he boarded the Larne to Stranraer Ferry and he's ended up in Edinburgh. Some say he's been seen as far away as Dublin. And,' the old farmer paused for another sip of his drink, 'some say that where he's gone to he's going to be spared all his troubles till the day of the resurrection.'

'And what do you say, Bobby?'

'A-ha, now there's a question. Well, they say there's no bad blood like bad family blood.'

'Meaning?'

'Away with you, Mr Doyle, I don't draw pictures.'

'Did anyone else on the field see him later?' Doyle said, shifting tack in his attempts to introduce a fresh trail.

'Not that I'm aware of. We watched him go and that was it. Work broke up about half an hour later and everyone made their own way home.'

'This work-share thing that some of the neighbouring farmers have, how come you're involved in it?' the policeman asked. 'Sure you've no more farming of your own to do for them to be able to repay you?'

The orangeade was sickly warm and not the pleasant refreshing drink Doyle had hoped for.

'Ah, well now, it's not as simple as that, you see, is it?' Patterson began, stretching back in his chair. 'The father, the twins' father – Desmond was his name – he and I were great friends and always turned out for each other and when he died ... well, I felt obliged to show them that there are still people in their corner should they need, or ask for, any help. I'm sure Des would have done the same for our young Tommy should the situation be reversed.'

'Did anything happen on the field to warrant Joe leaving you all there still working? After all, wasn't he the host farmer?' Doyle prodded.

'Meaning?'

'Well, let's see now, this time on the field was the last time he was seen ... and it was strange that he would have left before the end of the working day. So, logic would lead me to believe that perhaps something happened. You know, something like a fight, a disagreement or being called away on an emergency. Did anyone come and fetch Joe?'

'No, no-one came to fetch Joe.'

'Did anything happen on the field that day?'

'You know, Inspector, I think that's a question you should ask Patrick,' Patterson replied, smiling to soften the blow of his silence on the matter.

'And what would be the significance of that, Bobby?'

'I'm saying not a word further on this one.'

Doyle stood to leave, thanked the egg-man for his hospitality, three mouthfuls of warm orangeade, healthy rustic smells and some unhealthy heat.

'OK, I may need to come back to ask you some more questions though, Bobby.'

'I'm not going anywhere – not unless my maker calls me,' the widower replied.

Chapter Twenty-Nine

Castlemartin looked different to Wee Doyle as he passed Moore's Railway Inn on his way back to the police station, the next building along on the Broadway. The village smelt different; the ambient sounds were different. It was like he was walking into a new town and taking it all on board for the first time. He supposed, when you had nothing much to do, nothing much apart from apprehending, for their own safety, men intoxicated while in charge of a bicycle, you do tend to view your surroundings with something amounting to apathy at best.

But now the colours of the Broadway and Pear Tree Roundabout were as vivid as he had ever seen them. He was tuning into all the street conversations going on around him. The smell of freshly baked bread from Rogers & Daughters' Home Bakery mixed very pleasantly with the fresh fruit and vegetables displayed on the pavement outside O'Neill's shop. Doyle even noticed people noticing him. He felt his back straighten; he felt like a man about to embark on a mission he'd been put on this earth to accomplish: to seek out and incarcerate those involved in breaking the law.

It was funny, but people in villages like Castlemartin ultimately believed that the law was there to defend and protect them. The community respected the police, just as they did their teachers, shopkeepers, solicitors and doctors. It was also true that the community feared the police, but it was a fear built up from the understanding that, yes, the law was there to protect the innocent, but that, equally, they were going to be relentless in tracking down and helping to convict the guilty. So heaven help you if you were guilty.

Doyle wondered who, if any, were the guilty parties in this rural drama, the disappearance of Joe Kane? He thought about this as he walked on down past the Station House to the south of the Broadway. Who would he talk to next? He had to be careful, for if he was not and things were amiss, then he may find people closing ranks around him. So this initial gathering of information, should there in fact be any at all, could be vital.

Doyle's decision was eventually made for him, as while walking down the Broadway he met Valerie Scott, herself a member of the Kane-family harvest team.

'Ah,' Doyle began, trying to appear casual, 'this is lucky, I mean, meeting you – I was going to try to meet up with you.'

'Really?' Valerie replied, smiling.

'Yes, look, do you have any time – I mean now? Let's see, we could go to Teyley's Café and have a tea or coffee or something?'

'Well,' Valerie replied, looking at her watch, 'I have to meet Wesley in about thirty minutes and I have to go home before that and drop off some shopping for my ma, but we could talk for about ten to fifteen minutes, if that would be any good for you?'

'Aye, that would be great,' Doyle replied, and with that they headed off to Teyley's, indulging only in small talk until they were seated in a quiet corner of the café, she with a tea and he with a strong coffee.

'Listen, Valerie, what I wanted to talk to you about was Joe Kane – you know, his disappearance.'

'Yes, it's awful, isn't it? No-one's seen him for ages.'

'I understand you were up on the farm the day he disappeared, working the harvest with a few others?'

'Yes, I was there with Wesley – he'd promised them he'd help 'cause they always return the favour and so rather than hang around under my mum's feet I went out as well. It's usually a great bit of fun. Well, a good bit of fun, particularly with the Lone Ranger and Tonto – they're such a scream!' Valerie offered, as she sugared her tea.

'Am, did Joe behave, you know … funny?'

'What, funny like the Lone Ranger and To—'

'No,' Doyle interrupted, 'I meant funny as in *strange*.'

'Well no … not really.' She paused.

'But?' Doyle probed, sensing a hesitation.

'Well, I'd never seen brothers fight before, I mean, fight with such savagery.'

Doyle nearly swallowed the entire contents of the coffee cup.

'What?' he asked, a little too forcefully.

'Oh, you didn't know … Well, am, you know, I mean, I wasn't really *that* close to the fight, so you should perhaps ask one of the others. It was during the last tea break and I was chatting with Wesley,' Valerie offered, making a clumsy job of trying to cover her tracks. She was acting very uncomfortably, perhaps because she was in a public café with a man other than her own, or maybe it was that she felt she had said too much. Doyle studied her in his attempts to work out which.

Valerie Scott was dressed in a pair of vibrant yellow slacks. Doyle was one of those people who sometimes made the mistake of thinking a woman had a poor figure, as was the case with Miss Scott, when in fact it was nothing more than an ill-fitting pair of trousers. She wore a red cardigan, which partially covered a white blouse, and a yellow head scarf that now lay on the table to her side, but which she would delicately place on her high bun of jet black hair to protect it from the lough winds. She wore a lot of make-up in the manner and fashion of the models used by cosmetic companies to display their wares on counter-cards and posters.

'Why were they fighting?' Doyle persisted, seeing the large catch struggling to break free of his line to head for the darker waters.

'Oh, I wouldn't know, I'm sure, Inspector – you should ask Pat.' Valerie was struck at that precise second with a thought, a thought she was compelled to voice immediately. 'Does this mean you've found Joe? Oh my God! Is he OK? It didn't twig with me until now that you were, you know, working on an investigation, what with your questions and all.'

'No, no,' Doyle said, suppressing her excitement. 'Joe hasn't been found and we don't even know if he's really missing yet or if he's simply gone away for a while; I've only just started to look into all of this. Am, Valerie, tell me: did you see who started the fight – was it Pat or was it Joe?'

Valerie started to giggle at the detective.

'What? *What?*' Doyle enquired in his ever-growing embarrassment. Her laughter had grown louder, attracting the attention of all the people in the café.

'No, it's just that just now you sounded like the Flowerpot Men, you know, "Was it Bill or was it Ben?"'

'Ah, I see,' Doyle lied, hoping she'd quieten down for good. 'Well, did you? See which one it was, that is – which of the twins started the fight?'

'No, I didn't. As I mentioned, I was a bit away from them with Wesley. The others were closer – why not check with them?'

'Yes, I suppose that's what I'll have to do,' Doyle said, backtracking. He relaxed into his chair and took a sip of his drink. 'So … when's the big day for you and Wesley?'

'First Saturday in November,' came the oft-used reply from the bride-to-be.

'And the honeymoon, where are youse off to?' Doyle asked, sending a few braves back through the long grass while he smiled at Valerie to distract her from the final couple of questions which were going to jump out (from the long grass) and hopefully (successfully) surprise her.

'Well, my father has a caravan down at the Port,' she began.

'Ah, a couple of weeks down at Portrush, that'll be grand,' Doyle interrupted.

'What? No, of course not, don't be silly! It'll be *freezing* – a caravan in November, oh, you are funny, Inspector. No, what I was going to say was that he rents it out to this wonderful couple from Edinburgh who have a guest house and as it's the closed season they've invited us to stay *there* for free. Wesley's older brother lives in Stirling and he and his wife have a car – a Ford A40, you know – well, they're going to show us around.'

'Oh,' Doyle offered, so involved in listening to the answer he nearly didn't give his braves the nod in time for them to come out from the long grass. 'That'll be nice. Have you ever been to Scotland before?'

'No, Inspector, never been out of Ulster. We were going to go to Donegal once but Wesley's grandmum took ill. It was sad – she died, you know.'

'Really?' Doyle couldn't believe it; she was off on another of her tangents. However, the surprising thing was not that she was off on one again, but rather that the detective was following her every step of the way.

'Yes, but Wesley was OK about it; I mean, she'd a good innings, hadn't she?'

'How old was she?'

'Three days short of ninety, can you believe that?' Valerie boasted.

'Aye, as you say, a good innings – more than most. Tell me, Valerie, when the twins were fighting, who stopped the fight?'

'Oh, Michael Gilmour, Bobby Patterson and our Wes–' Valerie paused, in sudden recognition of the brave who'd come to collect her scalp. 'Yes ... em, Bobby was there to help pull them apart, and our Wesley ran down the field to help in the separation as well.' Doyle had the decency not to pull her up on her little lie that she and Wesley had been further away from the fight than she'd originally let on. He was purely collecting information at this point and there was no need to be rubbing people up the wrong way, since news would travel. He certainly wanted to avoid, if possible, a village shutdown. However, he still had one more brave to use.

'Thanks for your time, Valerie. That'll do me for now – perhaps we'll talk again later,' the detective said, deciding a good chief knew when to keep some of his braves in the undergrowth. Knew when to leave them to fight another day.

Valerie Scott carefully floated the scarf over her head, barely tying the two tails under her chin, and with a brief smile, more like a grin, at Doyle, she swept out of Teyley's Café. She hit Briscoe Street at a skip, a more relieved girl than the one who had walked in. Doyle was aware that the police (himself included) had a way, an uncontrollable way, of making even the innocent feel guilty.

He was amused at her small fib, rather than overly concerned about it. He knew it had been told so that she and her husband-to-be would not be placed in a position where they were giving evidence against one of their friends. Castlemartin was a very small village and a community that needed to pull together, such as they had in the harvest, to get by.

After all, weren't the police paid to catch the criminals? So why on earth should the locals have to help them? They'd already paid the taxes which in turn paid the likes of Doyle.

And with that the inspector left the café with a resolve to earn his wages.

Chapter Thirty

'What kind of fresh hell is this?' widower Harry McKinney announced to his trusted companion, who immediately started to bark, showing he concurred with his master's annoyance.

The pair, Harry and Lioney, had just settled down to listen to the radio following their early supper. As the door was locked for the night, Harry had decided to ignore the knocking on his front door in the hope that whoever it was would go away. But no, the knocks persisted.

He rose from his chair and stroppily strode in the direction of the front door. Harry didn't open it, choosing instead to call through it.

'Yes, who's calling at this ungodly hour?'

'Inspector Doyle here!' the visitor announced, checking his watch and amused to see that it was still only 5:45 p.m. He then realised that the old man had probably been up since 5 a.m. 'Look, Harry, I'd like to ask you a few questions about—'

'Then come back tomorrow morning – I'm not going anywhere,' the old man grunted back.

'I wish you'd let me—' Doyle persisted.

'I'll tell you what,' came the muffled voice from inside the door, 'wish in one hand and pee in the other and see which one fills first. I'll see you in the morning. Now be off with you before I set Lioney on you.'

'Charming,' Wee Doyle thought to himself as he walked away.

He accepted that he wasn't going to have the same kind of luck twice in a row: walking into a potential witness on the street. So he decided to visit Patrick Kane next. Pretty soon the word would be getting back to the twin – the one still in residence on the farm – that questions were being asked about the town. The next obvious step, not to mention the decent thing to do – if only to keep ahead of the bush telegraph – was to pay him a courtesy visit and maybe even discover why he hadn't reported his brother as missing. At the back of Doyle's mind was the thought that there was still a very logical and acceptable reason for Joe Kane to be missing from the farm.

Chapter Thirty-One

S o, here's what happened next.

Patrick Kane and his wife Maggie greeted Inspector Doyle with a warmth typical of the Ulster farmers, who, legend has it, have hearts as large as the Sperrin Mountains.

'Come on in, why don't you,' Pat announced from the doorway.

The policeman followed the twin's wife into the small, but clean, living-room-cum-kitchen. Doyle could easily observe Maggie's touch around the house; everything had considerably lightened since the last time he was there, on the occasion of the twins' mother's funeral. Gone was the dark and oppressive wallpaper, the main advantage of which was making it hard for the dirt to show up – now the walls were covered with washable light-blue and yellow vertically striped paper. The doors and doorposts had recently been painted eggshell white, and Maggie had arranged a magnificent bunch of flowers in a yellow vase, which had vividly painted roses embossed on the sides. The only concession to the previous drab decor was the maroon floor tiles, which in their well-worn state – now so well polished that Doyle, with his leather-soled brogues, had to be very careful not to slip – subtly revealed the cottage's age. As the detective tentatively paced his way across the floor, he appeared like one in desperate need of the toilet.

The open fire was quietly crackling and gently smouldering at the far end of the kitchen. A copper kettle was coming to the boil on the ring atop the gas oven, which was situated to the right of the window, beneath which was the sink and draining board. To the left of the window was a latch door, which had seen one too many coats of paint and was on Pat's list of things to attend to. In fact it was on the second list – the first list consisted of things which had to be done immediately, like moving the toilet indoors. This was altogether a more complicated job than it had first seemed. Maggie had figured out that the toilet itself could stay where it was – about ten feet to the rear and the left of the house – and that all Pat had to do was build a little lean-to extension to the rear of the house, which would encompass the toilet. In the new space they'd created, they could have a bathroom. The old bathroom could then be knocked through into the kitchen, making their living area more inhabitable. In all of these renovations Maggie had also worked out the most cost-effective way to get them done. She had been around the various sheds on the farm and had ear-marked all the materials needed – bricks from here, rafters from there – and she planned to use the fittings from the current bathroom for the new one. They were not the best, but they would do until they could afford better. She hoped that by the time they *could* afford better it would be time for a new farmhouse, or perhaps even a new farm.

The second list consisted of things that Pat, and Joe, would get around to when they could, such as the aforementioned door.

'Tea?' Maggie enquired, smiling.

'Yes, that would be great,' Doyle replied. He was impressed at their unspoken togetherness. There was definitely a very strong bond between them and if either was concerned by the absence of the unmarried twin, neither was showing it. 'Actually, would there be any chance of a cup of coffee instead?'

'Yes, of course, I like coffee as well – I'll have one with you. Pat never touches the stuff so I tend to not drink it when he's around,' Maggie replied, as her husband sat in his favourite chair, a long-since-broken-in easy chair – his dad's – by the fireside. Doyle sat at the pine table slightly behind Pat, which meant in effect that the detective was looking at the right-hand side of the twin's face. Doyle would have preferred it to have been set up differently, but he'd have to make do.

'It's Joseph I've come to talk to you about,' Doyle began, and when neither the twin nor his wife acknowledged his statement he continued, 'I understand he's missing?'

'Well, we certainly haven't seen him around for a few weeks, so it would seem like he's done a bit of a Basil Bond on us,' Pat replied, as he stared into the fire.

'Basil Bond …?' the detective asked.

'Oh, sorry: famous French illusionist who specialised in disappearing – he might even have been a fictional character,' Maggie offered.

'Right … So … have you any ideas where Joe is?'

'No, to be truthful, we haven't a clue,' Pat replied.

'Has he ever done this before?'

'No, never.'

'Don't you find it all a bit strange, then?' Doyle asked, reverting once more to his best impression of a dentist, dragging out the discomfort.

Pat turned around, looked over at Maggie, who was turned towards the draining board preparing the tea, and appeared to be waiting for his wife to say something; when she didn't, he turned back to look at the dying flames and said, 'No, not really. I mean, it's been a difficult time for Joe. You know, what with Maggie and myself getting together, getting married and all that. There was obviously a bit of a pull there – you know, the twins thing everyone talks about: we'd been close all our lives and obviously I've been spending more time with Maggie since I met her. Then we thought it was all going to be OK 'cause he started courting Doris Durin, but they split up a short time before he vanished.'

Doyle added another name to his book. 'Right, let's see now, and he hasn't been in touch since?'

'No,' Pat replied.

'What about Doris – has he contacted her?'

'We wouldn't know – we haven't seen or heard from her in ages,' Maggie replied.

'I have to say,' Doyle smiled to try and make what he was about to say not appear rude, 'neither of you seems to be overly concerned about this, about Joe.' And then he thought, but he didn't say, they seemed incredibly cosy here, just the two of them.

'Look, it's probably something harmless – he's off down to stay with mates in Belfast. You know, kicking his heels, and when he's got it out of his system he'll come back again,' Pat offered.

'Does he have any mates in Belfast?' Doyle enquired.

'Yeah, a few of the people we went to the technical college with moved down there.'

'Can you give me names and addresses?'

'I can't really, to be honest. I mean, I remember some of the names, you know – they were friends at tech and you mean to keep up but your flippin' life happens and you don't. But let's try and see now who went to Belfast that Joe would have known. Am, Vincent Kelly – I think he's working for the BBC down there – and, ah, Jerry, oh shi—sugar … what was his second name now, let me think? Jerry Snow, that's it – Jerry Snow! But I wouldn't have a clue as to how to get hold of them,' Pat replied, his head twisted towards Doyle now.

Maggie brought two cups of coffee over to the table and invited Doyle to help himself to milk and sugar. She returned to her preparation area and brought Pat's mug of tea over to the table, added sugar and milk and took it over to the fireside to her husband. She also rescued a couple of day-fresh Paris Buns from a biscuit tin and offered them to Pat and Doyle, who both accepted.

Doyle washed a large bite down with hot coffee and then dropped his bombshell. 'So, Pat – what were you and Joe fighting about in the field on the day of the harvest?'

'Oh that? That was just a bit of fun, you know, we were just codding around.'

Doyle threw Pat one of his 'really?' stares but decided not to push that particular area until he had more concrete information.

'So let's see now,' Doyle started and paused, 'right, what about clothes – did he take clothes with him?'

'From what we can guess, just what he stood up in,' Maggie replied.

'And money – did he have much money with him?'

'Well, he'd a few bob with him, you know, but not a fortune. But then he could always pick up casual labour as he went along,' Pat answered this time.

'And what about a bike – did he have a bike?'

'Yes, he did.' Pat laughed.

'Did he take it with him?'

'No, it's still out in the shed,' Pat answered suddenly solemn.

'Tell me,' Doyle began, swerving as skilfully as Bobby Charlton, 'Joe's mood, I mean, did he say he was thinking about leaving?'

'Nah, we woke up the day after the harvesting and he was gone,' the twin replied.

'So that means he returned to the farmhouse later that evening, after he ran from the field.'

'Why yes!' Maggie started up again. 'He came back after everyone had left and we had his supper ready for him; he ate it and didn't say much, just went to bed.'

'Didn't say much ... so what did he say?'

'Oh, you know, that he was sorry,' Maggie continued.

'Why was he sorry – I thought he and Pat were just kidding around?' Doyle countered.

'Well, am, it started out that way and then it just got out of hand and I think that's why he left the field – he was kinda embarrassed,' Pat offered.

'So what exactly did he say when he came back?'

'Gee, Inspector, it's hard to remember *exactly* what he said – why do you want to know all this?' Pat enquired, as he arose from his very soft seat to return his empty mug to the sink and sit down beside his wife on the opposite side of the table from the detective.

'Well, I'm trying to get a picture of him just before he left. Was he sad? Was he happy? You know.'

'You don't mean you think that he could have done something flippin' stupid, do you?' Pat interrupted.

'Look, Pat, you have a man – a healthy man – and he just vanishes from the face of the earth. Now, he hasn't got the kind of money where he can just go and start a new life somewhere. He doesn't take any clothes with him. He doesn't take the only means of transport he owns with him. He doesn't appear to have anybody he knew so well he could stay with. His brother – his *twin* brother – takes a wife; the wife moves in to their small farmhouse. The equilibrium has obviously been upset. I mean, Pat, that's what I'm trying to find out from you. How upset was he? Was he upset enough to want to take his own life?'

'Je-sus, Inspector – you don't really think that, do you? Come on!' Pat said in controlled but raised tones.

'Something's happened, Pat, and I want to find out what. Some of these questions might be painful but I have to ask them. I'd love it if Joe walked in here right now, or tomorrow we found him shacked up with some farmer's daughter on the Glenshane Pass. Or you received a card from him saying he was over in England working on the roads or whatever, but, Pat, until then I've got to keep looking. He's been missing now for too long for us not to be worried about him.'

'Well, since he and Doris broke up, yes, he was a bit down-hearted, a little dejected – but we all go through that, don't we?' Maggie replied, taking her husband's hand.

'Did he have many girlfriends?'

'No, not really; it's not a glamorous job, you know, struggling to make a farm work. I was very lucky to find Maggie—'

'We were very lucky to find each other,' his wife interrupted as she squeezed his hand.

'Yes,' Pat agreed, 'we were indeed, very lucky, and as I was saying I, well, *we* really, yes, we thought he and Doris were good together, we thought they were getting on great and then it just seemed to end and he was a bit down. But he'd never, never ever take his own life. In the sweet memory of our mother and father he'd never be able to do any of that auld carry on. I'm sure he wouldn't even think of it.'

'Well,' Doyle said, standing up, 'you know, let's hope he turns up tomorrow and you'll all be able to get back to your lives and I'll be able to get back to the real crimes.'

And with that they all stood and smiled nervous smiles.

Chapter Thirty-Two

The following morning Doyle considered the amount of people he had to talk to and decided it might be time to enlist some help. If he thought the matter serious enough, he could apply for a constable, or maybe even a detective constable, from one of the neighbouring towns. Mid Ulster had a floating force as well as its skeleton local presence. At this stage, he decided he would make do with the station's regular constable, the one and only Constable Edward Hill.

Castlemartin's police station had a workforce of a mere six people: five men and one woman. There was Doyle, senior in rank and years; Sergeant Bill Agnew, from Cookstown; WPC Jill Watterson, Castlemartin's first ever WPC and, like the recently relocated Japanese family Hiydaka, she was currently a tourist attraction when in her uniform. She was pretty damned attractive anyway but the uniform gave everyone an excuse to gawk at her on her rounds. Then there were the three constables: Robin Irvine, Gavin McGee and the aforementioned Edward Hill. Rarely were all six on duty at the same time, except maybe during shift changeovers, but on that particular day Doyle comforted himself that even when he took Hill to work with him on the Missing Kane case (Doyle intentionally misspelt the name 'Kane' with a 'C' so that in years to come, should the case turn out innocently enough, he alone would know the file referred to the local twins' case, but there'd be no paper trails leading back to the Kanes themselves), that still left WPC Watterson and Constable Irvine in the station.

The first thing Doyle had to do was bring Hill up to date. Hill remained quiet while Doyle recounted the story so far as they made their way back to McKinney's.

'So, let me see now; let's find out more about the fight. You have two different descriptions of it: one says it was a bit of a lark; the other rated it high up on the brutal scale,' Hill offered, at the end of Doyle's summation.

'Correct and yes, that's what we need to ascertain. But we have to be careful how we go about it. At this stage no-one will be paying much attention to us paying attention to them so we can still probably creep around the bedroom without waking the wains. But at the point this moves up a peg or two and officially becomes serious, then just watch how quickly they all close ranks on us. Even now Valerie was blatantly lying about how close she and Wesley had been to the fight. No-one wants to be pointing the finger,' Doyle said, as he and Hill continued pacing down the pavement in the general direction of the widower McKinney's residence, which was a wee bit out on the Ballyronan Road.

'So, let's think about this; let's assume for argument's sake that the twins had a fight. OK?' Doyle theorised.

'Fine so far with me.'

'OK, so now we have to find out what sparked the fighting off. Was it a spur of the moment thing? Or was it something which had been brewing for as long as Old Man Patterson's mountain dew? It seems to me that there are three possible solutions to this, maybe four. But the fourth's too long a shot,' Doyle continued, his hands deep in his pockets with his jacket open, sides caught between either wrist and trouser pocket, while his tie blew freely in the wind.

'Four? I can think of three, yes, just the three,' Hill said.

The constable was excited about helping out the detective on a case. This was the first time it had happened and he found it hard to contain himself. So much so he wasn't, as usual, nervously picking his words with his superior. No, he was happily talking freely and, as it turns out, sensibly.

'And your three would be ....' the aforementioned superior quizzed as they passed Rogers & Daughters' Home Bakery. The smell of the freshly baked bread wafting out on the street was the best advertisement any of the shop traders possessed. People follow their belly and, as we all know, the belly has a great habit of following the nose.

'OK, so, one: they had a fight and Joe simply ran away to let things cool down, or to just get away 'cause he can't stand Pat any longer, or perhaps to punish Pat by leaving him to run the farm by himself for a while, and then maybe upon his return he would be able to get his own way with further threats of no labour. Two: they had a massive fight – before or after the fight on the field – and it led to Pat killing Joe, either by accident or on purpose, and he's buried the body. Or, three: he's found a woman and they're off somewhere practising the fiddler's elbow.'

'But there's still one more possibility, Hill,' Doyle continued seamlessly, 'Joe was down, sad, depressed even, according to his brother. He had just split up with this girlfriend, Doris Durin.'

'Oh, I know Doris – a friend of mine's elder brother went out with her; she's a bit tasty, sir.'

'Well then, there's your treat,' Doyle announced, 'after we see McKinney you can go and interview Doris, all by yourself.'

Hill smiled a huge grin.

'Let me see now,' Doyle continued, 'yes, as I was saying, he had split up with Doris Durin, he was down. It would appear Joe hadn't had many girlfriends. Pat had just married Maggie and was happy but was probably trying not to flaunt it. But equally he would not have been able to hide his happiness. So maybe, maybe, you know, Joe took his life. But there's one basic flaw to that solution.' Doyle paused at this point.

'Which is?'

'Well, simply, that we don't have a body; it's been three weeks since and if, heaven forbid, he's killed himself, I imagine someone would have found the body by now or at the very least a suicide note. So he's either gone AWOL or he's been murdered by person, or persons, unknown.'

'Or even murdered by his twin, sir.'

'Possibly, or possibly not.'

'Well they were seen fighting shortly before he disappeared.'

'Yes, but Maggie and Pat claim to have seen him after the fight,' Doyle cut in, impressed with how quickly Hill had taken on board all the facts. 'Now what if he was in trouble and Pat wouldn't help him and perhaps that's what the fight with Pat was about? Pat wouldn't help him get out of this trouble and left him to deal with the consequences on his own?'

'And the consequences were that, as you've already said, he was murdered by person or persons unknown,' Hill said.

'Exactly.'

'But surely then Pat would be more forthcoming with any information that would help us catch this person or persons unknown?'

'Well, not if in some way the trouble implicated either himself or his wife. Anyway, that's enough speculating for now – let's start amassing some hard facts,' Doyle suggested, as he knocked on Harry McKinney's door for the second time in as many days.

*

'So, you brought reinforcements with you this time,' McKinney announced, towering above them both, particularly Doyle. McKinney was tall, Doyle was short and McKinney was standing atop three high steps, which led into the narrow hallway of his house. They entered said house in ascending order of height, first Doyle then Hill, followed by McKinney.

'Sorry to disturb you yesterday evening,' Doyle offered as an opening.

'And so you should be – you might be the police, but God-fearing people have a right to their privacy,' McKinney offered sternly.

Doyle was about to get into it with him by saying that someone's life might be in danger and that those twelve hours of darkness may have been all he needed to save them. But, he argued with himself, McKinney was a man senior in his years and set in his ways. In the words of the song, he was too old to change and too young to die. So starting an argument with him, an argument where McKinney would use all the logic, answers and arguments he'd been making use of for his previous sixty-plus years, well, there was simply no point to it and nothing was going to come of it, except perhaps to antagonise a potential witness.

'Aye, Harry, as you say, there's always another day,' Doyle replied, accepting his chastisement graciously.

McKinney broke into a warm smile, appearing happy that the policeman had taken his hit on the chin. First blood easily went to the detective.

'Look, Harry, I don't want to waste too much of your time and it might all amount to nothing, but Joseph Kane has gone missing. Apparently you and your fellow harvest workers were amongst the last to see him.'

'Ah, the day of the scrap, don't you mean?' McKinney laughed.

'Yes, we'd heard something about that as well. What was it all about?' Doyle continued. He felt like he'd just sat down in the cinema and the movie had grabbed his attention in the opening thirty seconds and he knew he was going to be with it until the end. You know, no worrying about how hard the seats were, or the talking behind you, or the snogging in front of you, or even the noisy crisps or sweetie papers to your left and right. No, Doyle's eyes and ears would be committed, just as they were now committed to widower McKinney.

'Strangest thing. We were on a tea break and Joe's over with the Lone Ranger and Tonto, who are doing one of their routines, and Pat and Maggie are about fifteen yards away by one of the stacks having their tea. All of a sudden Pat screams at the top of his voice and comes galloping across the field like Lester Piggott and charges straight into Joe and they both fall to the ground in a heap of fists, feet and soil, knees and elbows and blood flying everywhere. Eventually they were torn apart. Pat came out of it the worst. He just wasn't able for his brother and if we all hadn't been there and the fight hadn't been stopped, I dread to think what would have happened,' McKinney recalled, obviously enjoying the hold he had over his willing audience.

'Did anyone know what it was all about? Had you seen it coming?' Doyle asked, annoyed that his voice was the noise to break the concentration of this unfolding epic.

'Listen to me, Inspector. Put one woman amongst two men and you are asking for trouble. There is no' – McKinney drew out the word 'no' into about three syllables – 'way that their situation was going to end in anything but tears.'

'Really?' Hill asked innocently.

'Really, lad. It wasn't a case of *if* the keg was going to blow, rather it was just a matter of *when*,' McKinney said, with all the confidence of the local clergy addressing their flock.

'So, did you see anything else which led you to believe that there was trouble up at the Kanes'?' Doyle was very happy to be hearing this information: whether it were true or gossip, it was still the kind of thing doing the rounds and somewhere in the middle of it all might be a hard fact, a straw for him to grasp at, which would point him in the correct direction.

Perhaps, Doyle thought, that's why he'd gotten so annoyed at Joan Cook. She was probably the biggest gossip in the village and it was she that was bringing him the news, news he didn't want to hear, news about – essentially – decent members of the community. He should have remembered the old saying 'There's no smoke without fire' before he nearly physically turfed her out of the station.

'Did Maggie say anything after the fight?'

'No, she took Pat into the house – Michael Gilmour helped her – and we never saw any of them again that day.'

'Did Michael say anything to any of you afterwards?' Doyle asked.

'No, in fact he seemed as shook up about it as Maggie; he went white as a sheet.'

'So up until this point, the point of the fight, Joe had been in good humour?'

'Yeah, as I said he was involved in the antics of those two clowns, Tonto and the geezer with sunglasses with holes in them,' McKinney replied, laughing at his own joke.

Chapter Thirty-Three

It was at this point in the initial investigation that Doyle split the team into two. He went to eat some humble pie with Joan Cook and he sent the young constable to interview Doris Durin.

*

'Oh, now, does this mean they've done away with Joe?' Joan Cook began as she opened her – well, actually, her ex–husband's – door to the inspector.

Doyle bit his lip and held his counsel.

'You see, I knew I was right. Oh, that poor man. Have you found him yet?' Joan whispered to the policeman on her doorstep. She half closed the door behind her leaving Doyle to believe she may have been doing a bit of entertaining herself. Most locals would have taken the police in, rather than be seen talking to them on the doorstep of their own house. But Joan seemed happy for this, in her mind, very public vote of confidence and would, no doubt, build it into her future gossip about the Kanes.

'Oh, let's see now, in answer to your question, no, not yet. But it would seem that Joseph is most definitely missing. I just wanted to see if you had any other information which may be of help to us. But if it's more convenient,' Doyle paused and looked at the half-closed door, 'I could come back at a later time.'

The inspector was convinced he'd heard someone creep down the stairs, which were only a few feet behind the door. Anyway, whatever – or whomever – it was, Mrs Cook's demeanour changed; it might have been simply the fact that she had made her point by having the detective calling at her door or maybe the fact that Doyle could have sworn that he heard the back door close – hell, maybe even a combination of both – but whatever the reason, she decided to invite Doyle into her house.

As he walked in, he immediately noted it was a very messy abode; in fact, there was not a single sign that Mrs Cook was house proud – the opposite was apparent, with most noticeably the half opened and staling loaf on the kitchen table. Doyle took one look at the stack of filthy cups in the kitchen sink and when he was offered a cup of tea he quickly, perhaps too quickly, refused. Her kitchen was so filthy he was convinced that any rats in residence were sure to wear aprons.

The draining board contained a few – five to be exact – empty Bass stout bottles and Joan was about to make it an even half dozen as she removed the cap of another with a bottle opener, which she found in her apron pocket, and poured it straight into a glass that she had briefly rinsed under the cold tap of the sink.

'You see, you could have saved yourself a lot of trouble and time if only you'd believed me the first time we talked.' She paused to afford herself a good mouthful of the stout. 'Goodness knows what she, or what she and Pat, have done with the body since.'

'Ah, come on, Mrs Cook, will you. I'm sure there's nothing like that going on.' Doyle tried to force a laugh, which came across as sincere as one of Hughie Green's 'And I mean that very sincerely, folks' retorts.

Joan Cook flashed WEE Doyle a knowing smile.

'Look, there's something afoot up there and I for one wouldn't be surprised if that Michael Gilmour, the matchmaker fellow, has something to do with it as well.'

'Michael? How so?'

'Well, you know, don't you, that he was trying to set up a match for Pat? Or maybe even the both of them. It was all very strange. He had me meet up with Pat. Did you know that?'

'Really?' Doyle feigned, omitting to mention that he'd clocked them on their 'date' in Bryson's.

'Oh, I've got your interest this time, do I?' Joan Cook gloated.

Doyle noted that her newly permed hair from her recent visit to the police station had now dissolved into more of a bird's nest than a groomed hairdo suitable for a matchmaking date.

'Are you sure about all of this?'

'I seem to remember you were in Bryson's the night the three of us met up.'

Doyle suddenly recalled fully the embarrassing – for Pat Kane, that was – episode.

'I told them I'd be nobody's skivvy. It seemed to me that they were just looking for someone to look after them. I told Pat it wasn't something I'd be interested in.'

Doyle unconsciously let his eyes wander around the kitchen and muttered 'obviously' under his breath.

'Well, come on, Inspector – you couldn't swing a cat in their small farmhouse and they never go out, the twins, do they? It's all work, work, work all the time, just to make ends meet. They only wanted me to help them with the work. And maybe even something else.' Joan gave the inspector a look which was usually accompanied by a blush. But Joan did not blush, not even a little bit. 'I'm quite liberal, I'll admit, but I'm certainly not up for threesomes, not in the way her ladyship was obviously up for it.'

Doyle's eyebrows involuntarily rose about half an inch. 'Surely not?'

'And wasn't she seen down at the Port gallivanting with the both of them? Wasn't she seen wearing a ginger wig when she was with Joe and her own locks when she was with Pat?'

'Sorry?' Doyle couldn't believe the can of worms he'd opened. It was like one of those sprung worms that clowns use in Duffy's Circus. When you released the lid and it uncoiled, well, you'd wonder how on earth you were ever going to get it all back into the same container. Doyle wasn't too sure whether this conversation had already gone too far as it was, but then he remembered what had happened the previous time he had cut Mrs Cook off.

'Oh yes ... a very good friend of mine saw the three of them – Pat, Maggie and Joe – down at the Port and she was sure as hell flaunting it. Brazen as brass. I mean, I can't believe it, can you? But then she did go to the tech and we all know what those girls are like, don't we?'

Doyle didn't, and even if he did he'd have refused to say. He didn't really know why, but he'd never really been attracted to girls, not at all in fact. Of course he'd wanted to, because he was aware of their beauty, but he had his life set up the way he wanted it: he had a great comfortable house, his prized books including a limited edition (not first editions mind you, his salary would never have stretched that far) set of the complete works of Arthur Conan Doyle, and he had a job which consumed what was left of his life. He often noticed the matchmaker eyeing him up, no doubt as a prospective client. But that whole route was far too unnatural for the detective. And what emotional, or physical, time he had left over to give to another person amounted to nothing more than a great big zero.

'But she's the matchmaker's sister-in-law – Michael wouldn't be involved in anything untoward,' Doyle found himself saying. He was uncomfortable – the *kitchen* was uncomfortable for him; the stale smell from the sink filled his nostrils and totally scundered him. The conversation was just as repulsive, which surely had a lot to do with the combination of gossip and innuendo. The main difference was that he would be able to get the stale smell to disappear with a few good wisps of clean air. But the conversation was eating its way into his brain as successfully as any of Roddy Yates' red-hot branding irons. There it would remain for at least the rest of this case and probably a good time beyond as well.

'Anything *un-to-ward!* Away with you, Inspector, you're too naive for your own good. Sure, he'd even make a match for his wife if the price was right. And don't get me started on his wife now – she's nothing more than mutton dressed as lamb. Sure, what does a mother of three want to go around showing off her legs in a mini-skirt for, and figure hugging tops, eh? You answer me that!'

'So what happened up at the farm then?' Doyle asked, ignoring the slight on the matchmaker's wife. He prayed for Pat's forgiveness as he asked the unforgivable question.

'Well, it's simple, isn't it? It doesn't take Detective Sergeant Lockhart to work it out for you, does it? She moves in with the both of them. Then she gets a wee bit too cosy with one of them, i.e. Pat. There's one too many in the new cosy nest and there's no hiding place for Joe, so they do away with him. And Pat and Maggie live happily ever after.'

'But where's the body?'

'Oh, we'll leave that wee bit of detective work to yourself, shall we? Who knows? They cut him in the Moyola, they cut him up into little bits and fed him to the cattle. They buried him: he'll help to fertilise next year's crops. I don't know, that's your job, isn't it?' Joan Cook replied, berating the detective.

Five minutes later the same detective was seen lingering on the footpath outside Rogers & Daughters' bakery, just so he could refill his nostrils with some pleasant scents. As expected, he was now haunted by a burning vision of Maggie and Pat Kane doing away with Joe Kane, in three separate and quite possible scenarios.

Chapter Thirty-Four

The other half of the team currently working on the Kane case was having an altogether more pleasant time with Doris Durin.

Constable Edward Hill felt a little self-conscious in his stiff black uniform with the light-green, not quite lime, shirt and black tie. It was hardly the way he would have chosen to turn out to impress a girl, and an older girl at that, like Doris Durin. However, she made him feel most welcome at her mother's house and immediately took him into the sitting room where she showed him to the sofa and disappeared 'for some refreshments'. Hill was sure, although he wouldn't have sworn to it, that when she returned her make-up had been touched up. Her fiery red hair had definitely been rearranged. She had released it from the black elasticated band, which had restrained it in a bunch at the back. Now her mane fell like flames warming up her cheeks.

'You were in the class a year behind me at school, weren't you?' Doris announced upon her return with a tray filled with a coffee pot, milk jug, sugar bowl, two cups and two saucers, all a very light blue with one white band towards the top. Hill detected this service to be her own for her personal use – he was sure that the mother of the house would have the more traditional white china service, or if not white then perhaps white with some red flowers. He also noted that the absence of any plates containing biscuits or cakes tallied with Doris' slim, but full, figure.

'Why, yes,' the young policeman replied, flattered that someone as stunning as Doris Durin would have noticed him. He supposed the other way he could have taken the remark was that she was making a claim to superiority, but he gave himself the benefit of the doubt.

When you are at school and a girl is a year older than you, it is a frightful thing, but these few years later it was altogether more exciting.

'You used to go out with my best friend's older brother.'

'Oh, who would that have been?' She smiled.

'Ivan Smart.'

'I don't ever remember going out with Ivan Smart.'

'No, I didn't mean Ivan – I mean his brother, Alexander.'

'That squirt!' she exploded in a friendly squeal. 'No, not guilty. He used to pester me all the time, send me wee notes and all that, but no, no and no. Sure hasn't he got a face like the moon? Craters everywhere.'

Edward Hill laughed loud and heartily. He liked this woman – he liked her honest way.

'God, I can't believe that. No, I'm sorry, of course I can believe that you never went out with him but I can't believe the lies he told us about all the times he went out with you.'

'And all the things we got up to together, I suppose?' Doris smiled impishly.

Hill blushed.

'I thought so. You know, if all the boys' boasts about the girls of Castlemartin were true, McKay's the chemists couldn't have possibly kept enough packets-of-three in stock.'

They both had a good giggle at that one. Once again Doris was captivating someone with her raunchy, infectious laugh.

When the laughter subsided, Hill reluctantly began the interview.

'I've come to talk to you about Joseph Kane.'

'Yes, I've heard the talk around town – he's gone missing or something, hasn't he?'

'Well that's exactly what we're investigating,' Hill boasted proudly.

He realised his job, as well as asking his interviewee questions, was to observe exactly how she answered them. This might prove to be difficult because Edward Hill, seeing Doris Durin dressed in her red figure-hugging slacks, simple white blouse and black slip-ons barely hiding her white bobby socks, was transfixed by this vision of smouldering innocence and was slowly, but surely, falling hopelessly in love with her.

'And you've heard that Joe and I were courting for a while, haven't you?' Doris teased.

'Well, yes. But listen, it's not that we feel you ....'

'No, no, but of course not.'

'When did you last see him?' Hill ventured forth with an official police-type of question.

'Let's see ... about two and a half weeks ago. Yes, three Saturdays ago we all went up to the Port,' Doris replied.

'And who would *all* be?'

'There was Maggie and Pat and Joe and myself.'

'And why did you go to the Port?'

'For a bit of fun, Edward – haven't you heard girls like to have a bit of fun every now and then?'

Constable Edward Hill was well aware that this was the new way of thinking but decided he would make himself appear to be more sophisticated should he just take it for the norm.

'Of course. And how did he seem?'

'Well, to be quite honest we had a blistering row. More as like I had the row – Joe, as ever, was quiet and broody,' Doris replied.

'You say you rowed – I mean, he didn't hit you or anything like that?' Hill enquired, hoping that 'or anything like that' would include any female matters, which he felt too uncomfortable to mention.

'No, no, nothing like that at all. I didn't have a motive to murder him, if that's where you're trying to go with it,' Doris replied, shifting her weight. She was sitting on a large brown sofa with white piping, her legs caught up under her. Her right hand held the coffee cup with the lightest of grips, so much so it appeared as though it was floating, hovering next to her mouth, waiting impatiently for the next time her beautiful, full red lips would make another mark on its surface. Her other hand was stretched the length of her body, clasping her ankle. Hill felt she was warning him off with her posture, but then maybe he was reading too much into this particular Desmond Morris *Naked Ape* pose.

'Now, if we had thought that, then I'm sure you're well aware it would have been District Detective Inspector Doyle who'd be sitting here questioning you, no?' Hill offered, trying to lighten things up somewhat.

'Yes, I'm sure. But I'm also sure the straw I drew isn't the shortest.'

She smiled her impish smile and once more broke into her throaty laugh. He felt like putty in her hands when she said things like that. And he knew he was a policeman and policemen were not meant to go falling for the first – the very first – witness they were sent to question.

'So the row?' Hill asked. He considered adding more to the question but decided to leave it hanging there. His vagueness may, he hoped, encourage her to open up.

'Well, Edward, it's like this you see … I started off wanting the relationship to work – I mean, I really did. They say there is someone out there waiting for you and I'm afraid I can't agree with that. So I had decided that I would lower my limits as it were, maybe settle for something which, while not perhaps perfect, was worth trying for. And along came Joe. We met – well, a friend of mine introduced us – and we hit it off pretty much immediately. I mean, it never was a terrible relationship or anything like that; it's just that it never went anywhere. It wasn't getting better. He wasn't slowly revealing himself to be this "perfect man". I'm not saying that he was the opposite or anything like that, but you expect, not unreasonably I think, that it … that the relationship is going to go somewhere. It's not that you're paying for an exciting bus ride, but you do want to make sure the darned bus at least starts up.' Doris paused to drain the dregs from her coffee cup.

Hill gallantly poured her some more and she patted his hand gently as he did so, sending a shock of electricity up his arm, across his shoulder and straight into his heart just like a cannonball.

'Joe wanted to have a relationship more just for the sake of wanting to be in a relationship. At the same time he made it perfectly clear that he neither knew nor cared about putting any effort into making a relationship work. It was like: it's here, we're in a relationship, let's just get on with it. I mean, he was just as obvious in the physical side as well, in that he was kind and attentive before, but bored and always restless afterwards,' Doris continued.

Hill couldn't believe it: here he was and this beautiful girl had, in so many words, admitted to him that she had gone the whole way with someone. Joe Kane was the lucky man, in fact, and it had all clearly happened before she was married. The young constable still couldn't help feeling shocked at that. Yes, he was aware that there were a few village bikes, but none of them could compare with Doris Durin. So what was wrong? Why had someone as beautiful as Doris had to do that to keep a man? If he'd had the courage to ask Doris this question, she'd have said something about wanting to be sure before she married and also why not have a bit of fun in the meantime? Men were not to have a monopoly on fun, well, at least not as far as Doris Durin and a few of her classmates were concerned. 'So it all came to a head down at Portrush did it?' Hill probed, as he refused to allow himself to dwell on such thoughts.

'Well, yes. I mean, Edward, it was really frustrating for me. It should have been a blissful time: here I was with Joe and he's a bit of all right. I've always thought that, you know, since our time in the tech. I remember I used to think he was deep, dark and mysterious and I'd never be able to get to know someone as cool as him. And then you do and at first, because of your earlier opinions, it's great and then you begin to find out that he's not deep, he's shallow, in fact, and then you discover that he's not dark—'

'What? He dyes his hair?' Hill asked and then blushed, realising the only way she'd really know the answer to that.

'No, no, you sweet man! *Dark*, as in possessing demons and revolutionary thoughts and being wild, but Joe's none of those things. It's like he's the day time and it appears that Pat turns out to be the night time. And it took Maggie Watson to discover it. Mind you, I think Joe's got a bit of a thing for Maggie on the QT. You should see the way he looks at her sometimes. Anyway, I was in a bit of a mood myself and so I started pushing him, just to see whether there was anything else there and whether he was really interested in trying to find a way of making the relationship work. And do you know what he said?' Doris asked.

'No?'

'Well, of course you wouldn't, not unless you and Doyle were down at the Port spying on me.'

'Of course not!' Hill began, then realised that the rise was being taken out of him.

'Good, glad we got that straight. Well, he said he thought it *was* working. Now, that one simple reply showed me the extent of how much it *wasn't* working and so I realised that it was a lost cause, a hopeless case.'

'Were you annoyed at him?'

'Well, naturally you want him to be so head over heels in love with you that he'll do anything for you and anything to be with you. And it's not like he's not seeing it going on around him – you know, Pat and Maggie are so into each other. There's a couple who would do anything for each other. And it's so obvious you'd think Joe should see it.' Doris stopped for a few seconds; she sighed as if accepting that was it. 'So I told him in no uncertain terms what a woman wants, expects and needs from her man, if only to make sure that at least his next girlfriend will stand a better chance. But that's maybe unfair, you know; Joe's not the only one – a lot of the men around this town are the same. They get themselves a new girlfriend like they get a new suit or a scooter, and then they end up doing all the things they're supposed to, like meeting the parents, getting engaged, getting married and having children, and then they realise there is absolutely nothing there *emotionally* for them. The only difference is that you can at least always buy a new suit or a new Vespa. Wives, however, are meant to last forever. But forever seems to be fast becoming a very short time indeed; some people, in point of fact, now seem to be able to fit three forevers into their one lifetime,' Doris said, as Hill flashed her a sympathetic smile.

'And Joe, you know, that's the sad thing; I bet Joe would have eventually wanted to get married and have children and then he'd have woken up one day and felt he was trapped. Then he would only have come near me when he'd have a pint of two, or he would have to beat me up weekly as his only way of expressing his frustration. He was shocked at me, at the fact that I was disappointed in our relationship as it was. He was annoyed that I wasn't prepared to accept what he was giving as being the "happy ever after package". He appeared to be listening to me and taking it all in, but then he just said nothing. And I mean *nothing* at all, Edward. He just turned and walked away. So I came home by myself and there's not been sight nor sound of him since.

'Then this chat started to go around the town that he was missing and at first I wondered if it had anything to do with me – you know, with me giving him a piece of my mind. Or maybe his disappearance had something to do with me walking out on him. And you know what – I'd even worked out what I was going to say should he come to see me again,' Doris continued.

The police constable leaned off his seat – matching brown and cream to her sofa – towards her, suggesting that he wanted to know exactly what she would have said, but because it was for personal reasons he dared not ask.

'I would have told him, gently, to look elsewhere. Initially I think he could have got me because I was *looking* for someone and I might have gone along with the flow. But I realised up at the Port, my reasons were all the wrong ones and I was lucky to have escaped. Better a wasted weekend at the Port than a lifetime on a dingy farm. Look, that's probably unfair – Maggie has worked wonders on the house since she moved in. But there's not going to be room for one more person, so Joe or Pat and Maggie are going to have to seek alternative accommodation whenever Joe finds his lady. Maybe that's what's happened. Have you thought of that? Maybe Joe didn't want to play happy families any more and is bitter about Pat finding someone while he couldn't, and so just to get a bit of his own back, he's not told anyone where he's gone, knowing his unexplained absence is going to make it very difficult for Pat and Maggie?' Doris said, suggesting another scenario to add to the short list Inspector Doyle had already made in his notebook.

Constable Edward Hill closed his own notebook.

'That'll do for now,' he began, finding himself, now that his official duty was at a close, awkward with his words. 'I'll trouble you no more.'

'No trouble, Edward. I have to admit I quite enjoyed talking to you about it. I mean, I talked because I have to, you being the police and all, but I was *happy* to have to talk about it. I haven't discussed this with anyone before, and it probably would have been better for me if I had. But now, here, voicing it all to you, it's kinda like putting the final wraps on it. You know, tying up the loose ends so that I can move on to the next thing.'

'You sound as though you know what the next thing is going to be,' he found himself saying as he rose from the chair.

'Oh,' and again she flashed him her impish smile, 'something's come up quite recently – I'm just going to have to wait and see how – no, not how, but if, yes *if* it develops into anything.'

Constable Edward Hill felt quite happy with himself as he walked back up the Broadway towards the Station House. All things considered, his first interview had gone quite well, he thought. He'd made a few observations he planned to pass on to his superior. On another front, the smitten constable felt that after their current meeting the next time he passed Doris Durin in the street with her red hair following in the lough winds, he'd have an excuse to stop and talk to her. Hell, if such a meeting took place when he wasn't on duty, he might even pick up the courage to ask her out for a coffee or a drink or a movie. He hoped he would 'accidentally' bump into her sooner rather than later, or at least before the police managed to discover the whereabouts of Joseph Kane. He tried not to think about the possibility of Joe returning and getting back together with Doris before he'd a chance of asking her out. He took some comfort from the fact that, due to the lack of current leads on the case, it looked like it was going to be a long time before any of the locals set eyes on Joe again.

If indeed they ever did.

Chapter Thirty-Five

Doyle didn't want to admit it, even to himself, but he was on an investigation: the first real one of his career. He did, however, admit to himself that a part of him didn't want Joe to 'turn up', just so he could have an, albeit temporary, missing person's case. However, he took comfort in the fact that only a small part of him wished for this outcome.

He and Hill then regrouped, exchanged information and headed off to see the man who might – if one were to take a grain of truth from Mrs Joan Cook's statement – have been the person who, unknowingly, with his attempts at matchmaking, had set off the entire the chain of events that had resulted in Joseph Kane's current 'missing' status.

Whether they had caught the matchmaker at an irritable moment or whether he'd thought his business with the police on this case was done, Michael Gilmour made both officers feel very unwelcome.

Doyle was somewhat rattled by this and went straight in at the deep end. 'So you didn't tell me that Pat Kane had come to you to do a bit of matchmaking for him.'

The matchmaker studied them both, mentally rubbing his chin. He looked like he was assessing whether the magnitude of his impatience should be in direct proportion to the length and detail of his answer. 'Don't you see,' he started, cleverly adopting the persona of his chosen profession, 'that there are two professions of people that one needs to remain discreet: those two people are your priest and your matchmaker. I mean, don't you think my business would disappear down the plughole if a potential client thought *his* business was going to be discussed with the entire village? People have to have absolute confidence in you, even if you don't manage to make a match for them. Which was the case, I can assure you, with Pat,' the matchmaker stated defensively.

They were in his professionally used sitting room and Michael had given a prearranged signal (of loosening his tie) to his wife that no tea or coffee was required, thereby advising her that he hoped it was going to be a short meeting.

Doyle had other ideas. 'Well now, don't you see, if it is relevant to this case then I wouldn't like to have to be charging you with withholding information,' Doyle announced.

'Don't come any of that old clap-trap with me, Colin. Don't forget I know you – I knew your parents. I say, I knew your parents. You asked me questions, I gave you answers. That is where my obligation begins and ends. It's not my fault that you didn't ask all the pertinent questions you now feel you should have,' the matchmaker replied, rising to the bait. He shifted uncomfortably in his chair, crossing his legs and arms.

Doyle discreetly nodded to Hill to take up the questioning and was very impressed with the speed of his response.

'Look, it's like this, you see,' Hill started. 'Joe Kane has gone missing, OK? We're trying to find him. There is a good possibility that he may be alive and well and just keeping his head down. Sadly, there is an equal chance that he may be in great danger or even, heaven forbid, already dead. It is our duty, and responsibility, to amass as much information about the missing person in as short a time as possible in order, hopefully, to help them. If it turns out we are too late to help him then it becomes our responsibility to track down and bring to justice the person, or persons, unknown who committed the crime,' Hill continued, borrowing more than a little from the manuals offered to anyone thinking of changing from police work to detective work. A change he was, in fact, dreaming of. He licked his dry lips before continuing. 'So, you see, we need to be made aware of every little thing that went on in Joe's life in order to assess the situation.'

'That's all very well, young man. Fair play to you. I'll sleep easier at night knowing that. Equally I have to tell you it is not my business to tell you Pat's business.' Michael made his last statement sound final, very final indeed.

'Am, Doris Durin told us,' Constable Hill, the man still on a mission continued, 'that Joe was very fond of Maggie.'

'Hey, what can I tell you? His brother was married to her. The quality of Joe's life has certainly changed for the better since Maggie moved in. You'd also be on his case if the town gossips were saying that Maggie and Joe *didn't* get on. She's now part of the family, so why wouldn't he like her?' the matchmaker replied.

'Yes, Michael, but there's liking and then there's *liking*,' Doyle rejoined, wringing every last drop out of the italics.

'Now listen, lads, that's my wife's sister you are talking about and don't forget the laws are there to protect us as well prosecute us, so I would advise you to be careful.'

'Michael, we're not on a mission – we just want to find out where Joe's gone,' Doyle offered in his best 'you know me' voice.

'Well, I wish I could help you because his disappearance has certainly become an annoyance, to all of this family, what with all the village tongues running riot. And when you do find him make sure you ask him why he's run off like this, knowing the trouble he'd cause. But as to where he is or what he's doing, well, I'm afraid I can't help you with that, much as I'd like to.'

As far as Michael Gilmour was concerned the meeting was over and he rose to his feet to ensure the members of the local constabulary were also aware of this fact.

Chapter Thirty-Six

'Well there's nothing like a warm welcome,' Doyle said, as they hit the street outside the matchmaker's house, 'and that was definitely nothing like a warm welcome.'

Doyle couldn't resist the habit of a lifetime and turned back to look into the window of the house they had just left. He saw the matchmaker's eldest son, Paul, studying them from behind the curtains. 'I suppose it's about time we paid another visit to Pat and Maggie then,' he announced as he led them left into Apple Orchard Lane; from there they would take a right into Railway Terrace, clockwise around Pear Tree Roundabout, left up into the Broadway, past the Station House and then just directly opposite Moore's Railway Inn they would take a right into Noah's Arc and then a quick left up Kane's Lane to the farm. It was a pleasant day for such a walk; summer was nearly over, but the coldness of autumn was yet to arrive.

'Now there's a thing,' Doyle announced, as they turned into Kane's Lane only to find the matchmaker's son Paul riding his bicycle towards them and away from the farm. 'Boy, he must have been quick – he'd have to have gone the whole way down Apple Orchard Lane, right into Garden Street, straight across the Broadway into Shore Drive, left up the Lough Road, first right into Noah's Arc and right into this lane.'

'Do you think Michael Gilmour sent him with a message?' Hill asked. 'Or is it just a coincidence?'

'There is no such thing as a coincidence,' Doyle announced, quoting the master. 'I'd say it was a written message. He wouldn't want his son to be involved in all these shenanigans. He probably had him watch us as he wrote the letter. Once they'd worked out which way we were going to get here, he sent his son by the southern route – longer, yes, but then Paul had the bike and much younger legs than ours. Well, let's see what kind of greeting we receive here, shall we?' Doyle said in a change of tone as he knocked loudly on the farmhouse's front door.

The greeting which Maggie Kane afforded the police was a warm and generous one. Not many farmers come home to a vision as beautiful as this one, Hill thought, as Maggie opened with 'Good day to you both, won't you come on in off the doorstep? What can I do for you today?'

'Good day to you, Mrs Kane. This is Constable Edward Hill and we've come to talk to you and your husband some more about Joe,' Doyle answered, as Maggie led them into the kitchen.

The smell which hit them as they entered the room was as good as a dozen walks past Rogers & Daughters' Home Bakery on the Lough Road. Maggie was obviously preparing lunch and had four large wheaten farls on the hearth rising to perfection. Meanwhile, she had a large pot of what looked, and smelt, like potato soup simmering to a peak atop the fire.

'Please take a seat and make yourselves comfortable. I'll do youse a cup of tea when I tend to my cooking here,' the farmer's wife said, wiping her hands on her apron for the second time since they'd arrived. The first time, Doyle noted, was probably to remove any flour before she shook his and Hill's hands. But was the second wipe to remove any contamination she may have received through the handshaking?

Close to the soup pot Maggie had a board of ingredients such as scallion leaves, onions, a little garlic and a few, Doyle counted eighteen, peas. The senior policeman found it very funny that someone would put so few peas into a large pot of soup.

Bit by bit Maggie added her secrets to the pot, stirring gently all the time, a few strokes clockwise and a few strokes in reverse. Occasionally she would break, always with a clean of her hands on her apron – once to put on the kettle, a second to remove the wheaten farls from the hot plate and a third to prepare the cups and saucers and milk in anticipation of the water coming to the boil. When it did, she applied a little of the hot water to the already rinsed-out teapot, swirled it around a few times and then deposited the hot water from the bottom of the kettle into the kitchen sink. Maggie now added three spoons of tea to the pot and then hesitated for a split second before adding another half spoon for luck. The boiling water was now applied to the teapot and a tea cosy was placed over the shining white vessel to let the tea draw.

During all of this preparation the three engaged only in small talk: about the village and the weather and how good the summer had been, and wasn't it sad now that it was over. Hill was transfixed by the woman as she moved effortlessly about her chores. Doyle couldn't help notice how intensely his junior was staring at the farmer's wife.

Was that what all of this was about? The beauty of this woman? Could she be so beautiful that she had driven two brothers – twin brothers at that – to bicker, to anger, to fight – hell, maybe even to murder? Doyle's problem was that he had so long since given up noticing women in that particular way that he hadn't even accepted this as a possibility. Not until now, that is, when he saw the effect Maggie Kane was having on Edward Hill.

Had Maggie Kane, *née* Watson, always had this effect on men? Doyle had seen her around the village over the years with this boy and that boy and then with this man and that man, but he'd never been aware, or told, that she was anything special. And if she had been special, then how come it had taken so long for her to have been 'snapped up', as the housewives say when they are gossiping by the grocery counter in Walter's Grocery and Hardware Store directly across the Broadway from the police station?

Or was it just possible that when women fall in love and marry they transform into these mystical beings who are beyond the logic, but not the attraction, of men. Oh, Doyle thought, men and women, and as he looked upon one of the finest of the other sex, he thought – for the first time in years – that perhaps he'd been hasty in giving up on the gentler pursuits all those years ago. He was amused that it had taken the possibility of a woman being so extraordinary that she may have caused one brother to kill another for him to consider such an opinion.

'Where's Pat?' Doyle enquired.

'Oh, he's tending to the cattle at the moment – he'll be in for his lunch shortly. Unless you're in too big a hurry to wait for him, of course – then I'll be happy to go fetch him?' Maggie replied.

'Well, let me see now, we do have a few other calls we need to make – perhaps I'll go and have a chat with him and leave you in the able company of my constable,' Doyle replied, rising from the table, annoyed that he was going to miss a cup of coffee but happy that he would get the chance to speak to Pat away from the company of his wife.

'Fine, Detective, but you'd better borrow those wellies by the back door – they're Joe's and they'll save your grand shoes and fine trousers from all the muck,' Maggie offered.

In two minutes the detective had changed footwear as directed and was looking every bit the country squire as he exited the back door.

He left his constable to indulge in not only the tea, but also a large piece of hot wheaten, so hot in fact that when he applied the butter to it – in large chunks – it melted into the heart of the wheaten immediately. Tea and hot wheaten bread by itself would have been perfect, but Maggie then went and spoilt him completely by giving him a little bowl of the magical brew of soup. It tasted so delicious that Hill did not want to swallow one drop of it. No, he just wanted to keep the lovely liquid in his mouth forever, savouring every single droplet. Fanny Cradock had nothing Maggie Kane couldn't do, and do better.

Five minutes later and Doyle was with Pat Kane who was, as his wife had predicted, tending the cattle by cleaning out the shed – a smelly and strenuous job, Doyle thought. It was obvious to the policeman that neither the smells nor the back-breaking work were a problem for Pat. To the farmer it was merely the smell of his cattle, a smell he had lived with all his life and, as Pat advised Doyle when he saw the policeman's nose take a turn heaven-wise, 'Ah, now, listen to me – there's beauty in this as well. You see all those beautiful roses of Maggie's around the back garden? Well, each and every one of those flowers owes their beauty to my fine cattle and their by-products.' Pat had a right old chuckle to himself on that one.

'True, true,' Doyle replied, as he manoeuvred his feet into a position where they weren't continuously sinking into the mire. He was concerned that, because the boots were too big for his feet, should he sink too deep then he might find his sock-soled foot leaving the wellies in their natural habitat. 'I also love a nice tender piece of chicken breast baked till it melts on your teeth, but that doesn't mean I'm going to chase those obnoxious little birds around the farmyard, craving their feathers!'

'Quite, Inspector,' Pat replied, as he carefully hung his pitchfork on two pegs on the inside of the corrugated iron shed. He walked towards Doyle, hands in pockets. 'However, I'm sure you've not come here to discuss your fantasies, no matter how close to earth they may be.'

'Exactly, Pat. This Joe thing – I have to tell you, the more I talk to people the more concerned I'm becoming.'

'Jeez, he's my brother, it's been a few weeks now – don't you think I'd like to know where he is too? Don't you think I'd like to wring his flippin' neck for all this grief he's been causing myself and, particularly, Maggie?'

'But, Pat—'

'But Pat nothing. Do you know what it's like for us to go into the village now? All the tut-tutting we've had to put up with, all the nudge-nudging and all the old biddies who should know better, coming on holier than thou – they'd be better spending their time finding out who their men are chasing at the local dances than concerning themselves with me and my wife. It's all so horrible. Maggie walks into a shop and gradually the conversation stops, and she turns and walks out, whereupon they all start to talk and buzz louder than before she entered. And it's simple: we haven't done anything. My brother, my dear brother, with all his non-communicative problems, has dropped us right in it. He was happy to be the one to always whisper in my ear – "do this", "do that", "ask them this", "ask them that", "find out if *blah blah*", but to leave me to be the one to deal with the village busy-bodies, particularly after the death of our parents …' Pat continued in a rant, although he managed to resist shouting.

Doyle put his questions to the back of his mind; he thought that now Pat was letting his anger out at last, perhaps he'd give something away.

'It's as simple as this, Inspector: I can't live his life – it's just that simple. I hope you're listening to me: I – can't – live – his – life. Heavens, it's so hard, nearly even impossible, to live your *own* life, pushing yourself all the time – how on earth can I live a life for a man who doesn't want to be involved in the world? I tell you, it was such a burden at the tech. I thought when we left the technical college that maybe, for the first time, we'd, you know, develop our own groups of friends, our own sets of interests. At the very least I thought it would be healthy and stimulating for the pair of us to come home and have discussions about all these new things and these amazing new people. But every time I turned, Joe would be at my shoulder, soaking up all I was taking in. I know this all probably sounds very callous to you, but I really want to like and be mates with my twin brother – not because he's my twin, or brother, or a member of my family, but because he's an interesting and stimulating person. But how can he be all that when all he wants to be is my bleedin' clone?'

Pat sat down on a bale of hay and pulled out a few strands before continuing.

'I kept thinking, is this really all there is to the big twin thing? I thought it was meant to be special, you know, being a twin? But from Joe's point of view I think he thinks it's about not feeling complete as a person unless you are with the other pea from your pod. Feck that for a life. I want a life of my own. I've carried him like a monkey on my back for much too long now. And I'm fed up of being polite to all of youse about the fact that he is missing. Hey listen, I've been missing as well you know; I've been missing the first twenty-nine years of my life and then I was found. A beautiful woman called Maggie Watson found me and saved me. And if part of the price to pay for Maggie finding and saving me was that Joe was going to "lose" himself just because he couldn't hack it any more 'cause I'm not around to live his life for him, well then I'm sorry but he's just going to have to accept the fact that he's lost. And once he knows he's lost, then perhaps he'll be able to start to put it all together again. Well not even "again", 'cause he's never been together in the first place. But maybe he'll be found by someone and they'll put it together and everything will be OK,' Pat said as he wove the strands of hay together.

Doyle watched him do this as he tried, unsuccessfully, to work out the method of his weave. The detective thought of saying something now but he felt Pat had more to add so he kept quiet, which turned out to be the right thing to do, as eventually the twin spoke again.

'You know what I'd really like?' he said, as he flung the failed weave down into the mire. 'What I'd really like is for Joe to find someone and go off and have a life and a family of his own, and then for us to start to deal with each other again as equals, not as competing twins. You know, twins who are meant to be in tune with each other's thoughts all the time. Of course, I knew what was on his mind all the time when we were growing up – he let me do all his thinking for him, didn't he? But if he'd his own family and interests and stories and yarns and jokes and I'd mine, then when we got together it would be a bit of a family hoot, wouldn't it? And that's what it's *meant* to be. But you know Joe's problem is he just doesn't *try*, and that's the sad fact. And it's probably partly my fault because I've always been there to do it for him before. You know what, with that wee girl Doris Durin? Gorgeous girl and really interested in Joe and I thought, you know, this could work; she seemed to really want it to work. But he just couldn't be bothered to put any time or attention or care into building a relationship with her. It was as if, OK, this is it, let's get on with it. And I'm thinking "Hello in there – is anybody in there paying attention? You're going to blow this great chance but don't be blaming me because it's all your own fault." And surprise, surprise when Doris found out, like I had, that Joe wanted me, or maybe in her case he wanted *her*, to do all the living and thinking for him, she was off. And you know what? I loved her for it. I loved her no-nonsense approach and maybe if I'd done the same around the time we were in the tech we wouldn't be having all these problems now.'

Pat paused for a few seconds as his face creased into a large smile.

'I was just thinking there,' the twin continued in the airy shed, 'of a time when we were nine – it was a May afternoon and no-one could find Joe and, as the evening wore on, Mum and Dad started to become worried. The three of us were out looking in all the sheds and all the ditches. It started to get dark and I wandered over to one of the paths I knew my parents had already looked up. And up in the top meadow there is this great chestnut tree with low branches and I decided to just go there – I don't really know why, I just ended up there, even though, as I say, my parents had already looked in that part of the farm. So I go to this tree and I climb up into the branches, the sun is going down and so I think I might get a better look at the surrounding fields to see if I could spot Joe. And who's in the bleedin' tree already but our Joe. He's just sitting there. And I say to him, "Mum and Dad were already up here looking for you." And he says, "I know, I saw them, but I wasn't lost, I was just waiting for you to come along and bring me home." I mean, can you believe that? And he's probably somewhere out there in the world – not lost, but waiting for me to find him again and bring him home.'

'Does he think you know where he is?' Doyle spoke for the first time in ages, thinking that this was just the saddest thing he'd ever heard.

Pat looked at the detective with a face that implied the officer hadn't listened to a word he'd been saying. 'Here's the sad thing, Inspector. *I don't care where he is.* And I certainly have no interest in finding him. I'll obviously be eternally grateful to yourself should you find him, because it will get all the village gossips from our back. But apart from that, it really is of no concern to me now. I have a life I have found, a life I might have a chance with if I put some energy and work into it. And I'm certainly going to give it my best shot, because with Maggie I now have a reason for my life and I'm certainly not going to waste any more of it. And speaking of Maggie, I'm sure I can smell her special soup – so it must be coming up to lunchtime.'

And with that they were off down the lane as quick as their legs would carry them. Doyle collected his junior at the back farmhouse door and Maggie and Pat, hand in hand and so obviously in love, bade them goodbye.

*

Halfway down Kane's Lane, Doyle said: 'I couldn't believe how much you stared at Maggie when we first went into the house.'

'But I couldn't believe it, I just couldn't believe it,' Hill replied in disbelief.

'Couldn't believe what?'

'Couldn't believe how similar Maggie Kane and Doris Durin looked – they could be sisters. Doris looks slightly younger, has flaming ginger hair and, personally speaking, has it for me, but basically it's like looking at the same woman,' Hill said, as he gently smiled to himself.

'Interesting … very interesting,' Doyle replied, realising where Joan Cook's report of Maggie wearing a red wig up at the Port had come from. He was happy now to be back in his brogues and moving at a more comfortable pace. 'You know what the other interesting thing is?'

'Yes?' Hill nudged, meaning 'no'.

'Did you notice when we arrived first at the farm, you know, and we announced that it was to speak about Joe?'

'Yes?'

'Well shouldn't her first question have been something like, "Have you found him?"'

Chapter Thirty-Seven

Then District Detective Inspector Doyle had a great idea. 'The obvious is so simple, and you always miss it because it's staring you in the face,' he announced to Constable Edward Hill as they entered the police station at 10 a.m. the following Monday morning to report for duty. 'OK, let me think now. If we're to believe Maggie and Pat, Joe left the house of his own accord three weeks ago last Sunday,' he continued.

'Correct.'

'And he left – if we are to believe the couple – just at the crack of dawn, because by the time they got up Joe was already gone.'

'Correct,' Hill replied. He hoped an occasional and well-placed 'correct' would be sufficient as his contribution to this investigation until he'd had, at least, his first cup of tea of the day.

'So, who else is up at the crack of dawn?'

'Unfaithful husbands,' Hill replied with a wry grin.

'Funny, and quite possibly true, but not who I was thinking of. No, I was thinking of the milkman, Mattie Stewart.'

'Of course!'

'So let's forget all this tea and coffee stuff for now and go and track down Mattie and buy ourselves a decent pint of fresh milk and put a little healthy liquid in our bodies,' Doyle announced as he led his junior down the steps of the Station House and out onto the Broadway.

Mattie Stewart was the legendary four-fingered, two-thumbed milkman of the district since probably before the year dot – there had been no-one but Mattie around before that time to testify any differently. No, since absolutely forever, Mattie, with Tommy, his trusted piebald pony, and solid cart had served milk to the locals of Magherafelt and

Castlemartin 364 days of the year. He even managed to fit in a double run on Christmas Eve. For a man with so few fingers, he was known for using under-arms, under-hands, and the occasional sky hook, to carry as many as seven pint bottles of milk at once. Rain or sunshine, snow or sleet, Mattie was always there with his faithful band of helpers; helpers whose only reward was a quick ride on the cart.

Mattie always left a crate-free space at the centre back of the cart for the helpers. He never moaned, he never groaned, he simply always had a warm smile for either side of the street. Mattie smiled most when the local horticulturists, and there was a growing number, came out on the street following the piebald with a bucket and shovel in search of Tommy's warm waste, which brought a decent flush to their roses or rhododendrons or whatever.

Yes, sure enough his piebald and he were the perfect team. Having worked together for so long, they both knew each other's habits and the pony would set off to the next stop, maybe a few houses away, maybe even a few streets away, with a click of Mattie's tongue. Mattie did so much tongue clicking on his round that by the end of his round … well … let's just say he'd developed quite a dry mouth. So dry in fact that a stop off in the pub for a pint or three (or four) on the way home was not out of the question.

It was also quite customary to see, around 3:30 in the afternoon, the faithful piebald pony head home, hauling the cart, now filled with crates of empty milk bottles, and Mattie fast asleep in the back on the helper's seat. The piebald always managed to show less caution solo than when clicked onwards by Mattie, and one couldn't work out if she were in a hurry to get home or hoped that the racket of the empty bottles in their crates might awaken her owner from his slumber.

By the time Doyle and Hill tracked down the milkman and his charge they were on the Lough Road gently winding their way about the streets and the sun was fast approaching noon time.

'Good morning, Mattie!' Doyle cried out, a little breathless.

'Good morning to yourself, Inspector!' came the warm reply.

'Could I just have a moment of your time, please, Mattie?' Doyle asked as they caught up. He gave Tommy, the piebald a pat on his hindquarters. The horse turned its head around close to a full one-hundred-and-eighty degrees and gave the detective a look which implied "What do you think *you're* at, sure we haven't even been introduced yet!"

'Certainly, always willing to oblige the law,' Mattie replied, as he himself gave the pony a pat. At this Tommy nodded his head up and down in a large arc a few times as if to say "Now that *is* OK."

Mattie Stewart used the police-induced stop in his round to tidy up his empties, raising the full crates of milk to the top to enable him unrestricted access to the fresh bottles.

'And how can I help?' he asked, as the two policemen stared at him in silence.

'About three weekends ago – three Sundays to be exact – would you have seen Joseph Kane out and about in the early hours around the village?' Doyle enquired.

'Couldn't quite tell you that, Inspector, to be sure. I've trouble going back a few days let alone a few weeks,' the milkman offered through his unshaven grin.

Doyle sighed as his shoulders dropped and his lead evaporated into the late morning air.

'But I could tell you about this morning if you want.'

'No, that'll be OK, Mattie,' Doyle said dismissively.

'It's just that I saw him this morning, over in Magherafelt,' the milkman replied to the disappointed, distracted and, ultimately, inattentive policeman.

Hill picked up on the milkman's reply though.

'What? You saw Joseph Kane this morning? In Magherafelt?' the junior said, jumping straight onto Mattie Stewart's revelation.

'Yep, the very same.'

'Are you sure it was Joe and not Pat?' Doyle quizzed, shoulders pucked up again.

'Oh, yes, that was Joe all right – always been a bit sour, if you know what I mean. When they'd both be my helpers, Pat would always have a nice warm smile for you, but not Joe – it would crack his face into smithereens to give you a smile, or even a grin.'

'Where did you see him exactly?' Hill asked. He couldn't believe the contained excitement in the air between Doyle and himself as this happy choresman gave freely of his information: information like none other Hill had known in his lifetime – information which was helping him and his boss solve their case.

'You know Tone Sounds – the music shop at the foot of Broad Street?'

Both the policemen nodded in unison.

'Yes, he was just going in there as I was coming out of Union Street at the foot of Broad Street, right in front of the Town Hall,' the milkman replied, as he returned to his crate and helped himself to another five full and fresh pint bottles of milk. 'Well, I'd better be getting on with getting the housewives *their* pints – so good morning to you both.'

The policemen watched Mattie waddle off to deliver his milk as he merrily whistled 'Diane', and pulled off a much superior version of the Bachelors' hit at that.

Chapter Thirty-Eight

'Yes, you're not kidding: Joe Kane *was* in here this morning, the upstart.'

Twenty minutes later, Doyle and Hill were in Magherafelt, courtesy of the inspector's green (close to lime) VW Beetle, and were talking to the rickety old shop assistant in Tone Sounds. The shop sold radios, record players, records (singles, EPs and LPs), jewellery, religious paraphernalia and various little gift-type trinkets.

'And you're sure it was Joe?' Doyle could barely contain himself.

'Well, yes.'

'How so?'

'Well, if only because he was buying a single for his brother's wife.'

'He told you that, did he? He told you that he was buying it for his brother's wife?' Doyle enquired.

'Well, not in so many words,' came the reluctant reply from the black-shawled assistant. Everyone knew she wasn't really an assistant – she was the owner's common-law wife and a right old battleaxe she was too. The only time she was happy was when she was selling wedding rings or Jim Reeves albums.

'Well, in *how* many words then?' Doyle said, growing impatient with the tooth pulling, especially when the roots were so obviously rotten.

'She came in here last week looking for it herself.'

'What – and you didn't have it? What single was she after?'

'No, we *did* have it. It was the Beatles' 'A Hard Day's Night', so it was,' the assistant replied.

'And why didn't she get it herself?' Doyle persisted.

'Well the shop was full, wasn't it? And I couldn't have her in here, could I? Bad for business with all the talk going around town about her and her husband and what they did to the brother.'

'Obviously not a lot if he was in here this morning and still large as life?' Hill interjected.

'Yes, but I didn't know that at the time, did I? We get a good class of people in here and I couldn't afford to lose any of my regular customers just because of that, could I?'

'Nothing like a good old bit of bigotry, eh, ma'm?' Doyle pushed.

'Now, listen here you, you may be the police but that doesn't mean you can come in here and insult me,' the old battleaxe started up.

But Doyle was in no mood for her. 'Yeah, but it's OK for customers to come in here and be insulted by yourself, is it? Just like Maggie Kane? What exactly happened?' Doyle pressed.

'Well, I told her quite simply that I wouldn't serve her. I told her she was barred,' the old woman said proudly.

'Yes, I bet,' Doyle replied. 'So what happened with Joe?'

'Well, he came in with the same request – I'd just one copy left and it was the display copy. Or at least the jacket was. When we first received our allocation from the suppliers, I took one of the Parlophone jackets from the single and wrote "In Stock" in large letters and stuck it in the window. You'd be surprised how quick the news goes around town – I don't even have to write the name "Beatles" on it any more. So I told him about the dust jacket being marked up and he said he didn't mind, he'd have it anyway. I offered him a few pence off, but he said he wouldn't be beholden to the likes of me. He paid me seven shillings, I gave him four pence change and off he went.'

'How was he dressed?' Doyle asked.

'Blue jeans, ah, let me think for a moment … a white shirt, dirty gutties and a blue jacket,' came the impatient reply. A queue of customers was building up and she was obviously anxious to take their money.

'Did you see where he went next?' the inspector enquired, taking great delight in taking his time.

'He said something about Bradley's; I assume he meant the café. Now, if that's all?'

'Well, that's all for now, ma'am. However, could you advise the owner that we shall be back, say, tomorrow afternoon, to check the stock? Particularly the jewellery – I'd like to make sure you have a receipt for every bit on the premises ….'

'You're not suggesting there's any stolen pro—' The old woman let the final word disappear for fear her customers would hear.

'Heavens, no, just a routine check, but I do have to protect your regular customers. Good day, ma'am,' Doyle replied, as he swivelled on his brogues and marched out of the shop, shadowed very closely by his constable.

Exiting the pokey shop, the two officers turned right, walked down to the foot of Broad Street, then took another right before heading straight down towards one of the infamous Three Spires of Magherafelt: St Swithin's Church. Just a few doors before the church hall was Bradley's Fish and Chip Café, the place with Mid Ulster's best example of that fine dish.

Now, Mrs Bradley, the sole owner of Bradley's, was a totally different kettle of fish to the previous servant of the public they'd come into contact with.

'Sit yourselves down – cup of tea? Your usual fish supper and beans?' was her greeting on being fetched from the living quarters towards the rear of the café.

'Well, it is nearly lunchtime. Let's see now. Yes, I think we will, but only if we can pay,' Doyle replied as he and Hill joined Mrs Bradley at the comfortable large corner table.

'Hmm, I wish they were all like you, Inspector. If that's how you wish it to be, that's how it will be.' Mrs Bradley smiled.

'That's how I wish it to be,' Doyle said, returning the smile. They gave their orders to an assistant the owner had subtly signalled for. Doyle had fish, chips and beans, as Mrs Bradley had predicted, supplemented by a bottle of Fanta, while Hill had simply beans and chips and a Coca-Cola. 'So, I believe you had an elusive visitor earlier on today?'

'Yes, and here was me thinking he'd been done away with,' Mrs Bradley replied.

'You and the rest of Mid Ulster,' Doyle consoled. 'So how was he?'

'He looked fine to me. Healthy, if a bit too slim.'

'How did you know it was Joe?' Doyle asked as his meal arrived. He wet the special Bradley's thick, crispy fish batter down with a generous helping of vinegar.

'I didn't, to be honest. I did one of those "Hello and you're …" and he filled in the missing "Joe" for me.'

'Oh, I see,' Doyle replied, pausing mid hot bite.

'But it was Joe, you know. He, well, *both* the twins used to hang out with my son and I remembered Joe as being the quiet one. Pat was always a little more loud, always a little more attention seeking. Joseph would always be deep in thought,' Mrs Bradley replied. The assistant, without being asked, had, while serving the two policemen, brought the owner about a dozen chips, which she was now dipping in Heinz tomato ketchup.

'Did he say where he'd been these last few weeks?' Doyle continued between tasty bites; he was really enjoying his lunch.

'Yes, we did chat a bit about that. He said he felt it was time to get out from under the married couple's feet for a while. He said they were being real nice about it and all but himself and Pat had started to get on each other's nerves and they'd even had a bit of a scrap up in the field – apparently they had to be pulled apart: Joe's words. Anyway, he said it was time for a change, and he didn't know if it would be a change for good, but he just wanted to check out what else he could do,' Mrs Bradley informed the two diners in between dunking and eating her chips.

'Did he have any work?' Hill, who'd cleaned his plate first, felt obliged to ask.

'Well, he said a mate of his from the tech was in a beat music group of some kind and whenever he wanted, he could go out with them to help with the equipment and make a few bob in the process, as well as having a bit of fun.'

Doyle stared at the remainder of his meal for a few moments before saying, 'This is great food, Mrs Bradley.'

'Why, thank you. Joseph said the same thing, you know, said he'd remembered the great taste of our thick, crispy batter from his school days and had a bit of a yearning for it. So he figured as he didn't know when he was next going to be back, he might as well have a tuck in,' the proud café owner replied.

'Tell me this, please, Mrs Bradley: are you convinced it was Joe who was here?' Doyle continued.

'Oh yes,' she replied confidently, 'do you see that quadrant of a tomato that was safely lodged on an island of a lettuce leaf that both of you scoffed down?'

'Yes,' Doyle replied, confused.

'Well, we do that with all our meals now. It's just a nice little touch. And they keep telling us we can't give our children enough greens and vegetables!' Mrs Bradley replied.

'Yes, and?' Doyle pushed, his attention fully held by where she may be taking this.

Mrs Bradley laughed. 'In fact, I remember that Joe didn't eat his earlier this morning and the only reason it stuck in my mind was I was here chatting with him when his food arrived, and when he saw the meal he asked for a small side plate. When the side plate arrived he carefully removed the tomato, still on its lettuce leaf, onto the small plate … said he'd never been able to abide the things, said even looking at them sometimes made him sick. So I had the girl take it away immediately. I remembered the twins from their school days. Pat would eat everything you'd give him; Joe always avoided tomatoes like the plague.'

'Thank you very much, Mrs Bradley, you've been very helpful, not to mention a fine host,' Doyle offered, making a wee note of 'Joe's aversion to tomatoes' in his notebook. By now the café was filling up with hungry lunchtime diners and the relative peace the three of them had shared was disappearing. Doyle paid for the lunches, two shillings for his and one and ninepence for the constable's, and he was just about to put the threepenny bit change in his pocket when he remembered another question. 'Would you know where he was off to next?' Doyle asked, change hand still deep in his pocket.

'Yes, he told me in fact. He said he was off on the noon bus to Belfast.'

So two contented and nourished policemen walked back out on the pavement outside of Bradley's.

'Thanks for lunch, sir,' Hill began.

'No problem. I enjoyed it too, particularly when we were able to wrap up our first case during it. Yes, quite productive, wasn't it? You see, it proves what Holmes used to say.'

'What's that, sir?' Hill asked, sounding like he knew he was about to be told anyway but wanted it on record that he was interested.

'He said that you shouldn't go off speculating on a case until you have amassed all the relevant information. To make any guesses or come up with any theories before that time is not only a waste of time, but could also be dangerous.'

'So the information we were missing on this one, sir – would that have been a copy of the Beatles' 'A Hard Day's Night' and a fish supper, sir?'

'Something like that, Constable, something like that. Let's get back to Castlemartin and the Station House.'

And with that they went off in search of the inspector's very own Beetle.

BOOK THREE
The Fairground Incident

Chapter Thirty-Nine

And so Castlemartin, this small rural cloister of houses, shops, farms, three churches and numerous streets in the heartland of Mid Ulster, returned to normality. People shopped in their usual shops and when they couldn't find what they wanted in Walter's the grocers, Francis' the jewellers or Smith's the newsagents (with their limited supply of books), then they'd wait until the weekend and head over to Magherafelt. And, heaven forbid, if they shouldn't be able to find their heart's desires in Magherafelt, then they would just have to wait until one of the two or three trips they made down into Belfast each year. Mind you, the clergy didn't encourage such trips because, they preached, 'there is evil awaiting you on each and every corner in the big city'.

Yes, life settled back into its tried and tested rural system. All sons eventually became fathers, each and every one nothing more or less than a middle man. Mattie Stewart and his trusted piebald pony continued to service the village with a daily supply of fresh milk. District Detective Inspector Doyle continued to dress exactly the same, re-read as much Sherlock Holmes as he could fit into a day and, without batting an eyelid, also help to clear up all the local petty crime. Constable Edward Hill helped the senior policeman in his endeavours but also found time to invite out the very beautiful, and even more eligible, Doris Durin.

Doris, of course, knew that Edward was going to ask her out, right from the moment they met in that first interview and she in fact, if truth be known, encouraged the invitation by accidentally (on purpose) bumping into the constable as frequently as good taste would allow. She graciously accepted his kind invitation for a cup of coffee in Teyley's and the romance, which would keep the village tongues wagging for a few weeks, began.

Doris, in the wisdom of her recently failed relationship, had decided to move cautiously at first because she had already determined that this young man cared enough about her to be her partner for life and she certainly didn't want to scare him off.

On paper it was a match: a match made between the two ginger-haired youngsters without the aid, services or interruptions of the matchmaker. Equally, it was a match that would stick and, as such, was another of those natural matches that worried the matchmaker.

In fact, Michael Gilmour had found that in recent years he and his little leather book were being called upon less and less. The 'now' generation were doing it for themselves. Michael took little comfort in the fact that they were not, by and large, doing the matchmaking as well as he would. But then people had to be allowed to make their own mistakes, didn't they? And make their mistakes they did.

The incident with the Kane twins hadn't been the reason for the decline in his business. No, his drop in matchmaking had started with the sixties. Michael often thought that one year, culturally speaking, in the sixties was equivalent to any decade previously. He'd been living with it for four years now and, yes, maybe the Kane twins' scenario would prove to be a bit of a watershed. However he'd already agreed with Dorothy that he would have little or no business to pass on to their eldest, Paul. They'd considered this to be OK, because Paul seemed to have a sharp brain for figures and a certain logic, which was fast finding the solutions to the problems he was encountering in his short life. Perhaps, thought Michael, Paul was a product of the 'now' generation and as such, he would be looked after by his own. But that was the whole thing about this new generation – sure weren't they capable of just looking after themselves?

Paul had been surprising his father recently. He had asked him two questions. Both questions came on the same day, in fact. Two questions which Michael, in all of his thirty-eight-and-one-half years on this planet, had never even considered. The first one Paul asked in the morning over the breakfast table.

'How do you think it felt to be the friend of the first person in the world who died?'

Michael looked at his son, then looked at his wife, then looked at his other two children to make sure they weren't disturbed as well, looked back at Paul and then looked, once again, at his wife for support; none was forthcoming and so he had spluttered out something in answer. 'Well, perhaps this friend, the one who was still alive, had already seen animals and plants die so he would have been familiar with the concept.'

Familiar with the concept indeed – a useless answer, Michael thought.

But Paul was not quite so dismissive. Without batting an eyelid or missing a spoonful of cornflakes he had continued: 'Yes, but he wouldn't have been able to talk to the plants or animals – well, I mean, he would have been able to talk to them, it's just that he wouldn't have been able to hold a conversation with them. It's just that, you know, one day you're talking to your friend, and laughing and joking with them, and then your friend is dead. He's cold. He doesn't respond to you in any form or manner. I mean, would the survivor have thought his dead friend was asleep? How long would he have left the body lying around before he would have had to bury it because it was getting smelly?'

'Paul!' his mother had cried out in exasperation. 'Not in front of the children.'

Michael wondered did Paul feel grown up at this stage. This was the first time he'd been allowed to be a part of an 'adult' conversation that excluded 'the children'. Usually these conversations covered people's wives or husbands carrying on with someone behind their backs. And there was a lot of s-p-e-l-l-i-n-g going on, sometimes bad spelling at that. In fact, sometimes the spelling was so bad that the other grown-up didn't have a clue what the first one was on about. But that was another life in a different childhood, Michael thought. Right now his eldest son was worrying him with a rather concerning question. And how did he answer it?

He had lived with the question for the rest of the day. He had tried to imagine himself in the situation and the thought that kept rising to the fore of his exploding mind was that he would probably think that *he* was next; he would probably have worried about the fact that he would also stop breathing and become cold and smelly and maybe even food for the animals that roamed around him. Did that say a lot about him? When he quizzed Paul further, Paul replied that he would have probably gone and found another friend to talk to.

Later on that afternoon, the afternoon of the big question in the morning, Paul had asked his father another concerning question: what his first thought had been. 'You know, Dad, the first time you were conscious of thinking, what did you think about?'

'Well, Paul, I was probably too young to remember.'

'No, no, I don't mean then – I don't mean idle thoughts. I mean the first time you were aware of the thought process and you used it: what did you use it to think about?'

Michael thought long and hard about that one. He thought about the question as much as he thought about the answer. What a question for a ten-going-on-eleven-year-old to ask! But then, at ten-going-on-eleven you do have a sharpness of vision, because you enjoy a sharpness not blurred by disappointment, a sharpness honed by the knowledge that you can and will do whatever it is you choose to do with your life, a sharpness forged to stone-piercing quality by the absence of one word: compromise.

Michael replied, 'Well, I probably thought I understood what my father did and started to work out how I could possibly do the same.' This would have been a sad answer if it hadn't been a correct answer. For as long as Michael could remember, matchmaking was all he *had* wanted to do; to do as his dad did. 'And what was yours? What was your first thought?'

'I remember thinking, I wonder what makes Mum sad. I thought if I could work out what it was, I could try and make her happy. I mean, it's not that she's unhappy all the time. It's just when I look at her sometimes, it's like, she's not there.'

Wallop! Whack! A mule-kick, smack right between the eyes. He was right on target without even taking the trouble to aim. Paul was a constant source of amazement to Michael. The father's pride wasn't that of the 'pat-on-the-head' kind. No, not at all, and in fact part of the pride must, deep down, have been based on a much more disturbing premise than that.

And then his son had a passion for music and really just one form of music: the Beatles. What was that all about? Paul was two years and three months away from being a teenager and yet he'd saved up his pennies, a total of one pound twelve shillings and sixpence, if you please, to buy their first long player, *Please Please Me*, and young Paul played it so often on their beat-up radiogram that Michael was already familiar with each and every one of the fourteen songs on it. Some of them great songs, mind you, like 'Do You Want to Know a Secret' and 'There's a Place', both written (so the sleeve told the matchmaker) by McCartney/Lennon. Paul even knew the names of each and every member and what instrument they played.

Now Michael had never seen that kind of attention before. Music was music and was for background entertainment. They had a couple of well-worn long players lying around – mainly Elvis Presley and Jim Reeves, battered by the years, along with Dorothy's favourite, an Emile Ford album which included her favourite song, 'What Do You Want to Make Those Eyes at Me For?' She'd heard a local showband, the Playboys, perform the song at a dance. They had announced the original recording artist and she wasn't happy until she'd managed to purchase a copy of the song. Luckily, this was the first track on the album and they weren't subjected to the rest of it. Michael doubted his wife had heard the other songs more than once. He equally knew that when Dorothy went into one of her repeated-playings of that song he should leave her alone, give her plenty of space. He was sure neither he nor his wife had once read a single bit of the information on the album jackets. But he was equally sure that Paul knew every word printed on the sleeve of *Please Please Me* off by heart.

He hoped this hero-worship thing was not going to make the 'now' generation into a flock of toothless sheep. It was more than evident to Michael that the followers of this new sound were looking for something, some kind of commitment from the art form they were now intent on idolising so much. He hoped with all his heart that they would not be disappointed. But if and when the disappointment came, it would be too far down the river of exchange for any of them to pull back anything worthwhile for their lives.

But what about the matchmaker himself? What about his life? He was too old to change, for he had certainly known nothing else in his life apart from matchmaking. When he was growing up he couldn't wait until he was old enough to start. He was in such a hurry to be a man, he'd forgotten his youth entirely and his father had not bothered to encourage him otherwise. Now he could never, ever reclaim the youthfulness that had once belonged to him. Yes, he too was too old to change and too young to die.

His family definitely wouldn't be going hungry, for the matchmaker had a soft mattress. His sleep would be a deep sleep brought on by the security and the softness of crisp crinkly blue ones, and lots of them. But what was he to do with the rest of his life? He'd worked out, with the certainty of his lifetime's experience, that by the time they came crashing into the 1970s his business would have all but dried up. Any matchmaking that needed to be done at that point would all take place at the annual fairs of that particular year, places like Lisdoonvarna where the first dance of the day is your best chance of the day.

And Michael couldn't farm. Yes, he loved helping Pat out but, as Michael knew only too well, at one stage, they hadn't enough of a farm to sustain two adults and a wife. What else could he do, he wondered? He liked working with wood but not enough to make his living as a carpenter. Perhaps he could get a job at Stewart Bros., the highly respected Castlemartin Carpenters who had converted the disused railway station house on the Magherafelt Road? But that would mean working for someone else and he wasn't sure that he could do that either. He'd had his independence now for too many years – all his life, in fact – he wasn't about to become beholden to someone else at this late stage, was he?

What about a pub – wasn't that what everyone said when they were retiring with a bit of money? How many times had Michael heard those very words himself: 'Oh, I think I'll open a pub, I certainly spend enough money there.' Wrong. What with Moore's, Morrison's and Brady's, Castlemartin had enough public houses to water the population several times over. And those not liking the decor at the above, and there were a few dissenters, would make their way over to Bryson's popular corner bar in Magherafelt.

He knew this was all stuff he should be talking to Dorothy about or, at the very least, you know, running it up the flagpole with Maggie, see how she reacted to it and then give his selective, watered-down version to Dorothy. But he rarely saw Maggie now. When he did, she was always with her husband, Patrick Kane.

Oh, how he missed their carefree long chats, and even longer walks. The happily married Kane couple was most certainly keeping a low profile since the Joseph incident. They weren't to blame and they seemed to take little or no pleasure at the announcement of Joe's, albeit brief, return to Magherafelt. Perhaps they'd been hurt too much by the words already spoken, but now Michael figured enough time had passed and he had tried to encourage the four of them to start socialising again.

Damn it, he'd take the bull by the horns himself and invite the two families to the fair, which was due to hit Magherafelt at the Fairhill the following weekend. It would certainly do them all the world of good to get out and about and, more importantly, be seen out and about *together*. He decided not to take no for an answer – he just wouldn't hear of it. It would give the girls a chance to doll themselves up, and they both certainly loved to do that. He and Pat could slip off and have a few drinks, the way men do, the way men *should* do. Perhaps, after all Michael had done for the twin, he'd have a few suggestions or ideas as to what the matchmaker should be planning to do with the rest of his life.

At the very least, it would be good to share his late-night thoughts, haunting as they were, with another human and not just the banshees of Lough Neagh.

Chapter Forty

The first you become aware of the fairground, even before you see it – in fact, way before you see it – is when you hear the noise of the records being played over the Tannoy. It obviously wasn't a faithful reproduction. The record in question as Pat and Maggie and Michael and Dorothy made their way up Meeting Street past the Fairhill School to Magherafelt's celebrated Fairhill itself, was the Rolling Stones' cracking single 'It's All Over Now'. The problem with the Tannoy system was that it had no facilities for the bass register of the record; consequently, all you heard was the crackle of Jagger's wafer-thin voice, a bit of the melody and not a lot of Brian Jones' excellent rumble-tumble production. But you felt the buzz.

That buzz hit you like you were splashing your head underneath the ice-cold waters of the River Moyola.

The buzz of the game of rings, where you had to throw a ring around a prize, a prize hardly worth the cost, but it was the winning that mattered, and it was yours to give to your sweetheart and claim your very own real prize – a kiss. A kiss, if you were lucky enough to find a receptive girl, was worth its weight in gold. Kisses were so valuable because they were not only the main event in horizontal recreation, sometimes along the banks of the same beautiful River Moyola, but they were, in the majority of cases, the *only* event: the sole game in town.

The buzz of the brightly painted swing boats, which took your breath away, leaving a hollow in the pit of your stomach, by just seeing how high they reached at either end of their arc. And the buzz of the noise of the dodgems, which were manned by a host of James Dean look-alikes, all with Surf-white T-shirts, tight-fitting blue jeans and equally tight-fitting DAs, slicked back either with lard or, for the wealthier boys, half a jar of Brylcreem.

The buzz of the harmless roundabouts with their exquisitely painted horses, unicorns or dragons; or the buzz of the chair-o-planes that swung out at right angles to the vertical when turning at full speed. God bless those who weren't chained in.

The buzz was of the noise, of the chat and of the laughter, not to mention the screeching of the poor unfortunates unlucky enough to be tempted into the ghost trains while believing they were going to be protected in the comfort of their sweethearts' arms. The Ulster Octopus ruled, and you'd better believe it.

Yes, the buzz was hypnotic and the attractions were as inescapable as Crumlin Road Jail. People who should know better and could ill afford nights at the fairground were drawn along the well-trodden grassy paths between one amusement and the next. 'Just one more turn in the swing boats, Mammy – *pleee-ase?*' was the most repeated request on fairground weekend, with 'No, I told you we can't afford any more' being the most common, and most feared, reply.

When the foursome hit the Fairhill that September Saturday evening, they did not have a collective care in the world. After the Stones' single, the Kinks were up next, pumping out Ray Davies' classic 'You Really Got Me'. The unmistakable distorted guitar intro led straight into the provocative 'Girl, you really got me now, you got me so I can't sleep at night,' pumping out the lewd suggestions all over the town as the ministers and village fathers and mothers wondered exactly what it was that was brashly hitting them smack between the ears. Then came the wildness of the guitar solo and for the first time in their lives the matchmaker and his wife and her sister and her sister's husband saw young people spontaneously break into dancing on the grass of the Fairhill, egged on by tonight's prime liberator, *Mr Ray Davies*.

The matchmaker was happy that finally, after such a long while, people were leaving them alone to get on with it. He hadn't seen Maggie so happy in ages and when Maggie was happy so was Pat Kane. Michael had little difficulty persuading Pat to join him for a pint of Guinness around at Bryson's, as the Watson girls had fallen in with a crowd of school friends, including Doris Durin, and they were more than happy to ogle the James Deans of Mid Ulster – the James Deans who, first thing Monday morning, DA free, would be back at their places of work, well-respected men one and all.

The usual crowd, plus some of the town's fairground influx, packed out Bryson's. Michael managed to find a space where they could at least hear themselves think and appreciate the pleasures of their rich pints of Guinness. 'Everything back to normal, then?' he began after his first full swig. He regretted asking the question the moment it had left his Guinness-moustached lips.

'I'll drink to that,' Pat replied without hesitation.

Both men did exactly so, as they clicked their pints together and wished each other good health.

'You must have been happy when Joe turned up, though?' the matchmaker added after their toast. His face was very red now, what with the excitement up on the Fairhill and the packed, and consequently very warm, atmosphere of Bryson's.

'Hey, Michael, you know, it would have been nice if he'd come out and told Maggie and myself exactly what he was up to, after all he'd put us through. I mean, I'm OK, I'm family, I've been dealing with him my whole life, but Maggie – what on earth has she ever done to deserve this?'

'Does this, the trouble between you, have anything to do with, you know, the thing we talked about the first time we met?' Michael enquired, his rasp falling to a near whisper.

'No, absolutely not. All that ended with Doris Durin. Yes, that was the end of all that nonsense. And then after having a chance with Doris, he goes and blows that as well. I couldn't believe it. All he had to do, it was so obvious to me, was pay the girl a bit of attention. That's all she wanted – she just wanted to be treated a bit special,' Pat replied, his tongue loosened by the Guinness. He took off his jacket, a blue denim, and hung it on the back of his chair where it dangled precariously close to the red-tiled floor, which was completely covered with sawdust and wood shavings. He undid the buttons on the cuffs of his blue shirt and rolled his sleeves up to his elbows, revealing solid weather-beaten arms. He undid the top button of his shirt and, now feeling quite ventilated, he helped himself to another swig from the earth's richest liquid.

'Aye, well, she's got someone else now paying her all the attention she wants. Fair play to Constable Edward Hill. Joe missed out badly there, I say, Joe missed out badly there,' Michael offered.

The matchmaker couldn't be sure but he thought, or imagined, that a couple of guys were talking about them, even looking their way – not exactly pointing or anything as rude as that, but every time Michael would follow his suspicions and look over at the pair of strangers, they would immediately turn away, a split second too late. He decided not to get annoyed at it, mainly because Pat seemed totally oblivious to the fact. But he wondered what they were gossiping about. Now that it was clear to everyone that Pat hadn't, in fact, done his own brother in, either with his wife's help or by himself, what could they possibly have to say? Gossips seem to enjoy a very selective memory. They certainly wouldn't let the fact that Joe had been spotted on three occasions – four, if you take into consideration the bus inspector who swore he saw him board the Belfast bus that lunchtime – get in the way of a good story.

Pat went to the bar for another two special soldiers in their unique white-topped uniform and Michael used the time to stare over at the strangers. They were both about Pat's age and well-dressed from a better wage packet than one picked up around here, he imagined. He felt like going over and asking the two chaps exactly what they were staring at, but that would only cause a scene, wouldn't it? It had taken Michael a lot of persuading to get Pat out tonight so he certainly wasn't going to allow a couple of city busybodies to spoil it for them. Michael decided that they should leave the pub after this next pint, before Pat picked up on what he'd been seeing and before the girls were getting into trouble up on the Fairhill. All the James Deans, combing their hair every two minutes, would be into overdrive with all the unattended woman – hey, and married woman at that. Hadn't Michael heard somewhere that married woman were considered easy prey by those very same Dodgem Romeos?

Sure enough, by the time the boys returned, the Fairhill proceedings were still buzzing wildly. Maggie, Dorothy, Doris and three other friends of the Watson girls were surrounded by the

Coca-Cola guys, the guys who could keep a bottle of Coke half full all night and at the end of the evening, when it had gone flat, they would merely blow their own bubbles into the black liquid using the straw and then at the appropriate moment down it in one for the benefit of the watching girls.

'So, when are we going to have this charge in the bumping cars?' Michael shouted, trying hard to make himself heard over the rising racket of the Honeycombs' debut single 'Have I the Right', featuring their female drummer, Honey Lantree.

'You're on!' Maggie shouted back, full of laughter. 'Me and Pat against you and our Dot.'

They were merrily banging half-heartedly into each other when Michael, again out of the corner of his eye, spied the two well-dressed chaps from Bryson's. He tried hard to dismiss them and insisted they all have another go in the cars, this time swapping partners – the boys versus the girls – in the hope the well-to-do lads would be gone by the time they got out.

Not so.

They were there waiting for them by the time the foursome were finding their land legs again. Michael was sure they were staring in their direction, whispering in a conspiratorial manner and nudging each other. Michael split up from the foursome when he spied the two heading in the direction of the rings. He quickly nipped around the other way and met them face on. 'OK, lads?' he began, hearing and fearing the tremor in his own raspy voice. 'What's up? What's all the whispering about? I say, what's all the whispering about?'

The well-dressed chaps were not used to being accosted in such a manner and started to laugh, to laugh out loud again, nudging each other playfully in the ribs.

'OK, I'm giving you one last chance: what's your business here? What's the story?' Michael continued, the interrogation starting to draw the attention of passers-by squeezing through the crowds.

The Savile Row mannequins started to laugh again, more helplessly than the first time.

Michael made to grab one of them, the bigger one as it happens, as he said, 'Now be off with you, we don't need your type here.' The matchmaker was still trying to contain the situation. He could see Pat and Maggie still over by the dodgems and still having fun. Michael just wanted these two people to go away; he wanted to prevent them from ruining Maggie and Pat's big night out. If only he could get them to go away, everything would be OK again. But he'd obviously grabbed the chap more aggressively than he'd meant to because he, in turn, lashed out in self-defence at Michael.

This was all the matchmaker needed to provoke him to the point of no return. He could see their perfectly great evening coming to a rude end just because these two city slickers were poking fun.

Well, Michael was having none of that.

He bopped the biggest of the two men right smack on the nose, a nose which immediately collapsed and would never again rise to its original proud form. Blood was flowing everywhere and several girls started to scream. As yet, Maggie, Dorothy and Pat were unaware of the scene unfolding nearby. Michael still hoped to contain the situation, although he didn't know exactly how he could achieve that – there was no carpet to dust his mess under and now the smaller of the two was making his way towards him.

Michael did not wait until Junior threw the first punch. He grabbed him by his coat lapels and head-butted him. Again more blood – there was blood everywhere. More girls began to let rip. Michael, being the local, immediately had everyone on his side.

'What were they doing, Michael?' someone asked.

'Shall we give them a good hiding?' one of the James Deans asked, in a 'can I hold your jacket?' kind of way.

Both of the visitors were on the grass now. They were not being encouraged to rise and any efforts in that direction were met with their legs being carried from under them, with Michael's well-aimed boot hitting them each in turn in the back of their knees.

Then the matchmaker made the mistake of standing between them. The smaller of the two leapt from behind Michael and grabbed him around both ankles, willing him to fall over. The matchmaker, just like a part-sawn redwood tree, very slowly at first, with his arms waving frantically in wild reverse windmills, eventually tumbled over and fell face first in the mud. Now he had got his wish, because a large crowd had gathered around him, shielding him and the two well-dressed lads, who were no longer well-dressed, from Maggie, Dorothy, Pat and the majority of the Fairhill crowd.

Michael couldn't wriggle his feet free from their captor and at the same time he could see the bigger of the two chaps rise from the grass and make his way toward him. He was sure he was going to get a good kicking, and a good kicking around the head at that if he couldn't free himself. But the other wee bastard still had his ankles secure in a vice-like arm lock. Michael could see the big lad rushing towards him. He clocked his fine leather shoes as they slowly made their way across the blood-soaked mud and he tried to calculate the effect one of them would have if it hit him in the head in the wrong place. He panicked. He thought of his children; he thought of Maggie and Dorothy together. He thought of Pat and wondered why he hadn't thought of Joe, but he accepted that by doing so he'd just thought of the twin. He broke into a cold sweat, genuinely fearing that his life was about to end. He tried to shake off the thought. He tried to resist images from his life flashing past him. He realised Dorothy was at the most twenty-five feet away, laughing and joking with her sister, totally unaware that her husband's life was about to end.

'Well feck this for a game of soldiers,' Michael shouted at the top of his voice while he used every ounce of energy he could muster to turn over onto his back. Junior still clamped his ankles, but now he was also facing up towards the sky. Michael summoned the energy required to sit up and leaned over and grabbed Junior by the lapels of his expensive jacket, returning once again to his emptying well of energy. With all the strength he could muster, and using his backside as a fulcrum, his legs as a lever and his upper torso weight as a counter-balance, he rolled backwards and at the very last possible moment he extended his legs to their fullest position.

Still lying on the ground on his back, he watched in amazement as Junior went airborne in real slow motion and landed feet first into his oncoming friend. Both collapsed in a heap on the ground. Michael jumped up immediately, preparing himself for more, but neither of the lads appeared to have the stomach to continue the fight.

The crowd shouted their approval for their local hero, even though not a one of them had seemed prepared to even up the numbers. The excitement over now, though, they started to wander away.

Michael knelt down between the two outsiders, far from the madding crowd – well, at least four feet. 'OK, lads ... what are you here for?' the matchmaker asked, indicating it was his final question of the night.

The smallest one dared to speak first – well, by the look of his comrade's face he was the only one capable of speaking.

'Well, sir, it's like this: we heard you were the matchmaker and, well,' now his voice dropped so low that Michael had to put his ear right close to his mouth to hear him say, 'we were trying to pick up the courage to see if you could, you know, suggest a match for us.'

Chapter Forty-One

Well, the matchmaker certainly had a bit of explaining to do, and then a bit more on top of that, by the time Dorothy got him home. Of course he would have to, wouldn't he? It went along the lines of something like:

'What on earth was that all about?'

'Well, they kinda started it.'

'They kinda started it? How so?'

'Well, don't you see? They were staring all the time at Pat and Maggie and they followed us up from Bryson's,' the matchmaker replied, standing firmly on his sticky wicket.

'Oh, Michael, you didn't start a fight in the pub as well, did you?'

'No, no. Nothing like that. But that's when I noticed them first and I thought it was about the Joe thing and I thought they were going to be clever about it. You know – bring it all back up again? And it was going so well, you know, with the four of us out having a great time and—'

'The four of us off having a great time my foot – more like you and Pat skiving off to Bryson's at the first opportunity. Michael, for heaven's sake, you're a father of three children: I've never seen you lift your fist in anger before and here you are at the top of the Fairhill in Magherafelt rolling around in the mud with two well-dressed men and them bleeding all over you. What were you ever thinking about? How embarrassing – we'll be the talk of the town by Monday morning, just you wait and see.'

'Oh, hush, woman, anything to divert attention from Maggie and Pat.'

'Oh, hush me, nothing. Since Joe was spotted in Magherafelt, you know, that morning on his way to Belfast, well, the chat and the gossip has all died down, or hadn't you noticed?'

'Well, look here now—' the matchmaker tried to cut in.

'No, *you* look here, Michael, I say, you look here,' Dorothy began, in a quiet but firm and stern voice, and mimicking Michael's habit of repeating himself, 'I don't know what's up with you but you've been different since all of this began. I can't quite put my finger on the exact moment, but it was around the time Maggie started stepping out with Pat Kane. You've been, well, distracted and at first I thought it was all to do with the Joe rumours, but then I realised you'd also been weird on me when Joe was still around. When we were up at the farm helping out and things you'd always be looking at Joe, always out of the corner of your eye. What on earth was that all about?'

'Dorothy, please, woman, you're giving me the beginnings of a sore head.'

'Aye, well you'd better watch out or I'll finish the job off properly. Now come on here, talk to me – what's been going on?'

Michael pondered for a few minutes as he sat in his favourite fireside chair pretending to sulk, but in reality he used the cloak to give himself a bit of space to think. Here he was, married to this woman for the last ten and one half years and he could feel the balance of power literally slipping away from him as they sat there in silence. He wondered where her new-found confidence had come from.

Dorothy had always been a good wife – an attentive wife, a trusting wife, yes, even an obedient wife. But in the recent month to seven weeks, Michael could see the wind of change blowing around his sitting room, like the winds on the lough shore unsettling the leaves each and every time they felt they had found a comfortable and secure resting place. All he wanted was peace. All he wanted was for Pat and Maggie to be left alone. Well, that wasn't really all he wanted: he also wanted Joe to be forgotten about and for things to be as normal. He wanted the only knock on the door to be from people who would say 'Is the matchmaker in?' and 'We were wondering would you ever put our names on your books?' Hell, he'd never grumble again about having to do up his tie – he unconditionally promised this to whoever was listening to his thoughts.

'Please, I promise, just let things be as they were.' He wanted Dorothy to go on as she normally would and make him a nice cup of tea and the conversation to go along the lines of 'Yes, dear, that was a nice evening, wasn't it? Didn't Maggie and Patrick look happy? They'll soon be thinking of starting a family, you know,' and on and on. And he would sit in his favourite fireside seat studying his book or the *Mid Ulster Mail* and nod here and grunt there and then have Dorothy say to him at the end of the conversation, 'You haven't been listening to a single word I've been saying, have you? Oh, I'm off to bed, dear. Don't be too late, please – we've all got a long day ahead of us tomorrow.' At that Dorothy would, as usual, kiss him on the crown of his head, just where the red spiky hair was making way for the skin to shine through, particularly on the evenings he'd consumed more Guinness than perhaps he should. And the matchmaker would say, under his breath, 'Now there's a thing, dear, as sure as light follows darkness tomorrow will only have twenty-four hours and we'll be asleep for at least eight of them, so it will be no longer or shorter than any of our other days.' And he would say, above his breath, 'Yes, dear, I'm just going to study my matchmaking book a wee bit longer. I won't be too late, but I'll try not to wake you.'

Instead, here was Dorothy, his wife, and she was demanding that her husband talk to her and tell her what was going on. And she said it with such a voice of authority that Michael knew – with a power of conviction based on the fact that at a certain point in your life you start to consider the days you have left rather than enjoy the ones you are in – that she was not going to be fobbed off on this occasion. No, this was a time he should note in his great book. This was the time the meek and mild-mannered wife of the matchmaker took over the leadership of their relationship.

Truth be told, Michael Gilmour, matchmaker of the parish of Castlemartin, was happy, in a way, to have someone to share his troubles with.

'Well, Dorothy, don't you see, it's like this,' and Michael proceeded to splutter out his excuses, his frustrations about matchmaking, or at the very least at the death of matchmaking as he knew it, and his want and need to protect Pat and Maggie. He refrained, of course, from telling her how Maggie and Pat had really gotten together and how he'd played his part in the *arrangement*. When he had concluded his explanations, after a few false endings, Dorothy tut-tutted a few times and replied.

'Michael, you've got three fine children you've got to be a better example to. What's Paul going to feel like when he goes into school on Monday morning and all the other kids start to have a go at him about his father scrapping on the Fairhill in Magherafelt? Eh? We've had our chance and all our energy now must go into – has to go into – making a future for the children. That's all there is, really: the children and what we give them to get them started in their own lives. That's where I want to see your energy going – not rolling around in some muck heap in Magherafelt. Leave Maggie and Pat to their problems – our Maggie is a survivor: she is well capable of looking after herself and her man. Believe you me, she will do anything she has to do to protect the both of them,' Dorothy said, as she started doing her last minute tidying of the night: putting the few remaining dishes away; the knives and forks and spoons in their relevant sections in the drawer; folding her apron and carefully placing it on the back of the door; picking up the newspaper; folding it back into its natural creases and putting it over by the wireless and moving the children's toys to one corner of the room, out of harm's way. All the time she was doing this she was addressing Michael.

'So listen good, Mr Michael Gilmour, I say, listen good, Mr Gilmour: I want to see you getting on with things – no more whimpering about the death of matchmaking or Maggie, Joe and Pat this, that and the other. Go and see Daddy if you want to talk to someone about what you should do if there's no matchmaking to be had. He'll have a few good ideas, I'm sure. I've enough to be worrying about without having to worry about you. And another thing, I don't want you sitting down here at night till all hours of the morning reading your little book with your matchmaking notes – get off to bed now with me: you'll feel much better after a good night's sleep, believe you me.'

Michael started to protest, but then thought better of it. Dorothy was right in a way: it was time to get on with it, to get on with the rest of his life. Actually, more exactly, it was time to get on with the rest of *their* lives. He lazily untied his boots and took them off like a man weary from a day's work in the field. He barely seemed to have the energy to lift them and put them under the stove to benefit from the dying embers inside. 'Aye, a wee cup of tea would go down well,' he said as he chanced his luck with his traditional late-night request. For one second Michael felt Dorothy was about to give the reply she had often given to the children on making similar requests: 'Well, you know where the cups and saucers are.'

Instead she replied: 'Well, you know, that's a very good idea – put your feet up there by the fire, Michael, and I'll make us a fresh pot to send us off on our dreams. Shall I?'

'Aye, fair play, that would be nice,' Michael replied, contented and happy for the remission. 'Aye, I say that would be very nice.'

As she went about her duties Michael thought that his wife's response had not been the one he'd expected. He concluded that now that she'd made her mark in the sand and donned the trousers in their relationship by stating what he should and shouldn't do, she seemed happy to adopt the role of supportive wife again. If anything, the matchmaker thought as he studied her closely, she appeared as though she desperately needed the bond of affection more.

'Aye, that'll be the mother of the family, won't it?' he said under his breath as she filled the kettle.

Chapter Forty-Two

Meanwhile, on the other side of Castlemartin as midnight's darkness fell, Dorothy's sister was quizzing her husband.

'So what was that all about with Michael and those two chaps?'

'I'm not exactly sure, to be honest. I mean, there was definitely a scrap about something, but by the time I went over there it had fizzled out. But it must have been *something* for Michael to take on the two of them,' Pat replied, still flush from his Guinness.

'You're not kidding, are you? I've known the man for ten years now. I mean, I knew of him before that, but I really got to know him properly since he and our Dorothy started going out. And in ten years I've never seen anything like that kind of behaviour from him. Did anything happen down at Bryson's?'

'No, not really,' Pat replied, shaking his head. 'I think I saw the two of them drinking there, but we'd nothing to do with them. We had our two pints and left – we didn't want to leave youse beautiful women with all those flippin' Romeos around now, did we?' Pat caught his wife as she passed his chair. He swung her back towards him so that she too fell into the chair on top of him.

'And are you sure it's only two pints of Guinness you've had?'

'Quite sure,' Pat replied as he nuzzled into her neck.

'Pat, stop that – you're tickling me!' Maggie spluttered playfully.

'No need to stop, Maggie – there's not a soul here bar us any more: it's our house and we can do whatever we want, wherever and whenever we want,' Pat whispered amorously.

'Aye, and what if Joe should walk in on us, just walk in off the street?' Maggie replied, offering little or no resistance. It was the end of the day and her clothes were going to come off anyway.

'No chance of that,' Pat said, clearly distractedly as he negotiated those damn difficult hooks.

'Oh *yeah*?' Maggie replied, surrendering completely.

'Oh yeah.'

'And why are you so sure about that?' she asked, appearing surprised at the confidence with which he spoke.

'Well, for a start, I've changed the locks on the front and back doors,' Pat replied, as he eventually succeeded in his claim on a prize, or two.

'Ah! And for seconds …?' his wife squealed.

'You don't know our Joe — we won't see hide nor hair of him until he's successful on his own terms. He'll come back again only when he can parade a floozy of some kind around, proud as one of my dad's roosters. Now stop blabbering, woman — let me taste those beautiful lips.'

'That was cruel! Why a floozy?' Maggie breathed after eleven and one half minutes of relative quiet — quiet from spoken words, not from the moans and groans of passion.

'Well, it's sad but true. That's how Joe thinks people will judge him, by how much money he has made and by how beautiful the girl on his arm is. So that's the kind of woman he's attracted to,' Pat replied. He was content, lying there in the arms of his wife, both of them still glowing from the sweat of their love-making. He wasn't exactly sure he should be discussing his brother at this particular point in the proceedings.

'Are you saying that your brother is shallow, Pat?'

'No, not exactly. But he is bleedin' selfish — I can tell you that for nothing. But I don't think he's shallow, no … I just think he doesn't know any different. He genuinely believes that those things matter, that that's the only way he'll be able to impress people. He's always … well, he's always lived his life like he gets it out of a book. Do you know what I mean?'

Maggie considered this for a minute or two as she lay, limbs entwined with her husband. Pat was quite prepared for her to say, 'No, I don't know what you mean,' but he could see by the look of realisation on her face that she indeed understood.

'But you're twins – how could you be so different?' was her eventual reply.

'Oh, maybe because he was the lazy one and he let me live his life for him.'

'How so?'

'Well, look – even that ludicrous business with the matchmaker. You know, about the two of us wanting one wife. I mean, I cannot believe that I allowed him to talk me into that – it was so crazy. I still shudder to my roots when I think of it. Ah, what I put you through.'

'Oh, don't worry about me, Pat – I knew what I was getting into. I knew exactly what I was getting into and I knew that the … the "thing" wouldn't last long. I knew it would all sort itself out and we'd be together. And as I told you, we never actually made love.'

'Yes,' was the hesitant reply.

'Pat, you believe that, don't you?'

'Of course.'

'I *need* you to believe that, Pat.'

'It's fine – *we're* fine.' The husband brushed his wife's hair back from her brow and kissed her gently on the forehead.

'Thank goodness for Doris Durin,' Maggie added.

'And for the matchmaker,' Pat replied.

'Ah, yes, thanks to Michael.'

'But even with Doris, that's what I mean about him – about our Joe not really living his life. He did all the things he thought he was meant to do with Doris; he believed that everything was OK. But he was never there for her any other way apart from physically. He thought that's all he had to do. He was ready, I believe, to marry her. And it's all to do with our childhood. You know, he'd encourage me to do all the leg work, and then he'd want to share *my* experiences and *my* friends. He didn't want to go out and do anything on his own or find his own friends. You know a sad thing? Our Joe does not have one single friend of his own who is not *our* friend. He doesn't have one single person he can talk to and share things with. Everyone he knows, he knows through me.'

'That's so sad.'

'But that's our Joe, and that's why we won't see him until he conquers the world, or at least Belfast,' Pat said, as he pulled his wife closer to him so that they could share their body heat. The room temperature was dropping fast now the fire was dying.

'But, dear husband, isn't Belfast the world?'

'Oh yes, it's the world as we know it today,' Pat joked in a fake BBC accent.

'Yes, I know, but until I met you, dearest, I always thought the world was Magherafelt.' Maggie mimicked a little lost girl voice.

'Yes, that was your geography lesson, now get upstairs, woman, for a lesson on the birds and the bees,' Pat said, chasing Maggie up to the bedroom and, in his haste, neglecting to bolt the new locks on the back door.

Chapter Forty-Three

The talk around Castlemartin the following morning (which was a Sunday) wasn't about the matchmaker's scrap with the two posh strangers, surprisingly enough. No, the church chat was far spicier than that.

Edward Hill had been walking Doris Durin home from the fair in the early hours of the morning only to be disturbed by noises coming from the rear of the Fairhill School. Being a policeman, he felt it his duty to investigate.

And who should he find creating the disturbance back there but Joan Cook and one of the James Deans, doing a bit of their own matchmaking. The only problem with the couple coupling, and them being disturbed mid-coupling, so to speak, was that they found it difficult to disengage. No, make that *impossible* to disengage.

Embarrassing wasn't the word. No assistance, discreet though it was, from Constable Hill nor his companion, Miss Durin, would prove successful and so the only thing for it was for them to be helped, under the cloak of Doris' raincoat, down to the police station where Hill was decent enough to see them straight through to the witness room.

A late-night call was then made to the local doctor, a Dr Taylor. He was totally unfazed by the whole situation and with the use of soap, water and, believe it or not, a mirror, and with Mr Dean suffering a considerable amount of pain, the doctor managed to effect a release, as it were.

The desk sergeant, through fits of giggles, couldn't help but add further insult to Joan's injury by advising the local gossip that he would be charging her with disturbing the peace.

Brass-necked as ever, Joan Cook complained that it had been *her* peace that had been disturbed that early morning, and that she would be seeking the opinion of her solicitor first thing Monday. The James Dean fellow had the sense to keep quiet, very quiet indeed, and consequently disappeared into the highly polished woodwork.

Now, the funny bit was just how quickly the story travelled and grew as it went around town. In fact, the locals didn't use the ad break during *Sunday Night at the London Palladium* to make their usual cup of tea – they used it to pass on the Joan Cook Report to whichever TV-less neighbour was out calling round those houses that had aerials to catch Brucie in his weekly antics.

But the *real* fun started Monday morning when the shops opened. While buying her *Daily Mirror* in William Harry Smith's, the newsagent's, Mrs Toner heard about Joan Cook's adventure with a man from the fair behind the Fairhill school. So, she reported it to Mrs Jones in Walter's Grocery and Hardware Store, only by this time Mrs Toner had made the coupling up to a threesome. Mrs Grimes, who was eavesdropping (it has to be said, not very successfully) reported to her very good friend Mrs Pickering, in a conversation in Richard Francis' jewellery store, that it was in fact Michael Gilmour who had caught Joan Cook with *two* men behind the dodgems marquee, and that he had given them a hiding because it had been well known that Michael and Joan had been doing a line for ages, and the reason he wasn't finding a match for her was because he wanted to keep her for himself. By the time Mrs Pickering had reached Rogers & Daughters' Home Bakery, three and one-half minutes later, she had it that Joan and Doris Durin were caught behind the Fairhill school with the two men *and* Edward Hill *and* Colin Doyle.

'Behaving like animals the lot of them – sure, didn't the desk sergeant have to get a couple of buckets of water to throw over them all, just like they occasionally have do with dogs on the street? But of course, the whole thing is getting hushed up because that young policeman, Hill, is involved. And sure, didn't I expect more from him? But then again he's hanging around with that Doris Durin and she's had more men than hot dinners, and didn't she go down to the Port with both the Kane twins?' Mrs Pickering eagerly relayed to the entire shop full of punters, including the young Gloria Rogers who didn't especially want to hear grown-ups talking about all that stuff, particularly in front of her father.

It was still only mid-morning and the pubs didn't open for a good few hours yet, so you could imagine what the story was going to become with all the blathering by the end of the evening. But anyone afforded the luxury of being privy to all of these rumours would perhaps have been surprised to discover that not in one single instance had anybody stood up in defence of the parties concerned. It didn't matter how ludicrous the story became: in fact, the more bizarre the tale, the more inclined the listener was to believe it. Incredible the folly of human nature, that we are all prepared to believe the worst of each other while at the same time paying little or no attention to the good deeds that so often go unreported.

The matchmaker and his son Paul, and the rest of the family for that matter, had been saved from their impending embarrassment due to the fact that the bigger splash of gossip had broken, and both sets of rumours only served to push the Joe and Pat Kane gossip even further into the annals of local history.

Castlemartin was a-buzz and all heads were a-turning at every strange man on the street: 'Was it him? Is that one of the men Joan Cook was with? Sure, there's not much to him, is there? She'd be eating him for lunch, wouldn't she?'

Did the village's infamous divorcée keep a low profile? Did she heck as like. In fact, she was seen parading around town with a new hairdo that very afternoon, proud as a peacock and twice as hard, and as shiny, as the brass fittings in the church. Joan Cook was totally made up, and why wouldn't she be? Sure, wasn't the entire town – every man, woman and child – talking about her. And if only she'd known it, people as far afield as Magherafelt were playing the exact same game of Chinese whispers as she sat drinking her coffee and puffing on her Woodbine in her favourite corner seat in Teyley's Café.

At lunchtime, in the same café, a group of schoolgirls, who had pretended not to hear their mother and father's whisperings about Mrs Joan Cook, were now getting to see the culprit firsthand and they wondered aloud what it was that all these cute fairground lads saw in one so 'obviously past it'.

'It's because she's easy,' Gloria Rogers had claimed. 'All the boys like a girl who's easy, don't they?'

'*Girls* I can understand,' claimed Audrey Driver – at fifteen years and three months, more worldly wise than the rest, 'but she's an old woman: it must be like doing it with your granny! Ugh!'

And all bar one in Teyley's burst into a combined high-pitched shriek of laughter.

Chapter Forty-Four

By the time the Watson girls and both their husbands got together at the matchmaker's the following Thursday – the last Thursday in September – the fuss over Joan Cook and the numerous boys, reported as many as a football team at last count, had all but died down again.

'We're all friends here, and it won't go any further than this room,' Dorothy began as they sat down to their meal of steak, peas and chips. The chips were a special request from Maggie on behalf of her husband: one was only really meant to have chips on a Friday night, usually with fish, but steak, peas and chips were Pat's favourite meal and Dorothy was happy to substitute the traditional 'boiled pratties'. 'But isn't the very same Joan Cook on your matchmaking books, Michael?'

Pat stole a glance mid-bite at Michael, who wasn't giving away a thing.

'If she was before the weekend – and for reasons of confidentiality, I'm not stating she was – she certainly isn't now, I can tell you,' Michael replied, much to the relief of at least one person present.

Pat was dying to make a chip buttie. Yes, he loved his steak, peas and chips, but his absolute favourite was a chip buttie, with the chips so hot they melted the butter into the bread. However, he was under orders from his good lady wife not to be going and affronting them in public by indulging in such common practices. His treat for such public compliance was not that which you might expect, because they both enjoyed that so much it was never used for favours. No, his treat for being 'a good boy' was to have Maggie cook him chips three nights of the week instead of their traditional sole Friday outing.

'A few months ago,' Dorothy began to offer up (the signal that she would continue was when the others saw her set her knife and fork down carefully on either side of her plate, wipe around her mouth with her napkin, place her elbows on the table and clasp her hands just under her chin. When she spoke at the dinner table, she was always sure to clear her mouth of food before doing so) 'I was making the Sunday lunch – Michael likes a nice wee bit of steak for his Sunday lunch – so I was making Sunday lunch, and Paul just says, matter of fact, "I'll have a bit of steak today, Mum, please." And he tucks in and demolishes it like he's been eating it all his life. Well, I didn't ask him about it or anything – I mean, I didn't want to put him off, so I just appeared to assume it was as natural as the moon and then one day he says to me, "Mum, when are you doing steak again?" So I tell him whatever the day was and he asks me would I mind doing it with chips and just peas – you see, I usually do it with carrots and parsnips, as well as the peas. So he says he wants it with chips and just peas and instead of having tea with it would it be OK to have it with Coca-Cola? Now, that wasn't all: he didn't want the Coca-Cola poured into a glass, oh no, he wanted to drink it straight from the bottle!' Dorothy continued her story as her food grew cold. But she preferred to let it grow cold rather than talk while eating. 'So I agree, you know, as I said, with the protein and all I'm more than happy for Paul to be enjoying his steak, so I ask him: is this how they have it at school? "Oh no," he says, "we never have steak for school dinner. It's the Beatles' favourite meal, isn't it." Well, God bless the Beatles, I can tell you – if they have the influence to start my son eating steak,' Dorothy concluded, as she picked up her knife and fork and started back into her own pile of steak, peas and chips. 'Though, according to our Paul, they wash it down with whiskey and Coke!'

'Whiskey and Coke? Ugh, I can't think of anything worse than drowning a good whiskey in Coca-Cola – maybe a little water, yes, but Coca-Cola … surely never?' Michael said, worrying not about the food already in his mouth.

'It's just that I've never been able to get Paul to eat steak before and it's so good for them while they are growing up, isn't it?' continued Dorothy.

'Well, this is delicious,' Pat began. 'You can see why they, the Beatles, and Paul, like it, can't you? It's very tasty.'

'So … any news from Joe?' Dorothy enquired somewhat self-consciously during another pause in her eating.

Before either Maggie or Pat had a chance to answer, Michael cut in about as subtly as a magpie visiting a thrush's nest.

'Of course not, woman.'

'Well, don't go biting my head off! I'm not to know, I'm sure,' Dorothy replied, visibly upset but also looking somewhat relieved.

'Don't you see, Dorothy? If they'd heard from Joe, don't you think we'd be the first to know about it, what with all the fuss that's been going on?' Michael replied, trying to put water on the fire he'd just ignited.

'Pat thinks Joe's not going to show up again until he's made something of his life,' Maggie offered, not exactly defending her sister but at least offering her some support.

'That makes sense,' Dorothy muttered, priming her knife and fork for action again.

'How does that leave you with the farm?' Michael offered, taking his turn at a question.

'Well, it leaves it that Pat and myself are working as hard as physically possible to keep the whole thing going and to work off the debts and all the time Joe still owns one half of it and is not putting a bit of energy into it, but he can come back any time he likes and claim his half, which, as I say, is increasing in value all the time by our efforts,' Maggie replied, not really out of anger but more as a statement of the facts as she saw them, and she certainly received no contradictions from her husband.

'Would it not be in your interest to have the farm valued now,' Dorothy offered, putting her knife and fork back on the table again, 'or find out what the value would have been at the point Joe disappeared and register that amount in a letter with your solicitor so when he does show up – I mean, the reality is it could be in ten years' time and God knows what you're going to be worth then, but you are certainly not going to want to have to sell up just to pay him his half? It would seem to me that he's certainly entitled to half the worth of the farm as it stands today, but that is all. And if you could get someone, say like an auctioneer, to officially acknowledge today's value in a document, then when he returns you can give him his fair share. It might even be worth your while to start to put some money into a fund or account to accommodate such an eventuality and then it won't bankrupt you down the line,' Dorothy concluded, showing a very clear and sharp mind and that her years at the tech were standing her in good stead.

'Our Dorothy's got something there,' Maggie enthused. 'Hasn't she, Pat?'

Pat didn't reply, for he was deep in thought.

'Hasn't she, Pat?' Maggie repeated.

'Mm,' Pat said, still pensive. 'She *has* got a point. But I don't think it's actually as simple as that.'

'How so?' the matchmaker enquired, obviously quite taken with his wife's insightful view of the situation.

'Well, Dorothy's right, of course, and we should consider protecting ourselves by using both her suggestions – the valuation and putting some money by. But what about the debts? At the minute, thanks to Maggie, we are starting to clear the notes held on the farm. So would we apportion the money we earn through working the farm that goes towards those debts? I mean, the actual value of the farm today is not really what it's worth to us,' Pat started, letting the words follow the idea forming in his mind.

'Pardon?' Dorothy asked. 'How do you mean the farm is not worth what it is worth?'

Maggie, Pat and Michael smiled at Dorothy's simplistic but honest interpretation of Pat's statement.

'Well, say we go to an auctioneer and he says the farm is worth, say, for argument's sake, one thousand pounds. OK?'

The trio nodded.

'So, at today's value Joe's half is currently worth five hundred pounds. However, before we could sell the farm today and receive one thousand pounds, we'd have to clear off the notes on it, which would cost us, say, for argument's sake, four hundred pounds, which would mean we'd only actually get six hundred pounds from the sale. And if, as we've just said, we put five hundred of that to one side for Joe, it would leave me and Maggie with one hundred,' Pat surmised.

'Good point, good point. But then surely all you have to do is have the auctioneer certify the net value of the farm today? You know, what it could be sold for, less the debts outstanding on it? Because, as you say, you and Maggie are now going to have to pay off the debts yourselves,' Dorothy offered.

'Yes,' Pat replied, drawing the word out to the length of a short sentence, leading his wife to believe that he was still troubled about some part of the theory. And she was right.

'But then there are other things to consider, like the grey area. You know, in a few weeks we'll be starting the prattie gathering,' Pat started up again.

'Aye, only a week to go now – Paul talks about nothing else. He's getting holidays from school for it and he's really looking forward to earning his first bit of money,' Michael's rasp announced, proud as a father could be.

'He'll earn it, believe you me,' Pat replied. 'Please warn him it's hard work, very sore on the back. You'll be with us as well, Michael, won't you?'

'Of course he will,' Dorothy cut in, having sat silent for a good time now as she finished off her dinner. 'He'll be out there with the best of them, earning a good few bob, I'm sure.'

'Great – we need everyone we can get. But, as I was starting to say, we planted the fields back in the springtime, Joe and me, using some of last year's spuds, which were obviously the property of both of us, and now we're going to pick them without Joe. So does that mean he's got an equal share of the crop? I hope bleedin' not 'cause I can tell you, there's going to be a right few bob from this year's crop and it will go a long way – even after paying everybody's wages and the Lone Ranger and Tonto for their tractor and digger – to paying off our debts.'

'Don't you see, Pat? You have to apply the same logic. When you planted the potatoes they belonged to both of you. However, when the crop comes out of the ground there is only one of you to claim ownership. There is only going to be one of you here, working it. So my view would be, Pat, that Joe should be credited with the spuds that were planted in the spring, but not with the crop you pick next week,' the matchmaker advised to nods of agreement from both women.

'It'll be great … I know this sounds cruel, Pat, but it's what I think,' Maggie began, looking to her husband for approval to continue. Such approval was forthcoming in the shape of a quiet discreet nod. 'It'll be great if he does stay away and then we can get all this farm stuff resolved. It's just that we're in limbo; we're here working away, starting to do well, and we just don't want him swanning back and claiming the fruits of our hard labour.'

'I know, Maggie, but it's not as simple as that.' Pat paused. It looked like he was about to tell them all something important and was considering the ramifications before he did so. He obviously decided not to, for he continued with, 'Ah well, we can't be too considerate about all of this stuff – we'll just have to get on with living our lives and working on the farm as best we can. We just need to take some steps to protect our future and get on with it.'

'Well, if I was you, I would make me plans based on the fact that you're not going to see Joseph Kane around here, not for a long time to come, I say, not for a long time to come,' the matchmaker proclaimed with an air of finality that only someone with a permanently hoarse voice like his could deliver.

Chapter Forty-Five

Now the dust from the recent gossip storms had passed over, Castlemartin's rich and colourful cast of characters had settled down contentedly. Winter was fast approaching, which was evident in the ear-blueing winds whistling around the village that had lost little of their bite and ferocity on the short journey from the lough shore, some three miles away.

Warm clothing was making an appearance all over the village, having been holed up the entire summer with only moth balls for company. Maggie Kane, *née* Watson, did what her mother used to do and hung the clothes out in the room the month before they were due to wear them, with the window opened wide in order to give them a good airing. At the very least, this meant that neither she nor Pat would smell like a stale half-sucked Polo mint.

In reality, most of the village did the same thing and the only ones who complained about having to wear the moth-ball-ridden layers were those approaching their teenage years – in other words, those keen on the new fashions as seen on the weekly edition of *Top of the Pops*. Obviously there was a lot of 'You're not going out wearing that large belt and calling it a mini skirt!' Or 'You're not going out in a skirt so short everyone can see what you've had for your dinner.' The boys didn't get off easy either. 'What are they – hipsters? But shouldn't you have hips to be able to wear them?' Or 'Bell bottoms? Bell bottoms, sure – there's enough extra material there to clean all the windows in Magherafelt.' Then came the Beatle boots and winkle-pickers, the toe point getting sharper and sharper every three months until eventually you could have used them to thread a needle, which had parents everywhere declaring: 'Oh, I *see*, it's so that you can pick your nose without getting your hands dirty. Well, I suppose at least that's an improvement.'

The brave teenagers, and sometimes their younger brothers and sisters, would proudly don their third-generation Carnaby Street outfits and wander up the town, turning heads and setting tongues wagging as they did so. They'd all end up in Teyley's Café, swaying around the jukebox to the Beatles *or* the Rolling Stones, for seldom would any youth claim to like both – it was always one or the other. Or there was the new exciting group from Belfast called Them. Again, this name was one to instigate their wise-cracking elders: 'Yes, I know you like *them*, but what are they *called?*' To add insult to injury, this was coming from the same generation who tried to convince you that Pat Boone and Cliff Richards (he soon lost the 's') and Ruby Murray and Teddy Carroll and … and a list as long as your arm … were the bee's knees.

It wasn't even worth trying to explain the intensity of the shiver running up your back every time you heard the guitar introduction to Them's version of 'Here Comes the Night'. Well, Paul Gilmour had tried, and he was only ten, but at least his mother listened to him.

In a way, Dorothy felt a little sorry for her son – he was a bit ahead of his time, in that he loved all this new music and knew everything about the new wave of pop stars, but he was just too young to hang out with the Teyley's Café crowd or to go down to the youth club to hear his favourite bands being played at ear-bleed-inducing levels while pulling on a bottle of Coke. But at least his mother supported him in his enthusiasm, even going as far as to buy him some of his records (more importantly, she didn't make fun of his attempts to grow his hair longer).

Each time he asked for a new single, the same discussion would always follow: 'Only two songs for six and eightpence when you can get ten, sometimes even twelve, on a full album for thirty-two and sixpence? Now that's either three and fourpence for one song, or two and sevenpence ha'penny a song.'

'Yes, Mum, but all the good songs are on singles, and this way I get to hear lots and lots of artists,' he'd claim, winning his argument. As far as his mother was concerned, he always won his arguments, but in her eyes the important thing was that he always did so with such beautiful logic, having all his facts and figures at hand to back himself up.

His aunt Maggie was also a supporter of this new influx of artists. She particularly liked the Beatles, and both Maggie and Paul played *A Hard Day's Night* until the scratches were louder than the songs. She promised to take him to see the film of the same name when it eventually reached Magherafelt – she'd even earmarked a copy of the same album for his impending eleventh birthday.

The older men – the men who stood and chatted on the street corners each and every day as they watched the village and life itself go by – saw all these changes too. From their vantage point, they witnessed the radical revolution in dress, in hairstyle, in the new sounds of the edgy English beat groups wafting out from Teyley's Café. If you bothered to solicit their opinion on the matter, they'd advise you that the music was too loud, much too loud, but the transformation of the village youth warmed their hearts. They watched as their youngsters tried out their legs, the way a newborn foal very shakily and unsteadily takes its first tentative steps: you want to reach down and steady it and help it up to its feet, but such support and comfort is neither sought nor welcome. Yes, these steps were their own steps, the first precious steps of the new generation – the first generation since the twenties not to live under the shadow of war; they were the generation with a voice, a voice not necessarily sure what it was going to say, but one that was convinced with absolute certainty it needed to be heard. And heard it would be, whether in the music blaring out from Teyley's, or in young men such as Paul Gilmour, whose wisdom only grew with their confidence.

The old street-corner men marvelled at the unfamiliar colours, fashions and sounds floating up and down the Broadway and around and around Pear Tree Roundabout so many times it made them dizzy – so dizzy they would have to repair to one of Castlemartin's finest (in the shape of Morrison's, Moore's or Brady's) for a taste of that fine black liquid with the snow-white top, which, by the time it had made its way down your throat, through your stomach and into your legs, gave you as solid a foundation and anchor to the ground as any corner boy could wish to have.

Following a pint or three of this magic liquid, a return to their favourite street corner would have them thinking they'd happened upon another planet – a planet so vivid with colour that it appeared not unlike the inside of the Big Top at Duffy & Sons' Travelling Circus.

Chapter Forty-Six

As village life ate its way into the sixties, farm life for Pat and Maggie Kane wasn't progressing with such reckless abandon. They were now preparing for the potato-gathering season and had high hopes for a plentiful crop, which would in turn furnish their coffers and reduce their debts.

Poor Maggie: she'd never owed anyone a penny. That's the way her dad had brought her up, and most days he'd come out with the same lecture: 'If you're buying something, pay for it; if you can't pay for it, don't buy it.' This no-nonsense approach had served her well, and she'd been able to put a few bob away before she'd married Pat. Mind you, it's easy to do a bit of saving when you're living with your parents and you've a list of well-paid jobs to your name.

Maggie had started off in McCelland's shirt factory, which was only a stone's throw away from the matchmaker's house. She found the work to be menial and tedious, but the craic with the other girls was ninety, and so she'd perhaps stayed on a bit longer than she should have, and a lot longer than her parents would have wanted her to. 'You're wasting all that fine education your father worked so hard to put you through,' her mother would say.

Next she secured a job at Dawson Bates', the grocer's, and had just about taken over the running of the shop when she decided to move on. The shop manager had tried desperately hard to persuade her to stay – he'd taken a real shine to Maggie (some had said in more ways than one), but she just couldn't abide the daily gossip that was paraded the other side of the counter by an ever-changing array of faces.

Next she'd gone to work in a bank in Belfast. Her mother was pleased to see her 'using her education for the first time'. She made good progress, but it wasn't long before she hankered for a return to village life. It wasn't that she was a country girl or anything like that – no, it was just that city life was much too impersonal for her. Sure, in a small village like Castlemartin everyone knew everyone's business and took great delight in poking around in it, but, equally, in Belfast you could drop dead on the street and people would merely step around you – or worse still, step right over.

Maggie had missed the fun of living in Castlemartin, and she'd really missed the weekly dances. In Belfast you didn't go to dances, rather you went to bops, and usually there were three or four musicians on stage, scruffy as Shetland ponies and playing only for themselves. But at the local weekly dances in the Dreamland Ballroom, out on the shore of Lough Neagh, you got the mostly sweet sounds of someone like the Playboys showband. In fact, all of the boys in the showbands were clean cut and wore matching suits. They played all the hits from the radio and even the older songs your mum and dad knew, and the lead singer was always quite cute to boot. The Playboys' singer had been off limits though – Maggie knew his girlfriend, Hanna Hutchinson, but that was another story.

Maggie was enjoying her morning trip down memory lane. She needed to focus on these moments for herself; she had discovered that the problem with running a farm was that, unless she set aside some personal time, she ended up spending all day every day working. There was always *something* to do on the farm. So at least once a week, but never more than twice, Maggie would make herself a fresh pot of coffee and settle down at the kitchen table with a Kit-Kat and allow herself some thinking time, prompting her thoughts with either photos or letters, or even some of her early diaries.

Just now she'd happened upon a photograph of the Playboys and she studied the lead singer, Martin Dean, and wondered how he and Hanna were getting on. She knew from experience that it wasn't easy dating a member of a showband.

Next she flicked through a recent diary from around the time she'd returned to Castlemartin and worked in an administrative role at Magherafelt Technical College, which was where she'd been when she'd met and married Pat.

Sure, married life had definitely been very different to living at home, and particularly in the early days when she was supposed to have two husbands. When she thought about *that* now – especially now that she and Pat were working so well together – it made her physically cringe. How could she ever have done that?

In a way, it now seemed a bit unreal – not quite as if it had never happened, but she'd have liked to reach the stage where she could just block it out of her mind entirely. But she accepted that would probably never happen. Now, though, without Joe around, the memories were less vivid. In fact, now she could analyse the whole thing with the coolness of a third person. And she took great comfort in knowing that she had met a man she dearly loved – in a way that she had dreamed of all her life.

She was so lost in this thought that she'd committed the golden sin of running out of coffee before she'd finished her Kit-Kat. It always did this to her, reflecting on her relationship with Pat – she always grew totally immersed in her musings.

The best thing about the relationship was that Pat loved her in the same way – of that she was convinced. They both knew that they would do anything for each other; they had a trust based on absolute love – a spiritual, physical and cerebral commitment – which doesn't come easy. So was it that which had forced her to go along with the bizarre situation? Had she been scared that she would lose this precious man? And how had that same man become embroiled in such torrid circumstances?

She and Pat had discussed it a lot afterwards, at first quietly while Joe would be in the next room but now, in his absence, openly about the house.

Pat claimed that when Joe had first suggested the idea, he'd gone along with it out of desperation. He knew that the whole system they had in place on the farm was going to collapse and that they would probably lose the lot to those who held the papers. So why not take a woman on? He was enough of a realist to realise that no woman was going to join them as a skivvy, so he knew marriage and a share in the farm would have to be part of the enticement package.

Pat even claimed – and his wife believed him – that he'd have been quite prepared to forego his part in the 'intimate' duties of marriage and leave all of that to Joe, if he so desired. He'd already gone so long without that luxury that if he'd had to go longer – indeed, forever – it wouldn't have been a particular hardship.

Pat had also become very depressed about the matchmaking meetings. He liked Michael but some of those 'dates', if you want to call them that, had been so humiliating and toe-curlingly embarrassing that he'd been tempted to tell Joe to go off and find a wife for himself. Pat didn't need or want to share her, just as long as she and Joe were happy and she took care of the domestic duties on the farm. He'd put up with that until such a time as he could afford his own farm or the current farm could support four adults.

But then the reality became that Maggie met Pat.

And everything changed.

Pat didn't want to lose Maggie.

Maggie didn't want to lose Pat. She'd spent her entire adult life searching for her soulmate, her life partner – she'd even got to the point where she'd convinced herself that such a person didn't exist. She'd been leaning towards the theory that love was merely a fanciful idea that society had manufactured to ensure the continuance of man- (and woman-) kind through procreation.

And, as if to confirm her suspicions, she knew she'd be letting herself in for a horrendous situation with Pat, but in all of that potential recipe for catastrophe she didn't once – they hadn't once – sat down and said that Joe would have to take a running jump into the lough if he didn't accept they'd fallen in love with each other. In all probability, perhaps that would have been the end of the situation. Yes, Joe might certainly have mumbled and groaned for a time, but if they had stuck to their resolve, he would've just had to learn to live with it. End of story, beginning of another. But neither of them had dared to entertain such discussions because the unwritten contract was that Joe *was* part of the package, although running and hiding their heads in the sand obviously hadn't helped matters.

Hadn't helped their matters of the heart.

They both figured that they would sort the whole despicable thing out within the marriage and somehow it would all be worked out to their mutual satisfaction.

And for Maggie's part, she'd never been unfaithful to Pat – she'd never made love properly to or had full sex with Joe. She had been worried, though, that eventually he would catch on to her trick and demand what he thought were his rights. And after the way she had seen Pat attack his brother in the hay field that day, when the whole thing had reared up again following the demise of the Doris Durin relationship, she had been thankful Joe was content with what little he *was* getting.

And what about Doris Durin coming along when she had? God bless the matchmaker, Maggie thought, and his subtle ways of matching the two of them without Joe ever having twigged. And if Joe had only paid Doris some attention, even just a wee bit, they'd all be living happily ever after now. It'd be a bit crowded, but at least they'd all be happy. Eventually the couples would have had to split up and move on, and Maggie knew that if she had needed to she could have gone to her father to borrow the money so that she and Pat could get a place of their own. Why else had her father worked so hard throughout his life if not to make his children's lives easier? It was just that she'd preferred *not* to have to do that. It was silly, she knew, but she had her own man now, and she wanted to show everyone, particularly her parents, that they could and would make a go of it, and that she wouldn't be running back to them every five minutes looking for help. Apart from anything else, Pat would have been too proud to have taken Old Man Watson's money. They had already gotten over the biggest hurdle in life – they had found each other – so after that there wasn't anything they couldn't accomplish *together*.

Now with Joe out of the picture, Maggie was determined that nothing else should ever be allowed to obstruct their way. They were happy, as happy as they ever had been. Pat, away from the pull of his brother, was blossoming into the wonderful man she'd always known was there.

But he sometimes had his darker moments.

On more than one late-night occasion she'd caught him alone in the kitchen, sitting in his chair – his dad's old chair – just staring into the flames of the fire. Maggie saw such a sadness in his eyes, and it wasn't even a sadness that people grow into (she'd sometimes seen

244

sorrow in the eyes of children – even Paul, her nephew). And when Pat would become aware of her presence in the room, he'd physically snap himself out of the trance with an utterance like, 'I was miles away.' Perhaps two people, even those in love, needed time to escape somewhere to be by themselves, whether in the same room or not.

And Maggie never pried or pushed Pat when he was in his flame-staring mood; instead, she left him to his space for as long as he needed, just like her and her coffee and Kit-Kat breaks. It wasn't like he was brooding or sulking; no, it was more that he was considering their lives, his parents' lives, the life of the farm, and maybe he was even thinking about Joe.

Did he have regrets about his brother? It wasn't as if he came out of these trances with any great revelation, such as 'I've been thinking about the price of fish and it's too expensive so what I've decided we'll do is go to the lough each Saturday and catch our own,' or perhaps 'You know the trouble with the Moyola River? It flows the wrong way; we just have to find a way of reversing the flow and everything will be fine.' To which Maggie would have replied, 'Yes, fine for everyone except the eels at Toomebridge who'd end up swimming on a dry riverbed.'

But that didn't worry Maggie; in fact, she felt this private space might be vital to their survival as a couple, and she knew her husband well enough to know that if he wanted to talk to her, then whenever he was ready he most certainly would.

No, she'd other, more important things on her mind – things in the short term, such as clearing away her coffee pot and Kit-Kat wrapper. Things in the long term, like building up the farm, paying off their debts, taking Paul to see *A Hard Day's Night* when it eventually opened, finishing off the new indoor bathroom, starting their own family (they'd agreed that when the time was right they'd like two babies, no preference for boys or girls: they'd just be happy they were healthy).

And in the immediate future, she had the potato gathering to get ready for, which was about to commence, weather permitting, the following Monday morning.

BOOK FOUR
The Lonesome Heart

Chapter Forty-Seven

Seagulls hovered around and about the Lone Ranger's Massey Ferguson tractor. It was, in fact, early Monday morning, the first Monday of October 1964. The prattie-gathering team was assembled on the smallest, but prettiest, of the several fields in which the Kanes had sown spuds in March that year. This particular field bordered the disused railway track on one side and the meadow on the other. It was only a five-minute walk from the farmhouse and Paul Gilmour, youngest gatherer on the team, worked out that it must have been this fact that earned the field the distinction of being the very first to be harvested. There was probably a bit of psychology going on as well: the field was quite small so it made for an easy first step to what would be a back-breaking, and certainly back-aching, fortnight.

The seagulls were after the worms that the new Thomas Potato Digger would throw up in its search for this year's crop of King Edwards, and the gatherers were after the potatoes. And the more they picked, the more they made. Pat Kane was paying twelve pence for each and every hundred-weight bag collected that year. Since they usually gathered in pairs, this meant a crisp red one (ten shillings) per gatherer for every twenty bags of potatoes. If you managed a full day's work – usually 8 a.m. until the light faded at about 5 p.m. – you could possibly raise that to a not-so-crispy green one (one pound) each. Paul had already worked this out as being twelve pounds for the better gatherers for the full two weeks' work.

By lunchtime he'd also calculated, by their current rate of gathering that he and his partner (who happened to be his father) could earn as much as nine pounds each. His dad though, probably wouldn't consider splitting the gains fifty-fifty – not that it really mattered much, because Paul planned to give most of the money to his mum anyway. Actually, he planned to give his *entire* share to his mum in the hope that he'd receive a luck penny from her for his efforts. This luck penny would hopefully stretch out as far as a couple of singles, possibly even a new shirt or two and he'd his eye on a leather jacket with white piping up in Magherafelt in Cuddy's drapery store, but he accepted that was probably going to have to wait until Christmas.

But all that shopping was ages away: first he had to earn the money to give to his mother to give back to him.

The tractor moved slowly and steadily through the drills, pulling the potato digger, which would open the drill directly below the tractor between its massive wheels, exposing the King Edwards for the pickers and the worms for the seagulls. Both gulls and pickers were equally greedy.

Each duo had their own section of the drill to pick and the secret to a successful gathering was to keep in time with the tractor ahead of you; that way, you finished your share of the drill before the tractor returned to commence spoiling the next one along. If you managed to fall behind the tractor, that is to say your work rate grew so slow that the tractor pulled way ahead of you, then you were guaranteed to do your back in, as there would certainly be no breathers between drills.

As well as picking the potatoes into crates, the workers had then to empty their contents into the hundred-weight bags. It took three full crates and a bit of a fourth to fill each one.

The bags were then stacked in each team's stash until the end of the day, when Maggie would wander round recording the number to be credited to each pair in her little book. Then the bags of potatoes would be taken by tractor and trailer back to the farm and stored in the relative warmth of one of the sheds, awaiting further transportation to the shops. Here they would then be re-bagged, by some poor shop-boy, into seven- or fourteen-pound plastic bags, where they would be sold to the villagers for a great profit.

Villagers such as his mum, Paul thought, as he worked with his back bent at a full ninety-degree angle to his legs, his arms dangling like a monkey's as he scooped up the potatoes. He spent some time studying the weird shapes of certain potatoes in the hope that he might one day recognise one, or some of them, on his dinner plate.

The sky was a blemish-free, pure blue and the rising sun added, not heat, but a wonderful golden hue to the field as the workers continued to collect the basis for the staple Ulster diet. Paul marvelled at his father's ability to scoop up so many potatoes in his huge hands – hands which were soon covered in dry clay. You had the feeling, as the clay stuck to your skin, that should you manage to bend one of your fingers it would crumble away from your hand.

Paul had lots of questions for his father.

'How did they do this before they had tractors and diggers?'

'With a horse-drawn digger?' the matchmaker guessed.

'And what about before they had diggers for the horses to draw?'

'They probably did them the same way we do them at home: dig up the drills with a spade.'

'Gosh, can you imagine doing a field this big with just a few spades? It would take forever,' the matchmaker's son said, as he stood up to survey again the size of the field. 'Is there a digger that can do both – you know, dig up the drills and pick the potatoes at the same time?'

'No, I don't think so – it would surely pick up hard bits of earth, stones and horse droppings as well.'

'Oh, gross – can you imagine boiled horse droppings for dinner? Eurgh,' Paul said, nearly spitting out the words.

'Yes, well,' his father smiled, 'you'd better not let your mother hear you going on about things like that.'

'This soil, you know, the earth – how old is it?' Paul enquired, as he held a piece in his hand and examined it closely. 'How long has it been lying here in Pat's field?'

'Now there's a question,' Michael Gilmour declared. 'I'd say a long, long time, but you should take it up with your geography teacher when you go back to school.'

'Where's Joe? Why is he not here helping Pat and Maggie?' another question from Paul's endless list. This time it wasn't such an easy one to answer.

'Oh, he's gone away.'

'Gone away where?'

'Maybe Belfast – maybe he even caught the ferry over to England.'

'Why?'

'Well, that's a good question,' Michael replied, only this time he was unable to fob it off onto a school teacher. 'I think it was some personal business between him and Pat and it was thought better if he went away for a time.'

'Had it anything to do with that fight they had when we were harvesting the hay?'

'Paul,' Michael replied with just the slightest hint of annoyance, 'grown-ups sometimes feel the need to be apart from each other, if only so they can breathe.'

'But they're *twins* – aren't they meant to be together forever?'

'Well, that's the thing with twins, you see. Because they are twins, they are rarely judged or treated as individuals: they are always referred to as "one of the twins". And you know, sometimes that just gets to be a little too much and, in order to survive, they need to spend some time apart.'

'What, you mean if they hadn't parted, if Joe hadn't gone to Belfast or England, they would have died?'

'No, not exactly. It's a bit like drowning in a way, I suppose; it's like when someone is that close to you, like a twin brother, and you're in the water. Now not only do you have to protect yourself from drowning, but this other weight, in this case your twin, could also weigh you down and if you are not careful you could go under with him.'

'So Pat had to get rid of Joe or he was going to drown?'

'Not in so many words, but maybe it is better for both of them that they spend some time apart before anything bad *did* happen.'

'How long will he be away for?'

'Oh, I think it could be a very long time before we hear of Joe again,' Michael announced, as he saw the opportunity arriving for a timely interruption in the shape of the first tea break. Maggie and Dorothy were crossing the field towards the workers with a large white milk urn filled with tea and a large box containing, hopefully, sandwiches. Michael hoped that the Lone Ranger and Tonto would get up to some of their wild antics and take Paul's attention away from his never-ending, not to mention hugely awkward, interrogation.

'What's the difference between a banana and a bunch of grapes?' the Lone Ranger asked Tonto as they all gathered around the parked tractor trailer in the middle of the field.

'Oh, I don't know, Kemosabe,' the ever-loyal Tonto replied.

'You'd be a fine one to send to the greengrocer's!' the Lone Ranger replied.

And the workers chuckled a little before breaking into their various factions to discuss, amongst other things, the price of fish, the weather, Tonto's strange out-of-character pale complexion and, most covertly, the current whereabouts of Joseph Kane. In fact, luckily enough, it was only Michael, who had hoped all of that stuff had died down, who had overheard that particular conversation.

When he told his wife what he'd overheard on the field, her reply surprised him. 'Well, he should be here, shouldn't he? He knows what work goes on this time of the year – he's been on a farm long enough, hasn't he? They are talking about him because they all know he should be here helping out his brother and not sulking off to somewhere like Belfast.'

Michael didn't offer a reply. Instead, he threw the dregs of his tea over the opened drills and gazed into the distance beyond the meadow. He was so lost in his thoughts that he didn't notice his wife remove the empty cup from his fingers and head back down towards the farm with her sister and a load of dirty dishes, emptied of their food – the workers had been as effective in clearing up the sandwiches as the seagulls had been with the worms.

Luckily enough, his son was off on another tack – one of his statistic-collecting tangents – by the time they returned to their task. How many potatoes did it take to fill a bag? (About four hundred and fifty.) How many potatoes would the entire team gather in a day? (Nine thousand, if they were lucky.) How many potatoes would they collect in the full two weeks? (Approximately one hundred and eight thousand.) He further calculated that if the average person devoured three potatoes per day, then his and his father's hoard would last someone thirty-six thousand days, which was just under a hundred years, or twenty-five years' worth for a family of four.

Michael merely encouraged his son in his extravagant calculations, occasionally offering some assistance when required. He had to admit, he found the subject of long division altogether more enticing than the whereabouts of Joe, or one of the many variations on that theme.

*

The first day's gathering concluded without any further incident, and with a last-minute burst, they had just about managed to finish the small field, leaving pastures fresh, new and closer to the disused railway track for the morrow.

Paul and his father, should his father care to admit it, hadn't realised just how painful their backs would feel once repositioned in their natural upright position for the first time since they'd left home. A good soak in the bath would remove all of the dirt from their hands, faces, necks and fingernails, but it would serve to ease the tension building in the back only a little.

Dinner came and went very quickly. Paul excused himself for an early sleep and, in what seemed like only a few minutes, he heard his mother calling him from below. She was shouting something about breakfast being ready. Surely it must be a dream? A quick peek from under the bedcovers confirmed the worst. The new day had arrived. It was indeed time for breakfast and a return, dressed in dirty clothes, to the labours of potato gathering.

The teams sauntered onto the field at a much more leisurely pace than on the previous day. At 8 a.m. sharp the Lone Ranger was leading his Thomas Potato Digger through the first of many drills of the day. Paul, deciding to conserve all of his energy for the day's gathering, said little to his father.

Today the pair were on the drill next door to another father-and-son team – Tommy and Bobby Patterson – and Paul enjoyed hearing the gossip of the elders, but all the time he stuck to his mother's golden rule: children should be seen but never heard. And it was easy to keep quiet with all the information that was floating around – all the snippets and titbits he was picking up about this, that, whatever and whomever. It was all harmless innocent stuff, of course – otherwise his father would have steered the conversation in more child-friendly directions.

Paul had already decided, with the hindsight of the previous day's experience, that he wasn't going to eat as much lunch on the second day. The heaviness of his belly had slowed him down in the afternoon, he felt. Bending over had become uncomfortable. So he would take just a glass of milk and a sandwich or two to keep his energy up. And since he had some time to spare on his lunch break, he decided he'd go for a wander down by the old disused railway tracks.

Chapter Forty-Eight

It turned out that the Lone Ranger and Tonto had the same plan as Paul. However their plan was one gained from years, not just one day, of experience.

Paul found them sheltering from a rain shower under the little bridge that carried the railway track over a long-since dried-out river bed. He longed for the days gone-by when he could have sat under here, with or without the Lone Ranger and Tonto, and listened to the iron monsters passing overhead.

But instead he decided to tell the duo about some words he had recently learnt from a Bob Dylan song. Paul had discovered Bob Dylan in a John Lennon interview he'd read, and if this new raggedy American artist was good enough for one of the Beatles, then he was most certainly good enough for Paul Gilmour. The song, as near as the boy could recall, went something along the lines of 'The Lone Ranger and Tonto, were riding down the line/Fixing everybody's troubles, Everybody's except mine/Someone must have told them I was doing fine.' Castlemartin's Lone Ranger and Tonto had a rare old laugh at this one and very soon they had Paul teaching them the melody right there under the bridge, which ten years since would have supported the very line down which the masked one and his faithful companion might have ridden.

Ulster's Lone Ranger and Tonto soon got the hang of the lyrics and began to sing them quite easily to the melody the matchmaker's son had taught them. They weren't to know then that, soon enough, those words would prove somewhat ironic for a certain member of their community.

The three of them were sitting on a makeshift bench, a plank of wood stretched across two five-gallon cans. Their seat was unsafe at the best of times and when they all started laughing at their newfound harmonies – Castlemartin's answer to the Bachelors, they jested – their makeshift seat became precarious. So much so, in fact, that eventually one of the five-gallon cans gave way, which in turn caused the entire contraption to collapse, sending the three of them flying down to the dry river bed, only to land in a messy pile. Laughing more heartily than ever, they scrambled around on the ground trying to find their feet. Eventually one of them – it was the Lone Ranger they later agreed – surfaced from the muddle of bodies holding what looked like a short white stick in his hand. The laughter subsided and they all started to dust themselves off. The Lone Ranger studied the sick more closely and thought it may not, in fact, be a stick at all, as there was no give or bend in it.

'It's strong, strong enough to be a bone, Kemosabe,' Tonto reasoned.

Paul looked back to where they'd fallen and was surprised to see another, and then another, of these odd white lengths. And as they began to search the dry ground, they came across more and more pieces.

'I know what this is,' the Lone Ranger announced.

'And what is that, Kemosabe?'

'It's the winner of the 1949 Ulster hide-and-seek competition!' The Lone Ranger and Tonto collapsed in another heap of laughter. Only this time Paul wasn't laughing. He continued to look at the collection of off-white sticks, before saying in a voice so quiet neither Daniel Stevenson, aka the Lone Ranger, nor Ray O'Sullivan, aka Tonto, heard him.

'I know what these are. These are the bones of Joseph Kane.'

Chapter Forty-Nine

Events took on a life and speed of their own at this point. Paul Gilmour had never really considered himself to be a quick runner – long distance perhaps, but never a sprinter. Most definitely not. But he shot out from under the disused bridge like a bat out of hell. He'd been running for at least a minute when he realised he was running in completely the wrong direction – well, that was, of course, if he was planning on getting back to his parents. He seriously doubted that even his parents could protect him, but to their sanctuary he fled. He was running so fast that his own body couldn't keep up with the pace of his legs and he stumbled and fell several times, cutting and bruising his knees and the palms of his hands on the rough earth. Then he started to feel as though something was holding him back. He'd never felt as scared in his short life as he did the moment he realised the bones he and the Lone Ranger and Tonto had discovered were the bones of his uncle. He felt like Joe was running after him, deliberately willing him to slow down so that he could catch him. Then he realised that the Joe in his imagination was a skeleton and he immediately moved up a few gears, broke into a sweat and felt sick in the pit of his stomach.

His temples were pumping away as if they were about to burst through his pale skin. He felt the beginning of a small but extremely focused and sharp pain dead in the centre of his forehead. He spotted the main group of field workers, huddled around the tea and sandwiches area, way in the distance. He screamed and shouted at them and waved his arms furiously in the air to attract their attention. They ignored him and continued to laugh and chat with each other. He realised that waving his arms was slowing him down, so he stopped using them to get everyone's attention and was greatly relieved to feel his speed pick up again. He also realised that, although he could see the group laughing and chatting, he couldn't actually hear them so, consequently, there was a very good chance that they couldn't hear him.

He felt the copper-coloured hair on his scalp and neck quiver as if it was being violently grabbed in a bunch – not to remove it from his head but to direct the eerie shiver the whole way down his spine. He dared not look behind him for fear Joe's skeleton was gaining on him. His temples pulsed even quicker; his headache grew fiercer. He tried to scream out to his parents and the remainder of the group again but this time he was so hoarse no audible sound could escape his mouth.

Paul Gilmour felt his legs grow heavy; they felt like he imagined they would were he running through deep mud. Just as he was thinking that he had quit falling, he tripped over a large sod and fell flat on his face, which disturbed the earth and uncovered a pile of busy worms and he couldn't get the image of the worms eating away all the flesh from Joe's body out of his mind. He rose to his feet, spitting out imaginary bits of soil from his mouth in disgust.

This time he couldn't help it: he was sick on the spot. He tried to keep running and be sick to the side. He tasted the bile at the back of his throat and promised everyone, everything, every angel and every God he could think of, that he would be good – better than good as gold – if only he could just get back to the safety of his parents.

His prayers were answered because three-quarters of a minute later he ran into, and nearly knocked over, his mother.

And he was in such a state that he couldn't get a word out. His mother, with him in her arms, dropped to her knees on the earth and everyone fussed around him, offering various opinions.

'Give him air.'

'Hot tea with lots of sugar.'

'Holy Mary Mother of God, what's gotten into him?'

At the mention of the name, 'God', Paul's head swivelled a quick left and right several times and his eyes bored holes into his mother's, beseeching her with a silent: 'Help me, please, help me!'

'He needs a drink of water,' someone said very calmly.

'Stand back, I say, stand back,' the matchmaker ordered, although no-one did.

Eventually, when Paul's heart rate calmed down to mere double time, he pointed out across the fields in the general direction of the fast approaching Lone Ranger and Tonto and croaked, 'Uncle Joe … we found … we found Uncle Joe's bones.'

The workers were hit with a tidal wave of disbelief. It appeared that the very rumour that had been whispered in hushed tones for these many months, and as far afield as Magharafelt, had been confirmed.

Valerie Scott began wailing like a banshee. She later reported that she didn't know if her reaction had more to do with the fact that it had been Paul who had discovered the remains, or if she had been mourning Joe.

Tommy Patterson studied everyone and said nothing. Bobby Patterson stood in silence beside his father. They both looked like they were at a funeral just before the remains were removed.

'It's all over,' Pat Kane said, as he turned to comfort Maggie who was trying hard, although unsuccessfully, to contain her tears.

Nobody had ever seen Dan Stevenson or Ray O'Sullivan lost for words or short of antics to entertain a crowd, no matter how small. But here they were, acting as silent as the very ghost they had seen down in that riverbed.

Dorothy continued to mother Paul as only mothers can. She looked strangely at peace, since Paul had quietened down again and was back in the arms of his family.

On hearing his son's news, the matchmaker had hunkered down close to, but not right beside, his wife and son. He looked like an Indian brave, mid-battle – protecting his own, but equally keen to be able to get a move on and take them out of harm's way. He found he couldn't look Maggie, Pat or his wife in the eye. He wasn't sure if he was scared of what he'd see in their eyes or scared of what they'd see in his.

After a few minutes and without anyone saying anything more, the group started to disperse, perhaps to give each other a little space, maybe to take some time to formulate their thoughts.

On instruction from his father, Tommy Patterson had set off towards the village, heading straight in the direction of the Station

House. By the time he reached the Broadway he was out of breath and District Detective Inspector Colin Doyle had to give him a few minutes and a glass of cold tap water before he could spurt out his information. And spit it out he did, like someone vomiting uncontrollably, which left the detective having to remember it and put it all back together again before it made a jot of sense.

But sense it did make, eventually, and Doyle summoned Hill to accompany him back up to the farm.

On the way they passed Wesley McIvor and Valerie Scott walking down Kane's lane, Wesley trying, unsuccessfully, to console his sobbing girlfriend. When Doyle was assured they were not at the scene of discovery, he let them pass but advised that he would be calling on them later to take a full statement. He also cautioned them not to discuss any of the developments from the potato gathering. They agreed immediately. 'Aye, and pigs might fly,' he thought.

Bobby Patterson seemed to have taken control on the potato field, advising the remainder to stay there until the police arrived. Maggie and Pat were still distracted by their attempts to console each other. The matchmaker and his wife remained with their son and even Daniel Stevenson and Ray O'Sullivan had lost their usual zest for fun and devilment.

In view of the discovery, Doyle instructed Constable Edward Hill to 'Stay with Pat Kane at all times – do not let him out of your sight. If he goes to the toilet, you go with him.'

As they approached the group on the field, Old Man Patterson came to meet them. For the first time in living memory, Old Man Patterson didn't use his traditional greeting of 'So far so good' when someone (in this instance Doyle) asked him how he was doing.

'I've certainly been better,' he offered instead. 'I tried to get everyone to stay where they were, just like they'd do on *No Hiding Place*, you know, but I have to apologise for the fact that I didn't manage to keep Wesley McIvor and his girlfriend on site. Valerie was so upset, Wesley just totally ignored me and dashed her away, probably desperate to get the poor girl home. Dan and Ray were over there, under the old rail track with young Gilmour. I imagine they were probably loafing around when they discovered these bones. I think we all know whose bones they are – or, should I say, we all *think* we know whose bones they once were,' Patterson Senior continued, as he nodded an acknowledgement to his boy, who was still breathing heavily from his marathon dash into town.

Patterson Senior always had a smile in his voice and today was no exception. He was probably too old for gathering potatoes, if the truth be known. But he preferred the craic of the field to the company of his chickens. He looked like he was wearing several layers of jumpers and pullovers, the top one looking like it might have been hand-knit for him and once would have been vibrant with blue, yellow and red, but now it was caked in several shades of brown from the clay. He wore a heavy pair of corduroy trousers, so threadbare that they would've made a perfect runway down at Aldergrove. His feet were protected by a pair of wellies, turned down to half their length and then back up part-way to show a ring of inner – once white-as-snow but now a soily brown colour. His blue, thick woollen socks, again probably hand-knit as a Christmas or birthday present, rose out from his wellingtons to house the bottoms of his worn cords.

Doyle, who was ill equipped for the potato field, said in a voice just loud enough for Patterson to hear, 'Look, Bobby, this is very important: when young Paul came over with the information, what did he say?'

'Aye, well, he went straight to his mum, put his arms around her and said they had found Joe – he claimed they had found Joe's bones,' the senior of the two Pattersons present recalled.

'Did he mutter it or did he shout it out?' Doyle pressed.

'He said it quite plainly – hoarsely, yet clearly, but not too loud. Then he started to sob. Poor lad, imagine finding a body like that?' Patterson replied.

'Am … could you tell me how Pat, Maggie, Michael and Dorothy reacted?' the detective continued.

'Well, let's see now: I saw Maggie look at Pat and then she ran straight into his arms. They hugged and I'm pretty sure neither said a thing. Dorothy continued to comfort her son … and Michael? Well, I think he just looked off in the general direction of the railway bridge,' Bobby replied, scratching his day-old beard.

Doyle looked over to the people in question from his vantage point, about ten yards from the main group. It was a strategic spot – he hadn't wanted his conversation with the two Patterson men to be overheard. Mind you, it left him close enough to pick up the scents of the old man. But, thankfully, it wasn't an unpleasant smell: although there were traces of the aroma of sweat, sometimes the smell of an old man – assuming he and his clothes were clean – was somehow reassuring. His son, on other, had not yet acquired this attractive quality, since he stank of some kind of flowery soap – Lux, was Doyle's guess.

'Did any of the four talk while Tommy was coming down to fetch us?'

'Not a lot – they mostly seemed to be in shock, as we all were, Detective,' was the simple reply.

'OK, thanks, Bobby. Could you stay here with the main group and send Daniel and Ray over?' Doyle asked. He wanted to maintain a distance from Pat just now, but he also wanted the surviving twin to be in company.

The Lone Ranger and Tonto were now very much back to Daniel Stevenson and Raymond O'Sullivan – no longer a duo, but merely two pale-faced individuals without a sidekick to comfort them.

'Right, lads, let's go to where you found the bones,' Doyle announced as they approached him – very sheepishly, it has to be said.

'Yes, OK – it's this way,' Daniel replied and led the way across the half-ploughed field and along the railway track for about a hundred-and-fifty yards before they dropped down the steep siding into the dry riverbed.

Doyle was disappointed.

There, close to the makeshift, three-berth fallen seat was a small pile of about six or seven bones of various shapes and sizes. Perhaps they might have even been human bones at one time, but they were hardly in total the remains of one Joseph Kane.

The three of them, under Doyle's careful directions, gently rooted around in the dirt on the hunt for more bones, which was a good move, since they turned up another five. Doyle didn't say it outright, but he was convinced that if Joe had met his end here some time in the last two months, there'd be a lot more of him left. Unless of course, that was, he'd been cut to pieces and burnt and spread over the farm. Wasn't there that case in Dungannon where a man had murdered his wife and fed her to the pigs, Doyle recalled. He decided to keep his own counsel on it for now, but he was clearly a dejected man.

When Tommy Patterson had run into the police station some fifteen minutes before, a whole host of thoughts had run through Doyle's head: had Pat actually killed his brother? Perhaps Maggie had done it – perhaps they'd done it together? It had already annoyed him that he'd not been able to positively tie up the missing person's case, as he'd reluctantly had to settle for the couple of sightings of Joe around Magherafelt on that one particular morning, but there'd been nothing since. The sightings had been good, no doubt about that, and they'd been confirmed on three separate occasions: there'd been Mattie Stewart, the milkman; the staff in Tone Sounds; Mrs Bradley, the owner of the café where Joe had dined; and then finally, although it wasn't one hundred per cent definite, the Ulsterbus inspector had been sure he'd seen Joe boarding the noon bus. But, despite these confirmations, should he have double-checked the sightings, just like his hero would have done? Had he put it to one side because deep down he was happy to have an excuse to claim that Joe was still alive and, despite still being desperate for a big case, all the town mutterings would stop? But something had continued to niggle Doyle about Joe Kane's disappearance and he wished now he'd acted upon it.

But it hadn't niggled as much as the scene in front of him: a few pathetic, sad bones. For a few moments there, he thought his big case had finally come along – and perhaps it still had, he reasoned. He would, as ever, be diligent and tie up all the loose ends as efficiently and precisely as his hero would have, but the pipe-smoking man in the deer-stalker hat had always, at the very least, found some meat on the bones of his victims.

'Let's see now. OK, let's leave it like this for now and go back to the others – I'll have some people come up and dig up this area,' Doyle advised the Lone Ranger, who looked like he'd just lost his silver bullets.

He continued to study the area around which the bones had been discovered and he suddenly realised he wasn't really looking at what was actually before him. Rather, he was trying to put together a system under which to conduct his investigation. He'd read numerous books, both fact and fiction, on murder investigations. But now that he was confronted with a real scene of … he still struggled to call it a scene of crime, even to himself … but now that he was confronted with a set of *circumstances* that may or may not be suspicious, it was totally different from reading about it. He slowly collected his thoughts and decided to revert to what his hero would have done. He would collect all the facts and clues available to him and he would not consider any conclusion, including the fact that Joe may or may not be still alive, until he made a full assessment of all the information available to him.

He surveyed the scene once again with new eyes and a clearer head. The earth didn't look like it had been dug in recent memory, but you never knew. If the bones before him were in fact Joe Kane's, then where were the rest of his remains? He swore under his breath; they'd also have to search the farm, its outhouses and sheds and, heaven forbid, the pigsties, if the Kane farm had any.

As the small group strolled back across the field, Doyle had the pair of witnesses recall every single thing that happened under the bridge one more time – just in case they had missed something or he'd failed to pick up on some vital nugget of information. He noticed a few people had, annoyingly, gathered on the other side of of the hedge, near the Kane's lane entrance. Joan Cook's theory that Maggie had taken on two husbands seemed to be gathering strength around the town whisperers recently.

'God, that was quick!' he shouted to Hill. 'Go and warn them all off – tell them we'll get them on trespassing charges or something. People are so morbid around here.'

'Aye, there's not a lot more for them to do, is there, though?' Old Man Patterson confirmed, with a smile still in his voice.

'Get rid of them, for heaven's sake,' Doyle ordered Hill impatiently, 'and then come and see me in the farmhouse – I've got a wee job for you.'

Hill nodded before scurrying off towards the gathering crowds.

'OK, let's leave it for now,' Doyle continued, mentally addressing his checklist. 'Daniel, Raymond, Bobby, Tommy and Harry, I'll come and see you all later on today. The rest of us should return to the farmhouse for a chat and maybe a wee drink of something warm,' he said, addressing the second request to Pat, Maggie, Dorothy, the matchmaker and his son. They, Doyle was sure, would all have a different story to tell, and no doubt a different interpretation of his request for 'a wee drink of something warm'. His own preference was for a cup of coffee but Pat and Michael, and maybe even Paul, looked like they could do with something stronger.

With that, the dazed group moved towards the farmhouse.

The detective himself wasn't dazed – no, far from it, for he had been so focused on trying to do everything by the book, and in accordance with his new slowly-but-surely approach, that he had completely forgotten possibly one of the most important points on his mental checklist.

Chapter Fifty

'Je-sus, he's not letting go – he's going to haunt us forever,' Pat said to no-one in particular once they had all reached the sanctuary of the farmhouse.

'Don't, Pat,' Maggie whispered softly.

They both looked at Doyle and shut up.

Dorothy was the one who took control indoors. She started organising tea. Doyle felt about as welcome as a hen at a roosters' party. The two sisters and their respective husbands were paying so much attention to each other, that they did not notice or care about the detective as he wandered around the kitchen, seemingly casual but noting everything – he'd settle for *anything* he could use as a lever to pry more information out of the foursome.

That was the big secret in all of this.

Whatever happened had already happened, so the facts were already there, lying somewhere nearby, waiting to be uncovered. All he needed to do was know where to look and what questions to ask. As Doyle looked around the room he convinced himself that there could be clues, perhaps items, that would point him on his way. But because he didn't know what these items were, or their significance, his eye passed quickly over them, whereas Pat, looking around the same room, might be cringing, praying the detective wouldn't pick up on anything untoward – should there be anything untoward, of course. If he could take the room as it was now, wind back the clock to that morning and let Pat know what would unfurl that day, down by the old railway bridge, what would Pat hide? Or what would he remove altogether? Doyle thought that the room's secrets would present the truth if he could do such a thing as turn back time. The farmhouse kitchen was a well packed but orderly room. The walls were pretty bare, apart from a couple of religious pictures and a photo of Pat's parents, blown up and neatly framed, enjoying pride of place over the fireplace. On the mantelpiece were a couple of small framed photos of Pat and Maggie on their wedding day, and a single framed photograph of Pat, Maggie and, surprisingly, Joe. There was also an unframed photo of the Gilmour children – Paul, Nick and Marianne – all dolled up in their Sunday best. The photographs' companion on the mantelpiece was a clock, set centre-stage and constructed from black wood. It had obviously once borne a white face, which was now browned with smoke and age. Alongside the clock, at either side of the mantel, were two matching vases in the shape of smiling dogs and a letter rack, made from untreated or unpainted wood and again, like the clock face, showing its age in a fire-smoked yellow.

To the left of the fire was a black coal bunker filled with peat and wood. To the right was Pat's chair, amply cushioned. To the left of that was a pair of red tartan bedroom slippers. All they needed was a small circular book table with large pipe and magnifying glass and this could have been a perfect spot for Holmes, a place by the fire for his considerations, deliberations, violin playing and drug-induced forays into the mind. But there was no table, no pipe or baccy, wacky or otherwise. But there was a small ottoman, which also served as a seat, covered with a pink and blue flowery material. The edge of a newspaper, probably the *Mid Ulster Mail* Doyle noted, stuck out from beneath the lid.

Working his way around the room to his right, Doyle then came across a large chest of drawers, pine wood, with a smallish mirror resting on top. Then, still travelling to Doyle's right, came a door – closed – and next, in the corner, was a vintage gramophone with a built-in radio. The lid was down and there were a few singles, EPs and albums scattered across the top. Doyle noted Jim Reeves' album *Gentleman Jim Reeves*; the Drifters' single 'Under the Boardwalk'; Peter and Gordon's 'World without Love', which he duly discovered was written by none other than Lennon and McCartney, according to the credits (and he had no reason to doubt them); Cilla Black's 'Anyone Who Had a Heart'; and, partially hidden under the Jim Reeves album, the Beatles' single 'A Hard Day's Night' with a Parlophone Records dust jacket. The final single, the detective noticed was also housed in an identical Parlophone green-tinted sleeve – Matt Monro and his top-ten hit 'Softly As I Leave You.'

To the right of the corner that housed the gramophone, and taking up nearly the entire wall, was a large sofa covered with the same material as the ottoman. The next wall along was the one with windows, back door, sink, cooker and work surface, complete with a set of cupboards under the sink and worktop. A plate and cup rack, also made from pine wood, sat to the right of the window. The plates were obviously old, white with dark-blue patterns, and probably originally owned by the Kanes' parents, or maybe even their grandparents. On the window-sill was washing-up liquid; a cup with no handle containing pens and pencils; several plastic roses – given free with Daz washing powder and now waterless in a long thin blue, with infrequent white hoops, clay pot. Doyle figured the pot was probably made by one of the twins – or even one of the sisters – in a long-since-forgotten pottery class.

As Doyle looked around he noticed again that the house was benefiting greatly from the feminine touch. Maggie's efforts to restore the farm*house* to a *home* seemed to be very evident. He wondered again whether, like the gossips suggested, this was the very core of the unravelling problem.

The kettle had boiled and Dorothy made the tea. Doyle so wished they'd offer him coffee: tea just went right through him, and it was difficult when you were trying to ask people questions, listen to their answers, judge their reactions as they answered and think up your next question, while at the same time trying to push your knees through one another in order to delay the much-needed toilet visit. Oh well, he mused, he didn't have to drink it – he could just politely sip.

'Oh, let me see now,' he began, directing his question to Maggie, 'is there another room we could use?'

'Yes, there's the parlour,' she replied, nodding towards the door between the chest of drawers and the gramophone.

The detective could hear Hill walking across the yard towards the back door and he wanted privacy for his one-on-one interviews. If he had Hill entertain the remaining three adults and one child while he was asking questions next door, it would ensure that stories weren't agreed upon and compared in advance. The other thing he was anxious to do was to gather (carefully, of course) the bones and take them back to the police station. He had already decided to use, for the sake of privacy, a potato sack and that he and Hill would do this on the way home. Daniel and Ray – and Paul Gilmour, for that matter – were the only other witnesses to the remains, and the Lone Ranger and Tonto were too dejected for anything other than a stop-off at Moore's public house for a bit of private drinking.

Doyle chose to talk to Pat Kane first, mainly because he might also need to speak to him last, following his chats with Maggie, Dorothy, Paul (with his mother sitting in, of course) and the matchmaker. Then, if information gained warranted it, he would take Pat Kane into the police station for further questioning.

It was difficult, all this; at least Sherlock Holmes rarely knew his criminals, Doyle thought. Once Holmes' clever detection was accomplished, he would hand over the culprits to Scotland Yard and he and Dr Watson would head off to celebrate. But Doyle lived in this village, no more than a few miles, in fact, from the very farm that had now become the centre of his investigation. For heaven's sake, he had even grown up with (although he was older than) Pat and Joe Kane. After this case was done and dusted, he was going to have to continue to live and work in this area with all these people. Oh yes, they were very delicate eggshells he was about to set his brogues upon, aye, and he could hear them start to crack from just looking at them.

Chapter Fifty-One

'This is not looking too good for you, Pat,' Doyle offered quietly when they were safely behind the closed parlour door.

Doyle thought he saw a look in the twin's face of 'Oh God, all of this, and you too.'

Pat buried his face in his hands and remained like this for ages. The detective took the time to check out the second room he had been invited into in the farmhouse: the parlour. And what a room it was. Doyle felt like he had just stepped back at least one hundred years by coming through the door. Certainly the twins' grandparents, or possibly even great-grandparents, appeared to have been more prosperous farmers.

Doyle looked at Pat Kane – the heir apparent – slumped on a beautiful rosewood easy chair with a woven cane back, seat and sides puffed up with black cushions, each decorated with a solitary large red rose. The detective studied him intensely and then wondered when the last time was that anyone had been allowed in this room dressed in anything other than their Sunday best. Above the cleaned-out fireplace was a beautiful Charles McAuley painting of men and women gathering potatoes under a blue cloudless sky – a scene, excepting the dress, very much like the one he had come across earlier, he thought. The other big change, of course, was the fact that the potato digger, out of sight in the painting, would have been horse-drawn instead of today's tractor-drawn version.

On the mantelpiece itself was the Kane family heirloom: the silverware, all proudly polished and looking as good, if not better, than the day it was bought. Doyle didn't know much about silver, but he was sure the two candlestick holders, the two decanters, the two tulip-shaped vases and the solid silver horse – which was about ten inches high and fourteen inches long – would have been enough, if sold, to purchase a tractor for those potato gatherers in the McAuley painting.

And there was more. An incredible rosewood sideboard was covered with hand-carved ornamentation, one of which was a symmetrical affair that came out of the sideboard carvings, rising proudly from the rear and above to support an oval mirror. The oval mirror had a single rose engraved on it, similar to those on the cushions. Beneath the mirror, on the sideboard top, was a silver punch bowl with a silver ladle and fourteen silver punch cups hanging from hooks, evenly placed around the perimeter of the bowl. Alongside this was a matching fruit bowl, the silver tone of which had never been blemished once by the acidic juices of fruit.

There was another easy chair, identical to the one Pat was slumped in, and a similar sofa, a three-seater. These two chairs and sofa were placed around the fireplace in a wide arc, showing off a rug about eight foot by twelve. It was breathtakingly beautiful. The weaver had managed to illustrate a country scene, not unlike some of McAuley's work, with green and brown fields, blue skies, white fluffy clouds and in the foreground on the right-hand side a large rose, to match the others in the room. Beyond the rug was a well-worn and well-polished wooden floor.

Around the room were lesser pieces of rosewood furniture – a corner and shelving units; a proud ticking grandfather clock; several little magazine tables with racks underneath and a bookcase with glass doors. All of these units were packed to overflowing with ornaments and bric-a-brac, which included glasses, old watches, various clocks and egg-timers, letter-openers and crockery – cups, saucers and plates. The walls were covered with sepia-coloured framed photos, framed maps of the local area and beyond, along with a framed embroidered Red Hand of Ulster and more frames filled with what looked like deeds, letters and other official-looking documents. This room and its entire contents would have an antiques dealer thinking he'd died and gone to heaven.

This was Pat and Joe's heritage. Here, about the walls, you could see where, and whom, they'd come from. One got a great sense of history and also of the toil and sweat – of four generations of Kanes, if the papers and photos on the wall were anything to go by – that must have gone into the farmland over the last hundred years. Was this long proud line now about to end with one twin killing the other? What a sad scene, Doyle thought. All of this, as he looked around the walls one more time, just to end with the death of one brother at the hands of the other. The bones of a member of the once proud Kane farming family to be found under a railway bridge by the Lone Ranger and Tonto. Goodness.

But what was in Pat's head? Not once since the bones had been found had Pat seen fit to deny that they were in fact the bones of his brother. Nor had he denied that he had been responsible for the bones being found there. Doyle felt this was a bit of a tenuous theory to have. Sure, Pat certainly hadn't denied such an accusation, but then the accusation had been made only in the minds of the majority of gatherers up on the field.

'Oh, let me think now, Pat,' Doyle began as he sat down in the chair identical to the one his interviewee was in, 'yes … we need to talk about this.'

Pat Kane took his face out of his hands, shook his head severely a few times as if to clear his mind and looked Doyle straight in the eyes, as if to say, 'OK, I'm ready for you.'

Doyle took it as his sign to go ahead. 'Do you know anything about these bones, found down under the railway bridge?'

'No, Inspector, not a thing – just as much as the rest of youse.'

'Do you think they are Joe's bones?'

Kane's eyes answered that one for Doyle as the twin shot him an 'are you crazy?' look.

'Be careful how you answer this one, Pat: have you any reason to believe that they are Joe's bones?'

'I have no reason whatsoever to believe that they are my brother's bones. Following the Magherafelt sightings, I, like everyone else, believed he was in Belfast,' Pat replied, quite solemnly.

'When was the last time you were under the railway bridge?'

'Whoa,' Pat blew the word through his lips, 'let's see now … about two year since. A cow wandered under the bridge and couldn't flippin' get out – the sides were too steep – and so I had to pull her out with a tractor.'

'And you haven't been there since?'

'No, Inspector, I haven't been there since,' the twin replied firmly.

'Look, Pat, please give me something here. Give me *something* to work on. You know, could your brother have fallen in with a bad crowd? Maybe something went wrong, they did this to him and perhaps threw the body under the bridge?' Doyle pleaded, wanting – with all of his being – to believe that Pat hadn't had anything to do with the death of his brother. All the contents of the parlour they now shared, the detective and the surviving twin, would have led anyone who cared to believe that it just wasn't possible for this man to have killed his brother.

'I'd love to be able to say something like that; it would get all of this from our doorstep, Maggie's and mine. But hand on heart, Colin, I just can't. There is nothing I'm aware of; there are no *people* I am aware of who would wish to do my brother harm.'

'Did you know that Daniel Stevenson and Ray O'Sullivan would go there today?' Doyle enquired, shifting track.

'Well, they always have quick light lunches so they usually go off for a lark somewhere. There was a bit of a rain shower today so they probably, I imagine, just stumbled under the bridge for shelter. Other days they've used the hay shed, or the cowshed, or they've just slunk under one of the big trees. Usually, it's wherever they can get their biggest audience assembled,' Pat replied, allowing his warm smile to creep over his face for the first time since young Paul had come running across the field earlier that day.

'Aye, they're a pair, aren't they?' Doyle said, encouraging a lighter side to the conversation as he sat back in the chair and crossed his legs.

'That's true, but people don't seem to realise that they are also very, very good at their work. They lark around quite a bit, but their equipment always works well and they do most jobs a lot quicker than you'd expect. That equipment, you know, all the harvesting gear, doesn't come cheap to rent, so the quicker they are the better for me, better for the farm,' Pat replied, appearing happy to be talking about something other than the disappearance of his brother.

'They were also on the field when you and Joe had the big fight. At the time you were harvesting?' Doyle started, trying to find a direction to take the questioning, a direction that would give him some much-needed information.

'Like I told you before, that was just a bit of a brother kinda scrap.'

'Well, Pat, that's not exactly what the other people on the field tell me. They, that is to say, some of them, were shocked by how violent you were to each other. And,' Doyle continued cautiously, 'they say it had something to do with Maggie, about Joe and Maggie.' Doyle pushed himself even further into his extremely comfortable chair. He'd thrown the stone in the water, a rather large stone at that, and he wanted to sit back now and observe how far-reaching the ripples ran.

At first Pat looked at the detective as if to say 'What are you on about?' But he didn't explode as Doyle thought he might. Perhaps he was even happy to have it out in the open, Doyle surmised.

'Look, all that carry-on was nothing really. Joe was quite down. He'd just split up with Doris Durin. Maggie and I thought they were great together; we thought they would make a go of it. But for some reason they didn't. They broke up, didn't they? Joe was down. He saw how happy Maggie and I were together. He must have developed some fixation on her. At first we laughed about it. But then he took it to a point where we couldn't really ignore it any more, you know, laugh about it and pretend it wasn't happening. So I warned him off, simple as that. I warned him off. I wasn't aggressive or anything about it: I just wanted him to know that I was serious and it had to stop.'

'What had to stop?' Doyle asked. He was reluctant to interrupt Pat now he was on a roll, but it was just too good an opening to pass up.

'You know, him bleedin' messing around.'

'Like how, Pat?'

'You know, getting frisky, chasing her about like I wasn't there. Behaving like a man does to a woman, but never to a woman who already has commitments, commitments like a bleedin' husband, for instance,' Pat grunted.

'OK, let's just stay with this point for a while – I'd like to get this clear in my mind. Your brother was coming on to your wife?' Doyle asked, making the question as direct as he knew how to. He found himself with his elbows on the arms of the chair, his hands involuntarily clasped in front. He stole a glance at his fingernails to see if they were clean – as usual they were spotless. But what did it matter? Here he was, finally getting somewhere with this case after several long and trying months, and all he could do was worry about trivial matters such as his fingernails. It's not as if Pat was going to jump up and run out of the room declaring, 'I couldn't possibly talk to you – your personal hygiene is deplorable.'

Doyle found that sometimes he could have such a clear vision and sharpness of mind that he could just focus on something being said and at that same time, maybe because he was so tuned in, as a trained officer, he could have all these other observations running around his mind at the same time. It was like he could be looking at the door for two months or more, and he could think he knew all there was to know about that door: you know its shape, its structure, where the handle is, what type of handle it is, the colour of the door and its surround. But, because he had been looking at it for two months or so, he was no longer really looking at it. You know it's there and your mind fills in all the features allowing, and maybe even encouraging, your eyes to be lazy. But then one day you look – really look – at the door again, and it's opened just a little. You don't know how or why it's opened, but your distraction ensures you start to really look at it again, as though you are looking at it for the first time. But now the shape is different, and the different shape ignites a whole other series of ideas in your brain and so your sharper vision is called upon. Could be that, Doyle thought, or it could just be that some days you are lazier than others.

'Well, not exactly – more like horsing around a bit, if you know what I mean.'

'What, he wasn't being *too* physical with her or anything like that?' Doyle continued.

'No, no. It was more kinda just unwanted attention … He was making Maggie uncomfortable. And I spoke to him about it. I hoped that when I made him aware of it he would realise what he was doing and back off,' Pat answered, trying really hard to shut the metaphorical door.

'But he didn't. He didn't back off, I mean?' Doyle said, trying to push his toe in the same door, just a little to keep it open. He didn't want it slammed in his face. Figuratively speaking, of course, he reminded himself.

'Well, no. Not really. If you must know, he started on about it again that morning with Maggie in the kitchen, when I was out starting work. She didn't tell me about it until later that day. In fact she didn't really tell me – she'd never have volunteered it. But I could sense something was wrong by the way she was behaving. Not her usual self. Maggie is usually a fun person and not a lot bothers her or gets her down. But she didn't know how to handle this. I mean it was awkward for her, wasn't it? I'm her husband, he's my brother, we were all living under the one roof, and so she didn't want it to blow up into anything. But it had to be dealt with,' Pat started, moving around a bit uncomfortably in his chair. Doyle noticed for the first time that he had put a newspaper on the chair in order to protect it from his dirty clothes – probably something his mum had always insisted he do and it had turned into a habit. The rustling of the newspaper underneath the twin had stopped so he must have found a comfortable position.

'So I prised it out of Maggie and went over to Joe to have it out with him and the closer I got to him, the madder I became. By the time I reached him I was so mad I just tore into him; once it started, it was hard to stop – all our pent-up frustrations with each other just came flooding out. I'm sure other brothers do the same, especially twins. We had a bit of a scrap, we were pulled apart and, I didn't say it to you at the time, but I felt that was why he'd run off. So if I'm honest, I'm glad in a way we had a fight, since it kinda brought everything to a head. In fact, if it hadn't been for the village gossips bugging Maggie it would have been perfect, because the fight meant that Joe went off, leaving us by ourselves for the first time. But then the rumour mill went into overdrive and threatened to spoil everything on us,' Pat offered, twisting once again in his chair.

'Look,' the twin continued, rising from his seat, 'if there's nothing else, I'd really like to get out of here with these dirty clothes. There are the potatoes to be dealt with – I've got to bring them into the shed; now they're out of the ground, they're going to need protecting from the cold night air.'

Doyle nodded – he had more questions, but they would keep. 'Could you send your wife in, please?'

As he awaited the arrival of Maggie Kane, whose significance in the case had just grown in the previous few minutes, the policeman wondered if the recent loosening of Pat's tongue was a result of the discovery of the remains under the railway bridge?

Chapter Fifty-Two

Maggie Kane, *née* Watson, walked into the parlour a few minutes later looking every bit a worried woman – a very worried woman. She caught Doyle over by the sideboard, studying one of the family photos closely. The policeman decided not to push home his advantage; he knew Pat would have had a few words with her and given her a heads-up on the direction his interview had taken.

'They're amazing some of these photos, aren't they?' Doyle opened, inviting her to look at the pictures.

'Yes, every single time I come into this room I'm in awe of everything in it. It's like it's from another world. Even Pat says it's like going into another house. We don't really know what to do with it, but somehow it definitely seems wrong to change it,' Maggie offered in a quiet voice.

Doyle hoped she would relax now she was aware they were not going to get straight into the heavy stuff.

'That's Pat's great-grandfather. Pat is named after him. And did you know he lived until he was ninety-nine? That's a shame that, isn't it – that he didn't make another few months which would have won him a telegram from the queen? And they say that he was as sharp as a razor the day he died. He read all the papers, local and national, and he could have a conversation about any topic he chose. Pat says on the morning of the day he died, he was engrossed in a conversation with his son – you know, Pat's dad – about wasting money on new curtains,' Maggie said, and then she broke into laughter.

Doyle looked at her, eyebrows arched.

'You know what he used to say? He used to say that the reason he lived so long was because he smoked like a train and drank lots of

Guinness and poteen, but that he always made a point of visiting his place of worship every Sunday morning,' Maggie said, recalling the oft-told bit of Kane family folklore for the detective.

'How did he die?' Doyle asked.

'What, you mean apart from old age?' Maggie laughed. 'He went for a nap that afternoon as usual and died in his sleep, real peaceful like – no fuss, no agony, no pain. He just fell into the big sleep.'

Maggie was one of those people who when she smiled or laughed her face was totally transformed. She'd long, straight, naturally blonde hair, characterful brown eyebrows and a small snub nose, which enhanced the fullness and magnetism of her lips, which infrequently shielded her perfect snow-white teeth. This woman – and in her late twenties she surely was a woman, although she retained some girlish qualities such as her innocence and inquisitiveness – with her full but firm, maybe even perfect, figure was stunning when she laughed. No wonder Joe had turned his attentions to her. Who wouldn't have been attracted to this woman, Castlemartin's answer to *Peyton Place*'s Barbara Parkins.

But then Doris Durin wasn't exactly a bag lady and Joe had lost his chance with her. So why did he think he had any rights with a married woman; and particularly one who was married to his own twin brother? There was something missing, Doyle thought – something *big* missing.

Maggie sat down in the chair her husband had left moments before, as though to acknowledge to the detective that she was ready for his questions.

Doyle made his way to his seat and started, 'Oh let me see now … so tell me about you and Joe?'

Maggie laughed nervously. 'Well, it's difficult really. He split up with Doris and, as you know, he seemed to take a shine to me. I warned him off, he wouldn't listen, and then Pat warned him off when he *still* didn't listen. They had a fight on the harvest field and Joe left the following morning. That's it in a nutshell,' Maggie offered.

Doyle smiled wryly. It sounded very much like Pat had managed to pass the very same 'nutshell' of information onto Maggie during the few seconds their paths had crossed between interviews – any more than that and Edward Hill, keeping an eye on the gathering of witnesses in the next room, would have become suspicious. Doyle immediately regretted his lack of diligence in ensuring his interviewees be kept apart during questioning, but it was too late for that now. More important was the question of why had Pat been so desperate to pass this information on to his wife.

'Was there ever anything going on between you and Pat?'

'Yes, quite a bit actually: he's my husband,' Maggie said, breaking into one of her wonderful smiles again.

'Sorry! I mean Joe, of course – what I meant to say was, was there ever anything between you and Joe,' Doyle repeated, somewhat embarrassed by his faux pas.

'No, certainly not!' Maggie lied, sounding fully composed and prepared for the question.

'It's just, you'll forgive me, it seems a bit weird, someone – anyone – coming on to their sister-in-law without some kind of stimulus. For instance, had you ever dated when you were in the tech or anything like that?' Doyle pressed.

Questions and answers – that's all it was down to. Questions and answers. As his hero never tired of saying, you needed to amass as much information as possible before you started working on your theories. If you developed a theory, or three, too soon in the case, the fear was that you might try to tailor your information to support those theories.

'Believe me, Inspector, there never was anything of substance between Joe and me,' Maggie replied, throwing the detective a clue too opaque even for one with their full headlights on.

'But I find it—'

'Look, sir,' Maggie interrupted, 'you have to realise, with Joe it's not exactly, well, he wasn't exactly on the same page as the rest of us.'

'Oh?'

'Yes.'

'As in?'

'Well, if you check with Doris Durin – and I'm sure in light of the circumstances she won't mind me telling you this – Joe was incapable of having a proper relationship. He just didn't get it, or know how to do it. And he hadn't a clue that anything was wrong either – Doris told me that Joe had been genuinely shocked when she broke it off. He really thought that what they had was a proper relationship. So you can't tell me that someone, someone like that, is going to be bothered about brothers and wives and marriage and all that goes into it. Doris ditched him and I was the nearest female to him. The fact that I was married, let alone married to his brother, didn't even come into it. He wanted to, and that was enough for him. But don't you see, sir, you have to understand that in his mind it *is* enough. His interpretation of a relationship is different to ours, so therefore he is not bound by the confines and rules we place on ourselves. I imagine if he and Doris hadn't split up, it wouldn't have become an issue and he'd still be here and we'd all be peacefully getting on with our lives,' Maggie surmised. She was fidgeting with her hands now, turning her wedding band around and around on her finger. 'The other thing that is worth pointing out to you now, and it has been mentioned to me by so many people, it's not something I can ignore anymore ....' Maggie stopped talking for some reason.

'And this "thing", Maggie?' Doyle pushed, hopeful of a big revelation.

'Well, it's just that everyone keeps saying how much Doris and myself look alike,' Maggie replied, somewhat bashfully, which led Doyle to believe that Maggie thought Doris was beautiful, which by association meant she was also claiming that tag for herself. Perhaps this was the reason for her apparent hesitation.

'So do you think ... is there any chance that Joe continued to bother Doris?' Doyle asked, recalling that Joan Cook had mistaken Doris Durin up at Portrush for Maggie Watson in a ginger wig.

'Good question, but I'm afraid I don't know the answer. I've never asked her. She started dating your constable so quickly I thought it might be inappropriate to bring up Joe's name again. But I can see what you're thinking.'

'You can?'

'Well yes: say Joe was bugging Doris and Doris had a new boyfriend, a policeman, well, perhaps it could be another reason for Joe's disappearance,' Maggie offered, posing yet another theory that Doyle hadn't considered.

'You're not suggesting … ' Doyle started to reply halfway through a smile and a look of sheer disbelief. 'But sure Constable Hill didn't meet Doris until he interviewed her about Joe's disappearance.'

'I'm not suggesting anything, Inspector. I'm merely implying that you can take a few facts and, with only a little twist to them, you could get the town gossips' tongues wagging two to the dozen. Perhaps you might now appreciate how Pat and I have been feeling for the last few weeks,' Maggie grandstanded.

Doyle nodded and looked down at his notepad. 'I do understand. But I have to ask you a question now that I hope won't upset you.'

Maggie nodded wide-eyed, which Doyle took as his cue to continue.

'Is there any chance that Pat could be responsible for Joe's bones being found under the railway bridge?'

'Are they definitely Joe's bones?' Maggie asked, in a quiet, reverent voice.

'Well, we don't know for sure until all the tests are done, but the evidence seems to point that way,' Doyle responded, feeling sorry he'd phrased his original question in such a clumsy way. And to make matters worse, Maggie wasn't about to let him off with his reply either.

'And what evidence would that be, Inspector Doyle?'

'Well, the argument, the fight, Joe chasing you, him supposedly running away,' Doyle said, reeling off as many points as he could think of as quickly as he could on the rebound.

'Well, I think you may be getting a bit ahead of yourself there. The argument – the fight and Joe chasing me, as you put it – are all the same thing and it was dealt with and ended up in said fight. That was the end of it. That was two brothers dealing with something that was not pleasant for either of them. That was both of them dealing with the same thing, but in their own different ways – Joe, because he couldn't get what he wanted, and Pat, because the squabble was threatening to hurt our marriage and the peace around here. But to suggest he, or we, would deal with the issue by doing something, well, I don't really know what you are suggesting … Can you really sit there and tell me you suspect Pat or myself, either together or separately, of being guilty of getting rid of Joe permanently?'

Doyle didn't reply – he merely stared expressionlessly at Maggie.

'Well, I'm speechless, to be honest. And what about Joe turning up in Magherafelt a few weeks ago?' Maggie snapped so loudly that Doyle was scared they'd be heard in the kitchen and someone would come running in. He didn't want to be disturbed at this point in the questioning. Not when it was just getting interesting.

'It would seem to me that our recent discovery throws a different light on all of that,' Doyle offered, trying hard to keep the edge from his voice. He was keen to return the interview to its chatty form, whereby Maggie's responses would be less considered and she might let something slip out.

'Jeez, this is all new to me, Inspector, and I apologise for interfering, but I would have thought that before you started running off and getting excited by all of this – you know, over Joe's remains – shouldn't you at least try and get some proof that they are in fact Joe's remains. I mean, it seems to me that the minute Paul – a ten-year-old, mind you – the minute he ran onto the field, crying that he'd found bones, everybody immediately assumed that they were Joe's. Isn't that a bit like putting two and two together and getting a pint of milk?' Maggie replied, chastising the policeman, albeit in a friendly manner. She had taken her boots off and left them at the back door and she had a pair of, Doyle assumed, her husband's thick blue socks on over her stockings. The socks came up to her knees and, in theory, under her dress, a frail-looking dark-blue effort with white spots. However, the more animated she became in her answers, the more her dress rode up, exposing a little bit of leg for the detective's attention. Intentional? Perhaps a little, Doyle thought, but she definitely wasn't flirting with the policeman. She was treating him as an equal, which he liked – not too argumentative but on the other hand she wasn't being subservient to his badge.

Doyle's unintentional glimpse of Maggie's stockings sent him rocketing back to a time in the distant past. He'd been seventeen and he was lying on the banks of the Moyola with a young lady called Colette, also seventeen, a blonde who in hindsight was quite possibly *the* love of Doyle's life. Doyle had been throwing stones into the crystal clear waters of the gushing Moyola when Colette laid back and encouraged the young Colin to do likewise. Then they kissed, in an awkward kind of way. He sat up again, uncomfortable about what he would, should or could do next and he noticed that her skirt had risen up her legs, exposing nothing more shocking than her stocking tops and snow-white thighs. Colette's eyes were closed and her companion continued to steal glances at the wondrous sight while simultaneously pretending to be preoccupied with his stone-throwing.

Doyle quickly snapped himself out of such mind wanderings, pleasant though they were. 'Surely that begs another question, Maggie.'

'Which would be?'

'If those aren't Joe's remains out there, then whose are they?'

'Gosh, now there is a good question – a great question, in fact. Or do you mean what else have Pat and myself been up to?' she asked, but she didn't expect, nor receive, an answer. 'Oh come on, Inspector, this is Castlemartin, not New York, London – or even Belfast for that matter! Things like finding dead bodies under railway bridges just don't happen here. Everyone knows everyone else too well to consider murdering them. It's just not an option or a solution to problems around here. When's the last time someone was murdered in Castlemartin? Come on now, Inspector, answer me that?'

Doyle thought long and he thought hard. 'A-ha! What about John Preston?'

'Well, number one, that was ten years ago and, if my memory serves me correctly, *one* theory certainly was that he was murdered,' Maggie started as Doyle afforded himself a little, just a little, smile of smugness. 'However, the other, and the more plausible view, was that he'd been cycling home from the pub a little too worse for the wear; he'd fallen off his bike into the hedge; bumped his head on a stone and had knocked himself out. By the time he was found the following morning he'd died of hypothermia.'

'Yes, but then explain if you can why his bike was found a good ten feet from his body?'

'Oh, I'm sure that's a job for the experts such as yourselves. But, if I were to hazard a guess … perhaps the bike just kept going a bit when he fell off? He was going down a hill at the time, wasn't he? But it's really not important. My point is – and you've just helped me make it – people don't get murdered around here. The last one was ten years ago and, as we've just discussed, it's still very debatable whether John Preston died in the elements or if, in fact, he *was* murdered. Castlemartin is too close a community for such terrible crimes. Sure, they happen in those Sherlock Holmes wee books you are always reading, but not around here, sir – we don't have any strangers; or long-moustached Chinamen; or devious characters who answer to the name of Moriarty; or people with ginger hair; or even cocaine addicts – oops, sorry … that was Sherlock Holmes himself, wasn't it?'

They both laughed at that one. Doyle was thoroughly enjoying himself with this fine woman. Why hadn't he been able to find such a lovely lady to share his life with? He'd been sure no such person existed when he decided not to bother with women any more. But then again he'd known Maggie Watson a good few years, from afar at least. Most villagers guessed, before she married Pat Kane, that she was too fussy and was going to get left on the shelf, so to speak. So why hadn't he approached her then? Under careful consideration, the answer was really a simple one. When she met and married the twin she became another person. Or maybe she just blossomed into the person she was always going to become when she met her soulmate.

Doyle wondered if a similar kind of metamorphosis would have happened to him if he'd met his perfect woman? And if so, how apparent would the changes have been? For the most part, he actually enjoyed his single life. It meant he could do whatever he wanted – if he fancied a drive to the sea for a walk along the beach, he'd do it. If it was a stormy day, he'd find a nice quiet little café, order a coffee and do a little reading. Why would he drive all that way just to read? Simply because he could.

But, of course, that type of thinking didn't solve his problems. He was thirty-four going on seventy and he'd missed out on his youth in his attempts to reach the higher echelons of the Royal Ulster Constabulary. This was, of course, not something to be sniffed at. But he *was* set in his ways, no doubt about it, and that ran right from his everyday uniform of Donegal tweed jacket and grey flannel trousers, to his inability to rid himself of his sweet tooth and his late-night sugar binges, despite the knowledge that they were doing him no good at all. No, to make changes at this point in life – for a woman or anyone else – would be completely out of the question. He was a detective and, above all else, that is what he wanted to be. He felt very lucky and privileged to be able to work at, and make a living from, something he loved with a passion. Here he was now with a proper case, possibly the first real case in which he was going to have the chance to put his considerable skills to proper use, uncovering the mystery behind Joe Kane's Basil Bond trick. Only with Basil Bond, his vanishing acts were nothing more than an illusion – exceptional illusions but still illusions nonetheless. The vanishing of Joseph Kane, on the other hand, had not been a trick, of this Doyle was certain. And with today's interviews, particularly that with Patrick Kane, the detective was convinced the mystery could be solved on the Kanes' farm and, might possibly even be resolved on this very day.

'A question I asked your husband, Maggie. Do you know anyone who would have any reason to do Joe harm?'

'Like how?'

'Well, you know, maybe he just fell in with the wrong crowd and, who knows, maybe he backed out of one of their schemes or whatever and they felt he knew too much about them and—'

'Much too fanciful, Inspector, I'm sure,' Maggie cut in. 'You have to realise Joe didn't make friends. He let Pat make friends for both of them. It's been the same all their lives – the way it was with them. Joe doesn't have any "Joe" friends, if you know what I mean. I'm sure nothing like you've just described could happen.'

'It would explain a lot, Maggie.'

'Don't you mean it would be convenient? It might be convenient, sir, but it's couldn't have been a reality,' Maggie concluded.

Doyle was impressed with the way the second of his prime suspects had reacted. He had just offered her what might have been considered by some to have been a lifeline, a theory that presented a way out of the whole sorry affair for herself and Pat. Yet she had avoided the lure to clear her name. Either Maggie wasn't involved in the disappearance of her brother-in-law or she was clever, very clever.

'That'll do for now, Maggie – no doubt we'll talk again later.'

'No doubt. I don't know about you but all this talking has me parched – come through to the kitchen and I'll make you a cup of tea before you start your next interview.'

Doyle accepted the offer, since the break also gave him a chance to study Maggie and Pat, husband and wife, together. They were tight, very tight. Not in a lovey-dovey kind of way, but their closeness was evident in the little sparks of magic flashing between them: a glance, a look, even just a brief touch that showed what they had was the real thing. Whatever the real thing was, Doyle thought. But might the protection of this loving partnership have become the motive behind something much more sinister? Could they have murdered Pat's own twin brother, Maggie's brother-in-law, to protect their marriage? Had either one of them been responsible for Joe's death – assuming he was dead, of course – and the other knew about it, then surely they'd be struggling to maintain the tightness clearly visible between them now. Coming to this conclusion, the detective was left with three, maybe four, possible scenarios. One, Pat was responsible for Joe's death and Maggie knew nothing about it. Two, Maggie was responsible and Pat knew nothing about it. Or, three, husband and wife were jointly responsible and were so in love they felt the end justified the means, leaving them both with a clear conscience. But it would only be a matter of time before one of them started to wilt under the pressure and their guilt would rise to the surface. Perhaps there'd be a fight, which would sow the seeds of disquiet. Months or even years might pass, but the seeds would inevitably grow into an ugly shrub, the fiery leaves and branches spreading beyond control and eventually choking their caretakers. The detective knew that all he had to do was wait for the strangling weeds to do their work. And the fourth possible scenario? Well, that was perhaps the most intriguing, for maybe Joe's disappearance had nothing to do with either his brother or his sister-in-law. Maybe someone else entirely was to be held accountable for whatever had happened to Joseph Kane.

Chapter Fifty-Three

Dorothy Gilmour, *née* Watson, had always been somebody's something: her mother and father's daughter; Maggie's sister; the matchmaker's wife; Paul, Nick and Marianne's mother; or, most recently, Pat and Joe Kane's sister-in-law. She neither sheltered behind these names nor shunned them. Dorothy Gilmour was too strong, capable and determined to suffer from any such insecurity. She was a country woman, a woman of resolve.

She was also a woman who knew how to make people – even District Detective Inspector Colin Doyle – feel comfortable. She did this by being there for the people around her, by acting as a sponge to soak up all their problems, rantings, ravings, insecurities and fears, never once giving them a hint she might possess any of those imperfections herself, thus making her counsel all the more solid, offered from a position of strength and undiluted by personal flaws.

'Well, Inspector,' she began, wiping her hands on her apron, 'this appears to be a bit of a mess, doesn't it?'

'Mrs Gilmour, it certainly seems to be at the very least a mess,' Doyle replied, happy now that he'd a chance to wet his whistle. 'This is an incredible room, isn't it?'

'Isn't it just – all this family history in the one room. Certainly makes one feel humble, doesn't it?' the matchmaker's wife said, as she smoothed off her dark-blue apron, one she'd borrowed for the occasion from her sister.

'Did you know Joe very well?' Doyle enquired, anxious to start the questioning.

'How well do we ever know our in-laws, Inspector?' She smiled, a staged smile that broke into a laugh as she continued, 'in fact, how well do we ever want to know our in-laws? But you know, he'd been down to our house a bit with Pat, and then Maggie and Pat would bring him over to our house once in a while after they started courting. Then we'd see him up here at the farm. But I don't think we were here much before the wedding.'

'You knew Pat and Joe then, before your sister started going out with Pat?'

'Well ... knew *of* them more like. As you know, in Castlemartin you can't help but see people around. I was talking to Michael about this the other night and we probably know everybody in Castlemartin. In fact, everybody in Castlemartin probably knows everybody in Castlemartin. All our lives lived out in this fish bowl ... we were just wondering what it would be like to live somewhere like, say, Belfast, where you just know the people in your neighbouring streets and a few extra friends. Away from the pressure of everyone looking over your shoulder, would you live your life any differently? In Castlemartin, for instance, you wouldn't want to do anything wrong, would you? You'd die from the embarrassment of everyone knowing you. I always think that's why there's so little crime around here and so much in the cities,' Mrs Gilmour offered.

'Possibly, possibly,' Doyle replied, half-hearted, for he'd tuned into something Dorothy had said earlier in their conversation. 'My question about whether you knew the twins before Pat and Maggie started seeing each other – well, I asked it because you said that the twins were around your house a few times and you said *then* Maggie and Pat would bring Joe over once in a while, once they started courting. So, from the chronological order of your answer, I thought perhaps you knew the twins *before* Maggie and Pat became a couple, as it were?'

'No, I see what you mean. I mean, yes, the boys were over a few times to see Michael.'

'OK, let me see now. I just want to get this clear. Before Maggie and Pat started going out? The twins were at your house then, before Maggie and—?'

'Oh yes,' Dorothy cut in, clearly becoming impatient.

'But why would they be coming to see you if you didn't know them?'

'And you're the detective,' she smiled, 'Michael's work, of course. You know, matchmaking?'

'So, Michael matched Pat and Maggie?' Doyle asked in disbelief.

'Good heavens, no, Inspector – this was before Maggie and Pat started dating. They met up at our house one evening by accident and it all started from there. I don't remember what he was over for, but Michael will be able to tell you that, I'm sure. He's got the memory of an elephant.'

'Let's get back to Joe,' Doyle said, deciding he'd gained all the knowledge he was going to in that line of questioning, at least for now, 'you didn't know him very well then?'

'He's very quiet; he's hard to get to know. But I didn't really have to try, you know – we were never really in each other's company much. And when the twins were together, Pat always seemed to do all the talking. I think that's why he likes Maggie so much – she's a right old chatterbox, and for the first time in Pat's life, he didn't have to hold all the conversations; he most likely couldn't get a word in edgeways. Is it like that with all twins, Inspector, where one relies on the other so much?'

'I don't know,' was Doyle's honest reply, but he made a mental note to try and find out.

'It must be horrible, though, don't you think? Maggie's my sister and we are supportive of each other and all of that, but sometimes you just want to get away and be by yourself and do it by yourself. But it must have been hard up on the farm for Pat and Joe; I mean, as much for Joe as for Pat. When you depend on someone so much it must be really frustrating,' Dorothy said, and then cut herself off very quickly. 'Oh heavens! Of course I'm not suggesting it was so bad that, you know, either of them would have considered … oh heaven's no, Inspector!'

'I'm sure you weren't implying anything, Mrs Gilmour,' Doyle offered in comfort. He paused, rubbing his hands a little to warm them. The room on this autumn evening had a bit of a chill. 'I wanted to ask you about the fight. You remember? The day of the harvesting?'

Dorothy nodded in acknowledgement.

'Well, I've two questions really. The first one is: were you close enough to see it start?'

'No, not really – I was over at the other side of the field with Maggie, dishing out the tea and sandwiches, and suddenly we started to hear this commotion. It started quietly and then it just got noisier and noisier, until eventually you couldn't ignore it any more and all of a sudden it was a screaming match. Surprisingly, Pat wasn't fit for Joe – I mean in the fight. Pat came off the worse for wear and he certainly was saved from a real hiding by the men pulling them apart.'

Dorothy Gilmour now sat silent. Her hair was tied up in a practical style that was intended to keep it out of the way more than anything else. She had, Doyle was sure, several skirts on, the top one being a vibrant red, a colour which suited her well.

After a time she asked the detective, 'And your second question?'

'Oh,' Doyle replied. He'd been waiting to see if she was going to tell him any more about the fight, but it was clear that she was not. 'Yes, did you see what happened to Joe after the fight?'

'Well, the men held him down while Maggie and Michael took Pat into the farm. I followed – the men must have released Joe 'cause he came rushing past me and ran straight down Kane's lane.'

'Did you see him later that evening?'

'No, Inspector, I haven't seen him since.'

Doyle thought she'd finished her answer, but once again he was proven wrong.

'And if you ask me my opinion, I'd say that Maggie and Pat have been much better off and happier since he left to go wherever he went. They've been able to start behaving, for the first time as a proper man and wife. And if you want some more of my honest opinion, District Detective Inspector, I would say that Pat and Maggie wouldn't be as happy as they are if either of them had done anything – anything at all – to harm Joe. In all of this sorry situation, I'm totally convinced of that fact.'

Doyle was sure she had a point. But then again, as she had also pointed out, everyone was a lot happier now Joseph Kane was out of the way. 'The Case of the Missing Twin' was probably how Doctor Watson would have recorded it. Doyle tried to imagine, if his case *were* a Sherlock Holmes mystery, what thoughts such a title would bring to his mind. Without hesitation he answered himself with a succinct 'The surviving twin did it, of course.' Then a split second later, the niggling voice in the back of Doyle's head offered in a scornful voice: 'Then prove it, clever dick.'

'Well, Mrs Gilmour, that's all the questions I have for the minute.' Then the District Detective Inspector added as an afterthought. 'I'd like to speak to Paul now and I'd like you, as a parent, to be present, but could you do me the favour of letting him answer on his own: it's important you don't correct him or contradict him in any way. And don't be going worrying – I'll make sure my questions are safe for young ears.

*

Paul Gilmour seemed to be quite excited about at the prospect of being questioned by a policeman. The matchmaker's son wasn't nervous or anxious, but rather excited for his adventure to begin.

Doyle had the young boy sit on the sofa, at the end closest to his single chair, thereby placing the mother at the furthermost possible point from her son. But he needn't have worried: Paul Gilmour, soon to be eleven, was confident, bright and articulate and totally uninhibited by his mother's presence. And for the second time in today's interview session, it was the witness who started the ball rolling.

'So, do you really think those were Joe's bones, the ones we found under the railway bridge?'

'Oh, we won't know that for a while, Paul. Why did you think they were Joe's bones?' Doyle asked, conscious he was guilty of patronising the young lad.

'Well, it's quite simple really. On the first harvest day someone tried to poison him. On the next harvest day he and Pat had a big row. Boy, that was a big fight. I'd never seen adults behave like schoolchildren before. It was quite amusing until I realised that they were really hurting each other. And, finally, Joe hasn't been seen since,' Paul replied, completely unfazed by District Detective Inspector Doyle but, at the same time, causing his mum to lose one of her nine lives.

'Back up there a bit, please – the poison? Who was trying to poison Joe?' –

'I don't know exactly, but someone put something in Joe's sandwich and when he took a bite he started vomiting. It must have been very strong the poison, or they used too much, because Joe started to be sick immediately.'

Doyle stared at Paul and then at his mum in disbelief. He suddenly noticed that he was rubbing his hands feverishly. He hoped Dorothy and son hadn't noticed. He looked again to the mother for some kind of explanation.

'Is it OK for me to speak? It's just that you said you wanted me to keep quiet.'

'No, no, please, it's fine,' Doyle replied, now anxious that the mother should intervene.

'Joe is allergic to tomatoes. Somehow a tomato or part of a tomato came to be in his egg sandwich and he was very, very sick there and then on the field,' Dorothy informed the detective.

'I don't like tomatoes, Mum, but they don't do that to me.'

'Yes but there's a big difference between not liking something and being allergic to it,' Dorothy replied immediately from her corner on the triangle. 'When you are allergic, like Joe is to tomatoes, it's a physical and chemical reaction. Joe's suffered from it all his life and he warned us about it, so I don't know how the tomatoes came to be in the sandwich.'

Doyle made a mental note of the word 'tomato' as he recalled Mrs Bradley's story about the tomato on a lettuce island being removed from Joe's fish-supper plate.

Content with his mother's explanation, Paul turned back around to face the detective for his next question.

'Let's see now, oh yes. Paul, do you remember the day the constable – Constable Hill and I – passed you out on the lane – Kane's lane?'

'Yes, I do, I was on my bike.'

'How did you manage to get up to the farmhouse before us? You were at your house when we left.'

'Well, you came in the top way, didn't you? By Railway Terrace up the Broadway, right into Noah's Arc and left into the farm lane?' Paul enquired, taking his turn to quiz the police officer.

'Yes, that's correct.' Doyle smiled.

'Well, I went down the bottom way – you know, Garden Street into Shore Drive, back towards the centre by Lough Road and then right in to Noah's Arc and right into the farm.'

'You must have been quick to beat us though … You took the longer route and you left after us?' Doyle suggested.

'Yes, but it's easy to get along that route quickly; I miss all the traffic by keeping away from the Pear Tree Roundabout,' Paul boasted.

'So you managed to get the note to Pat before we arrived.'

'Yes,' came Paul's quick and proud reply, but then a look of disappointment set in on his face, very slowly, but equally transparent.

Well, that's the cat out of the bag, Doyle thought. But which cat precisely? 'OK, let me see now,' he continued, trying to move up a gear. 'Today, when you found the bones … can you tell me how it happened?'

'Actually it was more of an accident really. The Lone Ranger and Tonto were larking around. We were all on this seat, a plank across a couple of five-gallon cans. One of the cans rolled out from under the plank and the three of us went flying into the dirt. One of them, the Lone Ranger I think, surfaced with this white stick in his hand. Well, we *thought* it was a white stick but then he said it was too stiff for a stick and as he was trying to work out exactly what it was we found another one and then another one. Then one of them had the joint, you know the thicker bit at the end, still intact and that's the one I knew for sure was a bone. Then we looked some more and found lots of bones and that's when I twigged that it must be a body. And then I felt very sad all of a sudden when I realised that they must be Joe's bones.'

Doyle switched track, only this time a little too quickly. 'I hear you like the Beatles?'

'Yeah.'

'Yeah, yeah, *yeah*,' Doyle replied, in an attempt to prove his youthful credentials to Paul, but failing miserably. Dorothy gave a little laugh of encouragement. 'Which one do you like the best?' he continued.

'George, George Harrison, I like him the best,' Paul replied swiftly.

'Really? What does he do? I've never heard of him. Isn't it Paul Lennon?'

'John Lennon and Paul McCartney,' came the knowledgeable and patient reply.

'Yes, that's it, but who is George Harrison?'

'He's the guitarist. The other two, Paul and John, they write all of the songs – they always seem to be competing with each other when they're on TV. George seems happy to stand back and get on with it and play guitar, and I like him for that. Brendan Quinn, the guitarist out of the Breakaways showband, says George is a very good guitarist, and he should know – he's a great guitarist himself.'

'You know Brendan Quinn?'

'No. I go to school with Philip Kerr – his father is Dixie Kerr and he plays saxophone with Brendan in the Breakaways showband.'

'Oh, I see. Tell me, Paul: is there a new Beatles single out?'

'Well, there was one out in July, a song from their film.'

'Yes, that's the one. What's it called again?'

'It's "A Hard Day's Night", sir.'

'Yes, "A Hard Day's Night", that's the one. Do you have a copy of it?'

'No. Maggie has it and we swap – she likes the Beatles as well. My dad puts all Maggie's good records, particularly the Beatles, on the tape recorder for me. You're not meant to do it but they're in London – they're never going to find out, are they?' Paul replied.

'Were you with Maggie when she bought the single?'

'No, I don't know when she got it. We talked about it when it first came on Radio Luxembourg and she said she'll take me to see the film when it eventually reaches Magherafelt. Maggie jokes that Nicholas will probably be in long trousers by then. I was over there one night with my mum and she played it for me. She's also got the "Long Tall Sally" EP,' Paul enthused.

'Really,' Doyle replied, as he realised he was getting way off track. 'Had you ever seen Pat fight before that day on the field – you know, with his brother?'

'No, I mean, it's probably a bit like me and our Nicholas: you know, you get on each other's nerves a bit, and there's a bit of a shout, but then we're brothers and that's what brothers do. Isn't it?' As he asked his question he turned to face his mother, who rewarded him with a warm smile.

'How did you get on with Joe?'

'Very well. He was always friendly to me, especially up on the farm. My dad says I sometimes ask too many questions – I just like to find out about things. But Joe would always take the care and time to explain things fully to me. Pat is OK too, you know, but mostly he's just being soppy with Maggie. I kid Maggie about that too. But she always says, "Just you wait five or six years." Joe was fine with me – we'd always chat. He'd ask me about school and stuff and tell me about his own school days. He was quiet though. When anyone else was around he wouldn't say much, ever,' Paul recalled.

'Did you talk to him about him being sick on the field?' Doyle asked, liking this boy more and more. The detective wasn't sure if it was his honesty or his innocence he liked most. And his mother was as good as her word, sitting back to allow her son to open up to the policeman. Sometimes just a little clicking of the tongue or a tut-tut from an elder would be enough to ruin a child's confidence and reduce all their answers to a simple 'yes' or 'no'.

'No, I felt too bad for him and I didn't want to remind him about it. But I felt real sorry for him. From the look in his eyes I really thought he was going to die. He just kept on vomiting and vomiting. You don't eat a lot of food, you know, in the course of a day. I worked it out once you know and ....' Paul seemed to think better about this and his sentence just died out.

'OK, Paul, that's it. You've been very helpful and, I tell you what, I'll take a look at this George Harrison fellow the next time the Beatles are on TV,' Doyle concluded, before awarding himself two black marks for managing to allow Paul to both start and finish the interview with the upper hand, so to speak. But it was too late to make amends and he didn't want to dig a bigger hole, so he turned to the mother. 'Could you send your husband through, please?' he asked, thinking that an in-depth chat with the matchmaker was bordering on being overdue.

Chapter Fifty-Four

The matchmaker was heard before he was seen. He was growling, clearing his throat, as he walked through the parlour door. 'My turn?' He smiled to the detective as he sat down where his son had sat less than a minute since.

'It is that. I've just had a very interesting conversation with your son.'

'Oh yeah?' the matchmaker replied, appearing a little concerned. 'You have to realise he's still relatively young and perhaps embellishes things a wee bit.'

'Yes, well, we were discussing the Beatles and he was trying to persuade me that the guitarist, Harrison, was the best. Now little and all as I know about the current pop scene, I do know that goes against the grain. It's usually John or Paul who get the vote. So this shows me that Paul – your Paul, that is – is prepared to think things through for himself and form his own opinions. So maybe we shouldn't be too dismissive of what he says,' Doyle said, carefully forming his sentence and trying to gauge the matchmaker's reaction at the same time.

'Fair play. I say, fair play to you, Colin. Don't you think, though, he could also have a preference for George Harrison simply because it makes him different from the majority of people?' The matchmaker was back to his usual painful-sounding rasp. He clasped his hands together and put them around his right knee, leaning back so that his right leg lifted off the ground in an uncomfortable stretching exercise.

Doyle looked at the matchmaker and offered, 'Back?'

'Yes. Don't you see, I'm not as young as I used to be and the old back doesn't recover from all the prattie gathering the way it did when I was younger. Take young Paul, for instance: first thing the following morning he's fit as a fiddle and rearing to get back on the field again, whereas I have to calculate every move and assess the potential damage before I go ahead. It works out that by the time you get on to the field and you've just about uncracked all the joints, it's time to bend over and start again. I sometimes think it would be easier if I could stay bent double all day. I'm OK until it comes time to stand up straight again!'

Doyle grimaced in sympathy before returning his thoughts to the job in hand. 'What was in the letter you sent Paul to deliver – you know, on his bike – to Pat Kane that morning when we came to interview you at your house?' Doyle rarely leaned back in his chair. He preferred to sit closer to the edge, alert and ready to spring at any second, as a cat would after a mouse.

'What? Oh *that*! That was just of a personal nature,' the mouse replied, his raspiness making him sound more like a lion.

'Am,' Doyle huffed, hoping he was making it clear he was far from satisfied with the reply, 'you know when you help Joe and Pat with their harvest?'

'Yes,' the matchmaker replied tentatively.

'And Dorothy helps Maggie with the food and drink?'

'I'm still with you.'

'Do they prepare the food in the morning or the night before?'

'A bit of both, I think. Dorothy will do a bit up at our house the night before and we'll bring it over with us in the morning, then they'll do the fresher things at the farm that same day,' Michael replied, moving his clasped hands to his other knee.

'Oh, let me think now. So, the sandwich which made Joe sick – that was an egg sandwich, wasn't it?'

'I believe so, but I can assure you I wasn't looking too hard at what he was throwing up or trying to identify the contents.'

'And the same egg sandwiches would have been made on the morning up on the farm?' Doyle persisted with this point. He wasn't even sure where he could take it. He hoped that the matchmaker would think *he* knew where it was going and then cut the detective off at the pass. Then at least he'd know where the pass was.

'I believe so, but Dorothy or Maggie would be in a better position to answer that question,' the matchmaker replied, appearing to feel safe on what he considered to be solid ground.

'It's just that young Paul thinks Joe was poisoned and I just wanted to establish the preparation process,' Doyle stated, showing at least one of his cards, if not his ace.

'I see.' The matchmaker smiled, but instead of commenting on the detective's not-so-subtle suggestion, he continued, 'Paul thinks Joe was poisoned, does he?'

'Yes.'

'And did he have an idea who might have poisoned Joe?'

'Well,' Doyle replied, not entirely sure he was the one who should be answering the questions, 'he connected Joe's disappearance with Joe being sick on the field, the fight on the field and the bones they found today. I think he has his suspicions but he didn't take me into his confidence on that one.'

At that point, they both heard music drifting through from the kitchen. Doyle couldn't work out what it was.

'Can we talk about your work a bit, Michael?'

'Sure, as long as you don't want me to betray any confidences,' the matchmaker replied defiantly.

'People come to you when they need help in finding a husband or a wife.'

'That's basically correct, but it's not as simple as that. That implies that they have tried other ways and means of finding a partner and on being unsuccessful they come calling on me, the matchmaker. And, yes, some do it that way. But equally some see me as being the *only* way of finding a husband or wife.'

'Pat and Joe came to see you in your professional capacity?'

The matchmaker looked initially confused, then disturbed and finally amused. 'Paul – Paul again?'

'No, actually your wife, in a roundabout way. She told me that she was aware of Joe being at your house, with Pat, before Pat and Maggie started to ….' Doyle searched for words, for his mind was concentrating on where he was taking this.

'Started to become Maggie and Pat,' the matchmaker offered helpfully.

'Yes, exactly.' The policeman smiled. Unlike Maggie Kane, Colin Doyle had an ugly smile. When his face cracked into its humour lines it was transformed hideously. Children were known to break into uncontrollable sobbing at such a sight. So he had learned to guard his smiles.

'So the twins came to see you?'

'Correct.'

'And did you help them?'

'Well, I tried – not with much luck, it has to be said – and then Pat met up with Maggie and, as they say, the rest is history.'

'So you'd nothing to do with that?'

'Colin, *plea*-se. We're talking about Maggie here: she's my sister-in-law, not to mention a good friend.'

'But surely Pat's a great man: why wouldn't you want to see your sister-in-law happily settled down and married? And if you could help the process along a little, professionally speaking, then why not?'

'Because I'd still want to stay married to her sister. If her sister for one moment ever had the idea I'd … goodness, perish the thought. No, suffice to say, Maggie and Pat met up at our house one night and after that they began stepping out,' the matchmaker said, physically shuddering at the detective's suggestion.

'What was Pat doing up there that night?'

'Look, if you must know, he'd come up to tell me how one of his dates had gone. Not too well, I hasten to add, and he was seriously considering giving up on the matchmaking,' Michael replied, still appearing troubled by his back.

Doyle had a long way to go yet and bad back or no bad back he was, he hoped, glory bound.

'And Joe, how did Joe fit into all of this?'

'Sorry?' The matchmaker sighed.

'Your wife told me that Pat and Joe together visited you at your house.'

'Oh, I see what you mean. They came together, probably to give each other moral support. At that point they were both after wives. I realise it is quite a big thing for a man or a woman in these days to come along and see me, don't you see? But the farm wasn't doing too well and they had to work all hours just to make ends meet and they didn't have time to go and hang around the ballrooms and pubs and bars. So I imagine they were here backing each other up. I know Pat would have come by himself but I don't think Joe would have come near the place without his brother.'

'Wouldn't it be a little tight up here for two married couples?' Doyle pressed.

'Oh, I don't know, I've seen worse – and in this village too, at that.'

'So did Joe have any matches?'

'Well, not really,' Michael replied hesitantly.

'Not really? Surely either he did or he didn't?'

'Well, he'd … What's the best way I can put this? … He behaved like he thought it was a shop. You know, come visit me in my house and buy a wife the same way you would buy a loaf of bread. He didn't really want to know about the dating and getting to know somebody, anybody. I got the feeling Joe was emotionally detached from all things matrimonial. Maybe even from all things. I know it sounds like a funny thing to say, Colin, but I really do think he would have preferred to have walked into our house and bought someone and took her straight home.'

'And then brought her back for repairs when it all broke down,' Doyle offered sympathetically.

'Exactly, I say exactly!' the matchmaker replied joyously, like a preacher who'd just made a successful connection with his congregation. 'Eventually, as soon as he realised it wasn't going to work that way, he just stopped coming to our house. Then Maggie and Pat started dating and he just dropped out of the scene entirely.'

'Was he jealous?'

'Ah, now, there's the 64,000 dollar question, I say there *is* the 64,000 dollar question,' Michael replied and stopped sharply, to think about either his answer or the implications of it. 'Honestly speaking. I'd have to say yes, I think he probably was.'

'Did you ever discuss this with Maggie or Pat?'

'No, never. It never came up. I can tell you that they were and are very happy. If I had been responsible for the match I couldn't have made a better one. I don't think even my father could have made a better match and there was none better than my father in these parts at matchmaking.'

'OK, let me see now, yes … let's backtrack a bit. Before he gave up on the matchmaking, was there anyone he tried to date? I'm thinking of … I'm looking for anyone who may have had a reason to do Joe some harm. So if he was seeing someone through you, with the intention of a possible match, and maybe even marriage, and say for whatever reason he didn't go through with it, perhaps maybe she had wanted to, you know, go through with it, and then she was bitter or upset or whatever?'

'And killed Joe?'

'Perhaps, Michael. Perhaps. At this stage I have to consider all options – and that would have to be an option.'

'No, it never really got that far, if you know what I mean,' Michael replied as he leaned over in his seat to get closer to the policeman. Instinctively Doyle leaned in as well to share what he hoped was going to be a revealing secret. 'I sent Pat out on a few dates, three to be exact. I went along on the first one, as I usually do, to allow them the opportunity to get to know each other, and then if it's going OK I let them go on one by themselves. Well, after every first date Joe would say to Pat, "She'll do, fix it up." And I'm sorry to say that happened three times before I realised he wasn't kidding – he just didn't want to be bothered with it all.'

'He couldn't have been that naïve, Michael?'

'That's what I thought and I even kidded him about it.'

'What did he do?'

'Just stormed off without saying a word.'

'So there's no-one?'

'Nope, sorry. Then he started dating Doris Durin and that seemed to be at least getting started, but then they split up.'

'Do you know why?'

'No, but I imagine it was back to the same old thing, you know, him being unable to connect with the wemen.'

'With women or with people?'

'I'd say with wemen. I mean, he wasn't the most communicative of men but with the rest of us men, up on the field, he'd get by and, strangely enough, Dorothy says he gets on well with our Paul. But not with the wemen.'

'Have you had similar cases in the past?'

'No. I've had very shy men before, and women to a lesser degree, and they need a lot of coaxing or a couple of pints or whatever, but eventually they get there.'

'How was Pat in all of this?'

'I think in the beginning, before he met Maggie, don't you see, he was keener to see Joe married off than to be worrying about himself – he only went on the dates because Joe didn't want to. Then he met Maggie and events took over for them both,' the matchmaker reported.

'So you definitely didn't set up Maggie and Pat on their first date?'

A simple 'no' and a smile was all Doyle received in answer to his question.

'The thing that bothers me in all of this, Michael, is how calm everyone is. You know what I mean? We might just have found the remains of Joseph Kane and no-one seems to be particularly bothered about it. It's like no-one is grieving for him or worried that he has been missing so long. Doesn't that bother you?'

'I think you'll find he wasn't close to anybody: it's as simple as that really. The sad thing is that there is no-one *to* miss him.'

'Not even his brother?'

'I'm not my brother-in-law's keeper.' The matchmaker grinned. 'That's a question for Pat.'

Both interviewer and interviewee sat in that room of history contemplating each other and the twins, and not necessarily in that order. Doyle struggled to find his next question for the matchmaker. He knew where he needed to go. It was just that he had not thus far made enough progress along any of his lines to warrant the step to the next question. Then suddenly he heard his voice ask, 'Have you ever had a situation like this before, like, where you were asked to make a match for twins?'

'Brothers and sisters, yes, but never twins.'

'Tell me,' Doyle continued, now picking at a thread, 'did Joe and Pat mention to you whether or not they were interested in sisters?'

'Well, if they'd got here twelve years earlier they could have gone for Maggie and Dorothy!' The matchmaker laughed, and when Doyle didn't join in with his laughter, he continued. 'No, I don't remember that was ever a topic of conversation.'

'What about two sisters going after the one husband or, say, two brothers looking for the one woman – you ever encounter anything like that?' Doyle asked, appearing the more uncomfortable of the two.

'The thing about wolves in sheep's clothing, Inspector, is that they're always given away by their shoes,' the matchmaker replied slyly, as he stared down intently at Doyle's dirty brogues.

'So the rumours of the twins looking to share a wife ….'

'I'm not even going to dignify that question with an answer. Next!'

'Well there is a certain kind of logic to it, isn't there? Economics, space ….'

'Listen, Colin, if the wife heard you talking about this, we'd be out on our ears, I say, we'd be out on our ears and no mistaking it. Can we move on, please?'

'Was it even discussed?'

The matchmaker totally blanked the detective.

'Would you even admit it to me if the rumour was true?' Doyle pushed.

For his sins, the detective received not even a flicker of acknowledgement from the matchmaker.

'OK, Michael. So when did you last see Joe?'

'Same as I told you last time, Colin,' the matchmaker replied, offering a look that said 'and we both know it'. 'It was on that day on the harvest field, you know, when he and Pat had the fight.'

'You haven't seen him since?'

'No.'

'Have you spoken to anyone who *has* seen him since?'

This time the matchmaker hesitated, ever so slightly, before replying with a 'no'.

'Did you cause him any harm?'

'No.' The matchmaker's answer came very quickly and impatiently.

'Do you know anyone who might have caused him harm?'

'I am unaware of anyone causing Joe harm. However, it's a small village, so it is quite possible that it could turn out that the person who caused Joe harm is a person with whom I'm familiar. I know that may sound like a weird answer, but, don't you see, it's the most honest way I can answer your question.'

'Do you think those bones, the ones found by your son, the Lone Ranger and Tonto, are the remains of Joseph Kane?'

'I really wouldn't have the slightest idea,' Michael replied, once again straining his knee against his clasped hands.

Doyle loved to note and examine the body language of the people he was interviewing – particularly his subjects' hand gestures. Why had the matchmaker his hands so firmly interlocked around his knee? The detective felt these gestures sometimes gave away more than the words spoken. Supposedly the matchmaker was trying to relieve the pain in his back. But Doyle wondered what the subtext was? Subconsciously, was Michael trying to prevent his hands betraying him. If only Doyle had been able to decipher the secrets of this body language, he felt he'd know exactly what the matchmaker was trying to hide.

Doyle realised that he was coming to a natural close with his final witness of the day, so he used the time to have another look around the room. He walked over and closely inspected the photographs. He looked at a photo of Pat and Joe and their parents. The twins took after their mother. 'What would happen if Joe showed up tomorrow?' he finally asked.

'Oh, there'd be a few days of idle chat and gossip, a little bit of inconvenience to the twins and Maggie but eventually things would settle down again,' Michael predicted confidently.

'Would he move back into the farmhouse again?'

'I don't know. I doubt it. I think you might find that Maggie and Pat are enjoying their newfound space so much so that they might push to change the domestic arrangements somewhat. But again, that's a question they'd be best to answer.'

'But you wouldn't be surprised if he came strolling back up the Broadway tomorrow?'

'Quite frankly, yes, I would be surprised. He's been away for too long now without any communication. What's he doing for money? Have you thought of that? Sure, he could have got a job but that would only have paid his living expenses – what about clothes and accommodation?' the matchmaker asked quietly.

'So you think he's dead.'

'Yes. I do now. At first I thought he'd run away and maybe that's because it's more of a preferred option to me, but now I'm convinced he's dead – I say, I'm convinced he's dead.'

'Do you have any idea how he came to die?'

'I haven't a clue. I wouldn't even know where to start guessing.'

Doyle decided it was time to collect the remains from up on the field and return to the police station. He thanked the matchmaker for his time and they both returned to the kitchen where Doyle bade his goodbyes and he and Constable Edward Hill stepped out into the surprisingly chilly air after the heat of the farmhouse.

But they were in for a big surprise.

Chapter Fifty-Five

'So what conversations were going on in the kitchen then?' Doyle asked his junior as he buttoned up his coat. Evening was falling. They were out at the time of day when it was easy for their eyes to adjust to the failing light. Should they be indoors now and looking out it would appear to be dusk, if not dark outside. Equally, the light escaping from the Kanes' kitchen window in a full downward beam was yellow, as opposed to the white it would become the darker the evening became.

Kane's lane narrowed as it passed along the south-side of the farmhouse where it became a real lane. The black tarmac stopped directly at the back wall of the house and changed into a fine reddish-brown gravel, which continued to the limit of the outhouses where it then changed back to the original dirt track. This dirt track originally (and up to as far back as ten years ago) had extended the entire way back to the junction of Noah's Arc. The lane eventually ran into the railway track about another quarter to half a mile back and the junction was in fact (henceforth) the now infamous railway bridge.

The bridge had obviously been built in the twins' grandparents' day, and the stream it passed over had long since dried up. The dry bed made it possible to cross under the railway line without going the whole way back into town via Kane's lane into Noah's Arc, taking a right onto the Broadway and then straight over the larger bridge where that road turned into Toome Lane. So where the farmland had dipped down to form a natural mini valley, to accommodate the stream, the North Western Railway company had built a bridge strong enough for the trains to traverse and just about large enough for a tractor, trailer and farmer to pass underneath.

On one of his fact-finding trips, Paul Gilmour had noted, to all who would listen and a few of those who wouldn't, that the stone the bridge was constructed from was exactly the same grey stone used to build the two churches and one prayer house now standing proudly on Church Street.

By the time District Detective Inspector Doyle and Constable Edward Hill reached the very same bridge, Hill had established that his witnesses had remained fairly quiet in the kitchen. Well, at least on the police matter in hand – they had covered a great deal of other, more trivial subjects, such as the weather; the potato gathering; the Lone Ranger and Tonto's equipment; the Beatles; what they were going to have for dinner (for Maggie had invited the matchmaker and his family to stay on); how much everyone on the field was owed and the historic contents of the parlour.

Doyle contemplated his sadness that no-one seemed overly concerned about Joe Kane, before he was interrupted by a late thought from Hill.

'Oh, one thing of note, though,' he added: 'when Pat came out from his interview with you he went straight to Maggie and said something like, 'I told him that Joe was chasing you. I had to. He needed to know the real reason for the fight on the field. So I told him that Joe was bothering you, after he and Doris split up, but that nothing had happened.' Or words to that effect. And that was it really. Those two are very affectionate with each other – not in a soppy way, it's just … well, there's genuine tenderness there.'

Doyle nodded and began to distil the highlights of the interviews he'd conducted over the previous hours into a bite-size chunk for his constable.

'I think it must be pretty cut and dried though now, don't you think?' Hill began, as he digested the information.

'You think?'

'Well, it would appear that Joe was after Maggie for some reason. I mean, it would be obvious why he was after her if she had been single, but she wasn't, she isn't – she's his brother's wife, for heaven's sake. This, this unwanted attention clearly wasn't going down too well. Pat tried to poison his brother, thinking that everyone on the field that day would believe that his brother was just experiencing another of his bad reactions to tomatoes, although this time it was intended to be fatal. As we know, it didn't work, but maybe that kept Joe quiet for a while. But then, just before that day's harvesting – the day of the fight – Joe started up again. He and Pat had a massive brawl on the field in front of loads of witnesses. Later that night, or early the next morning, Pat murdered his brother and hid the body, but not well enough.'

'OK, let's see now, yes, all fine, except for one important point. Joe was spotted by three people in Magherafelt, four if we include the Ulsterbus inspector, *after* the time you supposedly have him being murdered by Pat,' Doyle said, hands deep in pockets, tie blowing furiously in the wind behind him.

'Good point, good point. OK, then after the fight Pat warns Joe off. Joe goes away to Belfast or wherever. But Joe returns.'

'But he boarded the bus for Belfast.'

'Yes, but he also bought a present, the Beatles single for his sister-in-law, so he must have intended to come back at some point. Maybe he wasn't living in Belfast? Maybe he was living closer but on the same Belfast bus route – Toome for instance?'

'Possible.'

'So maybe later that day he returned to Castlemartin – Pat didn't want any more grief with his brother, so he murdered him, hid the body and the man with the silver bullets – well silver tooth fillings at least – found Joe's remains, over there under the disused bridge,' Hill concluded as the bridge came into sight – barely, though, due to the lack of light.

But as they drew nearer, something began to make Doyle nervous.

It was the bones.

There weren't any.

They were missing.

'I was sure we left them on a pile over here – by that green BP can,' Doyle announced, the panic rising in his voice. He couldn't believe he'd been so stupid. Here he was working on his biggest case, the Case of the Missing Twin, and he'd left valuable evidence, vital evidence – you couldn't get any more vital than the remains of the missing person – unguarded. And some bleeding git had gone and stolen it. He was now fit to be tied.

He silently berated himself for the error. But he couldn't very well have taken the bones up to the farmhouse – that would've been just a bit too insensitive and he'd already pushed Pat and Maggie enough. And there was no way he could have left Hill to guard the bridge – he'd been needed to keep an eye on the witnesses in the kitchen. All the other officers were busy on their own cases or manning the Station House. That was another problem with being a police officer in a small town – the lack of resources when a big case such as this *did* come along. What he should have done was hidden the bones – that would've been the perfect solution. Yes, a perfect solution, but he should have thought of it three hours ago.

He admitted this to himself as he and Hill continued to search under the bridge. They were using Hill's police-issue torch and the batteries were going flat so he had to keep hitting it every few minutes to reactivate the beam.

Then he had another panic attack. Up until that point, he was sure that one of the four adults he had just interviewed was responsible in some way for the death of Joe Kane. Yet they'd all been under Hill's supervision. So if it wasn't one of his prime suspects who had swiped the bones, who was it? District Detective Inspector Doyle suddenly realised that his case was falling apart at the seams.

Then Doyle had another brainwave.

What if the bones found under the bridge were not those of Joe Kane? This would explain a lot. This could put his prime suspect – one of the four he'd just interviewed – back to the top of his list, though it left him without a body. It could also mean that the bones belonged to someone else and the person responsible for *that* murder had come and removed the evidence while he and Hill had been distracted up at the farmhouse.

Two murders in Castlemartin.

And two unsolved murders at that.

Chapter Fifty-Six

'We've lost the body, sir,' Hill said. He'd wanted to find some words of comfort to offer his superior but these were the words which spurted from his mouth, with more spittle than sense.

'Really – tell me something I don't know,' Doyle hissed impatiently. 'And neither Pat, Maggie, Dorothy nor Michael left your sight?'

'Well, they did, sir.'

'Oh, they did? I thought I told you – Oh, which one for heaven's sake?' Doyle's sadness quickly turned to joy as he realised that the witness who'd escaped from the kitchen was probably the murderer. It was probably a bit more Agatha Christie than Sherlock Holmes, but anything was better than the dejection he'd felt a few minutes before.

'Well, they all did, sir.'

'What? They all left together? What on earth were you thinking?' Doyle snapped, seeing his case-closing clue evaporate as quickly as steam from a boiling kettle. But hang on a minute, he thought, they can't all be in this together? That would be just too bizarre, like the death of Julius Caesar, but instead of knives, this gang – Maggie and Pat and Dorothy and the matchmaker – had used a series of farming implements: perhaps a grass hook, a scythe blade, a gullet knife and a pair of sheep-shearing scissors. And the bloody hacking had the victim resorting to the immortal words, 'Et tu, Dorothy? Then fall Joseph.'

'I was just following your orders, sir. They went in to see you one by one,' Hill revealed hesitantly.

A flood of relief washed over the detective. 'Yes, yes, of course they did,' Doyle repeated, regaining his composure. Now he was back to his two separate murders, and the panic attack this evoked made a return.

'That's apart from Paul, of course,' Hill added, quite matter of fact.

'Paul? What do you mean?'

'Well, he asked if it was OK to go out and play. And I couldn't see anything wrong with it, you know, him out by himself – there's nothing he could do and he couldn't possibly be a suspect. Could he?'

'No, but he might just be *related* to the suspect, not to mention the deceased,' Doyle replied. 'Did you notice him talking to anyone immediately before he sought permission to go out to play?'

'He was with his mum the most, I guess. But he was generally roaming around the kitchen. To be honest, I thought the adults might talk a bit more freely in his absence so I was quite keen for him to go as well.'

'Great: not only does the suspect manage to sneak Paul Gilmour out to destroy or hide the evidence, but my constable encourages him to do so,' Doyle moaned, as he threatened to do serious damage to his brogues with all the stones and dirt he was kicking up.

'Oh God!' Hill shouted in a panic as he dropped the torch. The fall obviously banged the batteries into life because the beam now shone its brightest ever. It shone up into the roof of the bridge, which caused a series of eerie shadows on the stonework.

'What? What is it? Have you found them?' Doyle half shouted, half whispered, a shiver mainlining his spine.

'Look,' Hill hissed out of the side of his mouth, 'over there.' The terrified constable nodded in the direction of the opposite exit of the tunnel under the bridge.

Doyle looked over and saw an apparition so thin he thought it might have been a banshee come to claim the spirit of Joseph David Kane. Now it was moving, moving towards them.

He stood his ground.

It wasn't as if he was brave or anything like that. He just found himself anchored to the earth and unable to move a muscle.

'Is this what you're looking for?' the wraith's high-pitched tone enquired.

Hang on, Doyle thought, I recognise that voice. 'Hello?' he shouted.

'Inspector Doyle – is that you?'

The detective breathed a huge sigh of relief. The voice was not a ghostly call from the dead at all, but one of a child. And not only was it a child's voice, but it was also a child's person, and he soon came into view.

'With all the nosy parkers running around I thought it might be safer if these were rescued before they disappeared,' Paul Gilmour offered, as he handed over to the district detective inspector a small white flour sack containing, the detective deducted from the brittle rattling, the selection of bones discovered some hours earlier, just inches from where the police and the matchmaker's son now stood.

Doyle was hit by a rush of relief so violent to his system that he had to sit down on the single up-ended oil drum that was still standing.

'Good thinking, Paul. That could have been very embar—ah, it could have held up our case quite a bit. Good thinking indeed. We're indebted to you,' Doyle said loudly and clearly, his voice echoing around the grey stone walls. Under his breath he added in a mutter only Hill could hear, 'For saving our bacon, not to mention our careers.'

Chapter Fifty-Seven

By the time Doyle and Hill had walked back into Castlemartin, darkness had fallen over the village. It was one of those nights where the moon highlighted the movement of the clouds. A night for a fresh, brisk walk, Doyle noted, as he observed several people about the streets of the village.

Now he thought about it, there were a lot of people about the streets of Castlemartin and it was Hill who commented that the chatter seemed to get lower, the closer the both of them got. The buzz would then start up again a few seconds after they passed the various groups. Suddenly Doyle realised that none of the people on the packed street was out for a walk. Everyone was stationary.

It appeared to Doyle that perhaps every single member of the village was gathered on the streets of Castlemartin tonight. He was sure he even recognised a few faces from Magherafelt, Ballyronan and even one couple, a husband and wife, he was sure came all the way from Cookstown.

The muttering that followed the two police officers grew in volume, just like tumbleweed blowing through a ghost town, as they walked down the Broadway. They couldn't exactly decipher the words offered in their wake, but then a Guinness-proud voice said: 'Now that you've found poor Joe, aren't you going to throw Pat in jail?'

And then: 'And throw away the key?'

Then: 'Bury him under the bridge and see how he likes it!'

Then came the first female voice: 'Aye, and that Maggie too.'

'There's no smoke without fire, you know,' the original voice added.

Then a different female: 'Ah, they're all the same, the Watsons.'

Overlapped with, 'I blame the Kane twins.'

Followed immediately by, 'There have been strange comings and goings on their farm since their poor parents passed, God rest their souls.'

At that point it became impossible to make out one comment from the other.

Doyle felt nauseated at the thought of walking through the village with the bones of Joseph Kane in a flour sack; a sack gingerly held at arm's length to ensure that the flour would not soil his grey flannels.

All the brave spokespersons refused eye contact with either of the policemen. On a few occasions Doyle turned around to ascertain the speaker of the libellous words, only to find a serious amount of either shoe- or star-gazing going on. At one point, just as he was about to cross over the Broadway to the Station House, he felt compelled to say 'OK, that's enough. There'll be no more rubbish or we'll see if we can get a few of you charged with inciting a riot.'

That quietened them for a short time but about halfway across the road, the police were hit on the backs of their collective necks with: 'Just don't forget who pays your wages!'

Doyle was seldom as happy to enjoy the refuge of the Station House, and he was happier still to be greeted by Sergeant Bill Agnew, as solid as any foundation this side of the Empire State Building.

'The natives are ugly tonight, Bill,' Doyle offered with a smile.

'Sure, they've looked like that all their lives, but it's nothing the Avon Lady couldn't help them with,' Agnew replied, returning Doyle's smile as he added, 'as long as she brought along her husband's trowel to apply the make-up.'

'I haven't seen as big a crowd since the Christmas-tree gathering on the Diamond at Magherafelt last year. What's gotten into them?' Doyle asked, as he planted the flour bag on the desk in front of Agnew.

'I blame the television myself. There are only a few who have one, but they all talk about what's on it each night and they've been watching all this strike action and people gathering on the streets to show their opinion, support and strength of voice,' Agnew offered helpfully.

'Aye, but that's different: that's people-power being used as a positive to keep mines open, to get fair wages,' Doyle stated, his heart not really in the conversation. He was wondering what to do with his bones – well, the bones in the flour bag. He was also wondering should he inform someone, someone in Belfast, someone perhaps like his superior, the fire-breathing Regional Commander Stroke-Rees. Actually he wasn't really a fire-breathing demon – more like an ex-naval pussycat who had the odd rant and rave just to 'put the wind up the lower ranks', as he put it. 'It always worked on the high seas when discipline was the best, and sometimes the only, weapon with which to greet the enemy.'

No, Doyle thought after some consideration – informing Stroke-Rees could wait, at least until tomorrow. Then he considered Pat Kane. Should he be brought in? Perhaps even as much for his own safety as for Doyle's good. He could just imagine a conversation with Stroke-Rees: 'Well, a bit of good news and a bit of bad news, sir … We found the bones of Joe but we've lost all of Pat's.' But then, Doyle reasoned, no-one in the gathering mob – probably, at a guess, there were thirty maximum – would wish to commit bodily harm to Pat. The old street rhyme came into his mind: 'Sticks and stones will break my bones but names will never hurt me.' The detective could appreciate its sentiment, but he wasn't altogether sure that he agreed with it entirely. It was a rhyme usually recited by those close to tears as they ran to the comfort of their mum's apron strings. Their only crime? Accused of being a 'Cowardy, cowardy custard, your mammy can't knit, and your daddy can't go to bed without a dummy tit' if they refused to knock (and run) on the door of one of the local teachers. Mind you, such non-offenders could be forgiven their fear. One local teacher, a lanky Mr Ronnie Sperrin, caned each and every one of the pupils who lived on his street, since he knew it was one of them who had called him a name one night as he parked in his drive. He knew not which one it was so he caned them all just to be sure he got the culprit. A few of the parents had visited the Station House to report the incident, but Doyle had been unable to do anything about it, although he certainly knew what he would have liked to have done.

But Equally, Doyle knew that if he brought Pat Kane into custody then the village would see it as a sure sign of guilt. Even if the surviving twin was let off later, the locals would, as sure as a cat loves the shade, blame the failure to prosecute on the 'inefficiencies' of the police force before they'd accept, or even consider, Pat's innocence.

But could the surviving twin's life really be in danger? Doyle didn't think so. There was most definitely no-one who would risk their own freedom to avenge Joe's death, since he hadn't appeared to have a real friend in the world. And, anyway, Doyle had other considerations. Considerations such as if the bones in his flour bag were, in fact, Joseph Kane's, then what progress was he making in apprehending the murderer?

Absolutely none.

He went into his office, cleared his desk and unfolded three double-page spreads from the current edition of the *Mid Ulster Mail* across it. On top of this he carefully placed the bones from the small flour bag. Doyle positioned the largest on the left, working his way to the shortest on the extreme right. He looked to try and recognise at least one of them from a long-gone and very much forgotten biology class. 'God,' he proclaimed to the bones, 'you are all strangers to me.'

On the other hand, his suspects were anything but strangers. Essentially, at this stage in the investigation, if you knew Joe Kane you could very easily find your name on the list. Doyle wrote out the names on the left-hand corner of one of the pages with his Parker fountain pen. The ink seemed to flow easily on the newspaper and the initially thin-lined and beautiful handwriting became thick and spidery.

When he'd finished, the detective couldn't believe he'd as many as seven names on his suspect list. He read and re-read them several times to no avail. He thought about re-doing his list, this time alphabetically – anything for a bit of inspiration, he thought.

Suspects – alphabetically

This was as far as he'd gotten when the fountain pen's splodges, just like ivy clinging to a stone wall, started to grow on his nerves. He opened his drawer, took out a fresh notebook (ruled) and started again, recalling an incident when Dr Watson did the same to great effect in one of his and Holmes' famous cases. Mind you, with Holmes' brain-power, all he would need to do was study the subtext that came through in Watson's handwriting to determine the name of the culprit. Doyle smiled at this thought. His mind wandered to the bones and once again to Holmes' expertise in this area. Doyle decided to clean up his thoughts a bit, start to put things in some kind of order. That was what the art of detection was all about: order. Do this and the solution to the puzzle will never be too far away.

He returned to his list,

The Case of the Missing Twin. October 1964.

List of suspects – in order of suspicion

1. *Patrick Kane.*
2. *The matchmaker, aka Michael Gilmour*
3. *Maggie Kane.*
4. *Dorothy Gilmour.*
5. *Doris Durin.*
6. *Pat and Maggie.*
7. *Maggie and Dorothy.*

When he'd completed his list he had a few thoughts about it. He supposed it was natural to start it off with the twin brother. He knew Edward Hill would be none too happy should he see Doris' name at number five on the list. Doyle duly noted that Maggie Kane was on the list three times. The detective glanced at suspects number six and seven again. He supposed he could have put Pat and the matchmaker as a couple as well, but he determined that a combination of the matchmaker and Maggie or Pat and Dorothy was out of the question and, consequently, these were out of the running.

Notwithstanding any of the above, the single fact that amazed Doyle the most when he studied his list was the absence of a full stop following the name of suspect number two. Was this an omission, the Freudian slip Holmes would have pulled him up on? Perhaps so, because when Inspector Doyle rewrote his list on a clean page – only this time listing the suspects in order of priority – number two had moved up very swiftly to number one. Great news if you were the Beatles. Not such great news, however, if you were the father of one of their biggest fans.

Chapter Fifty-Eight

By midnight on the day of his vital discovery, Doyle was systematically working his way through three large medical books. He had tried to determine what part of the body he had in his possession, his logic being, that if the bones came from an arm, or perhaps a leg, then this would tend to suggest that the body had been cut up and hidden around the farm. He'd then have no option but to put together a search party and scour the farm for the remainder of the body.

'OK, let's see now,' he kept repeating to himself throughout the process.

About 2:30 a.m. he thought he'd cracked it. The second to largest specimen looked like it might have come from the lower leg – well, that was apart from a wee bit that stuck out at the end.

At 3:22 a.m. Doyle fell asleep at his desk whilst leaning over the evidence, his two lists of suspects, his three medical books and the loose pages from the *Mid Ulster Mail*.

Station Sergeant Bill Agnew woke up the district detective inspector at 7:45 on the Sunday morning. A cup of strong coffee and some toasted wheaten with dollops of melting butter created the rich smell that returned Doyle to the land of the living. He devoured the wheaten, barely satisfying his overnight hunger, and washed it down with the coffee, which certainly kick-started all the detective's motors. This was going to be a big day, so he returned to his cottage for a wash and a shave.

The walk down the Broadway shook the remainder of the sleep fog from his head. It was a stunning morning, bitterly cold – so bitter, in fact, that he could see his breath before him. The sky was a sweet blue, free from the blemishes of clouds, and the sun cast warm shadows around the streets of Castlemartin. There wasn't another soul on the streets save one stray dog, a sad old black mongrel with a white flash on its head. The mongrel adopted the detective and the pair lazily strolled down the Broadway, past Walter's Grocery and Hardware store. They circumnavigated Pear Tree Roundabout to the right until they came back onto the Broadway (second exit) where they hung a right down past Francis' the jewellers on the left and the bus station on the right, both of which were still securely locked up. Man and mongrel crossed Broadway just south of the bus station and then took the next right into Garden Street. It was a journey Doyle had made many times in his life but today, for some reason, he was aware of every building he left in his wake. He crossed Garden Street directly in front of his house, let himself in with his key but left his new-found best friend whimpering on the doorstep.

Two and one-half minutes later he returned with a bowl of scraps for the dog. He was conscious of all his movements, as if he were the subject of a documentary. Just over a year earlier, in a different country, Lee Harvey Oswald's every move had been corroborated and detailed by friend and foe alike. So, was Doyle now in fact creating a similar picture for the world to view and analyse forever more? Meanings would be read into what Oswald had eaten for breakfast, the direction he'd taken to work, his movements about the Dallas book depository that morning, the journey to the Coca-Cola machine. Now in Doyle's mind's eye he followed Oswald. Did he take a bottle of Coke before fetching his newly purchased rifle and assuming his spot at the window from which he supposedly blew the head off the president of the United States of America?

Was the discovery of the bones down at the Kanes' farm part of something much bigger? Bigger in the same way that, some said, Oswald was merely the window-dressing for the biggest conspiracy the world had ever seen? But what could twelve bones be the window-dressing for? The detective afforded himself a smile as he considered the possibility that they could be the remains of the twelve apostles. Or even perhaps the bones of a being never before seen? Well, he'd not been able to make a match from his three big medical books so what else could the bones be the remains of?

At least when they, whoever they may be, came to make the documentary about this day, they'd have to report that Doyle had been kind to the mongrel. He removed his coat, tie and shirt and visited the bathroom for his least favourite body repair – the removing of the stubble from his face, by means of metal and water. Doyle's problem with shaving was that he really needed at least three, possibly even four, days' growth before he was able to administer a good one. When it was possible to afford himself this luxury, then it was an invigorating experience and his skin felt as new, refreshed, like he'd shed a skin. When, as with that Sunday morning, he didn't have a proper growth, more like a five o'clock shadow (and in Doyle's case a midnight shadow), the process was akin to peeling the skin from his face using a fragment of broken glass. Pleasant it was not. Would this fact be recorded in the documentary?

'What documentary?' the detective enquired of his mirror-image face, so soaped up he looked more like Father Christmas. The mirror image selfishly refused to reply.

Then Pat Kane re-entered his thoughts, and he didn't know why: was the twin responsible for Joe's death? Or, if he wasn't responsible, was he aware of any facts that might help Doyle solve this case? Was there more to it all than met the eye? He tried to imagine the scene in the house, with Pat and Joe continuing the fight they'd started on the field that harvest day. A day that now seemed so far away. Maggie might have been there, or perhaps Pat had persuaded her to go with Dorothy and Michael to their house so that he and Joe would have a chance to sort it out once and for all.

Doyle could picture the scene now – as clear as any documentary. The discussions had started off civil enough. The fight on the field would have cleared the air to some degree. They would have eventually gotten around to the reason for the brawl: Maggie. In the detective's imaginings, the conversation maybe became heated again. Pat, aware that Joe had gotten the better of him on the field, would have been partly cautious, partly seeking revenge. A push here, a shove there, perhaps even mock playfulness at first, but the anger and aggression would have crept in.

To a degree, Pat had revealed the frustrations that came with being Joe's twin. Nearly thirty years of putting up with that had gotten him down, especially now that his twin appeared also to want his wife. Perhaps Joe had pushed Pat to the floor. Pat, fired by his resentment, adrenaline pumping, had retaliated with all the strength he could muster. Joe wouldn't have expected such a vehement show, so

Pat's shove would have been doubly effective. Perhaps Joe had gone hurtling across the room, hit his head on the table/hearth/chair and fallen to the floor. The anger might have continued apace, with Pat shouting at Joe as he lay lifeless. After a time, perhaps Pat would have said something like, 'OK, stop bleedin' foolin' around now – you can get up. It's over.' With no reaction from Joe, Pat would have gone over to his brother's side and shook him a few times. Perhaps at that point, both brothers on the floor, Pat would have noticed a trickle of blood either on the floor behind Joe's head, coming from the side of his mouth or coming from his ear. Doyle always felt that bleeding through the ear was a very fatal sign. The saddest thing in the above scenario was the fact that either twin could have been the one killed.

Panic would have set in at this point and Pat would probably have tried to shake some life back into his brother's still body. Perhaps the realisation of what had happened would have caused Pat to cradle his brother in his arms, only to find that the special bond of twins was now broken, broken at last.

Then Pat's survival instincts would have kicked in, and it might have been at this point he panicked and thought about disposing of the body. After everything they'd been through, it would have been tough to persuade anyone that his twin's death had been an accident, so, he'd have to deal with it his own way.

But it was the scene of Pat cradling Joe in his arms that stuck fast in Doyle's mind. He tried hard to shake himself loose from it. The harder he tried, the more vivid the poignant tableau seemed.

*

Twenty minutes later, the unpleasant chore over with, Doyle indulged himself in a more pleasant daily experience: a fresh clean shirt. Today's was identical to yesterday's and would also be identical to tomorrow's. Was this another possibly important, not to mention revealing, fact to be uncovered during the research for the impending documentary? At 8:35, freshened in both body and mind, District Detective Inspector Colin Doyle left his house to continue with his life and his work, which at that point was dominated by the Case of the Missing Twin.

Chapter Fifty-Nine

Doyle resumed the previous evening's work the minute he walked into his office. He tried another bone to see if he could find a match in one of his books. His main problem was he wanted to check the three books simultaneously. It was a problem he also had when trying to read a newspaper – his eyes would wander to the next story before he'd finished the one he was on. The detective always promised himself he would go back to the original story at a later time but he seldom, if ever, did, since it'd be old news by the time he'd eventually get around to it.

Then he had a brainwave, and he nearly kicked himself for not thinking about it earlier, so simple and logical was the solution. Of course: he should take the bones to his good friend Doctor Taylor. Holmes had his Watson to call upon, so why should Doyle not call to witness the expertise of Dr Taylor? 'Why not indeed,' he said to himself as he gathered the bones up and placed them once more in the small flour sack.

Most Sundays you could find Taylor indulging in his favourite pastime: tending to his racing pigeons. Many were the times when Doyle and Taylor had sat in Bryson's arguing about how the pigeons were able to find their way home from all those miles, not to talk about different languages, away in France and beyond. Needless to say, the Guinness-drinking duo failed to find a solution to this particular mystery, which had flummoxed countless men and women before them over several centuries. 'Knowing mankind, it's probably a good thing that this puzzle has never been solved. If we knew the answer, some of us would try and find a way to cheat. This sport is pure; let's leave it that way, shall we? My round is it not?' would be the final statement on the matter from Dr Taylor.

As expected, Doyle found Taylor cleaning out his pigeon loft. When the good doctor spied Doyle at the other end of his well-kept, colourful garden he waved to the detective to join him. The stranger in the loft caused the usual commotion, nigh-on stirring up World War Three. Wings bustled furiously, feathers slapping feathers in soft thuds. Small bits of feather and fluff rose from the loft floor in the resultant up-draft, which also helped to circulate the floor's rich aromas, those which the doctor was trying to clear away. It was useless for them to speak until the pigeon banter died down – there was more coo-cooing than Joan Cook and her chatterbox friends at their daily tea-and-sandwich sessions.

'It's the bag in your hand,' Taylor announced in his dry theatrical tones. 'You've got them spooked – they think you've come for one of them.' He laughed.

But Doyle did not, for he had visions of Hitchcock's *The Birds* whenever he entered this pigeon loft. 'Maybe I'll wait out in the garden,' he volunteered.

'OK, old chap. Just give me a couple of minutes to clear up this mess. Do you notice the way they keep their droppings out of their own nests?' Taylor replied.

'Yes. Maybe they've heard the one about not shitting on your own doorstep. Perhaps they should have told that to Pat Kane,' Doyle said, as much to himself as Dr Taylor.

Taylor's eyebrows rose involuntary into a well-rehearsed 'What?'

'I'll tell you when you come outside,' Doyle muttered as he carefully left the loft, the cooing already dropping down to a much more civilised aristocratic-tea-party level.

The autumn air was colder than you would have imagined – the sunlight made it all very deceptive. Doyle was happy when Taylor joined him after a few minutes. The loft noise now dropped to that of a manger on Christmas Eve. Taylor brought out a pigeon with him. He held it gently, but firmly, in one hand. He grasped the beautiful bird's legs between his first and second fingers, palm up, and the pigeon's head closest to his body. He used his thumb to hold the pigeon's wings in place, freeing up his second hand to negotiate the loft door and then examine the bird's beak, eyes and wings.

'Ah, the famous Silver Mealy,' Doyle noted.

'Yes, he was first in the Penzance race two weeks ago – a full twelve and a half yards per minute quicker than the second bird. He's looking good. If he keeps in this shape he'll be off to Oakhampton week after next,' Taylor boasted, before offering his hand and pigeon up to the skies. The Silver Mealy flapped heavenward, working up to quite a few yards per second very quickly. The bird circled a few times and then dived straight back to the loft, where it quickly popped through the wire trap.

'Yes,' Taylor observed, 'he's in a hurry to return to a bit of a romantic engagement.'

'Lucky for some,' Doyle announced.

'Let's get indoors to a bit of heat and a brew up.'

'No arguments from me on that one,' Doyle answered, as both men headed into the doctor's quaint cottage.

Doyle used the time Taylor took to wander around his kitchen to bring the doctor up to date with the Case of the Missing Twin.

'I'm intrigued, Colin. But you don't honestly think it was Pat?'

'That was my first reaction. But it has to be somebody, and we have to suppose that Pat's name must be on the suspect list. Anyway, can you look at the bones for me and tell me what part of the body they come from?'

'Surely, old chap – please spread them out here on the table.'

One by one, Doyle placed his twelve bones on the table. One by one the doctor eyed the bones and then eyed Doyle, encouraging him to produce the next one.

'I couldn't find them anywhere in any of the station's medical books,' Doyle said, trying to break the silence and get the conversation going.

Taylor looked at the detective and back at the bones on the table. He looked back to Doyle and said, 'You might find that you'd have had better luck if you'd checked in a zoological journal.'

'What?'

'There's no easy way to tell you this, Colin, but your collection of bones are from a cow.'

'Ohmigod!' Doyle declared, and not as a hallelujah for the Sabbath. He sank into his chair, his shoulders nearly disappearing into his arms.

Was there anywhere left to turn as the walls came tumbling down around his ears? The Case of the Missing Twin, Doyle told Taylor, was now exactly nothing more than a twin who was missing. He'd simply gone AWOL or was having a bit of fun but, most likely, nothing more sinister than that.

Doyle, being the professional he was, put his personal pride behind him and immediately left the good doctor to visit the Kane farm – he needed to tell Pat and Maggie of his, or more accurately Dr Taylor's, findings. Maggie smiled her warm smile and then started to laugh, a laughter brought on by the long-awaited relief from the tension that must have been building up on the farm since the potato gathering had been so rudely interrupted. Pat shrugged his shoulders and thanked the detective for coming up to tell them.

If the detective had been expecting Pat to be happy too, he was in for a big disappointment. But why should Pat be happy, Doyle considered as he walked back into Castlemartin en route to the matchmaker's house to give the Gilmour family the news. There was certainly more of his business known around the village than he would have liked due to all the recent investigations.

The village gossips, clearly tiring of the Maggie-sleeping-with-both-twins story, were now on to how many women the matchmaker had fixed Pat up with before he had to resort to the desperate measure of matching Pat with his sister-in-law. Well, they would soon have something else to natter about. He found himself quickening his step to the matchmaker's. Was this in order to give the good news (if, indeed, the news was good)? Or was his hastening of speed designed to ensure he made it back to the Station House before the streets were peopled again?

His welcome at the Gilmours' house was nowhere near as warm as the one he'd received at the Kane's farm. The matchmaker failed to invite Doyle into his house, so they had their conversation on the doorstep.

'Don't you see – you're a bloody idiot?' Michael began in his distinctive rasp, rougher than ever due to both the early morning and perhaps the anger he was now spitting at the helpless detective. 'Aye, I say, a bloody idiot. You think you're in London or Belfast or somewhere, with all your running around accusing all and sundry of murder and upsetting people's lives. Don't you realise how long it will be before Pat Kane and Maggie can live a normal life again in this village? Forever, that's how effing long. And it's totally your fault – I hold you personally to blame, and I shall be writing to your superiors, whomever they may be, to advise them how reckless, tactless and inconsiderate you've been and you are. And that's a fact.'

Doyle said nothing. In a way he felt the matchmaker was entitled to his gripe. But the matchmaker wasn't finished with the detective yet, not by a long chalk.

'Do you realise you had enough information to stop this stupid business of yours when you questioned me? I told you what I knew. I told you that Joe had gone away to clear the air, to put his life in order, to find a woman, to get away from his brother and that we wouldn't be seeing him around these parts again until he made his fortune and found his woman. But would you listen? Oh, no way, that would be too effing easy, I say, that would be too effing easy for you. You're too busy trying to be Sherlock Holmes when in fact you're more like those other two cowboys in town, the Lone Ranger and Tonto.'

Doyle was about to interrupt and advise the matchmaker that Tonto was a red Indian so that made one cowboy and one red Indian. However, he thought better of it and let the matchmaker continue.

'The main difference is at least they're harmless and always, but always, amusing. You're neither. You're a nuisance. Don't you see? I say, you're just a nuisance. And then you weren't content to talk to just me. Oh no, you then felt that you had to interrogate my wife and then, if that wasn't enough, you gave my son the third degree!' The matchmaker was not quite full throttle, but he was very close. Doyle could tell that he'd left something in the tank for the final blast.

The matchmaker chuckled in his morning rasp, which sounded like a cross between a wheeze and a squeak. 'And then,' he announced, so that those indoors could surely hear him, 'to top it all, our Paul, fair play to him, had to save your job by securing the evidence. You were in such a hurry to get up to the farm to cross-examine all of us that you left your precious *cow* bones unguarded. Cow bones! And you call yourself a district detective inspector! I could have told you they were cow bones if you hadn't been so secretive and hid them from all of us. *Pat* could have told you that they were cow bones.'

Once again Doyle decided to keep his mouth shut and not interrupt the ranting matchmaker to advise him that two experienced farmers, namely the very same Lone Ranger and Tonto, had examined the bones closely and neither of them had come to that conclusion.

'But did you check with any of us? Oh no! Sherlock bloody Holmes had other ideas, didn't he? Oh yes, he's after promotion, isn't he? He's pining for police work in a bigger pond than here, isn't he? He wanted to solve the murder mystery single-bloody-handed, didn't he? Well you know what, Colin, talking about single-handed, I've never trusted a man who doesn't seek the company of women. They're much too in love with themselves, I always say. And nothing you've done over the last few days is likely to change my opinion one little bit.'

The matchmaker glared directly into the police officer's eyes, took one step back through his doorway, military fashion, and slammed the door in District Detective Inspector Doyle's face.

'OK, let's see now. I guess I'll have to put it in my report that you were a little upset,' Doyle announced quietly to the closed door. He'd been hurt by what the matchmaker had said and he'd been equally hurt by the fact that it had been Michael – usually a reasonable man – who had said it. It wasn't the bit about being compared to the Lone Ranger and Tonto that had upset Doyle. He actually found that part of the diatribe quite amusing. No, it was the bit about not trusting a man who didn't seek the company of women. Now that was cutting, not to mention disturbing. Particularly since earlier that morning when Doyle had been up on the Kane farm and Maggie had broken into her glowing smile, he'd thought, 'Now there's a woman it would be great to come home to. Imagine opening the front door and being greeted by a smile like Maggie's, a smile as big as the mountains around the homes of Donegal.'

Her smile had more or less carried him from Kanes' to Gilmours'. He hadn't notice the space pass him by. His only thought had been that he was walking at quite a pace. And, in fact, he'd been thinking about the lack of a woman in his life. But the matchmaker wasn't to know that his comments had been so ill-timed. The district detective inspector had stopped looking for a woman because he'd convinced himself that there wasn't one out there waiting for him. He'd deduced that if there was the possibility of a woman, your soulmate, being out there waiting for you, then there also must be the possibility that, if you were out of time, there was a good chance you were never going to meet her.

Doyle felt he was out of time.

He had too many consuming interests to play at relationships with women. He'd never met a woman with whom he could feel completely at ease, in romantic terms anyway, for he had many great friendships with women. Better than men, in fact, since he found them to be more supportive than men. He marvelled at the fact that they were prepared to, in essence, give up their lives and live solely for their children. To Doyle that was the biggest sacrifice. But the most incredible thing was than none of the mothers he knew actually thought of it as a sacrifice.

And women, unlike men, Doyle felt, *could* keep a secret.

In fact, thinking about it, as he had been, it was the biggest disappointment of his life to accept the fact that he was never going to find the right woman. However, he was not prepared to waste the rest of his life in a string of failed relationships with the wrong women. But what made him so special that he set himself aside from all of this? Every time he thought of Maggie, smiling on the farm, he wondered if he had made a mistake giving up. Maggie had been around all the time and it wasn't until she and Pat got together that it clicked for them. So who's to say that Doyle and Maggie wouldn't have been great together? She was happy and attractive because she was content with her man. And now the matchmaker was claiming that Doyle couldn't be trusted because he didn't seek the company of women. 'Ah, he was just lashing out in anger,' Doyle said aloud to no-one but himself, the wind-filled aching trees of Apple Orchard Lane and the birds circulating noisily above.

But *had* the matchmaker just been lashing out in anger? Had his anger given him licence to tell Doyle a truth? Had the matchmaker been saving that one up to hit Doyle with it when it would have its greatest impact?

To the matchmaker, it was one of the many things he had said as he vented his anger. He had probably, by this time, forgotten he had said it. But it would be a long time, if ever, before Doyle could forget it. The arrow, sharpened by a need to wound, had found its mark, doing much more damage than perhaps intended. Rarely did Doyle regret his decision to 'avoid the company of women'. He had a job he loved and he was happy and content to put all his energy and emotion into his work. And his work had in turn served him well. Served him extremely well until this very morning, in fact, when it had all come crashing down around his head and the Case of the Missing Twin had been blown wide open.

'Feck the missing twin!' Doyle called back to the matchmaker's house, venting some of his own anger. 'Joseph Kane can feckin' go and find himself!'

Doyle laughed aloud as he considered this scene for a time. He imagined Joe going up to someone and saying, 'Excuse me, do you know where I am?' He would be answered with, 'Yes, sir, you are here at the moment.' 'Oh, that's good I thought I was lost,' Joe would reply. In Doyle's mind's eye, the stranger was in fact his twin brother.

Then, in the way dreams have a habit of rewriting themselves as you are viewing them, the scene was rerun. This time Joe was saying to Pat, 'Look, you go up and ask that man where we are.' Pat would push Joe away with, 'I know exactly where I am – *you* go and ask him yourself.' 'Where are we then?' Joe would tease. 'I don't care where *we* are. *You* are nowhere. I, on the other hand, am very happy where I am,' Pat replied as the dream dissolved, leaving Doyle standing on the pavement looking at his own reflection in the window of Harry Smith's the newsagents.

The detective went inside and bought a couple of papers before starting the short walk home, stopping off in the Station House to enlighten all and sundry about Dr Taylor's remarkable findings. He knew they'd find time to have a great laugh at his expense, but only when he wasn't present.

*

The remainder of that day passed very slowly for Doyle. He continued to torment himself with his troubled thoughts while he played his current favourite album, *The Freewheelin' Bob Dylan*, over and over. He found solace there. It took him away from himself, into someone else's vivid world.

As darkness fell, Dr Taylor came calling, followed shortly thereafter by another knock on Doyle's front door. He answered it to find a young boy of about seven or eight years old who immediately went into a well-rehearsed speech. 'Me daddy says me mammy's a poor cow. He wants to know: does that mean it's not murder if he kills her?'

Doyle had to laugh, as did his visitor, Dr Taylor, when the detective reported the incident to him.

'It's started,' Doyle began. 'The heat's off Pat and it's now on me – they're turning their attention to me. I thought it would take a day at least before they got it up and running.'

'Water off a duck's back, if you ask me.'

'It's always different when you're the duck whose feathers are being tested,' Doyle offered in a feeble attempt at humour.

They were in the cosiness of the detective's living room, amongst all his books and bits and pieces and extremely comfortable old leather chairs, which his parents had left to him. Doyle had just about worn out his father's indentations from the bucket of the chair and had worn his own in. This chair was so comfortable it greeted Doyle as warmly as any friend, encouraging him to float into its depths and to leave all his cares, woes and aches behind him.

'Ah now, I could tell you a tale or two,' Taylor began, 'like the woman who sent the wrong son to me for treatment. He was so anxious for a week off school and the other brother was so scared of doctors that they both went along with it. That was until it was time for the first injection – then you should have seen him run.'

'Hardly a mistake on your side,' Doyle offered, snuggling into his armchair. He had decided to stay there for the night. It would take a crane and more to draw him out.

'Oh, there are a few of those as well, old chap. Like the time I mixed up the case notes between mother and daughter. The mother was pregnant and the daughter needed her tonsils out. Well, I looked down the mother's throat using my light and holding her tongue back and said, 'Well, we'll soon get that removed for you.' She, quick as a flash, replied, 'These new delivery techniques – they're getting better all the time, aren't they? I'll be able to walk immediately, but I'm sure I won't be able to talk for a month.'

That was enough to get Doyle going, and he laughed until his sides hurt, as much at the doctor's famous delivery (of the non-natal kind) as the story itself. The storytelling continued into the early hours of the morning before the doctor bade his friend goodnight and vanished down Garden Street.

*

The following day was worse for Doyle, though. It seemed everyone in the village knew all about the cow bones. He was sure he heard a few not-so-discreet 'moos' as he walked up the Broadway to the Station House. When he arrived, there were already quite a few calls, all to do with mammals of the bovine variety, waiting for him. Through his office window, Doyle could see a never-ending stream of station callers, all no doubt with different variations on the current popular theme – like the farmer who came in to ask, 'My calf would like to know when she can come and collect her mother's remains?' or the shopper who brought in her recent purchase from Young's Butchers wanting to know if Inspector Doyle needed any more evidence. Or the teenager who presented a small piece of rope frayed at one end, with claims that it was the now infamous cow's tail.

Bill Agnew had the good humour to deal with each and every one of the callers, never once losing his patience and even offering as good as they were giving: 'Away with you or I'll lock you up for crimes of impersonating a comedian.' But, most importantly, he never bothered Doyle with any of them, allowing his detective the space and privacy he needed.

Doyle considered going away to Donegal for a few days, just until it all died down. However, eventually he ruled it out for two reasons: one, he loved being in Donegal and he didn't want to ruin any time there worrying about what was going to face him when he returned to Castlemartin; and two, should he go away for a time, the flack would only be greater upon his return. No, the best plan was to stay put, to just grin and bear it. Luckily enough, as things were quiet on the criminal front, there wasn't any need for Doyle to be out and about too much.

The week passed slowly enough. On Thursday, when the street taunting died down a little – except for market day, when the sight of cattle being moved resurrected the locals' humour – Doyle thought the worst of it might be over. But he was wrong. That was when he noticed the posters pinned to various lampposts in the village. There was a crude drawing of a cow's head with the word 'REWARD!' in large letters above it. At the bottom, the word 'WANTED' (in the same size lettering) was emblazoned across each poster, and under that in smaller lettering was the script:

> *Dead or alive! Castlemartin's Cow Assassin. Believed to work under the shadows of railway bridges. No description available but it is believed the assassin eats a good part of the evidence. All claims for the reward should be made in person to District Detective Inspector Colin Doyle at the Station House.*

Someone even had the cheek to pin one of the posters to the Station House notice board. Doyle felt as though all the waters from Lough Neagh were flowing very slowly down this particular duck's back.

On Friday night, he ventured over to Magherafelt for what he hoped might be a quiet pint in Bryson's. He could hear a bit of murmuring and muttering behind him and then he was approached by one of Bryson's regulars, Andy Charles, who said, through barely controlled snorting, 'Is there any truth to the rumour you caught the murderer of the cow but he might get off with a lesser charge of cowslaughter?'

Doyle smiled as the entire pub broke into boisterous laughter. He returned to his book, secretly hoping that the waters of the lough would soon hurry up and dry out. He finished his pint, didn't rush it, but as he made to leave, Andy Charles came up to him again, only this time with a fresh pint of Guinness and said, 'No hard feelings, only joking. OK?'

'Sure, none taken. Cheers for the pint.' Doyle replied politely. As he raised his drink to Andy, all the drinkers in Bryson's lifted their own to return the cheers. It was like Doyle had been on a bucking bronco and he had managed to hold on for dear life and ride the horse to a standstill. He was now officially considered a 'good egg' for putting up with the week's jibbing with such apparent good humour. The bucking bronco was now happy to quietly graze upon the grass – the little that was left – and he would soon be looking for pastures new.

Heaven help whoever it finds to pick on next, Doyle thought, as he sipped contentedly on his Guinness.

BOOK FIVE
Cold Cold Night

Chapter Sixty

Doyle found himself sitting in Teyley's Café using a coffee to wash down a Kit-Kat the following Tuesday afternoon. The detective was unaccustomed to solo trips to these surroundings. But it was 3:30 and he felt like a snack, so he'd decided to follow the much younger crowds to Teyley's to see what the attraction was. Well, it was pretty clear upon arrival: the main attraction seemed to be that there were lots of other young people there as well. The attraction for Doyle, for by the time he'd reached the last stick of his Kit-Kat he'd decided he would be coming back, was that he could listen to all the new pop singles. Add to this the fact that a lot of the tracks were being paid for by other punters feeding the jukebox, and the place had him hooked.

Several times, Doyle tried to pick up enough courage to select a few singles he'd like to hear again. Songs like the Kinks'; 'You Really Got Me'; Roy Orbison's 'Oh; Pretty Woman'; 'Needles and Pins'; by the Searchers and the number-one choice on the jukebox over the previous few months, Wink Martindale and his monologue 'Deck of Cards'. Apart from the last one, Doyle sensed a new movement. He couldn't really articulate what it was – he felt a little too told for that. But there was a genuine whiff of real change in the air.

Even teenager-in-waiting Paul Gilmour, the matchmaker's son, was hooked on the new music and he knew all the names of the Beatles' band members. The music clearly had a power of some kind, in that it was uniting youngsters of all ages. Doyle's generation tended to be able to 'take or leave' their popular songs. But the new generation had a passion for their music; it bonded them and appeared to serve them as a life blood, an energy source even.

Who could blame them when you heard the raw power of a band like the Kinks?

Putting the draw of the jukebox to one side, Doyle considered that perhaps he had another motive for visiting Teyley's. Could he be subconsciously taking the matchmaker's words to heart and forcing himself into more sociable locations? He afforded himself a detached smile as he imagined his next move would be attending dances out at the Dreamland Ballroom on the lough shore and cutting loose on the dance floor to the sounds of the Playboys.

Just then the Beatles hit the speakers, exploding with the infectious sound of John Lennon's distinctive chunky, twangy Rickenbacker chords before the Fabs raced off at ninety miles an hour. Doyle really tuned into the lyrics for the first time: clearly the song's hero was glad to get home to his companion at the end of a hard working day. More evidence, if indeed it were needed, of the pleasures of having a woman waiting for you to return from a day at the office. Roy Orbison had also boasted about his 'pretty woman' and Ray Davies was confessing to the world that his woman had 'got me so I can't sleep at night'. So clearly it was women who made the world turn.

Someone, Doyle thought, had the good taste to play the Beatles' 'A Hard Day's Night' single over again. Doyle submerged himself entirely in the sound of the four lads from Liverpool. He had to admit it *was* a great sound, especially when there was more than one voice on the go. God, Doyle speculated, if they were capable of music as great as this so early in their career, what would they be able to do a few years down the line? They were already hugely popular – a popularity which had never been seen before. The woman at Tone Sounds had told him, all she had to do was stick the record label's dust jacket from any Beatles' single in her window with the words 'Available Now!' in large felt-tipped letters and they would sell as many of them as they could get their hands on. The band's name wasn't even mentioned.

Then the penny dropped.

It dropped with such an almighty clang that Doyle was surprised that all the other visitors to the café didn't stare over to his corner to see where the almighty noise had come from. How could he have missed it? It was so obvious, too obvious in fact. He remembered his own advice: 'Always look at the simple solutions first.' It had been there all the time, clear as the lough's waters, and he'd missed it – repeatedly. It had taken John, Paul, George and Ringo to open the door for him.

Doyle jumped up with a start. He'd no time for hanging around street cafés, educational though they might be. He had work to do.

Chapter Sixty-One

This time the journey to the Kane twins' farm was a more pleasant one, much more pleasant altogether.

Maggie was preparing dinner – this same meal (which they ate at around 5:30) was called 'tea' on a Saturday and Sunday, when dinnertime was in fact lunchtime (at around 1:30). For the Ulster children trying to become accustomed to this confusing, yet rewarding, meal arrangement, it was important to note that breakfast was always at breakfast time and supper was always at supper time. The smell of freshly baked wheaten bread, potatoes coming to the boil and a frying pan packed, as tightly as Bryson's on a Saturday night, with bacon, sausages and liver, not to mention the delicious aromas of an apple tart in the oven – thirty minutes short of peaking – took Doyle's mind (not to mention stomach) off the job in hand.

Maggie was shocked by Doyle's quick return but immediately invited the detective in and sat him at the kitchen table with the promise of a cup of coffee but with the caveat, 'I must get on with this – Pat will be in from the fields in about fifteen minutes.'

Wisps of hair kept falling from her crown, causing her to infrequently release her vibrant red clasp, pull her hair back into a tail, wrap it around a few times and clasp the arrangement back on top with a few more hair clips. Every time she elegantly accomplished this task, Doyle was afforded a view of her beautiful neck. Such a regal neck, Doyle thought. Seeing her now in her blue apron, red top and three-quarter length, free-flowing, blue and white dress made Doyle doubt his chase from the race for the second time that week.

'So what's the news, Inspector?' Maggie said with a distracted tone but a heart-warming smile as she delivered his coffee cup to the table, along with a plate of homemade buns.

'Oh, I just wanted to tie up a few loose ends,' Doyle replied, reluctantly forcing himself back into an official capacity. 'Could I look at your record collection, please?'

'Ah, I *see* – you're working for the taste police now. Well, I will come clean and admit to a Malachy Doris, a Matt Monro, a Nina & Frederik and I'd like three further charges of Bridie Gallagher to be taken into consideration. However, I have to state now, in my defence, that they're all me mother's,' Maggie replied, pausing to redo her hair arrangement one more time, sending another shiver of heat directly to Doyle's formerly icy heart.

The detective tried, in vain, to warm to her humour and offered a polite laugh in return.

'Fine, of course, Inspector,' and she waved him in the direction of the corner of the room where the records were kept.

Doyle soon found the record he was looking for. The distinctive yellow pound-sterling sign on the black centre circle caught his attention. The green dust jacket was in perfect condition, apart from one flaw, which happened to be the exact thing he was searching for. Patrick Kane chose that same moment, the moment Doyle had his prize in his hands, to walk through the back door.

If the twin was annoyed at the detective being back in his house he did a very good job of hiding it. He smiled immediately at Doyle and was about to offer to shake hands but he hesitated, looking down at his dirty mitts and explaining, 'I'd better give them a lick of water first.' He then headed towards the kitchen sink, and as he did he added, 'What brings you out our way?'

'Oh, he's just tying up loose ends on the Joe thing,' Maggie offered helpfully on the policeman's behalf.

'Actually, I came to find this,' Doyle began, as he proudly held up the Beatles' single 'A Hard Day's Night'.

'What? You want to borrow it?' Maggie offered, slightly confused.

Pat, hands and soap still circling in the warm water, turned to look over at the detective. He was stooped over the sink and in an awkward position. Every time he concentrated on what Maggie and Doyle were doing, his hands came out from the flow of water and when he put his attention back to washing his hands he could see neither his wife nor the detective.

'No, not exactly,' Doyle replied. He returned to his position at the table, bringing the popular single with him. Pat's curiosity got the better of him and he dried his partially washed hands on the brown towel hanging on a peg on the cupboard door beneath the sink.

The three of them were now sitting around the table staring at the Ringo Starr-inspired title. Neither Maggie nor Pat knew what they were looking for.

'It's a Beatles single,' Pat offered, trying to break the silence.

'It's from their fil-um,' Maggie claimed, adding the Ulster 'um' in her broad accent.

Pat lifted the Fab Four's eighth single, flipped it over and read the title of the B-side. As he did so he remembered Maggie and Paul's running joke while talking about B-sides. 'Yes, I know that's the B-side but where's the C-side?' Maggie would declare. 'It's most probably up at Portrush,' Paul would answer and both of them would fall about laughing every time. Now Pat read the second title aloud: 'Things We Said Today'.

'Has it got anything to do with this?'

'No,' Doyle answered as he reclaimed the single from the twin. 'I'm more interested in this,' the detective continued, as he pointed them both to the large hand-written words on the front of the single sleeve. He read them out: 'Available Now!' and then he looked at husband and wife, searching for some sign. He thought he saw a flicker of something in Pat's eyes but he couldn't be sure. They both sat in continued silence so the detective felt compelled to continue.

'You see, this is the copy of the Beatles single ostensibly purchased by Joe in Tone Sounds when he visited Magherafelt for the "Three Sightings of Joe, four if you count the Ulsterbus Inspector's trip" some time back. The shop assistant told me Joe bought the single for you. She told me it was the last copy and that's why it has this,' he pointed to the hand-written note, 'on it. At the time it should have twigged with me that if Joe was buying the single for you, why had he gotten straight back on the Belfast bus without visiting you first?' Doyle revealed.

Now he had their attention. Now the fun had gone out of the air somewhat. Again they both remained silent so the detective continued.

'So either you lied and Joe *did* come back to visit.' Doyle paused to see what reaction this would get. None, absolutely none, so he pushed further. 'Or, and as is more likely the case, Joe didn't visit Magherafelt that morning. You, Pat, went to Magherafelt, pretending to be your brother to effect the supposed sightings. You couldn't resist going to Tone Sounds to get the single because they'd been so rude to your wife. And the Bradley's fish-and-chip lunch was an exquisite touch, especially leaving the dreaded tomato. You couldn't have done it in Castlemartin because everyone would have made such a fuss – they would've recognised you. But the people in Magherafelt – Mrs Bradley and the shop assistant in Tone Sounds – wouldn't have known you well enough.'

'It's not what you think, Detective,' Maggie began as she rose from the table and went over to the stove to remove both the frying pan and the potato pot from the heat.

'Oh? Could you tell me what it is then?'

'It's nothing to do with her, Inspector … It was my idea. Maggie had absolutely nothing to do with it,' Pat volunteered.

Great, Doyle thought – here comes the confession.

Chapter Sixty-Two

'It's important that you know Maggie didn't have anything to do with this, Inspector Doyle,' Pat asserted.

All the mistakes Doyle had made on this case flashed through his mind in a split second. He decided he would do it all by the book from here on in, and so removed his fountain pen and notebook from his inside pocket, flipped the book open, set it down (clean page up), unscrewed the top from his pen and prepared to take Pat's statement.

'Tell me what happened, Pat.'

'Well, we were getting bleedin' fed up with all the fuss about Joe, you know, what had really happened to him and all the gossip. All the muttering every time Maggie or I would go into the village. And it was starting to get on top of us. Joe was off swanning around somewhere, and we're left here to run the farm ourselves and face all this crap. It just wasn't fair. The gossips can be evil at times,' Pat started.

'Don't I know it,' Doyle replied, thinking this wasn't exactly the confession he was expecting or needing. He decided to hold his counsel and let Pat say whatever he was going to say and take it from there.

'So, we were sitting around, the four of us, talking one night about the petty cruelty of village life and how it would be great to live in the city where no-one knew you or bothered about you. You could just get on with your life without all the interference. Who needs it? And I kinda got the image in my head about walking around unknown, or walking around as someone else and, am, we chatted a bit more about it and then Dorothy said, and only as a joke mind you, "Why don't you pretend to be your brother?" Then it was only a small step to thinking, well, if I could pull off being my brother then I could be seen in a few places and people would think he wasn't missing. Then they'd leave us alone to get on with our lives. It was a deception, I know, but I thought it was a small price to pay to bring a bit of normality back into our lives. I didn't want my wife and I to have to be looking over our shoulders forever more. I didn't want people pointing at us for the rest of our lives.'

'OK, let's see now. Are you telling me, are you seriously telling me, Pat, that this is all you are guilty of – impersonating your brother?' Doyle asked, dumbstruck.

'Why yes. Of course. You didn't think that … you're surely not saying, not still saying, that you think I had anything to do with my brother's … my brother's dea– disappearance?' Pat replied, breaking into a look of disbelief.

Maggie was concentrating on Doyle's every move. He was aware of her examining him continuously; it made him more than slightly uncomfortable. Why was she doing it?

Doyle gave a 'well why not' type of shrug.

He had thought, with his fabulous Beatle clue, that he had literally cracked the case. And he still wasn't positively sure that he hadn't. Was it all a great bluff? Give him a few morsels: 'Yes, you've found me out – it was me impersonating my brother. Well spotted, sir – it's a fair cop, guv,' and all that rubbish. 'But that's the lot. There's nothing more to give.' Clever, Doyle thought, very clever. There was definite evidence that Pat had pretended to be Joe. Sure, Maggie and Pat could have claimed that Joe dropped the single through the letterbox, mailed it to them or had someone else deliver it. So he owned up to it immediately. No reason not to with his clever excuse.

Doyle certainly knew what it felt like to have the village gossips on your back. If he could have pulled a scam like Pat's during his week at their mercy, he would've gladly taken the bait. And Pat's logic for the impersonation was sound, plus it would probably stand up in court. But Doyle had nothing that would even stand up in a vacuum, let alone a court, to prove that Pat had killed his brother. There was no proof, no witness and no body. Great. How was he meant to progress? He could keep running around in circles for years and never move forward an inch on this case. Joe Kane had seemingly vanished from the face of the earth.

Doyle had interviewed everyone who had ever come into contact with Joe: school friends, colleagues and every acquaintance he could find. But they couldn't add anything and, sadder still, none of them had really shown any interest in trying to discover Joe's whereabouts. He hadn't received one single reply to the advert he'd taken out in the *Belfast Telegraph*, which offered a reward for anyone who could come forward with any information. He'd been expecting at least a few hoax replies, but his inexpensive advert hadn't attracted a response – not one single reply. Sad really.

'You can't possibly still be on about that, Inspector?' Pat said, smacking his lips. 'Look, Inspector, I'm a bit hungry – why don't you stay for dinner. There's enough, isn't there, Maggie?'

'Indeed there is, and you'd be most welcome.' Maggie smiled as she rose from the table and returned to the stove to heat the food up.

'So, it's settled then, Inspector: you'll join us for dinner. You can ask away at your questions and our food won't be ruined. I'm famished – I could eat a horse,' the twin claimed.

Doyle wondered had Pat's appetite returned because the twin had come to the same conclusion as the detective: that after owning up to impersonating his twin brother, there was literally nowhere else the police could take the case.

'I'm afraid I can only serve you a little bit of a pig.' Maggie laughed, her back to both of them as she opened the oven.

'At least neither of you suggested it should be a cow,' Doyle offered, lightening the atmosphere a little. 'I hate to be morbid over dinner,' Doyle began, stabbing a well-cooked sausage with his fork as he cut the end off with his knife, meaning that he was going to be exactly that: morbid over dinner, 'but did Joe ever suffer from depression?'

'What, you mean you're now thinking that he may have taken his own life?' Maggie asked.

'Well, it could be a possibility, couldn't it?' Doyle mouthed as he munched away on his sausage. It was exactly the way he loved them: dark, crisp on the outside, firm and light on the inside.

'We were discussing this with Michael and Dorothy,' Pat began, as he made himself a bacon and sausage sandwich with the newly baked wheaten bread. When Doyle saw the way the butter melted deep into the bread from the heat of the meat he was most envious but politeness (unnecessarily) prevented him striking up his own buttie. However, he resolved to do so at the next possible opportunity in the privacy of his own home.

'I think it was Michael who suggested it first, but then we came to the conclusion that no matter how and where Joe might have done such a thing, his body would surely have been found by now.'

'True, true.' Doyle nodded between bites

'Unless, of course ...' Maggie started, but seemed to falter and looked to her husband for approval. Pat smiled at her, encouragement enough to continue. 'Unless of course he went and did it in the lough.'

'Did what in the lough?' Doyle asked.

'Went and threw himself into the lough,' she replied solemnly.

'Yeah, but even if he had done that, after a while, ten days they reckon – and I hope this doesn't put you off your tea – but the body starts to give off gases and such, which cause it to float to the surface. There's still a good chance he would have been found,' Doyle replied.

'Unless he did a Virginia Woolf,' Maggie offered.

'Which is?'

'Filled his pockets with stones to keep himself down.'

That was as far as the conversation went. The dinner finished pleasantly enough after that. Although what Maggie had said niggled at Doyle as he walked from the farmhouse; sure, someone other than Joe himself could have been responsible for attaching weights to his body. Lough Neagh is the biggest freshwater lake in Europe: it would certainly take a lifetime to drag it to search for a body. Nonetheless it was a possibility that Doyle was going to have to consider – not the dragging of the lough, but the fact that the remains of Joe Kane may be lying at the bottom of the lough wearing a pair of matching concrete wellies. Stranger things had happened.

The district detective inspector had the uncanny feeling that he was on the verge of something. He wasn't sure of exactly what, but if he wasn't careful there was a good chance he could stumble all over it without even knowing he was doing so.

Perhaps it was time to dander over to the matchmaker's house again to share Pat's admission. Just to see the reaction. He might give something away – that was, if he *had* anything to give away. Doyle was now convinced that the case would be cracked through information he received at either the matchmaker's house or the Kane Farm. The problem, as ever, was going to be recognising the genuine clues in the information he collected as genuine clues. The Beatles' single had been available to him for some time now; it was just that he hadn't focused on it. But perhaps that in itself had been a red herring? Did this same clue have another interpretation? Could that possibly have been the reason why the Kanes had been so hospitable towards him? Could Pat have realised the detective was on the wrong track, and, as such, posed no threat to him, his wife or their freedom? These thoughts and the beauty of the sunset filled the detective's head as he made his way to the house of Michael Gilmour.

Chapter Sixty-Three

Dorothy Gilmour greeted Doyle at the front door. She was standing on her doorstep, arms folded in a kind of unconscious, self-protective way, bidding farewell to a friend.

Doyle and the matchmaker had not spoken since the blow-up. The detective had committed every word of the matchmaker's speech to memory, and the words still hurt. Particularly the part which went, 'I never trust a man who doesn't seek the company of women.'

But the matchmaker and his wife couldn't have been nicer on this occasion. They even offered him a cup of tea. Politeness ruled and he accepted. It was one of the many reasons Doyle had decided he'd hate to be a man of the cloth. He hated the stuff, tea that is, and yet that was all people seemed to offer their visitors with the usual greeting of 'Sure, you'll have a wee cup of tea in your hand'. What it actually meant was that rather than go through the whole hoo-ha of setting the table and sitting down properly, he who aped Johnny Cash's well-honed, man-in-black impersonation, would be expected to sit back in an easy chair, cup and saucer in hand and a small plate with a Paris bun and a sandwich – maybe even both – precariously balanced on his knees.

'I just wanted to keep you abreast of new developments on the Joe Kane case,' Doyle started, once the pleasantries were over.

'What – he hasn't turned up has he?' Dorothy enquired, somewhat nonchalantly, maybe as if she was tired of all of this by now.

'No, he hasn't. But Pat has now admitted to us that he impersonated Joe that morning in Magherafelt.'

'Fair play to him. I say, fair play to him. Don't you see, though, he had to do it to shake off all the gossips. Sure Paul even came back from school one day saying he'd been taunted about his Auntie Maggie riding two brothers. The gossips were malicious and vicious. But what Pat did, what he has now admitted he did, sure that was all harmless, I say, it was harmless,' the matchmaker enthused, his rasp seeming particular throaty that evening.

'Perverting the course of justice – I think that's how my superiors would see it,' Doyle lectured, somewhat in vain. 'I understand you and your wife were involved in the conversation where this plan was conceived?'

'Actually, I think it might even have been my idea,' Dorothy confessed.

'Oh?'

'Well, they were at their wits' end. I couldn't believe how cruel some of the locals were being. It just seemed like a good idea to me – there has to be some advantages to being an identical twin. It seemed harmless. Who was he hurting? It definitely was effective though, wasn't it?'

'Well, apart from anything else *you* were perverting the course of justice. Which all means, in effect, you were trying to throw us off the trail. Now as I mentioned before, this is all very well and good and, as you say, your Maggie and her husband Pat were getting unmercifully hammered by the gossips. However, let's say for instance that we hadn't thought that Joe was innocently walking around Magherafelt in perfect health, eating a plate of fish and chips, no tomato, and buying a single from a record shop. Let's say that, at that point, he might still have been in trouble and we had kept the pressure on to find him: maybe, just maybe, we might have found him before any harm came to him,' Doyle claimed, before sipping some more and reasoning that perhaps this was how men of the cloth got through the constant cups of tea: by talking so much their mouths become dry, so they needed to wet their whistle and make frequent trips to the toilet. It must have been hell, though, some ten years since, when all the toilets were outdoors.

'Fair play, I say, fair play to you, Colin, and that makes perfect sense to me. I've been thinking about this a lot – well, we all have, I say, we all have, Inspector – and I'm being drawn back to my original theory that Joe has gone and we won't see hide nor hair of him until he's been successful on his own terms, whatever that will come to mean. That's, of course, if he ever comes back at all. He could be as far away as Australia by now,' Michael said, leaning back in his chair, indicating that, at least for him, the matter was closed.

'OK, let's see now, there's another thing I have a problem with. If he went to Belfast, he'd need a fare, he'd need money to live on, he'd need somewhere to live, he'd need clothes. If he went to London, he'd need more money. If he went to Australia, sure he'd need as much as the farm was worth to make that trip. Where did the money come from?' Doyle asked, appearing as much to offer up a topic for conversation as to question the matchmaker directly.

'Thieving would be an obvious way,' the matchmaker leisurely replied.

'Again, if he were going to London or Australia, robbing a sweetie shop just wouldn't cut it. It would need to be something major – say, robbing a bank for instance. And, personally, I just don't think that Joe would have what it takes to pull off an armed robbery or anything else on that level.'

There was no response from either the matchmaker or his wife at this so Doyle continued. 'The way I see it, Joe was much too dependent on his brother to be able to go it alone. People keep telling me that he lived his life attached to Pat's coat tails. So I'm having difficulty accepting the fact that this quiet, shy, retiring person just ups and goes off into the world on his own. There are no relatives, absolutely none: Joe and Pat are the end of the line. Well, maybe that should be *were* the end of the line until Pat and Maggie got married. The other thing that's troubling me is, as I have said, the money. Let's just say, for arguments sake, that, like you've suggested, Joe hit the road to fame and fortune on his own. He's going to have a hard life until he gets on his feet. Right?'

'Right,' Michael Gilmour replied, and his wife nodded.

'It would seem, from the recent fight on the farm, over chasing his brother's wife, that there would be no love lost between Joe and his brother. Correct?'

'Correct,' Dorothy replied very quickly, and this time the matchmaker nodded in agreement.

'So, the farm is worth a few bob – probably not a lot with their debts, but I'm sure they'd be able to raise some money on it. It's great land, prime location, so someone's going to want it. Joe's going to be desperate for money if he's off on his own. He's not going to be particularly interested in getting the best pound on the land. He's going to want a quick sale and his share of the cash to make his life in parts abroad that wee bit easier. Do you see what I'm getting at?' Doyle asked the married couple, hearing the ever-growing disturbance of the children in foreign parts of the house.

'I can see where you're going with this. I say, I can see where you're going with this.'

'Joe just ups and offs. Not a word to anybody. By Pat's own admission, he didn't even tell *him* he was off. They woke up the morning after the fight and he wasn't there. Pat and Maggie put it down to the fact that he'd been upset over the fight. They thought he'd be off cooling his heels somewhere and would return with his tail between his legs and an apology, and life would go on as before. But the days turned into a week, and the weeks to a month, and now it's several months since he's been seen around. He didn't even take a change of clothes with him. No, I'm sorry, Michael, I just can't accept your theory that he's in Belfast, or London, or even Australia. I mean, for heaven's sake, from the little I know of Joe he'd be petrified about moving to Magherafelt without Pat, let alone all these other amazing exotic locations.'

Doyle paused. No-one spoke, each of them apparently deep in thought.

'No, I'm convinced that some harm has befallen Joe,' Doyle said, breaking the silence.

'Well, without the corpse, you've got yourself a bit of a mystery there, Mr Doyle,' Dorothy said, as she rose from her chair and returned to the cooker. 'Fancy a fresh cup of tea?'

Doyle considered his answer. Was there any more information to be gained from these two? Was it worth a trip to the toilet? And yet another cup of tea? He decided it was.

'Yes, I will, if you don't mind. But in the meantime, may I use your toilet?'

'Certainly, it's through there,' Dorothy replied, pointing to the door furthermost from him, 'and then the first door on the left.'

Doyle took the door into the hallway and pulled it behind him. He didn't close it fully, though. He then walked towards the toilet door and opened and closed it, but rather than going inside, he remained in the hallway. He then tip-toed back to the kitchen door and prepared to eavesdrop on the Gilmours' conversation, but he heard nothing – no noises, no clues, no words, just a few muffled bits of conversations from the children upstairs and the sound of cups and saucers clanking together. In fact, the matchmaker and his wife didn't say as much as a single word to each other.

The hallway was cold and the tiled and uncarpeted floor made his breathing seem incredibly loud, as though it was the lough wind cruising down the Broadway. The hall was about six-foot wide and led from the kitchen straight to the front door. The glass at the top of the door welcomed the yellow glow from the streetlight to spill in. As you came in from the front door, the stairwell was to the immediate left. Then there were two doors on either side of the hallway, with the kitchen door at the opposite end to the front door. The yellow light picked out a coat rack packed to spilling with coats, jackets, hats, scarves and gloves. The walls were painted a deep brown with the doorposts white and the doors themselves a gentle green. The cream Marley floor tiles were well polished and slippery under Doyle's leather soles.

He returned to the toilet, opened and closed the door – this time very quietly – and he went into the room to pull the string on the inside left, which lit up the bathroom. Doyle quickly raised the toilet seat, did a number one, flushed the toilet, washed his hands and returned to the kitchen. He found the matchmaker and his wife sitting in a silence unbroken since he had left them.

'Actually, if you don't mind, I won't bother you about that cup of tea. I'll head off now. But thanks for your hospitality.'

'Oh that's fine, Inspector, any time,' the matchmaker said as he showed Doyle to the door.

They both stood on the doorstep for a time. Doyle wondered if the matchmaker was going to mention anything about their previous conversation, but nothing was coming from his lips so Doyle bade him goodnight and headed back up to Railway Terrace. When he got there, he hung a right back down to Pear Tree Roundabout, a left up the Broadway and back into the Station House, a man very much without a plan.

Chapter Sixty-Four

The following morning things were no better. On the other hand, they certainly were no worse. Doyle was convinced that Joe was dead. He had reached this conclusion mainly because he did not have one shred of evidence to suggest otherwise. Not one single piece. Everything circumstantial pointed to the fact that Joseph David Kane had passed over to the other side.

'So, who's in the frame then?' Constable Edward Hill asked of his superior.

'OK, let's see now. Here's the list,' Doyle replied as he handed Hill a folded piece of foolscap paper.

Hill carefully unfolded it. Doyle was studying him intently as he read the list of names.

The Case of the Missing Twin. October 1964.
List of suspects – in order of suspicion
1. Patrick Kane.
2. The matchmaker aka Michael Gilmour
3. Maggie Kane.
4. Dorothy Gilmour.
5. Doris Durin.
6. Pat and Maggie.
7. Maggie and Dorothy.

Hill then proceeded to surprise Doyle.

'Why on earth is Dorothy Gilmour's name on the list?' he asked his superior.

'Not what I expected you to say.'

'No, oh I see – Doris. Well, I didn't consider that to be serious. At that point on the list I assumed you'd run out of suspects, you know? That's why you've grouped Pat and Maggie and Maggie and Dorothy. But why no Michael *and* Maggie? Both names begin with M,' Hill offered, wanting to laugh but feeling it would be inappropriate if not unwise.

'Well, *why* Michael and Maggie?' Doyle quizzed.

'Doris tells me that Michael and Maggie were good mates until she married Pat. She made it clear that there was nothing fishy or any carrying on or anything like that – they were just good mates. But maybe they might have had a reason. You know? But still I repeat my question: why Dorothy?'

'Oh, let me think now. Well, she's the matchmaker's wife, she's Maggie's sister, she's Pat's sister-in-law, so there's a connection.'

'Yes, but equally, Paul's her son and he's not on the list,' Hill said, trying to shift the gear.

Doyle figured his junior was being cantankerous simply because the new love of his life, Doris Durin, was also on the list. He tried to explain. 'At this stage we're ... I mean, *I'm* stumbling around in the dark. Joe knew, it would appear, very few people. So few people in fact that anyone he did know, must automatically be on the list. Doris dated him – we know all about that, she's been very candid. Now I doubt, as much as you do, that she had anything to do with Joe's death but you know what? Deep down, neither of us really knows. People reveal to you what they wish you to know. Motives are always an issue.'

'So, OK, hypothetically speaking, let's discuss Doris' possible motive,' Hill prodded, removing his uniform jacket and putting it on the back of his chair.

'Fine. Let's do just that,' Doyle replied. He took a step back and perched on the edge of his desk. 'Doris Durin, from what we can gather, embarked on what was for her a serious relationship with Joe. It didn't work out. She and Joe fell out in a bad way up in Portrush. She felt aggrieved, bitter, let down. She was at the point in her life where she wanted a serious relationship. You see, Constable, there are two kinds of relationships in this world. There are those we fabricate for ourselves because we want and need that relationship at that point in our lives. Let's say all your friends have gotten married. You're the same age. You feel life is passing you by and you don't want to be alone. Socially speaking, you feel you should be with someone but you're scared there's no-one out there for you. This applies to men and women equally. So you seek out the company of men or women. You go on blind dates, you have your friends fix you up with their friends, you go to dances, you go to cafés or you go to parties. You might even pay a visit to the matchmaker. You *work* at getting a relationship together. I believe this was the kind of relationship Doris and Joe were involved in.'

'And the other type of relationship?' Constable Hill enquired, every bit the innocent.

'The other type is the type I would say you and Doris enjoy. I'll put Maggie and Pat in that same category. I'm talking about people who are meant for each other, of course. They are soulmates who are waiting to turn the corner of the same street of life, or at least that is how I believe the songwriters of today would put it. It's where two people, who may have been aware of each other for a time, maybe even a lifetime, just fall across each other while they are busy getting on with their lives. Something big clicks and it all snaps into place.'

'Is it not possible to have successful marriages from both kinds of relationships?' Hill said, warming to the theme.

'Quite possibly, only that doesn't concern us in our specific case,' Doyle replied.

'Does this then mean, in your hypothesis, you think Doris was *so* desperate to meet someone that when she eventually did meet someone and it didn't work out, she might have murdered him?'

'Desperation is a persuasive nightmare, Constable.'

'Well, knowing Doris the little I do, and in the short time we've been together, I'd say she was more game to try anything than desperate. She told me all about the big bust-up in Portrush. Do you realise that it wasn't Joe dumping her, it was her realising that this thing they had wasn't special, wasn't the real thing, and whereas Joe was prepared, even happy, to put up with it and get on with it, Doris accepted that the love just wasn't there, and without love there was no point in trying to force the relationship to work, no matter how convenient it was. She was anxious to get on with her life and not dwell on a relationship that just wasn't meant to be. Now perhaps your theory is correct, in that she took up with Joe, because she felt she needed someone, needed to be with someone. But now Doris is with me, and we met each other while busy going about our lives. On paper it shouldn't work, because she's older than me, but something *did* click, we both want to be with each other and I believe we'll be with each other forever,' Hill said quietly and candidly.

It was clear to Doyle that his constable's honesty came from his desire to remove his girlfriend from the list of suspects. Doyle had no reason to labour the point. 'Well, at least we've managed to shorten our list to six.'

Hill smiled.

'OK, what about the remainder of the list?' came the next question from the constable.

'Let's see now. Maybe we should start with some coffee,' Doyle replied, as he also took off his jacket, only this time it was a non-police-uniform jacket, whose resting place was on a coat hanger, which in turn was hung on the door behind which the district detective inspector disappeared in search of coffee.

'Name number one?' Hill began when Doyle returned to the office bearing gifts of Jacob's chocolate-coated orange-flavoured biscuits. 'I can see why he's there and why he's top of the list.'

'OK – why?' Doyle asked.

'Gee, why. Let's see. Put-upon twin, carried his brother all his life, brother takes a shine to his wife, financial implications, one person too many on a struggling farm, but mostly, from what I can gather, he was anxious to release himself from the chains of being a twin.'

'But not all sets of identical twins have horrible lives,' Doyle offered.

'True, but if what we hear is correct, then Joe was the dependent one: he lived his life through his brother, while adding a lot of pressure to Pat's. But don't forget that they were in fact brothers, so no matter how bad it might have gotten, Pat would always have felt protective of Joe to some degree.'

'Interesting,' Doyle said. 'Could it be possible that Pat *did* kill his brother, feeling that it was the best kind of protection he could offer him?'

'Possibly,' replied Hill automatically, trying to think this theory out fully.

'But now that he was sharing his life with Maggie, he had, for the first time since his parents died, an emotional commitment to someone other than his twin brother. You know what, Constable, that would make a lot of sense, because it would also account for Joe's illogical behaviour of wanting to get close to Maggie. By doing so, he could only but help to destroy the relationship between Pat and Maggie and thereby rebuild his own relationship with Pat. So Pat realised there was no happy ending for his brother. It was only going to get worse for Joe and Pat, more than any other on the list, knew just how bad.'

'So you're actually suggesting that Pat felt he was doing his brother a favour by killing him?' Hill asked in clear disbelief.

'Perhaps,' Doyle replied, sounding like he felt he should maybe give that idea some more consideration, 'but it still brings us back to the big problem, the problem everyone on the list shares.'

'Which is?'

'How was Joe murdered and where's the body?'

As Doyle said this he wrote down on the top of a new sheet of paper:

Method of murder.

And on another:

Location of body.

On this page he wrote, in his best handwriting:

At the bottom of Lough Neagh

and then:

Buried on farm.

On the first page he wrote:

Accidental death in fight

and then:

Manslaughter.

Beyond that, at this stage, he had no additions for either list. He hoped, however, that before the end of his conversation with

Constable Hill he would have a few more notes to add to the pages, perhaps even a few more names to remove from the suspect list.

'OK. Let's see now. We know that Joe was stronger than Pat, so that, and the fact that they are brothers, keeps bringing me back to the two of them continuing their fist fight indoors and Joe falling against something, banging his head and dying in front of Pat's eyes.'

'Then why not report it as the accident it was?' Hill enquired, enjoying the verbal sparring with his senior.

'Simple: he *knew* no-one would believe him. He panicked and got rid of the body, by which time it was too late to come clean.'

'Wouldn't this method require the cooperation of his wife, though?'

'Possibly. Or he could have shooed her off to Dorothy's when it happened so he had space to clean up the mess and dispose of the body.'

'Assuming of course she wasn't in the room with him when it happened?'

'Yes, exactly, in which case we then have to work on the theory that they were both involved. As we know, they are very much in love. She shared his joys and his pains and Joe was one of Pat's biggest pains. Perhaps they both discussed it and came to the conclusion that they would have a better quality of life if Joe wasn't around, and that's when they cold-bloodedly planned his demise. With an accomplice, Pat's inferior strength wouldn't have been an issue. Now, would this lead us to believe that the body is buried somewhere on the farm? It must be a strong possibility, mustn't it?'

Instead of answering the question Hill asked another one, 'The matchmaker – why is his name on the list?'

'Well, he was trying to make a match for the twins, although it didn't work out. Perhaps Joe was mad at the matchmaker, particularly when Pat and Maggie started stepping out. Maggie is, after all, the matchmaker's sister-in-law. Perhaps Joe felt that the matchmaker had made a match for Pat and Maggie behind his back and he went to see him about it. Perhaps even the very night of the fight on the field, when Joe was still mad, they started fighting. The matchmaker looks like he can handle himself in a fight – he seemed to make easy work of the two suits up on the Fair Hill – and Joe came off the worse. Again, maybe at best it's a manslaughter charge, but it must be a possibility we can't rule out.'

'And what would he have done with the body, sir?'

'Good question. OK, let's see now. Well, the first logical thing would have been to bury it in his back garden. But that's too obvious, 'cause it's the first place we would have looked.'

'But have we looked there?'

'No.'

'My case rests, your honour,' Hill boasted.

'We're not going to go digging up someone's garden without evidence, Constable!'

'Easier to dig up someone's garden than someone's farm, sir.'

Doyle thought about Hill's comment.

In his mind's eye, he saw a picture of Sherlock Holmes and Dr Watson enjoying a similar debate. What would Holmes say, Doyle wondered. And in that split second the penny dropped, the cannon fired, the thunder cracked, the lightning flashed, someone pulled the chain and Doyle knew exactly what Holmes would have said, to the point where he stated it himself. 'Easier still, Constable, would be to just dig up someone's grave. I do believe you've got it.'

'Got what, sir? You've lost me. What's happened? Why are you grinning so much?' Hill persisted with his questions, but his district detective inspector was already off on another track, another track entirely – a track that owed more than a little to the great Sherlock Holmes himself.

Chapter Sixty-Five

'You see, Constable, when you hit on the words "it would be easier to dig up a garden than a farm" you focused my thinking. Why should we have to do the digging, though? Why not get the murderer to dig up the body? That way we don't have to go digging up an entire farm or even a smaller garden, or for that matter dragging all of Lough Neagh. The murderer obviously knows where the body is and all he, or she, has to do is dig up the grave and save us all of lot of time. That's how Watson and Holmes would have done it, don't you see,' Doyle enthused, now truly excited for the first time since Joan Cook had visited him at what was the very beginning of this long and, so far, fruitless case. If only he'd been prepared to listen to her, village gossip and village bike, though she was. Might he have been able to do something to protect the well-being of Joe Kane?

'Yes, sounds great to me, sir. Just one little problem, sir.'

'Which is?'

'Correct me if I'm wrong, but wouldn't we need to know who the murderer was first, sir, before we could encourage them to embark on this incriminating digging expedition?'

'True, true, Constable, but it really is easier than that.'

'You've certainly got my attention, sir.'

'OK, let's see now. First things first. What do all the names on our suspect list have in common, Constable?'

'All the names, sir?'

'Sorry, all the names excepting that of Doris Durin.'

'That's much easier, sir. They are all members of two households: the matchmaker's house and the Kane twins' farm.'

'Correct! Now I'm pretty convinced our murderer is either one, or a combination, of the persons on that list, of the people living in either of those two homes. So what I propose we do, Constable, is play a Sherlock Holmes trick and announce that we know where the body is and that we are about to make an arrest.'

'Ha, now I get it! Then the murderer goes to dig up the body, to see if it's still there or to move it, or whatever, and we get him or her red-handed. Isn't it a bit too obvious, though, sir?' Hill asked.

'Don't knock the obvious, Constable,' Doyle continued, enthusiasm unabated. 'That's why the obvious *is* the obvious.'

The two of them sat in silence as Doyle finalised, in his mind, the details of his plan. Once he felt comfortable he had it down pat, he introduced it to his junior. 'OK, here's what we'll do. Later on today, we'll drop the word to the town gossips that we know where Joe's body is and that we are going to arrest the murderer within the next forty-eight hours.'

'How can we be sure that the word will get back to to the two households we need it to get back to?'

'Don't worry, Constable – in this village, with this case, that is the one, and possibly only, thing we can be absolutely guaranteed of. Tomorrow evening, you and Sergeant Agnew will cover ... heads or harps, Constable,' Doyle enquired, taking a penny from his pocket and spinning it in the air.

'Harps, sir,' Hill answered, as the penny spun to its loftiest position.

Doyle caught the coin in his right hand as it returned from its short orbit and placed it on the back of his left hand, still covering it with his right.

'Sure you don't want to change, Constable?'

'Positive, sir.'

Doyle removed his hand exposing the Irish harp.

'OK, your choice as to which one you and Agnew will watch,' Doyle asked, every inch the good loser. He had his suspicions and he was sure they were not the suspicions of his young constable.

'We'll take the Kane farm, sir, if we may?'

'Perfectly fine with me. Constable Robin Irvine and myself will cover the matchmaker's house,' Doyle replied, hoping there wasn't a bit of a smirk showing on his face.

Chapter Sixty-Six

So it's October, a cold October night. What's a district detective inspector going to wear other than his duffle coat? Doyle had no problems resisting the Inverness coat and deerstalker hat of his hero in favour of his warm, friendly duffle. And it turned out to be a winter coat that Constable Robin Irvine only wished he'd had the foresight to own. He had the standard issue police coat and he was freezing his whatsits off, and his ears weren't doing too good either.

The two policemen had positioned themselves south of the matchmaker's house, down Apple Orchard Lane, in the trees and bushes on the left as you looked back to the house. The moon was growing to its monthly fullness so, Doyle thought, it's going to be easy to see (advantage) and be seen (disadvantage). The other advantage was that the lough wind was blowing up a storm and the bushes and trees were creaking under the strain, so all human noises would be concealed by the gusts. On the other hand, the wind, as the locals would say, 'blew right through ye,' so it wasn't long before red noses were uniform. Doyle had the luxury of his cosy hood; Irvine had the luxury of his youth.

The detective inspector decided to place Irvine further into the field so he could see the back door, while he himself remained close to the hedge so he could view the seldom-used front door. Both kept eye-contact with each other. It grew spooky as the sounds of distant farm animals intermittently jutted into the night, shocking them from their calmness. Sheep seemed to be the worst. They were capable of a self-contained, sleep-disturbing racket. Doyle also noted a few dogs barking, pigeons cooing in the safety of a warm loft, cats prowling (every tom in town seemed to be on the prowl that evening) and an owl whoo whooing ... perhaps, although he was prepared to put that particular set of eerie sounds down to his imagination. But mostly the noise was from the wind's continued fight with the trees and bushes.

*

Meantime, Constable Edward Hill and Sergeant Bill Agnew were faring better, for they were enjoying the comfort and shelter of the cow shed. Well, comfort in turns that was: first shift Hill was behind the hedge in Kane's lane, about twelve yards from the front door. His main problem was that he was clearly visible in the bright moonlight to anyone who might happen along Noah's Arc. Normally this would be signalled by approaching conversations or the noise of boots trudging on the tarmac or, more traditional on unlit country roads, the sound of whistling, as if doing so would keep the evil spirits and banshees away. Holding the tune, or sometimes not even bothering with a tune at all, never seemed to be a priority. No, a high-pitched whistle that seemed to say 'I'm walking along this road by myself and I'm not afeared. To show you I'm not afeared I'm whistling loudly. So, leave me alone ... *Please*?' Every time Constable Edward Hill heard a whistle (and there were several), he hunkered down close to the hedge in the hope that he wasn't noticeable to the solo travellers a mere fifty or so yards away on Noah's Arc. If truth be known, had they spotted Hill in his hiding place, they would've probably put it down to the fact that they were seeing things, or that maybe the moonlight was playing games, if only to appease themselves for the rest of their isolated journey home in the dark.

Sergeant Bill Agnew, on the other hand, had located himself squarely in the cowshed, which afforded him a clear view of the back door of the Kane Farmhouse about twenty yards away. The aromas filling his nostrils left a lot to be desired but the body heat generated by the fine animals just about kept his rheumatism at bay. After a while, the smell of the cattle seemed to grow somewhat pleasant, similar to how one acquires a taste for Guinness.

Hill and Agnew had agreed to keep eye-contact and to swap positions every hour. The other agreement, which applied to both teams, related to there being four suspects, two in each house. Should one of them exit the house, then the officer monitoring the nearest station would follow them at a safe distance, while the other remained, in the hope of covering a possible exit by the remaining suspect. There was also the possibility that the murderer would be sly enough to expect surveillance, and might even send out the partner, albeit innocently, to lay a wild goose chase.

Just as Hill was about to make his way to the comfort and warmth of the barn, the hall light of the Kane farmhouse came on. The officer remained near lifeless in his location. Hill judged from the shadows on the oblique glass of the front door that there was some activity in the hall. And just as suddenly as the light came on it went off. Thirty seconds later the front door opened and one Patrick Kane let himself out. From Hill's distance he couldn't be sure, but the twin seemed to be taking care to keep his movements as quiet as possible and gently encouraged the door to shut, rather than banging or even slamming it. 'We're on!' Hill suggested to his newfound friends, the bushes, as Pat made his way down Kane's lane and towards Hill's location. Hill squatted down as low as possible and the twin passed him no more than three feet away. He could hear Pat's boots scrunching away as he disappeared down the lane. Hill could still hear the same sound on Kane's lane, but the bushes were now obscuring the suspect from Hill's sight. He decided to remain where he was until he could determine if Pat was going to turn right or left into Noah's Arc. Should he turn left he would come back into Hill's view and the last thing the young constable wanted was to be running down the field towards his suspect only to bump straight into him. Should the journey into Noah's Arc be right, which Hill guessed was most likely – there were better locations for hiding a body by the disused railway track or even further on out in the countryside – then the constable could quickly make his way down to the junction of Noah's Arc and then discreetly follow his quarry.

And then Hill had his answer: the twin turned left.

The officer could make his prey out, between the gaps in the hedge and with the help of the moonlight. 'So, you're heading for the lough,' Hill whispered to himself, wishing Doyle were with him. 'What if he goes out onto the lough on a boat? What am I meant to do then?' He saw visions of himself and Doyle out on the lough in a rowing boat, both dressed as Watson and Holmes, the evil mist rising from the water caught in Holmes' lantern as he stood on the bow of the boat peering into the distance as they rowed on and on and on.

Lough Neagh was a very big expanse of water to have to trawl.

By the time Pat reached the end of Noah's Arc he surprised Hill by not turning left and going out the Lough Road toward Lough Neagh; instead he took a sharp right on the Lough Road, heading back into the village instead of away from it as expected. 'Interesting,' thought Hill, still murmuring to himself. 'But then surely the best place to hide a body is the place one would least expect to find one. Goodness, the sly fox – he's hidden it in the middle of Pear Tree Roundabout.' No-one would ever have dreamed of looking there – it was right in the centre of the village. Surely someone would have seen him. 'God, he's got a nerve,' Hill whispered to himself, getting very excited by the prospect of such a find. In his first year on the force, he was going to apprehend a murderer digging up his brother's body in the bloody centre of the village. He couldn't believe it.

Then Hill had a crisis. Well, more like a problem really. He noticed, because he was a policeman and policemen are trained to notice and observe these things, that Pat Kane had neither spade nor shovel with him. Surely he hadn't forgotten an implement to dig his brother up with? He wasn't going to have to return to the farm to pick one up, was he? How embarrassing. Hill decided he'd better keep a discreet distance so that if Pat did have to make a quick return he'd not be caught out trailing him.

Then Hill suffered the second major blow in his attempts to be written into local folklore.

Pat Kane crossed to the other side of the Lough Road, bypassing the Pear Tree Roundabout entirely. He walked up to a frequently used rickety door, opened it and let himself into Brady's pub. The craic was ninety within but the noise quickly ebbed away as the door swung shut behind the former number-one suspect.

*

Simultaneously, District Detective Inspector Doyle was having, he thought, much better luck on the case, for the matchmaker had exited his front door, stick of some kind in hand, and walked briskly off up Apple Orchard Lane. Doyle pulled on his already extended hood, more as a gesture of his imminent movement than one of necessity, and moved off in hot pursuit.

Michael Gilmour soon crossed Railway Terrace at the top of Apple Orchard Lane and continued on past the former railway station, which now served as the headquarters and workshop for the highly reputed Castlemartin Carpenters.

'Great, so it was you all the time,' Doyle whispered to the cold night air. His words sent a vapour trail from his mouth, which was quickly blown past the right-hand side of his face by the wind. He felt guilty about his joy. He felt sad that someone had to die just so he could feel this good. Then he remembered his previous failed conclusions and immediately reined in his enthusiasm, as just quickly as the Lone Ranger reined in Silver.

By the time Doyle reached the Station House, the matchmaker was making his way down the railway line towards the Kane Farm. The matchmaker kicked the fallen dead leaves violently out of his way as he did so. Doyle felt a bit exposed. There was no cover until they reached the bridge at Moore's Railway Inn. Should the matchmaker look behind him, the game would be up. He decided not to follow his quarry down the disused line but to keep off it, to the right, moving nearer to Railway Terrace.

As he took the first step of his new route, he fell into a large hole that had been filled with what appeared to be at least the fallen leaves of two, possibly three, trees. Luckily enough the leaves cushioned his fall and no bones were broken, nor any strains or sprains felt. Could the matchmaker and Pat Kane be in this murder plot together, he wondered, from the confines of the ditch. The matchmaker was certainly heading in the general direction of the twin's farm.

Gilmour walked on at a feverish pace, leaves flying north, south, east and west. Funny how all the first letters of the points of the compass formed the word NEWS, Doyle thought as he half-ran, half-walked in chase. The matchmaker reached the bridge at Moore's Railway Inn, where the trains used to fly over the Broadway in long-gone days. There he did a strange thing. Instead of continuing his journey over the bridge to the farm, the matchmaker came off the railway line and made his way down the side of the embankment to the Broadway.

Doyle had made his way back over to the railway line but soon he was falling in a very undignified manner down the same embankment. Luckily no-one but his own pride witnessed his fall from grace.

'Why are you heading back into town?' Doyle asked quietly in the direction of the vanishing walking machine. 'Surely you are not heading to the Station House to give yourself up?'

The matchmaker then swung a left into Pear Tree Roundabout and then another into the Lough Road. By the time Doyle had reached the start of Lough Road he was just in time to see the matchmaker disappear into Brady's Bar. Doyle casually walked down the road and positioned himself in the doorway of Rogers and Daughters' Home Bakery.

'Snap,' a voice behind him whispered.

The detective nearly jumped right out of his clothes and very nearly had to send for his brown trousers. 'What the—?' he uttered as he tried hard to regain his composure.

'*Snap*,' Constable Edward Hill repeated, 'mine's gone in there as well.'

'God, don't ever do that to me again! I thought I'd been sent for. Pat's in there too, you say?'

'Yes, all of five minutes.'

'Mine led me a merry chase. Obviously out for a brisk walk, working up a thirst,' Doyle replied, his heartbeat now down to merely double normal. He felt as though his shirt must be rising at least three inches from his chest with each palpitation.

'So … you think they're in it together?' Hill asked in a stage whisper.

'It's possible, I suppose. But I'm having trouble working out the connection,' Doyle replied in the same hushed tones.

'Well, maybe he just wanted to help the husband of his wife's sister. Joe was becoming a problem for all of them and, you have to admit, it's better now that Joe is out of all their lives.'

'Murder's such a big step to take to resolve a bit of a disturbance, don't you think?' Doyle replied.

'Well then, maybe they couldn't afford to let him live. Do you know what I mean?'

'Not really,' Doyle whispered.

'OK, say for instance Joe knows something, something that the other two can't afford to come out – you know, something which would be embarrassing to Maggie and Dorothy, particularly Maggie. Like, say, the story about Maggie sharing both of them to start. Let's just assume that is true.'

'Shit.'

'Exactly! Now, if the matchmaker was the one who made the usual match, he wouldn't want his wife knowing that he fixed up her sister with two men, brothers – and twins at that. Maggie and Pat wouldn't have wanted it to come out; they'd have died from sheer embarrassment,' Hill enthused. There were still some baking-bread aromas floating around the doorway and it was making his hunger almost impossible to ignore.

'Right. That's figures. Joe, if you'll forgive me, had tried and failed with Doris, and was now upset by the happy family Pat and Maggie had set up. Maybe that's what the Joe hitting on Maggie thing could have been all about. He was trying to get back with her, back to the original set up, and now that Pat and Maggie were rid of it, they wanted to keep things that way and get on with a *real* life,' Doyle replied. He liked this theory, he was warming to it. He continued. 'So, who could they go to for help? The man who set it all up, the man who had as much to lose as Pat, if the secret ever got out. He'd be ruined around town. He'd never be able to do business again. And not just in Castlemartin. A juicy bit of scandal would travel around Ulster quicker than George Best could scoot up Windsor Park and put one in the back of the opponent's net. So they planned it together, and executed their plan, with or without Maggie and or Dorothy. I'm inclined to think *without*, myself. But then I've no references for this case, none at all.'

'Don't forget though,' Hill offered, as much as a distraction from his hunger pangs as from a belief in his logic, 'it was Dorothy who came up with the plan for Pat to impersonate Joe. So I wouldn't let them, or at least her, off so easily.'

'Possibly. Possibly. So they are in there now, trying to work out what to do next – what to do before the morning. They obviously think they are going to be arrested,' Doyle offered.

'Do you think they feel any remorse at this stage?' Hill asked in a quiet tone.

'OK, let's see now,' Doyle pondered, addressing that very subject, as if for the first time. 'Frankly, no. I imagine self-survival is uppermost in their minds at this precise moment. They'll be scared – so scared they'll be sweating all the time, no matter how cold it is. They'll feel very conscious of everything that is going on around them. They'll be super aware. They'll be just this side of panic. The fact that there are two of them will be of help to both: the comfort of a partner in crime keeps the panic somewhat in the background. Later, the fact that there are two of them will be a problem, but for now they'll take comfort in their numbers. They'll feel a continuous lump in their throats. At the time of the murder, they'd also have felt very powerful, the power of just having taken someone's life. Thus they'll be sharing some of Joe's life force and potency.'

'You don't mean like in the movies, when the Indian braves believe by taking their victims' scalps they also take some of their power?' Hill enquired

'Yes, a bit like that, I suppose. They'll also be feeling very randy, I imagine.'

'I don't believe you!' Hill said in disgust.

'Supposedly so.'

'Come on … you're kidding, right?' Hill pushed.

'No, apparently that's a fact. It's all to do with the power of taking someone's life. They say it engulfs you.' Doyle paused, as he noticed the door of Brady's Bar open, and who should step out but the two powerful and potent men the police had just been discussing. Doyle pulled his junior back into the shadows of the doorway, which went back about four feet from the pavement, affording the shop more display area. They could see by looking through the two windows, which were at right angles to each other, the two men talking on the street. The suspects seemed in no hurry to move off and continued to chat.

'They look so normal,' Hill whispered.

Doyle studied the two men as they talked, smiled a bit and kicked their feet against the walls of Brady's to get some heat into them. Suddenly they shook hands and Pat crossed the Lough Road to the policemen's side. For one horrible moment Doyle feared that he was going to come up the Lough Road and pass within inches of them. But instead he headed down the road, with Michael heading down the opposite side. Pat took a very quick left into Noah's Arc and called a final 'Goodnight' to the matchmaker.

Hill and Doyle waited until Michael reached the end of the Lough Road where he, as predicted, turned right along Shore Drive in the general direction of his house. Doyle and Hill picked off their men as before and headed away in pursuit for the second time that evening.

'Bang goes that theory,' Doyle said to a lamppost, as he very quietly turned into Shore Drive.

Chapter Sixty-Seven

Pat Kane returned to his farm. And the matchmaker returned to his house with no further detours, a fact Doyle was very grateful for. He checked with PC Irvine when he returned. No-one else had left the house in the meantime.

Just to ease the boredom, Doyle switched positions with Irvine, but not before producing a flask of steaming hot coffee from somewhere deep inside his duffle coat. It was just past 11:15 p.m. and Doyle had the growing fear that they were settling down for a long, cold, eventless night. If this were so, tomorrow would be humiliating. He'd announced to all and sundry that he would be making an arrest that morning, and right now the chances of that happening looked pretty slim. Ah well, he surmised, he could always arrest himself on the charge of impersonating a police officer. For some reason he thought this very funny and nearly burst out laughing. Then he started to think about other aspects of this stakeout. Had he really thought it through properly? For instance, what would happen if one of his suspects left their house and set off, spade in hand, to dig up the remains of Joe Kane? The corpse would be at least a month old and in very poor condition. Would he be able to stomach it? Would the suspect be able to stomach it? Would the suspect come willingly with 'It's a fair cop, guv,' or would they attack him with the shovel?

The wind echoed Doyle's anger – well, more frustration than anger – and was getting noisier and angrier by the minute as it picked up everything in its path and redistributed the rubbish of Castlemartin. But for some reason, perhaps it was the hot coffee, Doyle didn't feel any colder. In fact, he felt invigorated by the wildness of the night.

The clouds were moving at a great speed across the sky, occasionally blocking out the moon entirely.

The time passed: 11:15 became midnight, which became 1:00, which very nearly didn't become 2:00, for Doyle started to feel extremely sleepy around 1:45. The wind had died down and he'd found a comfortable place in the bushes, sheltered and shielded by a fine oak tree. His eyes grew heavier and he caught himself nodding off. He stood up straight, banged his feet together and helped himself to another cup of coffee. That did the trick.

Not long after this he noticed a shadow stealing away from the Gilmour back door under the cloak of darkness that the clouds had provided by helpfully concealing the moon at that moment. Doyle looked harder. Yes, there it was – a figure making its way across the back yard. It stopped briefly by a rose bush and picked up what looked like a shovel. Yes, it was definitely a shovel.

The trap was working.

The matchmaker was on his way. Doyle decided to give him a head start. He didn't want to be discovered in pursuit – it was important that he produce the body as well as the suspect: their destinies were intertwined as surely as those of the Lone Ranger and Tonto. The figure went through the hedge that bordered the field behind the house but then, instead of crossing the field in the direction of McCelland's shirt factory, it stopped and started to dig, just there on the other side of the hedge. The matchmaker was digging up the body of Joe Kane, and he had buried it less than fifty yards from his back door. Incredible, Doyle thought – nothing short of incredible. But he wasn't euphoric at the sight; rather he was sad that he was now finally going to find Joseph Kane's body.

The figure kept on digging. The wind, considerate as an accomplice, had decided that this was the precise moment to work its way back to its former gale-force and drown out the sounds of the silhouette at work by the hedge.

But there were still questions. Was Pat Kane involved too? Had the meet in Brady's Bar been arranged so they could formulate the next part of the plan: to dig up the body and then bury it elsewhere? Was the matchmaker going to carry the remains in his arms?

Gross!

Or did he have a wheelbarrow to hand?

Less than thirty minutes later, the shadowy figure was down to his waist in the hole he had just excavated, so Doyle figured it would be the same time again before the matchmaker got down to the full six foot. But six foot was the standard depth of an official grave. This was hardly that. Then he saw the matchmaker discard the shovel and squat down into the hole, disappearing from sight. Doyle crept forward and was soon within spitting distance, just the other side of the hedge. He could hear a lot of grunting and groaning from inside the grave but he couldn't see a thing. He decided now was the time to make the arrest. The digger could hardly have made a mistake, he reasoned, and there was no acceptable excuse for digging a hole six foot long, two and a half foot wide and three foot deep at three in the morning.

He saw his chance and sprung through the hedge. 'OK, Michael, the game's up,' he said, somewhat nervously.

But both the principals in our eerie scene were in for the shock of their lives.

The shadow looked up from the grave in terror and gave a spine-chilling, banshee shriek. It was certainly not the matchmaker's throaty rasp. Doyle looked down into the shallow pit. What he saw *was* the matchmaker's distinctive overcoat and hat, but they were being worn by a smaller, more feminine body. The face and hands were covered in dirt and mud and the hair was hidden beneath the large hat, but the features were the unmistakable features of a member of the Watson family.

Chapter Sixty-Eight

Dorothy Gilmour, *née* Watson, the matchmaker's wife, to be exact.

Chapter Sixty-Nine

The commotion brought out the cavalry in the shape of Constable Robin Irvine, followed, very closely, by the matchmaker, his tartan dressing-gown untied and flapping in the wind behind him.

Dorothy had been physically sick over the unearthed corpse of Joe Kane. Irvine was sick over his shoes as he looked down into the grave. Doyle was stunned into silence. The matchmaker merely said in a plea, 'Oh, dear God, Dorothy, no, I say, please no.' He too looked beyond Dorothy to the remains, as revolting and stomach churning a sight as he'd ever seen. The skin was black and eaten to nothing by the earth's subterranean creatures that had shown no reverence other than to their own need to eat in order to live. The eyeballs had fallen out of their sockets and it was pitiful the sight of Dorothy trying to uncover the earth from the body.

'Get out of there, please! NOW. PLEASE!' the matchmaker pleaded.

He offered his hand down to his wife – as if it were a lifeline, perhaps, just in time to save her from herself. She turned her back on her husband. She took one last look at Joseph David Kane, was sick again into the soil and then accepted the assistance of Doyle and Irvine in climbing out of the grave.

By then young Paul was at the back door, shouting into the darkness, 'Mum! Dad! What's going on? Are you OK?'

'Michael, go and attend to the children – keep Paul away from all of this,' Dorothy ordered firmly, suggesting to Doyle that she was referring to the whole sorry situation and not just the grave. 'I'm going straight to the police station.'

'Don't you think, Colin, you could let her stay the night – what's left of it? Let her stay here, please, I say, please let her stay the night?'

the matchmaker pleaded, his normal rasp now a whisper as he moved towards his house, obeying his wife's demand.

Before the senior of the two policemen had a chance to offer a very negative response, Dorothy Gilmour ordered in a tone not to be disobeyed, 'Michael – attend to the children. I'm going to the police station with Inspector Doyle. Now get back in the house before you catch your death.'

Doyle advised Irvine to guard the remains and confirmed he would send Hill up to him as soon as possible so they could secure the grave and cover it with canvas until the morning when it would be removed to the morgue in Magherafelt.

*

Fourteen minutes later, Doyle and Dorothy Gilmour were sitting in the interview-room-cum-stock-room at the police station. They were accompanied by WPC Jill Watterson, who was there to take down Dorothy's statement.

All of Castlemartin's police force was on duty that windy night. Some were surprised that Doyle's trap had worked; all, including the district detective inspector himself, were surprised by who the trap had caught. Doyle sent Constable Gavin McGee up to Kane's farm with orders for Sergeant Bill Agnew to return to the station immediately and for McGee and Hill to go straight to the gravesite at the matchmaker's house to help Irvine secure it.

Dorothy had a half smile on her face when she accepted Doyle's offer of tea. The matchmaker's wife had not said a word since she'd shouted at her husband. In a way, Doyle thought she was grateful to him for rescuing her from her late-night horror. He figured she'd been driven to dig up the grave, but in all honesty he couldn't see how she would have been able to move the remains out of the grave, let alone into a new one. It was though she'd dug down the three feet to see if the game was up, was really up. Quite suddenly she started to speak.

'You know, as I was digging, all the time I was digging, I was thinking there is no way anyone knows where this body is. I was thinking that no-one had been near the grave since I first dug it. But all the time I was compelled to keep digging to see if he was still there. I knew he was. The more I dug the more I knew he was, but I couldn't stop myself from digging to see if he really was still there.'

Dorothy's hair was up in a bun. She was wearing a pair of her husband's old denim jeans rolled up at the bottom and stuffed haphazardly into her gardening wellingtons, similar to a pair Doyle had borrowed on one of his visits to the Kane farm. She wore a black crew-neck jumper covered by a brown patterned cardigan buttoned up to the top. Her face and hands were still filthy; she'd refused an offer to visit the station's basic bathroom. But beneath it all, Doyle thought, she still looked like Maggie's sister.

'It was an accident, really,' she began, following a large gulp of tea. 'I realise, of course, you must hear that a lot. But in this case it's true.'

'We also hear that a lot as well,' Doyle whispered under his breath.

'I suppose I really should start at the beginning, shouldn't I?' she offered helpfully as she replaced a fallen wisp of hair back into her bun.

'Yes, that would be best,' Doyle replied politely.

'Well, it started, God, it started … I was going to say it started when Maggie and Pat were getting on well together and Joe was feeling left out. But that's not true. It started way before that. It started when I agreed to marry Michael and be the mother of his children. It was at that point that I stopped existing as myself, as an individual.' She paused, appearing to be trying to pick out the real beginning of her story. Suddenly Doyle realised that he was about to be confronted by the tale of a seemingly happy married couple who weren't … happily married. Previous to Dorothy's opening statement, Doyle would have happily bet his humble home on the matchmaker and his wife having one of the soundest marriages in Castlemartin.

The clock ticking away above them eventually prompted her to continue her confession.

'I was there for one reason and one reason only: to attend to the needs of my husband and my children. My children, well that's fine — they didn't ask to come into the world and I was responsible for them. I brought them into the world. But I never realised it would be the end of my life. I never realised that Michael would leave all the rearing of the family to me. He genuinely believed that his responsibility ended with putting the money on the table each week for the food and clothes. They say the farmer only walks his cows into town once a year, and that's always on a market day, and that's possibly true, but I can also tell you, with one hundred percent conviction, that the next time Michael attends to our family chores will be the first.'

'That's all about to change,' Doyle thought, but he decided against saying it out loud.

As if reading his mind, the matchmaker's wife paused and afforded herself a little smile before continuing.

'Until Pat came along, Michael lived in a perfect world. He had me to mother his children and feed him and tend his house and he had Maggie for all those long walks with intellectually stimulating conversations. Don't get me wrong, there was never anything sexual going on between them. Maggie would never. Ever! She just couldn't. But there was most positively an emotional thing going on between the two of them. And in a way that was worse, much worse. I always felt so left out, you know, when they went out for their walks immediately after dinner leaving me to do the feckin' dishes. Then Pat came along and, of course, when Pat came along so did Joe.'

'So did Joe,' Doyle repeated to himself, as WPC Watterson worked her shorthand to the limit.

'Part of me feels the need to protect my sister and part of me needs to tell the truth,' Dorothy carried on.

'Well, let's see now, you know, all of the details only need to come out when it's a plea of not guilty. I would imagine with the grave and all that, you're hardly likely to make such a plea. You seem to want to tell us the truth and I suppose what I am saying to you is that I will do my utmost to make sure that no-one is dragged into this who doesn't have to be, if you get my meaning. I mean, I think we can all agree that Pat and Maggie have been through enough over this sorry tale,' Doyle offered, hoping to clear the air and encourage Dorothy to tell the full truth, and nothing but the truth, for that matter.

Dorothy appeared to take the bait. 'So Maggie and Pat met. Up at our house one night, in fact. I don't know whether or not Michael staged it; I have a feeling not. But with Michael you never know. They hit it off instantly. Even the Castlemartin people with the white sticks were aware that the spark had struck and that it would soon break into a bonfire. Anyway, when Pat and Joe came to Michael looking for a wife they were looking for *a* wife. They reckoned they could only afford one between them. I couldn't believe it when Joe told me all about it later on – I couldn't believe that my husband would be involved in such a thing. Shows you how close men and women are in marriage really, doesn't it? You let your partner know what you want them to know. In my case, if I thought it would hurt him, I'd let him find out things he thought he wasn't meant to know.' Dorothy paused as if in reflection.

Doyle studied her again. She was once such a proud woman and he hated to see her there, dressed like a tramp, mud still on her hands. He wished she'd accepted his offer to have a wash. He generously offered her the station's limited bath facilities again.

Once again she declined.

'I suppose it's like I want to get the dirt out of my mind first – once I've done that, then I can wash my body and hopefully rid myself of all of this forever,' she'd said.

Doyle doubted that.

'Anyway, as Pat and Maggie grew closer they were calling around quite a bit and Joe would be with them some of the times, not all of the time. In fact, I think they were always trying to lose him and spend a bit of time by themselves. Visit the "ballroom of romance" out on the Ballyronan Road, you know? And I'd see Joe look at me with his dark sad eyes, but he'd be looking at me in a way my husband hadn't looked at me in years. And I mean years. It's very sad when you think about that: you know, the look of love – even the look of lust would have done – disappearing from your husband's eyes and I thought about it a lot. But you know, when you first meet your man it's so exciting, getting undressed, teasing him even, going to bed and spending hours exploring each other's bodies. And I was proud of my body and I could see how men and boys reacted to it. We feel good when men look at us that way – don't ever let anyone tell you different, District Detective Inspector.'

Dorothy stopped talking and stared at Doyle as if to emphasise the point. When it looked like she'd successfully made it, she continued.

'Anyway, that was all fine and dandy until I fell pregnant with Paul. Don't get me wrong, we planned to start a family and we planned Paul. But when I was heavy with Paul, it was like we had to stop fooling around, stopped having fun with each other. And I thought it was all to do with being pregnant and it would change after Paul came along. But that wasn't to be either. Sex after that was infrequent and functional – lacking in both romance and excitement. There was *definitely* no excitement in it for me. And Michael performed as though he was doing his duty, his duty in relieving himself without any care or thought for my feelings. Every time I would get restless with the situation he would tune into it and get me pregnant. After the birth of Nicholas *I* started to take the precautions, but I needn't have bothered because he barely came near me after that. Like I was saying, you go between the extremes of the pure excitement of the first time you make physical contact with your husband to it being about as exciting as sharing a bed with a side of beef.' Dorothy looked over to the WPC who was going as fast as the wind trying to capture on paper in her little marks, squiggles and signs every single word she was hearing.

'And then there was Joe. And Joe didn't look at me in that way.' Dorothy laughed. 'He didn't look at as he was a puppy in love with me. He just always looked at me like he wished he was doing the naughtiest of things to me. And I admit to you, I started to imagine all the naughty things he might do to me – and me to him. But nothing happened for ages. Not until Maggie and Pat got married, in fact. Part of the deal, part of the spin off, if you will, of both of them finding a wife – the same wife – was that Maggie would look after Joe every now and again, if you know what I mean. Well, twice a month, really. Joe told me it was horrible – she didn't have a clue. He just climbed on, she wriggled around for a bit and, a few seconds later, it was exit stage right immediately in a rush to the bathroom. Maggie and Pat were growing closer and closer, and as a result, Joe on one hand and Michael on the other were both being pushed away. Michael wandered around like a calf whose mother had deserted him, and Joe? Well, Joe came round here one afternoon in his dirty work clothes. He knew Michael wasn't in because he admitted he'd seen him in the village, and he knew the children were at school. He said I knew what he was after and he said he could tell from the way that I looked at him and acted around him that I was after the same thing. Not the best chat-up line I've ever heard, but it worked. We were rolling around on the floor within a few seconds, tearing each other's clothes off like two wild animals. It was lust, pure beautiful lust. In a way, I thought, he was having me because he couldn't really have my sister and I supposed I was the next best thing. But I didn't care one hoot. I was just so ...' Dorothy took care to elongate the word as if showing how much she meant it, 'happy. Happy that, that ... I still had those urges, those needs. It had been so long that I was scared my sex life might have finished for good. You just don't know, do you? Being perfectly honest with you, the bottom line was that we used each other. No love was lost; there were no deep, meaningful spiritual conversations. He *did* tell me about the situation up on the farm. He *did* say that he enjoyed being with me more than Maggie. He said he sometimes craved my body. And with the subtlety he showed around at our house, I believed him. He just didn't care whether or not Michael found out. He had me outside the back door once while we could hear the children and Michael talking in the kitchen. He started to pretend to be fond of the kids but it was all just to give him an excuse to be around me. On the rare occasions I went up to the farm without Michael, Joe would always offer to walk me home, but not before a slight detour to satisfy our lust.'

Now Dorothy blushed for the first time, either from the memory of a particular occasion or from realising exactly what she was revealing to two relative strangers. Doyle guessed she'd never discussed her dark secret with anyone before this point, and she was, in all probability, finding it quite a relief to do so.

'Then Michael, accidentally, if you know what I mean, matched Joe with Doris Durin. I would notice Michael and Pat talking away quietly in a corner and when I would come near them they would change the subject altogether. So I figured something was going on. And then Doris came on the scene and, to be honest, I felt sorry for her. I knew what she was looking for, what we're all looking for – for a great man – but I knew she wasn't going to find him in Joe. He was incapable of feeling love, of showing any kind of tenderness. He was as charming as one of the bureau boys, one of the dole boys. To him it was all very basic: you eat, you go to the toilet, you eat some more, you go to the toilet some more, you get a ride, you go to sleep, you get up. A caring word from Joseph was as rare as a man of the cloth in a pink suit. Anyway, now Joe had his own woman, not someone's wife, and he just stopped coming around. It wasn't planned, it wasn't discussed: one afternoon he was here tearing my clothes off for his ride and the next day he wasn't. Then the next day he still wasn't and a full week went by and I hadn't seen him and then I realised that I wasn't going to see him again.'

Doyle refilled Dorothy's teacup, knowing it would stop her talking for a moment to allow the WPC to catch up.

'That's when I started to think about what I'd done. What I'd been doing. To be honest, I didn't really care about Michael, although I surely didn't want him to know that I was seeing Joe. But I started to think of Paul and Marianne and Nicholas and I realised I was their mother and it wasn't just a name, you know, the word "mother". It's a person children depend on to look after them and help them with all their problems and difficulties. Then I had this real panic about what would happen if we were found out. The whole of Castlemartin would have known about it in seconds. There was already enough gossip to fill the *News of the World* for a month about Maggie and Pat and Joe and the goings-on up at the farm and I got the shakes when I thought how absolutely embarrassing it would be for the children. I was scared they'd be the butt of all the jokes. Michael would have to leave in shame. He's a good father to the children: don't get me wrong about Michael. Basically, he's a good man – he just doesn't know how to behave any differently. He's suffered, from being one of the first generation of men to be greeted by women who quite simply need more from their men. He's certainly not the emotional cripple Joe Kane is. And he does love his children and provides for all of us.'

'Joe Kane was an emotional cripple.' Doyle repeated Dorothy's words under his breath. He wasn't sure he could agree with this. The detective felt that Joe had suffered as much as Pat from being an identical twin. It couldn't have been pleasant for him either to *have* to depend on Pat as his crutch. But then he wondered, were these just pangs of sympathy for Joe now that his body had been found and there was no doubt about his death? Up until the grave-digging, there was always the chance that it was all a big mistake on Doyle's part and that, in fact, there was never a crime at all. Joe might have been in Belfast, or London, or even Sydney, and he would show up some day, perhaps even some day soon, and everyone would laugh with him and tell him the story of the bones being found under the bridge.

Now that theory had to be discounted.

Joe was dead and Doyle wondered if his death would be any easier on those who cared. Would the fact that Joe had been missing for some time make it any easier for Maggie and Pat to accept his death? Maggie truly loved her husband; her husband had lost his brother, so she must share his grief. Or would they be relieved that their problems had finally come to an end? Mind you, Maggie now had other problems, potentially bigger problems, with her sister. What was going to happen to Dorothy and Michael and the children? Too early to tell, Doyle thought, but whatever the outcome, he hoped that Maggie and Pat were enjoying their current sleep because it was the last peaceful one they would have for some time to come.

Meanwhile, Dorothy continued recalling her story, the story which would rock Castlemartin to its very foundations over the coming weeks.

'I was grateful, you'll never realise how grateful, that I hadn't been found out. I loved Doris Durin for taking Joe from my door. She was more than welcome to him. I swore there and then, never to put myself before my children again. I swore I would never do anything so selfish again in my life. I had made my carnal-free bed and I was going to lie in it for the rest of my days. But then I heard Doris and Joe had a falling out up at Portrush. Maggie told me some of the details, but I guessed not all. You have to realise, she wasn't aware of the sordid details I was aware of. I was expecting Joe to come back. I had a whole speech ready for him. But he never came. Although I was grateful, a small part of me was disappointed, if I'm being perfectly honest.'

'Disappointed?' Doyle found himself saying involuntarily.

'Yes, I suppose just a little. You know, vanity and all of that. Anyway, things were not good up on the farm; there were a few fights, – Maggie wouldn't say what they were about, but I had a good idea.

Then we were all up on the fields when Joe and Pat had that one really terrible fight. God, they were so vicious to each other. They had to be pulled apart. And the threshing had to stop. Michael stayed up at the farm with Paul. Nicholas and Marianne were already around at my parents'. They had wanted to go to the threshing with Paul, but Michael said they were too young: he promised them they could go next year. And Joe turned up at the house. He was still raging from the fight, raging at Pat. He was madder at Maggie. He kept saying they had a deal and they'd better stick to the deal if they knew what was good for them. He went for me in his usual subtle way, grabbed me by the hand and pulled me out the back door and over to the hedge where you found me earlier, Inspector,' Dorothy continued, as she stared at the table. It was like she was staring through the table into a scene she was recreating and recalling for the detective and the WPC. It appeared to Doyle that the images were difficult to put into words now. A few tears started to flow down Dorothy's cheeks. The tears washed away part of the dirt on her face in streaks. The tears followed the path of least resistance and soon Dorothy had a river and a few tributaries flowing. Doyle knew not to comfort her now. The dam would burst and she would break down and be incapable of finishing her story – maybe ever. In the cool light of day and with the safety of her children at stake, she might choose to rewrite the ending. Doyle handed her his crisp, clean white handkerchief. A few seconds later it was covered in brown smudges. He breathed a sigh of relief when Dorothy chose to continue.

'I gave him my well-rehearsed speech. And you know what? It felt glorious to have a chance to do it. It was like I was taking a stand for myself and for my children and I felt so proud. Joe on the other hand was livid. He went purple with anger. He went on about how much he loved Maggie and she'd better come to her senses or the village tongues would be wagging again, but wagging with the truth this time.

'He asked me how would I like it if he told Michael and Maggie and Pat about all our great rides and where we used to do it and how many times. He asked how Michael would react when he told him about the times my face would be covered in tears of pleasure, or how Michael would feel when he found out about some of the degrading things I had done and how willing and eager I'd been to do them. He obviously thought his threats would work 'cause he grabbed me and shoved me to the ground and then started his usual foreplay routine of unbuckling his belt and unzipping his fly. I pleaded with him to stop. I was crying. I told him no, but he just laughed and grunted – he said I knew that a good ride was all I really needed.'

More tears flowed down Dorothy's very messy face. 'Come on,' Doyle pleaded under his breath, 'you're nearly there … just a bit more to go and then we can stop.' He knew she would feel better to complete her confession.

'He was on top of me, pinning me to the ground with his weight. He was fumbling around trying to get my clothes off. I remember feeling a resolve – it came over me in a wave and gave me strength. "No!" I shouted. "No, Joe – you're not going to do this to me." And then he said, "Just shut up and open your legs." Charming or what?' Dorothy added, trying to be casual but not carrying it off. 'I kept saying over and over to myself, "You're not going to do this to me." I kept thinking about my children. My hands scrambled around the earth to either side looking for something, anything to hit him with. My right hand found something – it felt solid, but not heavy. I raised it up in my hand, closed my eyes and brought it down as hard as I could. Then I felt this powdered stuff falling over my face. I thought, "My God, I've smashed his crown and it's falling all over me." Then I heard his laugh and I opened my eyes only to realise I had hit him over the head with a lump of soil which had disintegrated into pieces, which were falling all about him. He was still struggling on top of me, trying to undo my clothes. I searched blindly with my hand for something else – I felt so helpless. If I could have gotten my hands on a gun at that stage, even if he had let me up, I swear I would have blown him to pieces. I know at that moment I would have taken a great deal of pleasure in blowing his brains out. Instead, all I could find was a measly piece of roofing slate. I tried to get a grip on that and banged that on his head too. It shattered into pieces.'

She stopped again. Doyle thought, surely this time it's for good. Luckily he was wrong.

'It had as much effect on him as a fly biting an elephant. The biggest piece remaining intact rested on his shoulder. It had kind of a jagged edged and a sharp point at one end. In desperation, I grabbed it in my hand. I thought if only I could stick it into him a little it would make him bleed and that might stun him back to his senses, if he had any. I knew it was my last chance: there was nothing else around, no stones or rocks. I swear to you, when you're not looking for them the garden is full of them. I grabbed the piece of slate in my hand so tightly I thought I was going to draw blood on myself before I drew blood from him. I swung my arm in with all the strength I could muster. I watched the slate go straight into his neck. It was about ten inches away from my face and it went into the skin, almost like it was in slow motion. It went in, in stages, a little, then a little more, then a little more. It just seemed to slide into his skin as easy as a knife through butter. I was surprised that no blood was coming out. The slate kept going into his neck, further and further, and it stopped only when my fist – the one tightly gripping the slate – hit his skin. At this point it seemed to have no effect on him. Still there was no blood flowing. "God, what's he made of?" I kept thinking. I panicked. I thought I was never going to be able to stop him. I had one final idea: I would withdraw the slate and stab him somewhere else, where it would be more effective.

'I started to pull it out – it was more difficult to remove. Eventually I managed to get it out. When it was totally free from his neck, the first thing I noticed was that it was covered in blood. Then blood started to spurt from his neck out to my right-hand side. His eyes went from shock, to panic, to fear – all in the space of a split second. He put his hand up to his neck to try to stop the flow of blood, but it seemed to find a way through his fingers and started dripping all over my face. He rolled off me. I jumped to my feet and stared down at him, rolling about on the ground, struggling to try to catch his breath. I just remember having my hands up to my face, screaming. I was willing the bleeding to stop so that he could go home and leave me alone.

'I kept thinking, "Let that be a lesson to you, don't be coming back here any more." I wanted *so* badly for him to get up and go. He started gurgling, you know, like you do when you're rinsing your mouth out after you clean your teeth. His face was contorting as he struggled, like he was trying to catch his breath. It was like he was drowning, but on dry land. Then he passed out. Well, I thought he passed out. But he never moved again. After a few minutes I realised he was dead. I remember thinking just before he passed out, when he was supposed to die – he had this strange look on his face; it was like, well, you know, the thing I always thought about Joe was that he didn't really want to be on this earth. He wasn't really happy with his life and I always figured, I don't know why I kept thinking this, I figured that he couldn't care less whether he was alive or dead. It's what made being with him exciting. But the look on his face in his last few seconds was that of someone who thought life was precious and didn't want to lose it, but it was like he was discovering this for the first time, just as he was dying.'

Doyle was totally gunked by that poignant thought and felt like he'd just experienced a mule kick to his solar plexus.

'For some reason, unknown to me, I then became incredibly calm. I went to the tool shed at the other end of the garden and fetched a spade. I dug a grave right beside the body. I didn't want to dig it too deep because then I'd have a surplus of earth and it would be very noticeable. I dug down about three feet, rolled him into the hole and then I filled it in. I don't remember being exhausted or anything – I was most likely totally charged with adrenalin. I scattered the bit of spare earth around the hedge. I went into the house and ran myself a bath. I took off all the clothes I was wearing and put them in the fire and then went and soaked in the bath for ages. I think I was still in the bath when Michael came home.'

And that was it. Dorothy Watson, *née* Gilmour, had completed her statement. It took the efficient WPC Jill Watterson only fifteen minutes to type it up, all very neatly, with no errors. Doyle read it back to the matchmaker's wife who duly confirmed all the facts were correct and added her signature to the three-page document.

Doyle didn't feel vindicated or victorious or the hero of the hour. In fact, he felt sad, very sad indeed. He felt more deflated than he'd ever felt in his entire life. He was convinced that the image of Joe dying and struggling for, what he'd just discovered to be, precious life would stay with him for the remainder of his days.

Chapter Seventy

Life went on in Castlemartin, like it had been doing for nearly one hundred and thirty years. That was how long it had been since the first church was built on this lush land, not so far from the lough shore, between two orchards, one with apples and one with pears. But things would never be the same again for several of the inhabitants.

Dorothy Gilmour was eventually charged with manslaughter. At one point there was talk of a self-defence plea, but apparently it wouldn't have stood up. She admitted the charges and was ready to accept the punishment she deserved in the interest of redemption. Oh, that wonderful feeling of redemption did a lot for her. She was sentenced to six years in Crumlin and with good behaviour did three years and eleven months. Upon her release, she didn't return to Castlemartin. Instead, every inch the broken woman, she went to Stornaway in Scotland, took up with, but didn't marry, a crofter and some say continued her punishment on the wind-swept slopes, never seeing nor contacting her children or the matchmaker again.

Paul Gilmour left Castlemartin at the first available opportunity. Six years later he bypassed Belfast and went straight to London to continue his studies. He was sponsored by ICL, where he hoped one day to be able to work as a computer programmer. He found it easy to forgive his mother for her crime and in fact he always protested that she'd only done what she'd done to protect herself and her family. But he found it a lot harder to forgive her for totally abandoning her family in the process. She never even wrote to her children once. At first Paul thought his father might have been behind her forced exile. But as he grew older, and was encouraged in conversations with his Aunt Maggie, he came to the conclusion that his mother had dropped out of her children's lives because she believed that was the only way to separate them, maybe even free them, from her deeds. He came to realise that his mother had loved him and his brother and sister *so* much that she was prepared to do anything for them, anything including giving them up so they could enjoy better lives.

Pat and Maggie Gilmour grieved for a time and then got on with their lives successfully, working the farm, acquiring a neighbouring farm and starting a large family, with the birth of three daughters in alternate winters. It seems they had a mind to enjoy the springtime.

Pat seldom thought of his brother, and when he did, it was without regret. He often told Maggie that he was convinced one of them, one of the twins, had to die in order for the other to survive. Maggie openly accused Pat of missing his brother a lot more than he let on. She tried to convince him that admitting to missing Joe wouldn't be a bad thing.

Edward Hill and Doris Durin, the ginger-haired couple, married in the spring of 1965 and Edward was transferred to Portrush where they bought a little cottage near a caravan park. Five years later Edward retired from the force. He and Doris had already bought the caravan park and soon after Edward's retirement they also purchased a café on the seafront where they made their fortune selling high teas and souvenirs to the tourists.

Joan Cook eventually found a man to marry her – without the assistance of the matchmaker. He was a local councillor, the recently widowed Mr Ivan Raleigh, and fifteen months after their holy union you could have heard the town gossips' tongues wagging as far away as Belfast when Ivan was elected the Mayor of Magherafelt. Lady Raleigh was in her element and positively thrived in public life.

Castlemartin tried to return to the sleepy slumber it had enjoyed before Doyle's Case of the Missing Twin. But with the sixties revolution now in full swing, it never really succeeded. Before the sixties were but a memory, there were three housing estates built around the perimeter of the village, bringing with them a whole new set of characters.

The matchmaker? Well, it took him a long, long time to even believe that Dorothy had done what she had confessed to. He eventually confessed to himself that perhaps he had never really known her. He could never accept that he'd been anything other than a good husband and father, if only because he felt he'd been the best kind of husband and father his parents had reared him to be.

As he had predicted, the matchmaking business ground to a standstill. Something to do with the times and something to do with his wife, he guessed. He tried opening a pub in a property he bought beside Walter's Grocery and Hardware shop. Unfortunately, he neglected to concede the implications of trying to run a public house directly opposite a police station. Business was bad; however, he did manage to sell his property to the grocer next door – who was expanding in order to accommodate the new influx – at a great profit and is still considering his next step. He is often seen in Bryson's in Magherafelt on a Saturday night. If the craic is ninety and he is a few pints of Guinness to the wind, he will recall for anyone who cares to listen some of his greatest matches. His tongue will be going like a fiddler's elbow and all such conversations start off with, 'My father, Mickey Gilmour, now *he* was the best matchmaker this country has ever seen. He could set up a successful match without even having to speak to either the man or the woman.'

A few of Bryson's regulars often wondered why, with all the matchmaking experience Michael had at his fingertips, he never again sought out female company for himself.

District Detective Inspector Colin 'Wee' Doyle enjoyed a considerable amount of celebrity for cracking what had become such a famous case. The Case of the Missing Twin even made it to the front page of the *Belfast Telegraph* on eight consecutive nights, excluding the Saturday and Sunday of course. He was offered a promotion, but it would have meant moving to Belfast. He declined the invitation, choosing instead to remain in Castlemartin. His good friend, Dr Taylor, often kidded the detective that he only remained in the Mid Ulster backwater so that he would have peace and time to read and re-read the Sherlock Holmes stories … and just in case Maggie Kane, *née* Gilmour, ever decided to leave Pat Kane. As well as reading the Sherlock Holmes cases, he also worked, over the years, on a few unusual cases of his own. Those other cases? Ah, now there's another story, or three.

And the Lone Ranger and Tonto? Well, they're still riding down the line, fixing everybody's troubles. Everybody's troubles except those of Joseph David Kane – someone must have told them that he didn't do so fine.